By Lee Child

Stories

Make Me

LEE CHILD

Delacorte Press | New York

Make Me

A JACK REACHER NOVEL

Published in the United States by Delacorte Press, an imprint of Random House, a division of Penguin Random House LLC, New York.

DELACORTE PRESS and the HOUSE colophon are registered trademarks of Penguin Random House LLC.

Library of Congress Cataloging-in-Publication Data
Child, Lee.
Make me : a Jack Reacher novel / Lee Child.
pages ; cm
ISBN: 978-0-8041-7877-8
eBook ISBN: 978-0-8041-7878-5
1. Reacher, Jack (Fictitious character)—Fiction.
2. Murder—Investigation—Fiction. I. Title.
PS3553.H4838M35 2015
813'.54—dc23   2015017106

Printed in the United States of America on acid-free paper

randomhousebooks.com

9 8 7 6 5 4 3 2 1

First Edition

Book design by Virginia Norey

For Darley Anderson,
twenty years my agent, with thanks

Make Me

Chapter 1

Moving a guy as big as Keever wasn't easy. It was like trying to wrestle a king-size mattress off a waterbed. So they buried him close to the house. Which made sense anyway. The harvest was still a month away, and a disturbance in a field would show up from the air. And they would use the air, for a guy like Keever. They would use search planes, and helicopters, and maybe even drones.

They started at midnight, which they thought was safe enough. They were in the middle of ten thousand acres of nothingness, and the only man-made structure their side of any horizon was the railroad track to the east, but midnight was five hours after the evening train and seven hours before the morning train. Therefore, no prying eyes. Their backhoe had four spotlights on a bar above the cab, the same way kids pimped their pick-up trucks, and together the four beams made a wide pool of halogen brightness. Therefore, visibility was not a problem either. They started the hole in the hog pen, which was a permanent disturbance all by itself. Each hog weighed two hundred pounds, and each hog had four feet. The dirt was always chewed up. Nothing to see from the air, not even with a thermal camera. The picture would white out instantly, from the steaming animals themselves, and their steaming piles and pools of waste.

Safe enough.

Hogs were rooting animals, so they made sure the hole was deep. Which was not a problem either. Their backhoe's arm was long, and it bit rhythmically, in fluent articulated seven-foot scoops, the hydraulic rams glinting in the electric light, the engine straining and roaring and pausing, the cab falling and rising, as each bucket-load was dumped aside. When the hole was done they backed the machine up and turned it around and used the front bucket to push Keever into his grave, scraping him, rolling him, covering his body with dirt, until finally it fell over the lip and thumped down into the electric shadows.

Only one thing went wrong, and it happened right then.

The evening train came through five hours late. The next morning they heard on the AM station that a broken locomotive had caused a jam a hundred miles south. But they didn't know that at the time. All they heard was the mournful whistle at the distant crossing, and then all they could do was turn and stare, at the long lit cars rumbling past in the middle distance, one after the other, like a vision in a dream, seemingly forever. But eventually the train was gone, and the rails sang for a minute more, and then the tail light was swallowed by the midnight darkness, and they turned back to their task.

Twenty miles north the train slowed, and slowed, and then eased to a hissing stop, and the doors sucked open, and Jack Reacher stepped down to a concrete ramp in front of a grain elevator as big as an apartment house. To his left were four more elevators, all of them bigger than the first, and to his right was an enormous metal shed the size of an airplane hangar. There were vapor lights on poles, set at regular intervals, and they cut cones of yellow in the darkness. There was mist in the nighttime air, like a note on a calendar. The end of summer was coming. Fall was on its way.

Reacher stood still and behind him the train moved away without him, straining, grinding, settling to a slow rat-a-tat rhythm, and then accelerating, its building slipstream pulling at his clothes. He was the only passenger who had gotten out. Which was not surprising. The place was no kind of a commuter hub. It was all agricultural. What token passenger facilities it had were wedged between the last elevator and the huge shed, and were limited to a compact building, which seemed to have both a ticket window and benches for waiting. It was built in a traditional railroad style, and it looked like a child's toy, temporarily set down between two shiny oil drums.

But on a sign board running its whole length was written the reason Reacher was there: *Mother's Rest*. Which he had seen on a map, and which he thought was a great name for a railroad stop. He figured the line must cross an ancient wagon train trail, right there, where something had happened long ago. Maybe a young pregnant woman went into labor. The jostling could not have helped. Maybe the wagon train stopped for a couple of weeks. Or a month. Maybe someone remembered the place years later. A descendant, perhaps. A family legend. Maybe there was a one-room museum.

Or perhaps there was a sadder interpretation. Maybe they had buried a woman there. Too old to make it. In which case there would be a commemorative stone.

Either way Reacher figured he might as well find out. He had no place to go, and all the time in the world to get there, so detours cost him nothing. Which is why he got out of the train. To a sense of disappointment, initially. His expectations had been way off base. He had pictured a couple of dusty houses, and a lonely one-horse corral. And the one-room museum, maybe run part-time and volunteer by an old guy from one of the houses. Or the headstone, maybe marble, behind a square wrought-iron fence.

He had not expected the immense agricultural infrastructure. He should have, he supposed. Grain, meet the railroad. It had to be loaded somewhere. Billions of bushels and millions of tons each year. He stepped left and looked through a gap between structures. The view was dark, but he could sense a rough semicircle of habitation. Houses, obviously, for the depot workers. He could see lights, which he hoped were a motel, or a diner, or both.

He walked to the exit, skirting the pools of vapor light purely out of habit, but he saw that the last lamp was unavoidable, because it was set directly above the exit gate. So he saved himself a further perimeter diversion by walking through the next-to-last pool of light, too.

At which point a woman stepped out of the shadows.

She came toward him with a distinctive burst of energy, two fast paces, eager, like she was pleased to see him. Her body language was all about relief.

Then it wasn't. Then it was all about disappointment. She stopped dead, and she said, "Oh."

She was Asian. But not petite. Five-nine, maybe, or even five-ten. And built to match. Not a bone in sight. No kind of a willowy waif. She was about forty, Reacher guessed, with black hair worn long, jeans and a T-shirt under a short cotton coat. She had lace-up shoes on her feet.

He said, "Good evening, ma'am."

She was looking past his shoulder.

He said, "I'm the only passenger."

She looked him in the eye.

He said, "No one else got out of the train. So I guess your friend isn't coming."

"My friend?" she said. A neutral kind of accent. Regular American. The kind he heard everywhere.

He said, "Why else would a person be here, except to meet the train? No point in coming otherwise. I guess normally there would be nothing to see at midnight."

She didn't answer.

He said, "Don't tell me you've been waiting here since seven o'clock."

"I didn't know the train was late," she said. "There's no cell signal here. And no one from the railroad, to tell you anything. And I guess the Pony Express is out sick today."

"He wasn't in my car. Or the next two, either."

"Who wasn't?"

"Your friend."

"You don't know what he looks like."

"He's a big guy," Reacher said. "That's why you jumped out when you saw me. You thought I was him. For a second, anyway. And there were no big guys in my car. Or the next two."

"When is the next train?"

"Seven in the morning."

She said, "Who are you and why have you come here?"

"I'm just a guy passing through."

"The train passed through. Not you. You got out."

"You know anything about this place?"

"Not a thing."

"Have you seen a museum or a gravestone?"

"Why are you here?"

"Who's asking?"

She paused a beat, and said, "Nobody."

Reacher said, "Is there a motel in town?"

"I'm staying there."

"How is it?"

"It's a motel."

"Works for me," Reacher said. "Does it have vacancies?"

"I'd be amazed if it didn't."

"OK, you can show me the way. Don't wait here all night. I'll be up by first light. I'll knock on your door as I leave. Hopefully your friend will be here in the morning."

The woman said nothing. She just glanced at the silent rails one more time, and then turned around and led the way through the exit gate.

Chapter 2

The motel was bigger than Reacher expected. It was a two-story horseshoe, a total of thirty rooms, with plenty of parking. But not many slots were occupied. The place was more than half empty. It was plainly built of stuccoed blocks, painted beige, with iron stairs and railings, painted brown. Nothing special. But it looked clean and well kept. All the light bulbs worked. Not the worst place Reacher had ever seen.

The office was the first door on the left, on the ground floor. There was a clerk behind the desk. He was a short old guy with a big belly and what looked like a glass eye. He gave the woman the key for room 214, and she walked out without another word. Reacher asked him for a rate, and the guy said, "Sixty bucks."

Reacher said, "A week?"

"A night."

"I've been around."

"What's that supposed to mean?"

"I've been in plenty of motels."

"So?"

"I don't see anything here worth sixty bucks. Twenty, maybe."

"Can't do twenty. Those rooms are expensive."

"Which rooms?"

"Upstairs."

"I'm happy with downstairs."

"Don't you need to be near her?"

"Near who?"

"Your lady friend."

"No," Reacher said. "I don't need to be near her."

"Forty dollars downstairs."

"Twenty. You're more than half empty. Practically out of business. Better to make twenty bucks than nothing at all."

"Thirty."

"Twenty."

"Twenty-five."

"Deal," Reacher said. He took his roll of cash out of his pocket and separated a ten, and two fives, and five singles. He laid them on the counter and the one-eyed guy swapped them for a key on a wooden fob marked 106, taken from a drawer, with a triumphant flourish.

"In the back corner," the guy said. "Near the stairs."

Which were metal, and which would make a clanging noise when people went up and down. Not the best room in the place. Petty revenge. But Reacher didn't care. He figured his would be the last head to hit the pillow that night. He didn't foresee any other late arrivals. He expected to be undisturbed, all the way through the silent plains night.

He said, "Thank you," and walked out, carrying his key.

The one-eyed guy waited thirty seconds, and then dialed his desk phone, and when it was answered he said, "She met a guy off the train. It was late. She waited five hours for it. She brought the guy here and he took a room."

There was the plastic crackle of a question, and the one-eyed clerk said, "Another big guy. A mean son of a bitch. He busted my balls on the room rate. I gave him 106, in the back corner."

Another crackling question, and another answer: "Not from here. I'm in the office."

Another crackle, but this time a different tone and a different cadence. An instruction, not a question.

The one-eyed guy said, "OK."

And he put the phone down and struggled to his feet, and stepped out of the office, and took the lawn chair from outside 102, which was empty, and dragged it to a spot on the blacktop where he could see his own door and 106's equally. *Can you see his room from there?* had been the question, and *Move your ass somewhere you can watch him all night* had been the instruction, and the one-eyed guy always obeyed instructions, if sometimes a little reluctantly, as at that point, as he adjusted his angle and dumped his bulk down on the uncomfortable plastic. Outside, in the nighttime air. Not his preferred way of doing things.

From inside his room Reacher heard the lawn chair scrape across the blacktop, but he paid no attention. Just a random nighttime sound, nothing dangerous, not a shotgun jacking a round, not the hiss of a blade on a sheath, nothing for his lizard brain to worry about. And the only non-lizard possibilities were a lace-up footstep on the sidewalk outside, and a knock on the door, because the woman from the railroad seemed like a person with a lot of questions, and also some kind of expectation they should be answered. *Who are you and why have you come here?*

But it was a scrape, not a footstep or a knock, so Reacher paid no attention. He folded his pants and laid them flat under the mattress, and then he showered away the grime of the day, and climbed under the bedcovers. He set the alarm in his head for six o'clock in the morning, stretched once, yawned once, and fell asleep.

* * *

The dawn came up entirely gold, with no hint of pink or purple. The sky was a rinsed blue, like an old shirt washed a thousand times. Reacher showered again and dressed, and stepped out to the new day. He saw the lawn chair, empty, oddly placed in the traffic lane, but he thought nothing of it. He went up the metal stairs as quietly as he could, reducing the likely clang to a duller pulsing boom, by placing his feet very carefully. He found 214 and knocked on its door, firmly but discreetly, like he imagined a bellboy would, in a fine hotel. *Your wake-up call, ma'am.* She had about forty minutes. Ten to get going, ten to shower, ten to stroll up to the railroad again. She would be there well ahead of the morning train.

Reacher crept back down the stairs and headed out to the street, which was wide enough at that point to qualify as a plaza. For farm trucks, he guessed, slow and clumsy, turning and maneuvering, lining up ahead of the weighbridges and the receiving offices and the grain elevators themselves. There were train tracks embedded in the black-top. It was a whole big operation. Some kind of a hub facility, pre-sumably, serving the locality, which in that part of America could have meant a two-hundred-mile radius. Which explained the large motel. Farmers would come in from far and wide, and spend the night before or after a train ride to some distant city. Maybe they would all come at once, at certain times of the year. When futures were for sale, maybe, in faraway Chicago. Hence the thirty bedrooms.

The wide street or the plaza or whatever it was ran basically south to north, with the railroad track and the shiny infrastructure defining the eastern limit, on the right, and what amounted to a kind of Main Street defining the western limit, on the left. The motel was there, and a diner, and a general store. Behind those establishments the town spread out in a loose westward semicircle. Low density. Sprawl, country style. A thousand people, maybe less.

Reacher headed north on the wide street, looking for the wagon train trail. He figured it would come in across his path, from east to west, which had been the whole point of wagon trains. *Go west, young man.* Exciting times. He saw a crossing fifty yards ahead, after the last of the elevators. A road, perpendicular, exactly east to west. On the right it was bright with the morning sun, and on the left it was long with shadows.

The crossing had no barriers. Just red lights. Reacher stood on the tracks and gazed back south, the way he had come. There were no other crossings for at least a mile, which was about as far as he could see, in the pale light. There were no other crossings for at least a mile to the north, either. Which meant that if Mother's Rest laid claim to its own east-west thoroughfare, he was standing on it.

It was reasonably wide, and slightly humped, built up with dirt taken from shallow ditches dug either side. It was covered with thick blacktop, grayed with age, split here and there by weather, and random like frozen lava on the edges. It was dead straight, from one horizon to the other.

A possibility. Wagon trains went dead straight when they could. Why wouldn't they? No one put in extra miles just for the fun of it. The lead driver would steer by a distant landmark, and the others would follow, and a year later some new party would find the ruts, and a year after that someone would make a mark on a map. And a hundred years later some state highway department would come by with trucks full of asphalt.

There was nothing to see in the east. No one-room museum, no marble headstone. Just the road, between infinite fields of nearly ripe wheat. But in the other direction, west of the tracks, the road ran through the town, more or less dead center, built up on both sides for about six low-rise blocks. The corner lot on the right had expanded northward about a hundred yards. Like a football field. It was a farm equipment dealership. Weird tractors and huge machines, all brand-new and shiny. On the left was a veterinary supply business, in a small building that must have started out as an ordinary residential dwelling.

Reacher made the turn and walked on the old trail, due west through the town, the morning sun faintly warm on his back.

In the motel office the one-eyed clerk dialed the phone, and when it was answered he said, "She went back to the railroad again. Now she's meeting the morning train, too. How many guys are these people sending?"

He was answered by a long plastic crackle, not a question, but not an instruction either. Softer in tone. Encouragement, maybe. Or reassurance. The one-eyed guy said, "OK, sure," and hung up.

Reacher walked six blocks down and six blocks back, and he saw plenty of stuff. He saw houses still lived in, and houses converted to offices, for seed merchants and fertilizer dealers and a large-animal veterinarian. He saw a one-room law office. He saw a gas station one block north, and a pool hall, and a store selling beer and ice, and another selling nothing but rubber boots and rubber aprons. He saw a laundromat, and a tire bay, and a place for stick-on boot soles.

He didn't see a museum, or a monument.

Which might be OK. They wouldn't have put either thing right on the shoulder. Back a block or two, probably, for a sense of reverence, and to stay out of harm's way.

He stepped off the wagon train trail into a side street. The town was laid out on a grid, even though it had grown up semicircular. Some lots were more desirable than others. As if the giant elevators had a gravitational system all their own. The furthest reaches were undeveloped. Closer to the apex, buildings were shoulder to shoulder. The block behind the trail had one-room apartments that might have started out as barns or garages, and what looked like pop-up market stalls, for folks who had given over an acre or two to fruits and vegetables. There was a store that did Western Union and Money-

Gram and faxing and photocopying and FedEx and UPS and DHL. There was a CPA's office next to it, but it looked abandoned.

No museum, and no monument.

He quartered the blocks, one after another, past low shacks, past diesel engine repair, past vacant lots full of weeds as fine as hair. He came out at the far end of the wide street. He had covered half the town. No museum, and no monument.

He saw the morning train pull in. It looked hot and bothered and impatient about stopping. It was impossible to see whether anyone got out. Too much infrastructure in the way.

He was hungry.

He walked straight ahead through the plaza, almost all the way back to where he had started, past the general store, and into the diner.

At which point the motel keeper's twelve-year-old grandson ducked into the general store, to the pay phone on the wall just inside the door. He dumped his coins and dialed a number, and when it was answered he said, "He's searching the town. I followed him every-where. He's looking all over. He's doing it block by block."

Chapter 3

The diner was clean and pleasant and attractively deco-
rated, but it was above all else a working place, designed to swap
calories for money as fast as possible. Reacher took a two-top in the
far right-hand corner, and he sat with his back to the angle, so he had
the whole room in front of him. About half the tables were taken,
mostly by people who seemed to be fueling up ahead of a long day of
physical labor. A waitress came by, busy but professionally patient,
and Reacher ordered his default breakfast, which was pancakes,
eggs, and bacon, but most of all coffee, first and always.

The waitress told him the establishment had a bottomless cup
policy.

Reacher welcomed that news.

He was on his second mug when the woman from the railroad
came in, alone.

She stood for a second, as if unsure, and then she looked all
around, and saw him, and headed straight for him. She slid into the
empty chair opposite. Up close and in the daylight she looked better
than the night before. Dark lively eyes, and some kind of purpose and
intelligence in her face. But some kind of worry, too.

She said, "Thanks for the knock on the door."

Reacher said, "My pleasure."

She said, "My friend wasn't on the morning train either."

He said, "Why tell me?"

"You know something."

"Do I?"

"Why else get off the train?"

"Maybe I live here."

"You don't."

"Maybe I'm a farmer."

"You're not."

"I could be."

"I don't think so."

"Why not?"

"You weren't carrying a bag, when you got out of the train. That's about the polar opposite of being rooted to the same patch of land for generations."

Reacher paused a beat and said, "Who exactly are you?"

"Doesn't matter who I am. What matters is who you are."

"I'm just a guy passing through."

"I'm going to need more than that."

"And I'm going to need to know who's asking."

The woman didn't reply. The waitress came by, with his plate. Pancakes, eggs, and bacon. There was syrup on the table. The waitress refilled his coffee. Reacher picked up his silverware.

The woman from the railroad put a business card on the table. She pushed it across the sticky wood. It had a government seal on it. Blue and gold.

Federal Bureau of Investigation.

Special Agent Michelle Chang.

Reacher said, "That's you?"

"Yes," she said.

"I'm pleased to meet you."

"Likewise," she said. "I hope."

"Why is the FBI asking me questions?"

"Retired," she said.

"Who is?"

"I am. I am no longer an FBI agent. The card is old. I took some with me when I left."

"Is that allowed?"

"Probably not."

"Yet you showed it to me."

"To get your attention. And for credibility. I'm a private investigator now. But not the sort that takes pictures in hotels. I need you to understand that."

"Why?"

"I need to know why you came here."

"You're wasting time. Whatever else your problem is, I'm just a coincidence."

"I need to know if you're here to work. We could be on the same side. We could both be wasting time."

"I'm not here to work. And I'm on nobody's side. I'm just a passerby."

"You sure?"

"Hundred percent."

"Why would I believe you?"

"I don't care if you believe me."

"Look at it from my point of view."

Reacher said, "What were you before you joined the Bureau?"

Chang said, "I was a police officer in Connecticut. A patrol cop."

"That's good. Because I was a military cop. As it happens. So we're brother officers. In a way. Take my word as a gentleman. I'm a coincidence."

"What kind of military cop?"

Reacher said, "The army kind."

"What did you do for them?"

"Mostly what they told me to. Some of everything. Criminal investigation, usually. Fraud, theft, homicide, and treason. All the things folks do, if you let them."

"What's your name?"

"Jack Reacher. Terminal at major. Late of the 110th MP. I lost my job, too."

Chang nodded once, slowly, and seemed to relax. But not completely. She said, but softer, "You sure you're not working here?"

Reacher said, "Completely."

"What do you do now?"

"Nothing."

"What does that mean?"

"What it says. I travel. I move around. I see things. I go where I want."

"All the time?"

"It works for me."

"Where do you live?"

"Nowhere. In the world. Right here, today."

"You have no home?"

"No point. I'd never be there."

"Have you been to Mother's Rest before?"

"Never."

"So why now, if you're not working?"

"I was passing by. It was a whim, because of the name."

Chang paused a beat, and then she smiled, suddenly, and a little wistfully.

"I know," she said. "I can see the movie in my head. The end shot is a big close-up of a leaning-over cross in the ground, two boards nailed together, with an inscription done by a hot poker from a camp fire, and behind it the wagon train clanks away and grows tiny in the distance. Then the credits roll."

"You think an old woman died here?"

"That's how I took it."

"Interesting," Reacher said.

"How did you take it?"

"I wasn't sure. I thought maybe a younger woman stopped to have a baby. Maybe rested up a month and moved on. Maybe the kid became a senator or something."

"Interesting," Chang said.

Reacher pierced a yolk and took a dripping forkful of breakfast.

Thirty feet away the counterman dialed the wall phone and said, "She came back alone from the train station, and headed straight for last night's guy, and now they're deep in conversation, plotting and scheming, you mark my words."

Chapter 4

The diner got less busy. The breakfast rush was clearly a crack-of-dawn thing. Farming, as bad as the military. The waitress came by and Chang ordered coffee and a danish, and Reacher finished his breakfast. He said, "So how does a private investigator like you spend her time, if you don't get to take photographs in hotels?"

Chang said, "We aim to offer a range of specialized services. Corporate research, and a lot of on-line security now, of course, but personal security too. Close personal protection. The rich are getting richer and the poor are getting poorer, and that's good news for the bodyguard business. And we do building security. Plus advice and background checks and threat assessments, and some general investigations, too."

"What brings you here?"

"We have an ongoing operation in the area."

"Against what?"

"I'm not at liberty to say."

"How big of an operation?"

"We have one man in place. At least I thought we did. I was sent as back-up."

"When?"

"I arrived yesterday. I'm based in Seattle now. I flew as far as I could and rented a car. It was a hell of a drive. These roads go on forever."

"And your guy wasn't here."

"No," Chang said. "He wasn't."

"You think he left temporarily and is coming back by train?"

"I hope that's all it is."

"What else could it be? This isn't the Wild West anymore."

"I know. He's probably fine. He's based out of Oklahoma City. It's entirely possible he had to run back for some other business. He'd have used the train, because of the roads. Therefore he'll come back by train. He'll have to. He told me he doesn't have a car here."

"Have you tried calling him?"

She nodded. "I found a land line in the general store. But there's no answer at his home and his cell is off."

"Or out of range. In which case he isn't in Oklahoma City."

"Would he have gone further afield? Around here? Without a car?"

"You tell me," Reacher said. "It's your case, not mine."

Chang didn't answer. The waitress came back and Reacher got a jump on lunch by ordering a slice of peach pie. With more coffee. The waitress looked resigned. Her boss's bottomless cup policy was taking a beating.

Chang said, "He was due to brief me."

Reacher said, "Who was? The guy that isn't here?"

"Obviously."

"Brief you as in update you?"

"More than that."

"So how much don't you know?"

"His name is Keever. He works out of our Oklahoma City office. But we're all on the same network. I can see what he's doing. He's got a couple of big things going on. But nothing out here. Nothing on his computer, anyway."

"How did you get the back-up assignment?"

"I was available. He called me personally."

"From here?"

"Definitely. He told me exactly how to get here. He referred to it as his current location."

"Did it feel like a routine request?"

"Pretty much. It observed the protocols."

"So procedure was followed, except the case isn't on his computer?"

"Correct."

"Which means what?"

"It must be a small thing. Maybe a favor for a friend, or something else too close to pro-bono to get past the boss. No money in it, either way. So it stays under the radar. But then I suppose it got to be a bigger thing. Big enough to justify the call for back-up."

"So it's a small thing that's gotten bigger? Involving what?"

"I have no idea. Keever was going to brief me."

"No idea at all?"

"What part don't you understand? He was working on a hobby case, privately, in secret, and he was going to tell me all about it when I got here."

"What was his tone on the phone?"

"He was relaxed. Mostly. I don't think he likes this place much."

"Did he say so?"

"More my impression. When he was explaining how to get here, he made it sound apologetic, like he was sucking me in to some sinister and creepy place."

Reacher said nothing.

Chang said, "I guess you military people are too data-driven to follow that line of thinking."

Reacher said, "No, I was about to agree. I didn't like the store with the rubber aprons, for instance, and I had some weird kid following me everywhere I went this morning. Maybe ten or twelve. A boy. A slow kid, I assumed, fascinated by a stranger, but very shy. He ducked behind a wall every time I glanced his way."

"I don't know if that's weird or sad."

"You have absolutely no information at all?"

"I'm waiting for Keever to brief me."

"Which means waiting for the trains."

"Twice a day."

"How long before you give up?"

"That's very blunt."

"I was kidding. This is like most bad things that ever happened to me, and to you too, probably, in your patrol car. This is a communications breakdown. A message hasn't gotten through. That's my guess. Because there's no cell service, presumably. People can't cope without it anymore."

Chang said, "I'm going to give it twenty-four hours."

"I'll be gone," Reacher said. "I guess I'll take the evening train."

Reacher left Chang in the diner, and walked back to the old trail, ready to look at the rest of the town. He didn't see the weird kid again. He turned in at the veterinary supply office and re-checked the left-hand side of the street, all six blocks, and saw nothing of interest. He continued onward, out into open country, a hundred yards, two hundred, just in case the railroad had dragged the center of town eastward, leaving relics behind in their original locations. If Chang was right and an old lady had died, her stone wouldn't necessarily be visible from a distance. It might be a low-built affair, a slab laid on the ground, an iron picket not more than a foot and a half high, all nested in a sea of wheat, with maybe a mown path leading to it from the shoulder.

But he saw no such path, and no stone, and no ceremonial iron fence. No larger structure either. No museum. No official billboard about a site of historic interest. He turned around and walked back and started quartering the southern quadrant, block by block, beginning on the east-west side street that ran behind the establishments directly on the trail. Which looked pretty much like its northern equivalent, but with more one-room places carved out of barns and garages, and fewer fruit stands. But no memorial stone, and no museum. Not where logic dictated. Mother's Rest had not always been a crossroads. Not until the railroad. It had been a random speck alongside endless straight ruts through the prairie. The stone or the legend had brought the town to it. The town had grown up around it, like a pearl around a grain of sand.

But he couldn't find it. Not the stone, or the museum. Not where they should be, which was a respectable distance from the original shoulder. Enough to create a feeling of excursion or pilgrimage. Which would be about a modern-day block behind the original shoulder, but there was nothing there.

He moved on, block by block, the same way he had before. He saw the same kind of things, and began to understand them. The town explained itself to him, gradually, street by street. It was a trading post for a vast and dispersed agricultural community. It shipped in all kinds of technical things and shipped out produce in immense quantities. Grain, mostly. But there was some pasture, too. Evidently. Hence the supply companies and the large-animal veterinarian. And the rubber aprons, he supposed. Some folks were doing well and buying shiny new tractors, and some folks weren't doing well, so they were getting their diesel engines repaired and sticking new soles on their boots.

Just a town, like any other.

It was the end of summer, and the day had stayed golden, and the sun was warm but not hot, so he kept on strolling, happy to be out of doors, until he found he had revisited every block he had been to, and seen everything again.

No memorial stone, and no museum.

No weird kid.

But there was a guy who looked at him oddly.

Chapter 5

It was two blocks off the old trail, on a parallel east-west side street, which had five developed blocks on one side, and four on the other. The semicircular shape was starting to bite. There was a bank office and a credit union. There were small lock-up workshops, all of them one-man businesses, with a blade sharpener, and a gearbox repairman, and even a barber with a lit-up pole. But in particular there was a spare-parts guy for several different brands of irrigation systems. He had a cramped store and he was penned in behind the register. Not a small guy. He was facing out and as Reacher passed by he got some kind of flicker in his eye, and he reached upward and backward for something behind his shoulder. Reacher didn't see what it was. His momentum had carried him onward. The front part of his brain didn't think much of it. But the back part nagged. *Why did the guy react?*

Easy. He saw a new face. A stranger. Did not compute.

What was he reaching for? A weapon?

Probably not. A random passerby was no immediate threat. And no one kept a baseball bat or an old .45 loud and proud on the wall. Not in plain sight. Under the counter worked better. Plus how dangerous was the irrigation business anyway? Bats and guns were for bars and bodegas, and maybe pharmacies.

So what was the guy reaching for?

The phone, most likely. An old-fashioned wall-mounted telephone. Shoulder height to most folks, for comfortable dialing. The guy grabbed at it backward because he was too cramped to turn all the way around.

Why would he make a call? Was seeing a stranger such an extraordinary event it required instant sharing?

Maybe he suddenly remembered something. Maybe he was due a sales call. Maybe he was supposed to send a package.

Or maybe he had been told to call in sightings.

Of what?

Strangers.

Told by who?

Maybe the weird kid, too. Maybe that was an attempt at actual surveillance. There's a fine line between showy shyness and sheer incompetence.

Reacher stood in the plaza and turned a full circle.

No one there.

At that point he figured a cup of coffee would be a good idea, so he walked back to the diner. Chang was still in there, at the same table. Late morning. She had swapped seats, so her back was to the angle. Where his had been. He threaded his way through the room and sat down at the table next to hers, side by side, so his back was to the wall, too. Habit, mostly.

"Nice morning?" he asked.

She said, "Feels like a Sunday from my freshman year in college. No cell phone and nothing to do."

"Doesn't your guy at least check in with his office?"

She started to say something, but stopped. She looked all around the room, and at the people in it, as if counting the number of potential witnesses to what might turn out to be an embarrassing admission. Then she smiled a complex and expressive smile, part bold, part rueful, maybe even a little conspiratorial, and she said, "I might have glamorized our situation slightly."

Reacher said, "In what way?"

"Our Oklahoma City office is Keever's spare bedroom. Like our Seattle office is my spare bedroom. Our web site says we have offices everywhere. Which is true. Everywhere there's an out-of-work ex–FBI agent with a spare bedroom and bills to pay. We're not a multi-layered organization. In other words, we have no support staff. Keever has no one to check in with."

"But he has big things going on."

Chang nodded. "We're the real deal and we do good work. But we're a business. Low overhead is the key to everything. And a good web site. No one knows exactly what you are."

"What kind of a thing would he take on as a hobby case?"

"I've been thinking about that, obviously. Nothing corporate. There's no such thing as a small corporate case. Some of them are like a license to print money. They go straight on the computer, believe me. It's like giving yourself a gold star. This one has to be a private client, paying in cash, or handwriting checks. Nothing shady, necessarily, but probably dull and possibly nuts."

"Except now Keever needs back-up."

"Like I said, it started small, and then it got bigger."

"Or the nuts part suddenly wasn't nuts anymore."

"Or got even crazier."

The waitress came by and started Reacher's second bottomless cup of the day. He pre-paid upfront, about four times the check. He liked coffee, and he liked waitresses.

Chang said, "How was your morning?"

He said, "I couldn't find the old woman's grave or any kind of information about the baby."

"You think either one would still be around?"

"I'm pretty sure. There's plenty of space. They're not going to pave over someone's grave. And there's always room for a historical plaque. You see them all over. Some kind of cast metal, painted brown. I don't know who makes them. Department of the Interior, maybe. But there isn't one."

"Have you talked to the locals?"

"Next on the list."

"You should start with the waitress."

"She has a professional obligation to give me the showbusiness answer. So the good word can get around, and then suddenly her diner is a tourist attraction."

"Hasn't worked so far."

"You think many people ask?"

"Probably about five out of ten," she said. "Except that's about eleven years' worth of visitors, right there. So it's a high-percentage, low-frequency proposition. Depends what you mean by 'many.'"

And right then the waitress set off toward them with the Bunn flask, for Reacher's first refill of the session, and Chang asked her, "Why is this town called Mother's Rest?"

The waitress stood back, favoring one hip over the other, like tired women do, with the coffee mid-air and level with her waist. She had hair the color of the wheat outside, and a red face, and she could have been thirty-five or fifty, and a thin person bulking up with age, or a heavy person burning down with work. It was impossible to tell. She looked very happy to take a minute, because Reacher was already her best friend forever, because of the tip, and because she'd just been asked a question that was neither offensive nor boring.

She said, "I like to think a grateful son in a faraway city built his mama a little country home to retire to, in exchange for all the good things she had done for him, and then some stores came to sell her what she needed, and some more houses, and pretty soon it was a town."

Reacher said, "Is that the official version?"

The waitress said, "Honey, I don't know. I'm from Mississippi. I can't imagine how I washed up here. You should ask the counterman. I think he was born in the state at least."

And then she bustled away, like waitresses do.

Chang asked, "Was that the showbusiness answer?"

Reacher nodded and said, "But from the creative side, not the marketing side. She needs to get with the program. Or go write for the movies. I saw one just like that. On the television set in a motel room. In the daytime."

"Should we ask the counterman?"

Reacher glanced over. The guy was busy. He said, "First I'm going to find some real people. I saw some candidates while I was out walking. Then I'm going to find a place to take a nap. Or maybe I'll get my hair cut. Maybe I'll see you at the railroad stop at seven o'clock. Your guy Keever will be getting out, and I'll be climbing aboard."

"Even if you don't know the story of the name yet?"

"It's not that important. Not really worth sticking around for. I'll believe my own version. Or yours. Depending on my mood."

Chang said nothing in reply to that, so Reacher drained his mug, and slid out from behind his table, and threaded his way back through the room. He stepped outside. The sun was still warm. *Next on the list. Real people.* Starting with the spare-parts guy, for the irrigation systems.

Chapter 6

The guy was still hemmed in behind his register. He had about two feet of room, which wasn't enough. He was close to Reacher's own height and weight, but slack and swollen, in a shirt as big as a circus tent, above a belt buckled improbably low, under a belly the size of a kettle drum. His face was pale, and his hair was colorless.

There was a phone on the wall, behind his right shoulder. Not an ancient item with a rotary dial and a curly wire, but a regular modern cordless telephone, with a base station screwed to the stud, and a handset upright in a cradle. Easy enough for the guy to flail blindly behind him, and then the numbers were right there, in the palm of his hand, for speedy dialing. Or speed dialing. The base station had a plastic window with ten spaces. Five were labeled, and five were not. The labels seemed to be the brands the guy sold parts for. Helplines for technical advice, possibly, or sales and service numbers.

The guy said, "Can I get you anything?"

Reacher said, "Have we met?"

"I'm pretty sure not. I'm pretty certain I'd remember."

"Yet when I walked by the first time you jumped so high you practically bumped your head on the ceiling. Why was that?"

"I recognized you, from your old pictures."

"What old pictures?"

"From Penn State, in '86."

"I wasn't smart enough for Penn State."

"You were in the football program. You were the linebacker everyone was talking about. You were in all the sports papers. I used to follow that stuff pretty closely back then. Still do, as a matter of fact. You look older now, of course. If you don't mind me saying that."

"Did you make a phone call?"

"When?"

"When you saw me walk by."

"Why would I do that?"

"I saw your hand move toward the phone."

"Maybe it was ringing. It rings all the damn time. Folks wanting this, folks wanting that."

Reacher nodded. Would he have heard the phone ring? Possibly not. The door had been closed, and the phone was all electronic, with adjustable volume, and maybe it was set to ring very quietly, in such a small space. Especially if calls came in all the time. Right next to the guy's ear. A loud ring could get annoying.

Reacher said, "What's your theory about this town's name?"

The guy said, "My what?"

"Why is this place called Mother's Rest?"

"Sir, I honestly have no idea. There are weird names all over the country. It's not just us."

"I'm not accusing you of anything. I'm interested in the history."

"I never heard any."

Reacher nodded again.

He said, "Have a very pleasant day."

"You too, sir. And congratulations on the rehab. If you don't mind me saying that."

Reacher squeezed out of the store and stood for a moment in the sun.

Reacher visited with twelve more merchants, for a total of thirteen, which gave him fourteen opinions, including the waitress's. There was no consensus. Eight of the opinions were really no opinions at all, but merely shrugs and blank looks, along with a measure of shared defensiveness. *There are weird names all over the country.* Why single out Mother's Rest, in a nation with towns called Why and Whynot, and Accident and Peculiar, and Santa Claus and No Name, and Boring and Cheesequake, and Truth or Consequences, and Monkeys Eyebrow, and Okay and Ordinary, and Pie Town and Toad Suck and Sweet Lips?

The other six opinions were variations on the waitress's fantasy. And his own, Reacher supposed. And Chang's. Folks were working backward from the name, and inventing picturesque scenarios to fit. There was no hard evidence. No one knew of a memorial stone or a museum, or a historical plaque, or even an old folk tale.

Reacher strolled back down the wide street, thinking: nap or haircut?

The spare-parts guy was the first to call it in. He said he was sure he had handled it safely, with the old football trick. It was a technique he had been taught many years before. Pick a good college team in a good year, and most guys were too flattered to be suspicious. Within an hour three more merchants had made the same kind of report. Except about the football. But in terms of substance the picture was clear. The one-eyed motel clerk took all the incoming calls, and he got the information straight in his mind, and then he dialed an outgoing number, and when it was answered he said, "They're coming at it through the name. The big guy is all over town, asking questions."

He got a long plastic crackle in exchange, calm, mellifluous, and reassuring. He said, "OK, sure," but he didn't sound sure, and then he hung up the phone.

The barbershop was a two-chair establishment, with one guy working in it. He was old, but not visibly shaking, so Reacher got a hot-towel shave, and then a clipper cut, short on the back and sides, fading longer up top. His hair was still the same color it always had been. A little thinner, but it was still there. The old guy's labors produced a good result. Reacher looked in the mirror and saw himself looking back, all clean and crisp and squared away. The bill was eleven dollars, which he thought was reasonable.

Then he strolled back across the wide plaza, and outside the motel he saw the lawn chair he had seen before, all alone in the traffic lane. White plastic. He picked it up and put it down again on the right side of the curb, on a patch of grass near a fence. Unobtrusive. In no one's way. He rotated it with his foot, until it was lined up with the rays of the sun. Then he sat down and leaned back and closed his eyes. He soaked up the warmth. And at some point he fell asleep, outdoors in the summertime, which was the second-best way he knew.

Chapter 7

That evening Reacher walked up to the railroad a whole hour early, at six o'clock, partly because the sun had gone low in the sky and there was nowhere left to bask, and partly because he liked being early. He liked enough time to scope things out. Even something as simple as getting on a train.

The elevators were still and silent, presumably empty and awaiting the harvest. The giant warehouse was all closed up. The rails were quiet. The vapor lights were already on, ahead of the dusk, which was coming. The western sky was still gold, but the rest of it was dark. Not long, Reacher thought, before nightfall.

The tiny railroad building was open but empty. Reacher stepped inside. The interior was all wood in a gingerbread style, and it had been painted many times, in an institutional shade of cream. It smelled like wooden buildings always did, at sundown after a long hot day, all airless and dusty and baked.

The ticket window was arched, but it was small overall, and therefore intimate. It had a round hole in the glass, for talking. But behind the glass the shade was down. The shade was brown and pleated. It was made from some kind of primitive vinyl. It had the word *Closed* printed on it, in paint that looked like gold leaf.

There were restrooms off a short corridor. There was a table, with a six-day-old newspaper. There were lights hanging from the ceiling, milky bulbs in glass bowls, but there was no switch. Near the door, where it should have been, was a blank plate with a message taped to it: *Ask at ticket window for lights.*

The benches were magnificent. They could have been a hundred years old. They were made from solid mahogany, upright and severe, only grudgingly sculpted to the human form, and polished to a shine by use. Reacher picked a spot and sat down. The contour felt better than it should. The shape was stern and puritan, but it was very comfortable. The woodworker had done a fine, subtle job. Or maybe the wood itself had given up the struggle, and instead of fighting back had yielded and molded and learned to embrace. From all the shapes and sizes, with their various masses and temperatures. Literally steamed and pressed, like an industrial process, in super-slow motion. Was that possible, with wood as hard as mahogany? Reacher didn't know.

He sat still.

Outside it went darker, and therefore inside it went darker, too. *Ask at ticket window for lights.* Reacher sat in the gloom and watched out the window. He guessed Chang was out there somewhere. In the shadows. That was how she had done it before. He guessed he could go find her. But for what? He wasn't planning any kind of a big long speech. Five more minutes of small talk wouldn't make a difference. He traveled. He moved on. People came and went. He was used to it. No big deal. A friendly wave would do the job, as he stepped across to the train. By which time she might be preoccupied anyway, talking to Keever, getting the story, finding out where the hell he had been.

If Keever was on the train.

He waited.

* * *

A long minute before the train was due Reacher heard the stones in the rail bed click and whisper. Then the rails themselves started to sing, a low steely murmur, building to a louder keening. He felt pressure in the air, and saw the headlight beam. The noise came next, hissing and clattering and humming. Then the train arrived, hot and brutal but infinitely slow, brakes grinding, and it stopped with the locomotive already out of sight, and the passenger cars lined up with the ramp.

The doors sucked open.

On his left Reacher saw Chang step out of the shadow. Like a reflex, because of the train. Out and back, like the flash of a camera.

A man stepped down from the train.

On his right Reacher saw the spare-parts guy from the irrigation store. He stepped out of a shadow and took one step forward and waited.

The man from the train stepped into a pool of light.

Not a big guy. Not Chang's guy. Not Keever. This was a person a little above average height, but some way below average weight. He could have been fifty, and what might have been called slender in his youth was starting to look emaciated. His hair was dark, but probably colored, and he was wearing a suit and a collared shirt, with no tie. He had a bag in his hand, brown leather, larger than a doctor bag, smaller than a duffel.

No one else got out of the train.

The doors were still open.

On his right Reacher saw the spare-parts guy take another step forward. The man from the train spotted him. The spare-parts guy said a name and stuck out his hand. Polite, respectful, welcoming, and humble.

The man from the train shook hands.

The doors were still open.

But Reacher stayed where he was, in the dark.

The spare-parts guy carried the leather bag and led the man in the suit toward the exit gate. The train doors sucked shut, and the cars whined and shuddered, and the train moved away again, slowly, slowly, car after car.

The spare-parts guy led the man in the suit out of sight.

Reacher stepped out to the ramp and watched the tail light dance away in the distance.

From the shadows Chang said, "They're heading for the motel."

Reacher said, "Who are?"

"The man from the train, and his new pal."

She stepped into the light.

She said, "You didn't go."

He said, "No, I didn't."

"I thought you would."

"So did I."

"I think I'm a nice person, but I know I'm not the reason."

Reacher said nothing.

Chang said, "That came out wrong. I'm sorry. Not that kind of reason. Which is presumptuous anyway. I mean, no reason I should be that kind of reason. And now I'm making it worse. I mean, you didn't stay just to help me out. Did you?"

"Did you see those guys shake hands?"

"Of course."

"That's why I stayed."

Chapter 8

Reacher led Chang into the silent waiting room and they sat on a bench, side by side in the dark. Reacher said, "How would you characterize that handshake?"

Chang said, "In what way?"

"The narrative. The story. The body language."

"It looked like a junior corporate executive had been sent to meet an important customer."

"Had they met before?"

"I don't think so."

"I agree. And it was nicely done, by the local guy. Wasn't it? A whole subtle performance. Deferential, but not obsequious. Different from when he shakes his buddy's hand, I'm sure. Or his father-in-law's. Or the loan officer at the bank. Or an old friend from high school he hasn't seen for twenty years."

"So?"

"Our local guy is a man with a wide variety of handshaking styles at his command, and we can assume he's comfortable about using all of them. It's part of his shtick."

"How does this help us?"

"I saw that guy this morning. He runs a store with spare parts for irrigation systems. I walked by his window, and he jumped and went for the phone."

"Why would he?"

"You tell me."

"How paranoid do you want me to be?"

"Somewhere between common sense and a little bit."

She said, "I would think nothing of it, if it wasn't for Keever."

"But?"

"You look like Keever. In a general way. Maybe Keever's been snooping around, and people have been told to keep an eye out for him, or anyone like him."

Reacher said, "I wondered about that, too. Didn't seem very likely, but unlikely things happen. So I went back later, to check. I asked the guy, why did you react? He said he recognized me, from college football in 1986. At Penn State. Apparently there were photographs of me in the magazines. He said he didn't make a telephone call. He said maybe his hand was moving because the phone was ringing. He said it rings all the time."

"Was it ringing?"

"I couldn't hear."

"You played football at Penn State?"

"No, I went to West Point and played football only once. Not very well, I'm afraid. I'm pretty sure I was never in a magazine."

"Could have been an innocent mistake. 1986 was a long time ago. Your appearance would have changed considerably. And you look like you could have played football for Penn State."

"That was my conclusion. At the time."

"But now?"

"Now I think he was covering his ass. He was hiding behind a bullshit story. Maybe it's a trick he learned. Don't waste time with awkward denials, but jump right in with a plausible excuse. Some guys might find it flattering. Maybe they wanted to be football stars. Who wouldn't? Maybe their heads get turned and the problem goes away. Plus he calibrated it to make me younger than I am. Which is flattering too, I suppose. I was already in the army in 1986. I graduated in '83. The guy put on a whole big performance."

"That's not evidence of anything."

"First up, I asked him, have we met? He said no."

"Which was true, right?"

"But a guy like that, a fan who remembers college players from thirty years ago, if I had asked him if we'd met, he'd have said, no, but I'd sure like to shake your hand, sir. Or as I was leaving. There would have been a handshake in there somewhere. This is a handshaking guy. It's important to some people. I've seen it before. Better than an autograph or a picture. Because it's personal. It's physical contact. I bet there's a whole long list of people, when this guy sees them in the newspaper or on TV, he thinks to himself, I shook that guy's hand once."

"But he didn't shake yours."

"Which was a slip on top of a slip. He knew I wasn't a famous football player. So now I'm back with your version. People have been told to keep an eye out for nosy strangers. Including maybe the weird kid from this morning. Plus no Keever on the train. Where the hell is he? So I stayed. One more night, at least. For the fun of it."

"Who was the guy in the suit, who got off the train?"

"I don't know. An outsider, I guess, here to do business of some kind. Not staying long, because of the small bag. Rich, probably. People that thin are usually rich. We live in strange times. Poor people are fat, and rich people are thin. That never happened before."

"Good business or bad business? Is it a coincidence the Penn State guy picked him up, or is he also connected to whatever Keever's looking for?"

"Could be either thing."

"Maybe he's just an irrigation manufacturer. The CEO of a big corporation."

"In which case I think the travel would have been the other way around. Our guy would have gone to a trade show somewhere.

Maybe he would have met the big boss at a cocktail reception. Thirty seconds, maybe less. During which time he would have shaken the guy's hand. That's for damn sure."

"I'm getting worried about Keever."

"You should, I guess. But only a little. Because how bad can this be? With all due respect, this is a private investigator taking cash or grubby checks from a lone individual. Who may or may not be nuts. Your own words. And such a guy would always go to the cops first. After trying everywhere else from the White House downward. But apparently neither the White House nor the cops were interested. So how bad can this be?"

"You think cops always get everything right?"

"I think they have a threshold, where they at least take a look. If the guy had said the warehouse was full of fertilizer bombs, I think they would have come right over. If he'd said the elevators were broadcasting to his root canals, maybe not so much."

"But the point is it seems to have been one thing, and now it's another. Hence the call for back-up. Maybe now it's over the threshold."

"In which case Keever can dial 911 like anyone else. Or he could call the FBI direct. I'm sure he still knows the number."

"So what do we do now?"

"Now we go back to the motel. I need a room for the night, apart from anything else."

The one-eyed guy was on duty in the motel office. Chang picked up the key to 214, as before, and waited. Reacher went through the same grudging negotiation. Sixty bucks, forty, thirty, twenty-five, but not for 106. Reacher couldn't let the guy win every round. He got 113 instead, middle of the opposite wing, ground floor, far from the metal stairs, and one away from directly under Chang's room.

He asked, "Which room is Mr. Keever in?"

The clerk said, "Who?"

"Keever. The big guy from Oklahoma City. Checked in two or three days ago. Came by train. No car. Probably paid for a week upfront."

"I'm not allowed to say. It's a question of privacy. For our guests. I'm sure you understand. And I'm sure you would appreciate it, if the shoe was on the other foot."

"Sure," Reacher said. "That makes sense to me."

He took his key and walked out with Chang. He said, "Don't take this wrong, but I want to come up to your room."

Chapter 9

They used the metal stairs on the right-hand tip of the horseshoe, and then Chang's room was right there, 214, one door from the last room of the row, which was 215. Chang used her key and they stepped inside. The room was like every other room, but Reacher could tell a woman was using it. It was neat, and it was fragrant. There was a small rolling suitcase, with things folded tidily inside.

Reacher said, "What kind of notes would Keever carry?"

"Good question," Chang said. "Normally we carry laptops and smartphones. So all our notes are entered by keyboard. Which can be laborious, but you have to do it anyway, because it all has to be in the record eventually. But the point of an under-the-radar case is to stay off the record, so why do all the typing? He's probably got handwritten pages somewhere."

"Where?"

"In his pocket, probably."

"Or in his room. Depending on quantity. We should check."

"We don't know where his room is. And we don't have a key. And we can't get one, because apparently the Four Seasons here has a privacy policy."

"I think it's 212, 213, or 215."

"Why?"

"I'm guessing Keever made your reservation, right? He probably stopped by the desk and told the clerk he had a colleague coming in. And this clerk seems to think if you have any kind of a vague connection, then you need rooms close together. You're in 214 because Keever was already in 213 or 215 or maybe 212."

"Why did you ask the guy, if you already knew?"

"He could have narrowed it down some. But mostly I felt like using Keever's name in public. Simple as that. If people are watching, then maybe they're listening too, in which case I want them to hear me say it."

"Why?"

"To give them fair warning," Reacher said.

Reacher and Chang walked two doors down, to 212. Which was easy to rule out. The drapes were closed, and the television was playing softly. Not Keever's room. Both 213 and 215 were empty. Both had open drapes, but both were pitch dark inside. Serviced that morning, Reacher figured, and subsequently undisturbed. Law of averages said one was a vacancy, and one was Keever's, paid for but not currently occupied, due to some kind of extraordinary circumstance. The vacancy would look completely bland, and Keever's room would show some kind of sign, however small, like pajamas sticking out from under the pillow, or a book on the night stand, or the corner of a suitcase, placed out of sight behind a chair.

But it was too dark to see.

Reacher said, "Want to flip a coin or wait for morning?"

Chang said, "And do what? Kick the door down? We're in full view of the office here."

Reacher glanced down, and saw the one-eyed guy dragging a lawn chair across the blacktop. It was the chair Reacher had slept in, by the fence. The one-eyed guy lined it up on the sidewalk outside his office window, and he sat down, like an old-time sheriff on his board-walk porch, just gazing. In this case not quite at room 214. Low, and a little right. Which meant not quite at 113, either.

Both rooms at once.

Interesting.

Then Reacher remembered the same chair, that morning, aban-doned in the traffic lane, and he glanced across at 106, and he ran the angles.

Interesting.

He rested his elbows on the rail.

He said, "I guess whether we kick the door down depends on how urgent you feel this whole thing is."

Alongside him Chang said, "No one gets those calls right. Not all the time."

"But some of the time, right?"

"I guess."

"So which kind of time is this?"

"What's your opinion?"

"I'm not in your chain of command. My opinion should carry no weight."

She said, "What is it anyway?"

"Every case is different."

"Bullshit. Cases are the same all the time. You know that."

"Cases like this are the same about half the time," Reacher said. "They fall in two broad groups. Sometimes you get your guy back weeks later, no harm, no foul, and sometimes you've lost your guy before you even knew you had a problem. There isn't much middle ground. The graph looks like a smiley face. Ironically."

"Therefore the math says wait. Either we're already beaten, or we have plenty of time."

Reacher nodded. "That's what the math says."

"And operationally?"

"If we move now, we're committing unconditionally into an unknown situation against forces we have no way of assessing. Could be five guys with convincing handshakes. Or five hundred, with automatic weapons and hollowpoint ammunition. In defense of something we never even heard of yet."

"Which could be what, hypothetically?"

"Like I said, not fertilizer bombs in the warehouse. Something else, that started out weird and then suddenly wasn't. Maybe they really are broadcasting to our root canals."

Chang nodded down toward the one-eyed guy, far away in his white plastic chair. She said, "You picked the right channel to broadcast Keever's name. This guy is in this thing hip deep."

Reacher nodded. "Motel keepers are always useful, in any endeavor. But this guy is not high up in the organization. He's squirming. He resents this. He thinks he's better than all-night sentry duty. But apparently his bosses don't."

"And they're the people we have to find," Chang said.

"We?"

"Figure of speech. A leftover from the old days. It was all teamwork back then."

Reacher said nothing.

Chang said, "You stayed here. I didn't see a gun to your head."

"My reasons for staying have nothing to do with how urgent you think this whole Keever thing is. That's a separate matter, and it's your call."

"I'll wait for morning."

"You sure?"

"The math says so."

"Will you sleep OK, with this guy watching?"

"What else can I do?"

"We could ask him to stop."

"How different would that be than unconditionally committing?"

"That depends on his response."

"I'll sleep OK. But I'm going to double lock the door and put the chain on. We have no idea what's happening here."

"No," Reacher said. "We don't."

"I like your haircut, by the way."

"Thank you."

"What were your reasons?"

"For the haircut?"

"For staying."

He said, "Curiosity, mostly."

"About what?"

"That thing with Penn State in 1986. It was really well done. It was a superb act. I'm sure he's done it before, and I'm sure he's practiced, and rehearsed, and critiqued himself, and relived his successes in his mind, and therefore I'm equally sure it's completely inconceivable he doesn't know there has to be a handshake in there. I bet every other time he's shaken a hand. But not with me. Why was that?"

"He made a mistake."

"No, he couldn't force himself to do it. That was my impression. Even to the point of compromising his art. He's into something, and right now it's under threat somehow, and he feels the people posing the threat are literally too loathsome to touch. That's the impression I got. So I was curious about what kind of a thing could make a person feel that way."

"Now I might not sleep OK."

"They'll come for me first," Reacher said. "I'm downstairs. I'll be sure to make plenty of noise. You'll get a head start."

Chapter 10

Reacher sat in a chair in his room, in the dark, six feet back from the window, invisible from the outside, just watching. Fifteen minutes, then twenty, then twenty-five. As long as it took. The one-eyed guy in his plastic chair was a pale smudge in the gloom, about a hundred feet away. He had gotten comfortable. He was tipped back a little. He was maybe asleep, but lightly. Noise or movement would alert him, probably. Not the best sentry Reacher had ever seen, but not the worst, either.

Above the guy and to the right, up on the second floor, the center room had a rim of light around the drapes. Room 203. The guy from the train, probably. The recent arrival, no doubt unpacking his little leather bag, and getting all his ducks in a row. Unguents and potions in the bathroom, some things in the closet, other things in the drawers. Although the size of the bag was a serious issue, in Reacher's opinion. It had looked like a high-quality item, well used, but not battered or destroyed. Heavy pebbled leather, brown in color, with brass fitments. A classic shape, presumably formed by hinges and some kind of an internal skeleton structure. But not large. And the guy was in town for at least twenty-four hours. Maybe more. With a bag too small for a spare suit, or spare shoes.

Which was unusual, in Reacher's experience. Most civilians carried spare everything, in case of spills, or changes in the weather, or unanticipated invitations.

Ten minutes later the rim of light clicked off, and room 203 went full dark. The one-eyed guy stayed where he was, tipped back, maybe watching, maybe not. Reacher gazed back from the shadows, fifteen more minutes, as long as it took, until he was sure there was nothing doing. Then he stripped and folded his clothes the way he always did, the same pants under a new mattress, and he took a brief shower, and climbed into bed. He left the drapes open, and set the alarm in his head to wake him at six in the morning, or if there was noise or commotion in the night, whichever came first.

The dawn was silent, and it was golden again, but infinitely pale. The elevators threw weak shadows long enough to hit the motel. Reacher sat up in bed and watched. The plastic chair was still there, on the sidewalk under the office window, a hundred feet away, but the one-eyed guy had gone. At four in the morning, Reacher guessed. The lowest ebb. To a couch in the back, no doubt.

Room 203's drapes were still closed. The guy from the train. Still asleep, probably. Reacher got up and came back from the bathroom with a towel around his waist. He opened his window. For the air. And for the sound. He could hear vehicles on the wide street. Regular gasoline V-8s, and thick tires pattering on the rail lines embedded in the blacktop. Pick-up trucks, probably. Heading for breakfast in the diner. People were up with the sun.

He sat and watched, without coffee. He ran a pleasant fantasy through his head, of calling the diner and ordering a pot from the waitress, his new best friend, and having her show up with it minutes later. Except he didn't have the diner's number, and there was no phone in his room. And he wasn't dressed. A hundred feet away across the horseshoe there was light in the office window. But no movement. Just a faded old motel, two-thirds empty, not long after dawn.

He sat and watched, patiently, expecting to be rewarded eventually, and eventually he was, after almost an hour. First the one-eyed guy came out his office door, and stood and sniffed the air, the way people do in the morning. Then the guy glanced all around, at the inside perimeter of his little domain, and his parking spaces, and the sidewalk passing the first-floor rooms, and the walkway passing the second-floor rooms, a leisurely visual inspection, born mostly of duty, Reacher thought, but with a small slice of pride in there somewhere. Then the guy remembered the unexamined territory directly behind him, and he turned around to check, and he saw his misplaced lawn chair. He dragged it back to 102, and left it lined up in perfect uniformity with all its ground-floor equivalents, which were all directly underneath their second-floor counterparts.

Which made it more duty than pride. Because he hadn't bothered the day before. He had left the chair any old place it had wanted to be. Wherever it hung its hat was its home. But this new day was different. Somehow. The guy was acting like a nervous CO ahead of a one-star's visit.

Reacher waited. The shadows retreated, yard by yard, as the sun climbed higher. He heard the seven o'clock train. It rolled in, and vibrated, and rolled out again.   .

He waited.

The drapes opened in room 203. The window was sideways to the sun, and like everything else the glass was covered in crop dust, but even so Reacher saw the guy clearly, in his suit, standing with his arms held wide, his hands still on the drapes, staring out at the morning, as if in wonder, as if it was a big surprise the sun had come up again. As if it had been maybe fifty-fifty at best. The guy stood like that for a whole minute, and then he turned away and was lost to sight.

A white sedan drove into the lot. A Cadillac, Reacher thought. But not new. It was from a previous generation. It was long and low, all road-hugging weight and boulevard ride. Like a limousine. Therefore an unusual color, outside of Florida or Arizona. An unusual sight in any case, in farm country. It was the first sedan Reacher had seen in about three hundred miles. It was pretty clean. Recently rinsed, at least, if not actually washed. Reacher couldn't see the driver. The glass was too dark.

The car swooped right and backed left and reversed into the slot below room 203. It had no front license plate. The driver didn't get out. Above the car, room 203's door opened, and the man in the suit stepped out. He had the brown leather bag in his hand. He stood still for a long moment, and did the air-sniffing thing. As if in wonder. Then he snapped out of his trance and headed for the stairs, definitely gaunt but light on his feet, and a fluent, fluid mover, not muscle-bound like an athlete, but graceful like a dancer, or a stage actor. He came down the stairs, and the driver got out of the Cadillac, to greet him.

The driver was a man Reacher hadn't seen before. He was about forty, tall and well built, not fat but certainly fleshed out, with a full head of hair, and a guileless face. Another junior executive, possibly. The man in the suit shook his hand, and ducked into the back of the car. The driver carried the brown leather bag to the trunk, and placed it inside, like a little ceremony. Then he got back behind the wheel, and the car pulled forward, and drove away.

No rear license plate, either.

Reacher went and took a shower.

Chang was already in the diner, at the corner two-top they had used before. She had her back to the wall. She had reserved the table next to her, by hanging her coat on the chair. Reacher passed it back to her and sat down, side by side, with his own back to the wall. Which was tactically sound, but a shame in every other way. Chang looked just fine in a T-shirt. Her hair was still damp, which made it look like ink. Her arms were long and faintly muscled, and her skin was smooth.

She said, "The guy in the suit left already. He took his bag, so he isn't coming back. Lucky him."

"I saw," Reacher said. "From my room."

"I was on my way back from the railroad. Keever wasn't on the morning train."

"I'm sorry to hear that."

"So now's the time. No more waiting for him. I have to start looking for him. His room is 215. I peeked through the window. There's a big shirt hanging on a closet door. Room 213 is completely empty."

"OK. We'll get in somehow."

"We?"

"Figure of speech," Reacher said. "I have nothing else to do today."

"Should we go do it now?"

"Let's eat first. Eat when you can. That's the golden rule."

"Now could be a good time to do it."

"Could be, but later will be better. When the maid has started work. She might open the door for us."

The waitress came over, with coffee.

Chapter 11

After breakfast they found the motel maid had indeed started work, but she was nowhere near Keever's room. She was fully occupied on the other side of the horseshoe, making 203 ready-to-rent again after the man in the suit's departure. She had a big stacked cart on the walkway, and the room door was standing open. She was visible inside, stripping the bed.

She would have a pass key on her belt, or in her pocket, or chained to her cart handle.

Reacher said, "I guess I'll walk over there and say hello."

He turned left at 211, and left again at 206, and he stopped level with the cart and looked in 203's door.

The maid was crying.

And working, both at the same time. She was a white woman, thin as a rail, no longer young, hauling a sack of towels from the bathroom. She was bawling and sniveling and tears were streaming down her face.

From outside the room Reacher said, "Ma'am, are you OK?"

The woman stopped, and let go of the sack, and straightened up. She huffed and puffed and took a breath and stared blankly at

Reacher, and then she turned and stared blankly in the mirror, and then she turned back again without a reaction, as if her appearance was already too far gone to worry about.

She smiled.

She said, "I'm very happy."

"OK."

"No, really. I'm sorry. But the gentleman who just checked out left me a tip."

"What, your first ever?"

She said, "My best ever."

She had a smock with a wide catch-all pocket on the bottom hem. She used both hands carefully and came out with an envelope. Smaller than a regular letter. Like a reply to a fancy invitation. On it the words *Thank You* were handwritten with a fountain pen.

She flipped up the flap with her thumb, and took out a fifty-dollar bill. Ulysses S. Grant, right there on the front.

"Fifty bucks," she said. "The most I ever got before was two dollars."

"Outstanding," Reacher said.

"This is going to make such a big difference to me. You can't imagine."

"I'm happy for you," Reacher said.

"Thank you. I guess sometimes miracles happen."

"Do you know why this town is called Mother's Rest?"

The woman paused a beat.

She said, "Are you asking me or are you going to tell me?"

"I'm asking you."

"I don't know."

"You never heard any stories?"

"About what?"

"About mothers," Reacher said. "Resting, either literally or figuratively."

"No," she said. "I never heard anything about that."

"Can you let me into 215?"

The woman paused a beat. She said, "Are you the gentleman from 113? And 106, the night before?"

"Yes."

"I can't open a room except for the registered occupant. I'm sorry."

"It was a corporate booking. We all work together. We need to be in and out. It's a teamwork thing."

"I could go check with the manager."

"Don't worry about it," Reacher said. "I'll go check with him myself."

But the one-eyed guy wasn't in his office. An impromptu absence, clearly, because the desk looked like work had been interrupted recently and temporarily. Files and ledgers were open, and pens were dropped on notebooks, and there was a go-cup of coffee that looked pretty warm.

But the guy wasn't there.

Behind the desk was a door in the wall. Private space, Reacher guessed. The sleeping couch for sure, and maybe a kitchenette, and certainly at least a half-size bathroom. Which was maybe where the guy was right then. Some things can't wait.

Reacher listened hard, and heard nothing.

He stepped around the desk to the private side.

He glanced at the ledgers. And the files. And the notebooks. Routine motel stuff. Accounts, orders, to-do lists, percentages.

He listened again. Heard nothing.

He opened a drawer. Where the guy kept the room keys. He put 113 in, and took 215 out.

He closed the drawer.

He stepped back to the public side.

He breathed out.

The one-eyed guy didn't come back. Maybe he had a digestive disorder. Reacher turned around, and strolled out of the office. He crossed the horseshoe and went up Chang's stairs. He showed her the key, and she asked, "How long have we got it?"

He said, "As long as Keever paid for. All week, probably. I'm taking over his room. The motel guy can't complain. He's had his money. And Keever isn't here to express an opinion."

"Will that work?"

"It might. Unless they get up a posse."

"In which case we call 911. Like Keever should have."

"The guy in the suit left a fifty-dollar tip for the maid."

"That's a lot of money. You give that for a week on a cruise ship."

"She was very happy."

"She would be. It's like a free week's wages."

"Makes me feel bad. I never leave more than five."

"He was a rich man. You said so yourself."

Reacher said nothing, and stepped up to Keever's door. He put the key in the lock. He opened the door and stepped back and said, "After you."

Chang went inside, and Reacher followed. Evidence of Keever was all over the room. The shirt on the door knob, a neat travel kit in the bathroom, a linen jacket in the closet, a battered valise open against a wall, full of clothes. Everything had been lined up with great precision by the maid. The room was clean and tidy.

No briefcase. No computer bag, no fat notebooks, no handwritten pages.

Not on open view, anyway.

Reacher turned back and closed the door. He had searched maybe a hundred motel rooms in his long and unglamorous career, and he was good at it. He had found all kinds of things in all kinds of places.

He said, "What was Keever, before he joined the Bureau?"

Chang said, "He was a police detective, with a night-school law degree."

Which meant he had searched motel rooms, too. Which meant he wouldn't have used anywhere obvious. He knew the tricks. Not that the room offered many opportunities. It was not architecturally complex.

Chang said, "We're fooling ourselves, surely. The motel clerk could have been in here half a dozen times already. Or let someone else in. We have to assume this room was searched long ago."

Reacher nodded. "But how well? That's the question. Because we know one thing for sure. Keever was in this room at one point, and then he left. He had three possible ways of leaving. First, he left on an innocent errand that turned bad later. Second, he was dragged out of here kicking and screaming by persons unknown. Or third, he was sitting here on the bed, running things through his mind, and he made a sudden random connection, like a real oh-shit moment, and he stood up and hustled over to the pay phone in the general store to call 911 without further ado. Except he didn't make it."

"Didn't make it? What are you saying?"

"I'm saying the guy is missing. Tell me where and why, and I'll close down the other theories."

"None of those three ways of leaving means we should expect to find something in this room. Something that everyone else missed."

"No, I think the third one does. Just possibly. Imagine the moment. *Oh shit.* You're stunned. And as of that split second you're in grave danger. The danger is so bad you need to run straight for the phone. But you'll be exposed. This is not the same as using a cell behind a locked door. This is a walk in the open air. Which carries a risk now. So maybe you're tempted to leave a marker behind. You scribble a note and you hide it. Then you go for the phone."

"And don't make it."

"That's what the math says. Sometimes."

"But this note is hidden so well no one has found it. But not so well we won't find it. If there is a note at all. If it was the third of the three possibilities. If it wasn't something completely different."

"It was a sequence," Reacher said. "Had to be, right? It was two oh-shit moments. A small one, maybe the day before, after which he calls you for back-up, and then the big one, after which he goes to call the cops."

"After leaving a note."

"I think it's worth considering."

When Reacher searched a room, he started with the room, not the contents. Hiders and therefore seekers tended to ignore the physical structure, which was often rich with possibility. Especially for a sheet of paper. An under-window HVAC unit could be opened up, and nine times out of ten there was a plastic pocket expressly designed to hold paperwork, often an instruction manual or a warranty card, among which an enterprising person could conceal dozens of pages.

Or if there was forced-air heating and cooling, there would be grills, easily unscrewed. Pocket doors were good for hiding papers. Ceilings had removable panels for maintenance purposes. A folding door on a closet had an inside face no one ever saw. And so on.

Only then came the furniture. In this case a bed, two night tables, an upholstered chair, a dining chair at the desk, the desk itself, and a small chest of drawers.

They looked everywhere, but they found nothing.

Afterward Chang said, "Worth a try, I guess. In a way I'm glad we didn't find anything. Makes it less final. I want him to be OK."

Reacher said, "I want him to be in Vegas with a nineteen-year-old. But until we get a postcard, we have to assume he isn't. Just so we stay sharp."

"He was a cop and a special agent. How far is it from here to the general store? What could have happened?"

"It's about two hundred feet. Past the diner. Lots of things could have happened."

Chang didn't answer. Reacher's hands felt dirty. From moving furniture, and touching surfaces not regularly cleaned. He stepped into the bathroom and flipped up the tap to wet his hands. The soap was a new cake, still wrapped in tissue paper. Light blue, all pleated and stuck down with a gold label. Not the worst place Reacher had ever seen. He pulled off the paper and balled it up. The trash can was under the vanity. The vanity was deep. A kind of underhand through-the-slot change-up was required. Left-handed, too. Which he executed. And then he washed his hands, the new soap hard at first, and then better later. He dried his hands on a fresh towel, and then his conscience got the better of him, and he bent down to check his tissue-paper spitball had in fact hit the target.

It hadn't.

The trash can was round, like a short cylinder, but it was jammed up in a left-hand corner, which meant there was a shallow space behind. The kind of space that got ignored, especially by maids with mops. Not for two-dollar tips. It was the kind of space that ended up the graveyard of errant throws.

Three of them.

One was his own spitball. He could tell by the dampness. One was an older version of the same thing. Bone dry. A previous cake of soap.

And one was a piece of furred paper, like junk from a pocket.

Chapter 12

The paper was a stiff white square, about three and a half inches on a side, with one gummed edge. A sheet from a memo block or cube. Reacher had seen such things before. It had been folded in four, and it had ridden in a pocket for a month or more. The folds were worn, and the corners had deteriorated, and the surfaces were rubbed. Reacher guessed it had been flicked toward the trash can, maybe two-fingered like a trick with a playing card, but it had sailed too far, and hit the deck in no-man's-land.

He unfolded it and smoothed it flat. What could be called the outer face was blank. Just a rub of grime, and faint indigo staining, probably from denim. From the back pocket of a pair of blue jeans, he thought.

He turned the paper over.

What could be called the inner face had writing on it. Ballpoint pen, a hurried note. A scrawl, really. There was a phone number, and the words *200 deaths*.

Reacher asked, "Is this Keever's handwriting?"

Chang said, "I don't know. I've never seen Keever's handwriting. And it isn't a great sample. So we can't be certain. Think like a defense attorney. There's no unbroken chain of custody. Anyone could have left this here. At any time."

"Sure," Reacher said. "But suppose it's Keever's. What would it be?"

"Be? A note, probably made during a phone call. In his office. His spare bedroom, anyway. Maybe an initial contact, or a follow-up call. High stakes, with two hundred deaths, and a phone number, which might be either the client, or a source of independent corroboration. Or a source of further information."

"Why would he throw it away?"

"Because later he wrote it up in longer form, so he didn't need it anymore. Maybe he was standing here at the mirror, checking himself over, like people do. Maybe he dumped his old Kleenex and took new, and maybe he checked his other pockets at the same time. Maybe he hadn't used those pants for a while."

The phone number's area code was 323. Reacher said, "Los Angeles, right?"

Chang nodded and said, "Either a cell or a land line."

"Two hundred deaths. That would qualify as serious danger."

"If it's Keever's. If it was about this current case. It could be anybody's about anything."

"Who else would pass through here with two hundred deaths on his mind?"

"Who says they did? Even if it's Keever's, it could have been an old case. Or a different case. Or it could have been a liability lawyer a year ago, chasing ambulances. How could there even be two hundred deaths here? That's twenty percent of the population. Someone would have noticed. You wouldn't need a private investigator."

"Let's call the number," Reacher said. "Let's see who answers."

Reacher locked up the room, and they went down the metal stairs, and a hundred feet away the one-eyed guy came out of his office and bustled across toward them, waving and gesturing. When he arrived he said, "Excuse me, sir, but 215 is not your registered room."

Reacher said, "Then amend your register. The room was paid for by an associate of ours, and I'm going to be using it until he returns."

"You can't do that."

"No such word."

"How did you get the key?"

"I found it under a bush. Just lucky, I guess."

"This is not allowed."

"Then call the cops," Reacher said.

The guy said nothing. He just huffed and puffed for a moment, and then he turned around and headed back, without another word.

Chang said, "Suppose he does call the cops?"

"He won't," Reacher said. "He would have made a big point of telling us he was about to, yes sir, right there and then. Plus the cops are probably fifty miles away. Or a hundred. They wouldn't come out for a room that was already paid for. Plus if these people have something to hide, the last thing they'll do is call the cops."

"What will he do instead?"

"I'm sure we'll find out."

They stepped out to the wide street and walked past the front of the diner, to the general store. The sun was up and the town was quiet. No activity, and no big crowds. There was a pick-up truck fifty yards ahead, making a turn into a side street. There was a kid throwing a tennis ball against a wall, and hitting the rebound with a stick. Like baseball practice. He was pretty good. Maybe he should have his picture in a magazine. There was a FedEx truck crossing the rails on the old trail, and heading into town.

The general store was a classic rural building, a plain flat-roofed structure end-on to the street, with a fancy gabled frontage made of lap boards painted dull red. There was a sign, painted in circus letters colored gold: *Mother's Rest Dry Goods*. There was a single door, and a single window, which was small, and purely for light, rather than for the display of tempting goods. The glass was covered with decals, all with names Reacher didn't know. Brand names, he assumed, for arcane but vital country stuff.

Inside the door was a boxed-in vestibule, which had a pay phone mounted on the wall. No acoustic hood. Just the instrument itself, all metal, including the cord. Chang fed coins in the slot, and dialed. She listened for a spell, and then she hung up without speaking.

She said, "Voice mail. The phone company's standard announcement. Not personalized. No name. Sounded like a cell phone."

Reacher said, "You should have left a message."

"No point. I can't get calls here."

"Try Keever again. Just in case."

"I don't want to. I don't want to hear him not answer."

"He's either OK or he isn't. Calling him or not calling him doesn't change anything."

She used her own cell to look up the number, but she dialed on the older technology. As before, she listened for a spell, and then she hung up without speaking. She tried a second number. Same result.

She shook her head.

She said, "No answer."

Reacher said, "We should go to Oklahoma City."

Chapter 13

The train would have been faster, but its departure was still eight hours away, so they drove, in Chang's rental car. It was a compact Ford SUV, green in color. Inside it was bland and unmarked, and it smelled strongly of upholstery shampoo. They were out of town within a minute, on the old wagon train trail, and then they turned south and west and south again, through the immense checkerboard of endless golden fields, until they found a county road that promised a highway entrance two hundred miles ahead.

Chang was driving, in her T-shirt. Reacher had the passenger seat racked back, and he was watching her. She had one hand low on the wheel, and the other resting in her lap. Her eyes were always moving, to the road ahead, to the mirrors, back to the road ahead. Sometimes she half-smiled briefly, and then half-grimaced, as thoughts ran through her head. Her shoulders were rolled forward an inch, in a tiny hunch. Which Reacher took to mean she wanted to be a smaller person. Which ambition he could not endorse. She looked exactly the right size to him. She was long-limbed and solid, but not where she shouldn't be.

I think I'm a nice person, but I know I'm not the reason.

He said nothing.

She looked in the mirror again, and she said, "There's a pick-up truck behind us."

He said, "How far back?"

"About a hundred yards."

"How long has it been there?"

"A mile or so."

"It's a public road."

"It came on real fast, but now it's hanging back. Like it was looking for us, and now it's found us."

"Just one?"

"That's all I can see."

"Not much of a posse."

"Two men, I think. A driver and a passenger."

Reacher didn't want to turn around to look. Didn't want to show either guy the pale flash of a concerned face in the rear window. So he hunched down a little and moved sideways until he could see the image in Chang's door mirror. A pick-up truck, about a hundred yards back. A Ford, he thought. A serious machine, big and obvious, keeping pace. It was dull red, like the general store. There were two guys in it, side by side, but far from each other, because of the vehicle's extravagant width.

Reacher sat up again and looked through the windshield. Wheat to the right, wheat to the left, and the road running dead straight ahead until it fell below the far horizon. The shoulders were graveled for drainage, but there were no ditches. No turns, either. The fields were endless. Almost literally. Maybe the same field ran all the way to the highway ramp. Two hundred miles. It looked possible.

There were no other cars in sight.

He said, "Did you train for this stuff at Quantico?"

She said, "To a certain extent. But a long time ago. And in a different environment. Mostly urban. With traffic lights and four-way stops and one-way streets. We don't have many options here. Did you train for it?"

"No, I was never any good at driving."

"Should we let them make the first move?"

"First we need to figure out what they've been told to do. If it's surveillance only, we can lead them all the way to Oklahoma City and lose them there. The only fights you truly win are the ones you don't have."

"What if it's not surveillance only?"

"Then they'll do it like the movies. They'll bump us from behind."

"To scare us? Or worse than that?"

"That would be a very big step for them to take."

"They'll make it look like an accident. Tourist lady fell asleep on the long straight road and crashed. I'm sure it happens all the time."

Reacher said nothing.

"We can't outrun them," Chang said. "Not in this thing."

"So let them get close and then switch to the other lane and hit the brakes. Send them on ahead."

"When?"

"Don't ask me," Reacher said. "I failed defensive driving. I lasted less than a day. They made me go qualify on something else. When they get big in the mirror, I guess."

Chang drove on. Two-handed now. One minute. Two. She said, "I want to see their moves. We need to force their hand."

"You sure?"

"They're the home team. We need to shake them up."

"OK. Speed up a bit."

She hit the gas and he turned around and stared out the back window. The pale flash of a concerned face. He said, "Faster."

The little green Ford jumped ahead, almost two hundred yards, and then the pick-up reacted, and its grille rose up, and it came charging closer. Chang said, "Give me a real-time distance countdown. I can't judge in the mirrors."

"They're at eighty yards now," Reacher said. "Which gives us about eight seconds."

"Less, because I'm going to slow down. This thing might tip over."

"Sixty yards."

"OK, I'm clear ahead."

"And behind. It's just the two of us on the road. Forty yards."

"I'm slowing some more. We can't do this over sixty."

"Twenty yards."

"I'm going to do it at ten yards."

"OK, now, do it now."

And she did. She swerved left and braked hard and the pick-up came within an inch of clipping her right back corner, but it missed, and it sped on ahead, braking hard but much later. Meanwhile the little green Ford did a lot of side-to-side rocking and tipping, but soon enough it was stopped dead, safe, back in the correct lane, a hundred yards behind the pick-up truck, their relative positions completely inverted after a noisy few seconds.

Chang said, "Of course, this begs the fairly obvious question, what now? We turn around, they turn around. And then they're chasing us all over again."

"Drive straight at them," Reacher said.

"And crash?"

"That's always an option."

But the pick-up moved first. It turned around in the road and came back toward them, but very slowly, just creeping along, barely more than idle speed. Which Reacher took as a message. Like a white flag.

"They want to talk," he said. "They want to do this face to face."

The truck stopped ten yards ahead and both doors opened. Two men climbed out. Sturdy individuals, both about six feet and two hundred pounds, both somewhere in their middle thirties, both with mirrored sunglasses, both with thin cotton jackets over T-shirts. They looked cautious but confident. Like they knew what they were doing. Like they were the home team.

Chang said, "They must be armed. They wouldn't be doing it this way otherwise."

"Possible," Reacher said.

The two men took up position in the middle of the no-man's-land between the two vehicles. One was on the left of the center line, and one was on the right. They stood easy, just waiting, hands by their sides.

Reacher said, "Run them over."

"I can't do that."

"OK, I guess I'll go see what they want. Any problems, take off for Oklahoma City without me, and best of luck."

"No, don't get out. It's too dangerous."

"For me or for them? They're just a couple of country boys."

"We should assume they have guns."

"But only temporarily."

"You're nuts."

"Maybe," Reacher said. "But never forget it was Uncle Sam who made me this way. I passed every other course, except driving."

He opened his door, and stepped out.

Chapter 14

The little green Ford had regular front-hinged doors, like most cars, and the doors had a restraint about two-thirds of the way through their travel, so stepping out meant stepping back too, which improved Reacher's angle. It put the engine block between him and the two guys. If they drew down immediately and started shooting from the get-go, he could hit the deck behind a bulletproof shield. If they had guns. Which was not proven. Except even if they did, he couldn't imagine why they would start shooting from the get-go. Which was gone anyway. They could have fired through the windshield. That was the real get-go. Unless they wanted to preserve the car for a convincing accident. It would be hard to explain bullet holes in the glass, if the tourist lady had merely fallen asleep at the wheel. In which case how would they explain bullet holes in the dead passenger? And they would have to get his body back in the car. Which wouldn't be easy. He would be a lot of dead weight.

He figured they weren't going to shoot.

If they had guns.

He said, "Guys, you've got thirty seconds, so go ahead and state your case."

The guy on the right folded his arms high across his chest, like a bouncer at a nightclub door. A show of support, Reacher figured, for the other guy, who was presumably the spokesperson.

The other guy said, "It's about the motel."

His hands were still by his sides.

Reacher said, "What about it?"

"That's our uncle who runs it. He's a poor old handicapped man, and you're giving him a hard time. You're breaking all kinds of laws."

His hands were still by his sides. Reacher stepped out from behind the door and moved up next to the Ford's right-hand headlight. He could feel the heat from the engine. He said, "What laws am I breaking?"

"You're in another guest's room."

"Who isn't using it right now."

"Doesn't matter."

His hands were still by his sides. Reacher took a step, and another, until he was level with the Ford's left-hand headlight, but much further forward, on a diagonal. Which put him ten feet from the two guys, in a narrow triangle in no-man's-land, the guy with the folded arms on one corner, and the spokesperson on another, and Reacher all alone at the thin end.

The guy on the left said, "So we're here to collect the key."

Reacher took another step. Now he was seven feet away. Now they were in an intimate little cluster. No other cars in sight. The wheat moved slowly, in waves, like an immense golden sea.

Reacher said, "I'll return the key when I check out."

The guy on the left said, "You're already checked out. As of right now. And you won't get a room if you come back again. Management reserves the right to refuse admission."

Reacher said nothing.

The guy on the left said, "And there's nowhere else in Mother's Rest. My uncle's place is the only game in town. You getting the message?"

Reacher said, "Why is it called Mother's Rest?"

"I don't know."

"Where is the message coming from? Purely your uncle, or the other thing?"

"What other thing?"

"Something I heard about."

"There is no other thing."

"Good to know," Reacher said. "Tell your uncle no laws have been broken. Tell him he's been paid for the room. Tell him I'll see him later."

The guy on the right uncrossed his arms.

The guy on the left said, "Are you going to be a problem?"

"I'm already a problem," Reacher said. "The question is, what are you going to do about it?"

There was a pause, hot and lonely in the middle of nowhere, and then the two guys answered by brushing aside their coats, in tandem, casually, right-handed, both thereby showing black semi-automatic pistols, in pancake holsters, mounted on their belts.

Which was a mistake, and Reacher could have told them why. He could have launched into a long and impatient classroom lecture, about sealing their fates by forcing a decisive battle too early, about short-circuiting a grander strategy by moving the endgame to the beginning. Threats had to be answered, which meant he was going to have to take their guns away, because probing pawns had to be sent back beaten, and because folks in Mother's Rest needed to know for sure the next time he came to town he would be armed. He wanted to tell them it was their own fault. He wanted to tell them they had brought it on themselves.

But he didn't tell them anything. Instead he ducked his own hand under his own coat, grabbing at nothing but air, but the two guys didn't know that, and like the good range-trained shooters they were they went for their guns and dropped into solid shooting stances all at once, which braced their feet a yard apart for stability, so Reacher stepped in and kicked the left-hand guy full in the groin, before the guy's gun was even halfway out of its holster, which meant the right-hand guy had time to get his all the way out, but to no avail, because the next event in his life was the arrival of Reacher's elbow, scything backhand against his cheekbone, shattering it and causing a general lights-out everywhere.

Reacher stepped back, and then he checked on the first guy, who was preoccupied, like most guys he had kicked in the groin. The guns were Smith & Wesson Sigma .40s, which were modern part-polymer weapons, and expensive. They were both fully loaded. Both guys had wallets in their hip pockets, with about a hundred dollars between them, which Reacher took as spoils of war. Their driver's licenses both showed the last name Moynahan, which meant they could indeed be brothers or cousins with an uncle in common. One had been christened John, and the other Steven.

Reacher carried the guns back to the little green Ford. Chang's window was down. He put one gun in his pocket and passed the other to Chang. She took it, a little reluctantly. He asked, "Did you hear any of what they said?"

Chang said, "All of it."

"Conclusions?"

"They might have been telling the truth. The motel might have been their only beef. On the other hand, it might not."

"I vote not," Reacher said. "The room has been paid for. Why get so uptight?"

"You could have been killed."

Reacher nodded.

"Many times," he said. "But all long ago. Not today. Not by these guys."

"You're crazy."

"Or competent."

"So now what?"

Reacher glanced back. The guy on the right was about to transition from unconscious to concussed. The guy on the left was squirming halfheartedly and pawing at everything between his ribcage and his knees.

Reacher said, "Shoot them if they move."

He walked ten yards to their truck and climbed in. The glove compartment had registration and insurance in the name of Steven Moynahan. There was nothing else of interest in the cab. He got straightened up behind the wheel and put the truck in gear. He steered for the shoulder and parked straddling the gravel, with the left-hand wheels safely out of the traffic lane, and the right-hand wheels deep in the wheat, and the nose pointing back toward town. He shut it down and pulled the key.

He dragged the guys one by one into the shade ahead of the front bumper, and sat them up against the chrome. Both were awake by that point. He said, "Watch carefully, now," and when he had their attention he took their key and balanced it on his palm and tossed it underhand into the field. Forty or fifty feet. It would take them an hour to find, even under the best of circumstances, even after they were operational again. Which might be a supplementary hour all by itself.

Then he walked back and got in the Ford, and Chang drove on. From time to time he turned around and checked the view. The parked truck stayed visible for a long time, dwindling to a tiny dull pinprick in the far distance, and then it fell below the northern horizon and was lost to sight.

It took nearly three more hours to get to the highway, and then the distance markers promised another two to Oklahoma City. The drive was uneventful, until a point about ninety minutes out, when all kinds of chiming and beeping started coming from the phone in Chang's pocket. Voice mails and text messages and e-mails, all patiently stored and now downloading.

Cell service was back.

Chapter 15

Chang drove one-handed and juggled her phone, but Reacher said, "We should pull off the road. Before the tourist lady gets in a wreck for real. We should get a cup of coffee."

Chang said, "I don't understand how you drink so much coffee."

"Law of gravity," Reacher said. "If you tip it up, it comes right out. You can't help but drink it."

"Your heart must be thumping all the time."

"Better than the alternative."

A mile later they saw a sign and took an exit that led to a standard linear array of pit-stop facilities, including a gas station, and bathrooms, and an old-fashioned plain stone building in a federal style somewhat disfigured by bright neon signs for modern chain store coffee and food. They parked and got out and stretched. It was the middle of the afternoon, and still warm. They used the bathrooms and met in the coffee shop. Reacher got his usual medium cup of hot black, and Chang got iced, with milk. They found a corner table, and Chang put her phone down. It was a thin touch-screen thing about the size of a paperback book. She swiped and dabbed and scrolled, first through the phone options, and then the text messages, and then the e-mail.

She said, "Nothing from Keever."

"Try calling him again."

"We both know he won't answer."

"Stranger things have happened. Once I had three police departments and the National Guard looking for a guy, and all of a sudden he showed up, fresh back from a vacation out of state."

"We know Keever isn't on vacation."

"Try him anyway."

Which she did, after a long reluctant pause, first on his home number, and then on his cell number.

There was no reply on either.

Reacher said, "Try the Los Angeles number again. From the piece of paper with the two hundred deaths."

Chang nodded, keen to move on. She dialed, and held the phone to her ear.

This time the call was answered.

She said, a little surprised, "Good afternoon, sir. May I know who I'm speaking with?"

Which question must have been answered in the obvious manner, the same way Reacher had, with a previous inquiry: *Who's asking?*

She said, "My name is Michelle Chang. I'm a private detective, based in Seattle. Previously I was with the FBI. Now I work with a man named Keever. I think he might have called you. Your number was found in his motel room."

Reacher had no idea what was asked next, all the way out there in Los Angeles, but he pretty soon realized it must have been an inquiry as to how to spell Keever, because Chang said, "K-e-e-v-e-r."

A long pause, and then a reply, almost certainly negative, because Chang said, "Can you be certain of that?"

And then there was a long conversation, mostly one-sided, definitely biased toward the LA guy doing all the talking, which Reacher couldn't hear, and Chang's facial expressions could have launched a thousand competing scenarios, so he got no real guidance from her. He had a sense the guy worked hard on one thing after another, episodically. And in great detail. Maybe he was an actor. Or a movie person. The context was unclear. In the end Reacher gave up trying to construct a plausible narrative, and just waited.

Eventually Chang said goodbye and clicked off the call, and took a breath, and a sip of iced coffee, and said, "His name is Westwood. He's a journalist with the *LA Times*. Their science editor, in fact. Not that it's a giant department, he says. Generally he writes in-depth features for their Sunday magazine. He says Keever never called him. His habit is to make a brief contemporaneous note of all incoming calls, straight into a secure database, because that's the kind of thing journalists have to do these days, he says, in case their newspapers get sued. Or in case they want to sue their newspapers. But Keever isn't in his database. Therefore he didn't call."

"This guy Westwood definitely isn't the client, right?"

Chang shook her head. "He would have said so. I told him I was Keever's partner."

"When we found it you said the number would be either the client, or a source of independent corroboration, or a source of further information. So if it isn't the client, it's one of the other two. Maybe Keever planned to call him next. After calling you. Or maybe that was your role. Liaison, with Westwood. About whatever."

"We have to face the likelihood that number was nothing to do with Keever. That note could have been in that room for months."

"What is Westwood working on now?"

"A long piece about the origin of wheat. About how early wheat was cross-bred and became modern wheat. Sounds like a puff piece to me. As in, we already genetically modified it, so let's go right ahead and do it some more."

"Is that significant? As in, we've just seen a lot of wheat."

"Enough to last a lifetime. But I'm voting with the defense attorneys. That note could have been in that room for a year. Or two. Any one of fifty guests could have dropped it. Or a hundred."

Reacher said, "How private would Westwood's number be?"

"Depends how recently he changed it. If it's old, it's out there. That's how it is these days. Particularly for journalists. It's on the internet somewhere, if you look hard enough. Which a lot of journalists like, in our experience. It gives them a network."

Reacher drained his coffee, and said nothing.

Chang said, "What are you thinking?"

"I'm thinking the defense attorneys would win their case. But a couple of jury members wouldn't sleep easy. Because there's an alternative story to be told, and just as convincing, they're going to think, at four o'clock in the morning. It starts with your own first impression, some squirrelly guy with cash or handwritten checks, on a lunatic quest, because the wheat is going to kill two hundred people. Or something. And to prove it, talk to this journalist, who knows, too. And crucially, here's his number. Which proves something to us, about the guy. He digs up the number from the internet. He's that kind of a guy. That note feels connected to me. The whole thing feels consistent. It's some weird lone-guy obsession that carries no possible threat, until suddenly it does."

Chang said, "We should get back on the road."

Chapter 16

The little green Ford had GPS in the dash and it found Keever's house with no problem at all, in a faded suburban development north of Oklahoma City proper. It was a one-story ranch on a dead-end street. There was a young tree in the front yard, doing badly from lack of water. There was a driveway on the right side of the lot, ahead of a single-car garage. The roof was brown asphalt tile, and the siding was yellow vinyl. Not an architectural masterpiece, but the late sun made it pleasant, in its own way. It looked like a home. Reacher could imagine a big guy going in the door, kicking off his shoes, dumping himself down in a worn armchair, maybe turning on the ball game.

Chang parked in the driveway. They got out together and walked to the door. There was a bell button and a brass knocker, and they tried both, but they got no response from either. The door was locked. The handle wouldn't turn at all. The view in the windows showed a dark interior.

Reacher asked, "Does he have family?"

"Divorced," Chang said. "Like so many."

"And not the type of guy who leaves a key under a flower pot."

"And I'm sure he has a burglar alarm."

"We drove a long way."

"I know," Chang said. "Let's look around the back. With weather like this, maybe he left a window open. A crack, at least."

The street was quiet. Just seven similar houses, three on a side, plus one at the dead end. No moving vehicles, no pedestrians. No eyes, no interest. Not really a Neighborhood Watch kind of place. It had a transient feel, but in slow motion, as if all seven houses were occupied by divorced guys taking a year or two to get back on their feet.

Keever's back yard was fenced to head height with boards gone gray from the weather. There was a patch of lawn, nicely kept, and a patio with a wicker chair. The back wall of the house had the same yellow siding. There were four windows and a door. All the windows were shut. The door was solid at the bottom, and had nine little windows at the top. Like a farmhouse thing. It led to a narrow mud room ahead of a kitchen.

The land was flat, the houses were low, and the fence was high. They were not overlooked.

Chang said, "I'm trying to figure out the average police response time in a neighborhood like this. If he has a burglar alarm, I mean."

Reacher said, "Somewhere between twenty minutes and never, probably."

"So we could give ourselves ten minutes. Couldn't we? In and out, fast and focused. I mean, it's not really a crime, even. He and I work together. He wouldn't press charges. Especially not under these circumstances."

"We don't know what we're looking for."

"Loose papers, legal pads, notebooks, scratch pads, anywhere he could have scribbled a note. Grab it all and we'll go through it when we're out of here."

"OK," Reacher said. "We'll have to break a window."

"Which one?"

"I like the door. The little Georgian pane nearest the knob. That way we can walk in."

"Go for it," Chang said.

The pane was the bottom left of the nine, a little low for Reacher's elbow, but feasible, if he squatted and jabbed. Then it would be a case of knocking out the surviving shards of glass, and threading his arm in up to the shoulder, and then bending his elbow and bringing his hand back toward the inside knob. He jiggled the outside knob, to test the weight of the mechanism, to figure out how much grip he would need.

The door was open.

It swung neatly inward, over a welcome mat in the mud room. There was an alarm contact on the jamb. A little white pellet, with a painted-over wire. Reacher listened, for a warning signal. Thirty seconds of beeping, usually, to let the homeowner get to the panel and disarm the system.

There was no sound.

No beeping.

Chang said, "This can't be right."

Reacher put his hand in his pocket and closed it around the Smith & Wesson. Self-cocking, and no manual safety. Good to go. Point and shoot. He stepped through the mud room to the kitchen. Which was empty. Nothing out of place. No signs of violence. He moved on to a hallway. The front door was dead ahead. The sun had dropped lower. The house was full of golden light.

And still air, and silence.

Behind him he felt Chang move left, so he moved right, into a corridor with four doors, which were a master suite, and a hall bath, and a guest bedroom with beds in it, and a guest bedroom with an office in it, all of them empty, with nothing out of place, and no signs of violence.

He met Chang in the hallway, near the front door. She shook her head. She said, "It's like he stepped out to pick up a pizza. He didn't even lock the door."

The alarm panel was on the wall. It was a recent installation. It was showing the time of day and a steady green light.

It was disarmed.

Reacher said, "Let's get what we came for."

He led the way back to the smallest bedroom, which was all kitted out with matching units, shelves above, cabinets below, and chests of drawers, and a desk, all in blond maple veneer, and a computer and a telephone and a fax machine and a printer. Investments, Reacher supposed, for a new career. *We have offices everywhere.* The Scandinavian look was calming. The room was tidy. There was no clutter.

There was no paper.

No legal pads, no notebooks, no scratch pads, no memo blocks, no loose leaves.

Reacher stood still.

He said, "This guy was a cop and a federal agent. He spent hours on the phone. On hold, and waiting, and talking. Did anyone ever do that without a pen and a pad of paper? For notes and doodling and passing the time? That's an unbreakable habit, surely."

"What do you mean?"

"I mean this is bullshit." He ducked away, to the cabinets below the shelves. He opened one after the other. The first held spare toner cartridges for the printer. The second held spare toner cartridges for the fax machine.

The third held spare legal pads.

And right next to them were spare spiral-bound notebooks, still shrink-wrapped in packs of five, and right behind them were spare memo blocks, solid cubes of crisp virgin paper, three and a half inches on a side.

"I'm sorry," Reacher said.

"For what?"

"This doesn't look too good anymore. This is a guy who uses a lot of paper. So much so he buys it in the economy size. I bet that desk was covered with paper. We could have pieced this whole thing together. But someone got here ahead of us. On the same mission. So now it's all gone."

"Who?"

"The how tells us who, I'm afraid. Keever is a prisoner. That's the only way this thing can work. They found notes in his jacket pocket, maybe torn out from a legal pad, and in one pants pocket they found his wallet, with his driver's license, which told them his address, which they assumed was where the rest of the legal pad was, maybe with more notes on it, and in the other pants pocket they found his house keys, which meant they could walk right in, even to the extent of these new alarms maybe having a thing you wave near the panel, to turn it off. A remote fob, on the keychain. A transponder. Which would be a mercy, I guess. It would mean they didn't have to beat the code out of him."

Chang said, "That's very blunt."

"I can't explain it any other way."

"It doesn't tell me who."

"Mother's Rest," Reacher said. "That's his last known location."

They went through Keever's house room by room, in case something had been missed. The mud room held nothing of interest. The kitchen was a plain space, not much used. There was mismatched silverware, and odds and ends of canned food, presumably bought with temporary enthusiasm, but never eaten. There was nothing hidden, unless it had been walled up and artfully painted over with a finish exactly resembling twenty-year-old latex base coat, complete with grease and grime.

The living room and the dining nook were the same. Searching was easy. The guy wasn't exactly camping out, but it was clear he had started over without much stuff, and hadn't added a great deal along the way. The guest room with beds looked like it had been set up for his children. Visitation rights. Every other weekend, maybe. Whatever the lawyers had agreed on. But Reacher felt the room had never been used.

The master suite smelled slightly sour. There was a bed with a single night table. There was a chest of drawers and a wooden apparatus that had a hanger for a jacket, and trays for watches and coins and wallets. Like in a fancy hotel. The bathroom smelled humid, and the towels were a mess.

The night table had a short stack of magazines, weighted down by a hardcover book. As he passed by, Reacher glanced down to see what it was. Purely out of interest.

He saw three things.

First, the magazine on the top of the pile was the Sunday supplement from the *LA Times*.

Second, it was only part consumed. There was a quarter-inch of bookmark visible.

Third, the hardcover book was also only part consumed. It had a bookmark, too.

The bookmarks were old slips of memo paper, folded once, lengthwise. They were the first paper Reacher had seen, anywhere in the house.

Chapter 17

The slip of paper in the hardcover book was blank, except for a single scribbled number *4*. Which was a number of moderate technical interest, and most famous for being the only number in the entire universe that matched the number of letters in its own word in English: *four*. But other than that, it didn't seem to mean much. Not in context.

Chang said, "I'm with the defense attorneys on that one."

Reacher nodded. But the next one was better. Much better. Purely in terms of function, at first. The *LA Times* Sunday magazine came open at the start of a long article by science editor Ashley Westwood. It was about how modern advances in treating traumatic brain injuries were giving us a better understanding of the brain itself.

The magazine was less than two weeks old.

Chang said, "The defense attorneys would start by quoting the *LA Times*'s Sunday circulation."

Reacher said, "Which is what?"

"Nearly a million, I think."

"As in, it's a million-to-one chance this is not a coincidence?"

"That's what the defense attorneys would say."

"What would an FBI agent say?"

"We were taught to think ahead. To what the defense attorneys would say."

Reacher unfolded the bookmark. It was blank on one side.

It wasn't blank on the other side.

The other side had two lines of handwriting.

At the top was the same 323 telephone number. Science editor Westwood himself, in Los Angeles, California.

At the bottom was written: *Mother's Rest—Maloney.*

Reacher asked, "Now what would an FBI agent say?"

Chang said, "Now she would tell the defense attorneys to bite her. Keever is due to call Westwood for corroboration of or information about something to do with the town we were just in. I think that's clear. Plus now we have a name. There could be people up there named Maloney. After all, we just met the Moynahans."

"But why was the bookmark at the front of the article?"

"He hasn't read it yet."

"Which is why he hasn't called Westwood yet. Let's keep an open mind about the client. Let's just call him passionate. A guy like that, he's on the phone all the time. He's telling the same story, to whoever will listen. Mother's Rest, two hundred deaths, if you don't believe me call this reporter in LA, and he gives out the hard-won phone number, and every single time Keever jots it all down, over and over again, because that's the kind of guy he is, which is why we've already found that number twice without really trying. So maybe at first this is a nuisance client. Which I'm sure you get."

"From time to time."

"But there's some little thing in what the guy is saying that sets Keever thinking. But he's still skeptical, so he tries a little test. And this is Oklahoma City, right? He's likely got to go all the way to the train station to get newspapers from other cities. But he does. He gets the *LA Times* one Sunday. He wants to see if this expert witness has any kind of credibility. Is he a serious writer, or is he something from a supermarket paper? Keever wants to decide for himself. How long ago was wheat first grown?"

"Depends where," Chang said. "Thousands of years, anyway."

"So it turns out Westwood is probably pretty good. He's done the brain, and now he's going back thousands of years. This is a smart guy. But Keever doesn't know that yet. Because he hasn't read the piece. Which suggests that whatever the client said was intriguing, but somehow not very urgent. Keever didn't hop right to it."

"It feels plenty urgent now."

"Exactly. We need to know what changed."

It wasn't a Neighborhood Watch kind of a place, but even so they saw no sense in lingering. They went out through the mud room and pulled the door behind them. They walked around to the driveway and got in the car.

Reacher said, "We should talk to Westwood again."

"Keever didn't call him yet," Chang said. "He has nothing to tell us."

"Maybe someone else called him. He can tell us about that."

"Who else?"

"We don't know yet."

Chang didn't answer. She took out her phone, and dialed it, and hit an extra button, and laid it on the armrest between the front seats.

"It's on speaker," she said.

Reacher heard the ring tone.

He heard the call answered.

"Hello?" Westwood said.

Reacher said, "Sir, my name is Jack Reacher, and right now I'm working with my colleague Michelle Chang, who spoke to you not long ago."

"I remember. We agreed her other colleague never called me. Keever, was it? I thought we established that."

"Yes, we accept that. But now we have a pretty clear indication he was intending to call you at some point in the future. Maybe next on the list, or maybe somewhere down the line."

Westwood paused a faint distant beat, and said, "Where is this guy now?"

Reacher said, "He's missing."

"How? Where is he?"

Reacher said nothing.

Westwood said, "Dumb questions, I suppose."

"The how part could be crucial. The where part was fairly dumb. If we knew where he was, he wouldn't be missing."

"You should look at the calls he already made, surely. Not the calls he was possibly going to make. At some point in the future."

"Our information is limited."

"To what?"

"We have to work this thing backward, Mr. Westwood. We think he was about to rely on you for some kind of expert insight or opinion. We need to know what kind of a thing you could have helped him with."

"I'm a journalist. I'm not an expert on anything."

"But you're informed."

"Anyone who reads my stuff is as informed as I am."

"I think most readers imagine outtakes get left on the cutting room floor. They assume you know more than was printed. Maybe there was stuff you couldn't print for legal reasons. And so on. And they assume you like this stuff anyway. And they respect your senior title."

"Possibly," Westwood said. "But we're talking about a conversation that never took place."

"No, we're thinking about Keever's client now. So far we're picturing a passionate person with time on his hands. We have evidence that he called Keever repeatedly. We get the feeling he's that type of guy. And clearly there's an issue he feels strongly about. I said I bet he's called everyone from the White House downward. And I bet he has. Hundreds of people. Including you. Why wouldn't he? You're the science editor of a big newspaper. Maybe you wrote something that had a bearing on his issue. I think maybe he found your number on the internet not to pass on to Keever, not originally, but to talk to you direct. I think he has some weird-ass scientific beef, and he thinks you would understand it. So I think maybe he called you. I think maybe you've spoken to him."

There was a short pause, thousands of miles away, and then Westwood's voice came back, a little strangled, as if he was fighting a smile. He said, "I work for the *LA Times*. In Los Angeles. Which is in California. And my number can be found on the internet. All of which on balance is a good thing, but it means I get strange calls all the time. All day and all night. I've heard every weird-ass scientific beef there is. People call to talk about aliens and flying saucers and birth and suicide and radiation and mind control, and that's only the last month alone."

"Do these calls go in the database?"

"They're most of the database. Ask any reporter."

"Can you search by subject?"

"We get lazy about details. These guys ramble on. We use categories, mostly. This type of crank, that type of crank. Sooner or later I block their calls. When they outstay their welcome. I have to sleep sometimes."

"Try Mother's Rest."

"What's that?"

"It's the name of a town. Two words. Like your mom sitting down in a chair. Capital letters."

"Why is it called that?"

"I don't know," Reacher said.

They heard keyboard keys clicking, loud on the speakerphone. The database search, presumably. By subject.

Westwood said, "Nothing there."

"You sure?"

"It's a fairly distinctive name."

Reacher said nothing.

Westwood said, "Hey, I'm not saying your guy's client didn't call me. He probably did. We all know people like that. I'm saying, how would I know which one he was?"

They drove out of Keever's dead-end street, and out of his development, and past an outlet mall, to the highway entrance. Five hours to the right was Mother's Rest, and ten minutes to the left was downtown Oklahoma City, with steakhouses and barbecue, and decent hotels.

But Chang said, "No, we have to go back."

Chapter 18

Instead of a steakhouse or a barbecue pit they ate in chilly fluorescent silence in a rest-stop facility run by a third-best national chain. Reacher got a cheeseburger in a paper wrapper and coffee in a foam cup. Chang got a salad, in a plastic container as big as a basketball, with a clear lid at the top, and a white bowl underneath. She was stressed and maybe a little tired from driving, but even so she was good company. She put her hair behind her shoulders and turned attacking her salad into a shared misadventure, with widened eyes and about six different kinds of half-smiles, ranging from rueful and self-effacing to amused anticipation, as Reacher picked up his burger and tried to take a bite.

She said, "Thank you for your help so far."

He said, "You're welcome."

"We need to think about a more durable arrangement."

"Do we?"

"We shouldn't start out working as a team if I'm going to finish up working alone."

He said, "You should call 911."

"It would be a missing persons report. That's all, at this point. An independent adult, gone for two days, in a business where there's a lot of short-notice travel. They wouldn't do anything. We have no evidence to give them."

"His door."

"Undamaged. An unlocked door is evidence of homeowner negligence, not foul play."

"So you want to hire me? How does that work, with the low overhead thing?"

"I just want you to tell me your intentions."

He said nothing.

She said, "You could get a ride back to OC from here. There would be no hard feelings."

"I was heading over to Chicago. Before the weather gets cold."

"Same answer. Hitch back to OC and get the train. Same train you got before. Won't get delayed again, I'm sure."

He said nothing. He had come to like her lace-up shoes. They were practical, but they looked good, too. Her jeans were soft and old, and they rode low on her hips. Her T-shirt was black, neither tight nor loose. Her eyes were on his.

He said, "I'll ride with you. But only if you want me to. This is your business, not mine."

"I feel bad asking."

"You're not asking. I'm offering."

"I can't pay you."

"I already have everything I need."

"Which is what exactly?"

"A few bucks in my pocket, and four points on the compass."

"Because I would need to understand your reasons."

"For what?"

"For helping me."

"I think people should always help each other."

"This could go above and beyond."

"I'm sure we've both seen worse."

She paused a beat.

"Last chance," she said.

He said, "I'll ride with you."

It was dark when they came off the highway. The county road ran onward through the vastness, visible only a headlight's length ahead, and unrevealed beyond. The little Ford hummed along, bouncing now and then on eroded blacktop, pale wheat stalks strobing by on both sides. Overhead were thin clouds, and a new moon, and a dusting of distant stars.

It was impossible to say when they passed the point where they had left the Moynahans. Every mile looked exactly the same as every other mile. But the dull red pick-up had gone. They saw it nowhere, not on the county road itself, or on the right-left-right-left local turns that led back through the fields to Mother's Rest. Which they saw a mile away, faint and ghostly in the night, the elevators by far the tallest things in the landscape. They came in on the old trail, through the widest part of town, six low-rise blocks, and they turned on the plaza and drove down to the motel. The light was burning in the office window.

Chang said, "Let the fun begin."

She parked in the slot under her room and shut down the engine. They paused a moment in the sudden silence, and then they climbed out. They put their hands on their captured guns in their pockets, and stood near the car, in the yellow nighttime half-light, from the glow of the electric bulbs in their bulkhead fixtures, one above every door, and all of them working.

No movement. No sound.

No Moynahans, no posse.

Nothing.

Then a hundred feet away the one-eyed guy came out of the office.

He hustled over, the same way he had before, waving and gesturing, and when he arrived he fixed his imperfect gaze on the ground, and he took a breath.

"I apologize," he said. "A mistake was made. It led to a misunderstanding. Room 215 is yours to use, until the other gentleman gets back."

Chang said nothing.

Reacher said, "Understood."

The one-eyed guy nodded, as if to seal the deal, and then he turned tail and hustled back. Chang watched him go, and said, "Could be a trap or an ambush."

"Could be," Reacher said. "But I don't think it is. He wouldn't want fighting inside the actual room itself. The furniture would get busted up, and he would be patching bullet holes in the drywall all winter long."

"You saying they've surrendered?"

"It's a move in the game."

"What's the next move?"

"I don't know."

"And when will it come?"

"Tomorrow, probably," Reacher said. He looked all around, all three sides of the horseshoe, downstairs and upstairs. There was a rim of light around the drapes in room 203. Where the man in the suit had stayed. It had a new occupant.

"Not before dawn," he said. "That would be my guess."

"Will you sleep OK?"

"I expect so. Will you?"

"If I don't, I'll bang on the wall."

They went up the metal stairs together, and pulled their keys, and turned their locks, side by side but twenty feet apart, like neighbors getting home from work.

A hundred feet away the one-eyed guy took the lawn chair from outside 102, which was empty, and hauled it over to the spot he had used before, on the sidewalk under his office window. He lined it up and dumped himself down, in the nighttime air, ready to obey the second of the evening's commands, which had been *Watch their rooms all night.*

The first command had been *Even if they come back, do not under any circumstances rock the boat tonight.* Which matter he thought he had handled in a satisfactory manner.

Chapter 19

As before, Reacher sat in his room in the dark, back from
the window, invisible from the outside, just watching, this time from
a second-floor perspective. Fifteen minutes, then twenty, then thirty.
As long as it took, to be sure. The one-eyed guy in his plastic chair
was the same pale smudge in the distance, a hundred feet away. The
rim of light around 203's drapes burned steadily. Nothing moved. No
cars, no people. No glowing cigarettes in the shadows.

Nothing doing.

Forty minutes. Room 203's lights went out. The one-eyed guy
stayed where he was. Reacher gave it ten minutes more, and went to
bed.

Morning came, and it looked as good as the previous morning. The
light was pale gold, and the shadows were long. As good as the first
morning ever, maybe. Reacher sat on the bed, in a towel, without
coffee, and watched. The plastic chair was a hundred feet away, outside the office, but it was abandoned again. Room 203's drapes were

still closed. No one was moving. There was traffic out on the wide street, heard but not seen, first one truck, then a couple more.

Then silence.

He waited.

And the same things happened.

The shadows retreated, yard by yard, as the sun climbed higher. The seven o'clock train rolled in, and waited, and rolled out again. And the drapes opened in room 203.

A woman. The sun was still on the glass, which made her dustier than she should have been, but Reacher could see her, pale, in white, standing like the guy the day before, with her arms wide and her hands on the drapes. She was staring at the morning, the same way he had.

Then the white Cadillac sedan drove in, and aimed right and backed left, into the same slot as before. Still no front license plate. This time the driver got out right away. Above his head the door opened, and the woman in white stepped out of her room. The white was a dress, knee length, like a sheath. White shoes. She wasn't young, but she was in good shape. Like she worked at it. Her hair was the color of ash, and cut in a bob.

She had more luggage than the previous guy. She had a neat roll-on suitcase, with wheels and a handle. Bigger than the leather bag. But not huge. Dainty, even. She set out toward the stairs, and the Cadillac driver anticipated her coming predicament, and he threw out a *Wait* gesture, and went up to meet her. He collapsed her bag's handle and carried it down, ahead of her, as if showing her the way. He put the bag in the trunk, and she got in the rear seat, and he got back behind the wheel, and the car pulled out and drove away.

Still no rear license plate.

Reacher went and took a shower. He heard Chang in the next-door bathroom. The tubs shared a wall. Which meant she hadn't met the morning train. Which was a rational decision. It had saved her a walk both ways. Maybe she had done what he had, and watched. Maybe they had been sitting side by side, in towels, separated only by the wall. Although she probably had pajamas. Or a nightgown. Probably not voluminous. Given the weather, and the need to pack small.

He was out before her, and he headed to the diner, hoping to get the same pair of side-by-side tables in the far back corner, which he did. He put his jacket on her chair, pulled down on one side by the Smith in the pocket, and he ordered coffee. Chang came in five minutes later, in the same jeans but a fresh T-shirt, her hair still inky with water from the shower. Her own jacket was pulled down on one side, by her own Smith. Like any ex-cop she looked around, the full 360, seven or eight separate snapshots, and then she moved through the room with plenty of energy, powered by what looked like enthusiasm, or maybe some kind of shared euphoria at their mutual survival through the night. She slid in alongside him.

He said, "Did you sleep?"

She said, "I must have. I didn't think I was going to."

"You didn't go meet the train."

"He's a prisoner, according to you. And that's the best-case scenario."

"I'm only guessing."

"It's a reasonable assumption."

"Did you see the woman in 203?"

"I thought she was hard to explain. Dressed in black, she could have been an investor or a fund manager or something else deserving of the junior executive routine. Her face and hair were right. And she has a key to the company gym. That's for sure. But dressed in white? She looked like she was going to a garden party in Monte Carlo. At seven o'clock in the morning. Who does that?"

"Is it a fashion thing? Someone's idea of summer clothes?"

"I sincerely hope not."

"So who was she?"

"She looked like she was headed to City Hall for her fifth wedding."

The waitress came by, and Chang asked her, "Do you know a guy in town named Maloney?"

"No," she said. "But I know two guys named Moynahan."

And then she winked and walked away.

Chang said, "Now she's really your best friend forever. I don't think she likes the Moynahans."

Reacher said, "I don't see why anyone would."

"Someone must. We should assume they have their own best friends forever. We should expect a reaction."

"But not yet. They both took a hit. It's going to be like having the flu for a couple of days. Not like on a television show, where they get over it during the commercial messages."

"But they'll get over it eventually. Could be a mob scene, between their friends and their co-conspirators."

"You were a cop. I'm sure you shot people before."

"I never even drew my weapon. It was Connecticut. A small town."

"What about in the FBI?"

"I was a financial analyst. White collar."

"But you qualified, right? At the range?"

"We had to."

"Were you any good?"

"I won't shoot unless they fire first."

"I can live with that."

"This is crazy talk. This is a railroad stop. This is not the OK Corral."

"All those places had the railroad. That was the point. The bad guy would get off the train. Or the new sheriff."

"How serious do you think this is?"

"It's on a scale, like anything else. At one end Keever's in Vegas with a nineteen-year-old. At the other end he's dead. I'm shading toward the dead end of the middle. Or maybe a little beyond. I'm sorry. It was probably an accident. Or a semi-accident. Or panic. So now they don't know what to do."

"Do we?"

"Right now we have a simple three-part agenda. Eat breakfast, drink coffee, and find Maloney."

"Might not be easy."

"Which part?"

"Maloney."

"We should start at the receiving office. Over by the elevators. I bet they know every name for two hundred miles. And it might be two birds with one stone. If there's something hinky about the wheat, we might pick up a vibe."

Chang nodded and said, "How did you sleep?"

"It was weird at first, with Keever's things in the room. His suitcase by the wall. I felt like someone else. I felt like a normal person. But I got over it."

The receiving office was a plain wooden structure next in line after the weighbridge. It was purely utilitarian. It was what it was. It made no concession to style or appeal. It didn't need to. It was the only game in town, and farmers either used it or starved.

Inside, it had counters for form-filling, and a worn floor where drivers waited in line, and a stand-up desk where deliveries were recorded. Behind the desk was a white-haired guy in bib overalls, with a blunt pencil behind his ear. He was fussing around with stacks of paper. He was gearing up ahead of the harvest, presumably. He had the look of a guy entirely happy in his little fiefdom.

He said, "Help you?"

Reacher said, "We're looking for a guy named Maloney."

"Not me."

"You know a Maloney around here?"

"Who's asking?"

"We're private detectives from New York City. A guy died and left all his money to another guy. But it turns out the other guy already died too, so now the money is back in the pot for all the relatives we can find. One of them claims he has a cousin in this county named Maloney. That's all we know."

"Not me," the guy said again. "How much money?"

"We're not allowed to say."

"A lot?"

"Better than a poke in the eye."

"So how can I help you?"

"We figured you might know a bunch of names around here. I imagine most folks must come through this office at one time or another."

The guy nodded, like a vital and unanticipated connection had been made. He hit the space bar on a keyboard and a screen lit up. He maneuvered a mouse and clicked on something and a list appeared, long and dense. A bunch of names. He said, "These are the folks pre-cleared for using the weighbridge. Goes faster that way. Which we need, at busy times. I guess this would be all the grain people in the neighborhood. From the owners to the workers and back again. Men, women, and children. This business is all-hands-on-deck, at certain times of the year."

Chang said, "You see a Maloney in there? We'd certainly appreciate a first name and an address."

The guy used the mouse again and the list scrolled upward. Alphabetical. He stopped halfway down and said, "There's a Mahoney. But he passed on, I think. Two or three years ago, if I remember right. The cancer got him. No one knew what kind."

Chang said, "No one named Maloney?"

"Not on the list."

"Suppose he's not a grain worker? Would you know him anyway?"

"Maybe socially. But I don't. I don't know anyone named Maloney."

"Is there anyone else we could ask?"

"You could try the Western Union store. With the FedEx franchise. It's more or less our post office."

"OK," Reacher said. "Thanks."

The guy nodded and looked away and said nothing, as if both enchanted and annoyed by the break in his routine.

*　*　*

Reacher remembered where the Western Union store was. He had seen it before, twice, on his block-by-block explorations. A small place, with a window crowded by neon signs, for MoneyGram, and faxing, and photocopying, and FedEx, and UPS, and DHL. They went in, and the guy behind the counter looked up. He was about forty, tall and well built, not fat but certainly fleshed out, with a full head of hair, and a guileless face.

He was the Cadillac driver.

Chapter 20

The store was as plain as the receiving office, all dust and unpainted wood, with worn beige machines for faxing and photocopying, and untidy piles of address forms for the parcel services, and teetering stacks of packages, some presumably incoming, and some presumably outgoing. Some packages were small, barely larger than the address labels stuck to them, and some were large, including two that were evidently drop-shipped direct from foreign manufacturers in their original cartons, one being German medical equipment made from sterile stainless steel, if Reacher could trust his translation skills, and the other being a high-definition video camera from Japan. There were sealed reams of copy paper on open shelves, and ballpoint pens on strings, and a cork noticeboard on a wall, covered with thumbtacked fliers for all kinds of neighborhood services, including guitar lessons and yard sales and rooms to rent. *It's more or less our post office,* the guy in the receiving hut had said, and Reacher saw why.

The Cadillac driver said, "Can I help you?"

He was behind a plywood counter, counting dollar bills.

Reacher said, "I recognize you from somewhere."

The guy said, "Do you?"

"You played college football. For Miami. 1992, right?"

"Not me, pal."

"Was it USC?"

"You got the wrong person."

Chang said, "Then you're the taxi driver. We saw you at the motel this morning."

The guy didn't answer.

"And yesterday morning," Chang said.

No reply.

There was a small wire-mesh holder on the counter, full of business cards supplied by the MoneyGram franchise. A side benefit, presumably, along with the commission. Reacher took a card and read it. The guy's name was not Maloney. Reacher asked him, "You got a local phone book?"

"What for?"

"I want to balance it on my head to improve my deportment."

"What?"

"I want to look up a number. What else is a phone book for?"

The guy paused a long moment, as if searching for a legitimate reason to deny the request, but in the end he couldn't find one, apparently, because he dipped down and hauled a slim volume from a shelf under the counter, and rotated it 180 degrees, and slid it across the plywood.

Reacher said, "Thank you," and thumbed it open, to where L changed to M.

Chang leaned in for a look.

No Maloney.

Reacher said, "Why is this town called Mother's Rest?"

The guy behind the counter said, "I don't know."

Chang said, "How old is your Cadillac?"

"How is that your business?"

"It isn't, really. We're not from the DMV. We don't care about the license plates. We're interested, is all. It looks like a fine automobile."

"It does its job."

"Which is what?"

The guy paused a beat.

"Taxi," he said. "Like you figured."

Reacher said, "You know anyone named Maloney?"

"Should I?"

"You might."

"No," the guy said, with a measure of certainty, as if glad to be on solid ground. "There's no one named Maloney in this county."

Reacher and Chang walked back to the wide street and stood in the morning sun. Chang said, "He was lying about the Cadillac. It's not a taxi. A place like this doesn't need a taxi."

Reacher said, "So what is it?"

"It felt like a club car, didn't it? Like a golf cart at a resort. To take guests from one place to another. From reception to their rooms. Or from their rooms to the spa. As a courtesy. Especially without the license plates."

"Except this place isn't a resort. It's a giant wheat field."

"Whatever, he didn't go far. He was there and back in the time it took us to shower and eat breakfast. An hour, maybe. Thirty minutes there, thirty minutes back. A maximum twenty-mile radius, on these roads."

"That's more than a thousand square miles," Reacher said. "*Pi* times the radius squared. More than twelve hundred square miles, actually. Connected with Keever's thing, or separate?"

"Connected, obviously. At the motel the guy acted the same way as the spare-parts guy who met the train. Like a lackey. And the spare-parts guy dimed you out because you look a bit like Keever. So it's connected."

Reacher said, "We'd need a helicopter to search twelve hundred square miles."

"And no Maloney," Chang said. She stuck her hand in her back pocket and came out with Keever's bookmark. *Mother's Rest—Maloney.* "Unless the guy is lying about that, too. Not being in the phone book doesn't necessarily prove anything. He could be unlisted. Or new in town."

"Would the waitress lie, too?"

"We should try the general store. If he exists, and he isn't eating in the diner, then he's buying food there. He has to be feeding himself somehow."

They set out walking, south on the wide street.

Meanwhile the Cadillac driver was busy calling it in. Such as it was. He said, "They're nowhere."

In the motel office the one-eyed guy said, "How do you figure that?"

"You ever heard of a guy named Maloney?"

"No."

"That's who they're looking for."

"A guy named Maloney?"

"They checked my phone book."

"There is no guy named Maloney."

"Exactly," the Cadillac driver said. "They're nowhere."

The general store looked like it might not have changed in fifty years, except for brand names and prices. Beyond the entrance vestibule it was dark and dusty and smelled of damp canvas. It had five narrow aisles piled high with stuff ranging from woodworking tools to packaged cookies, and candles to canning jars, and toilet paper to light bulbs. There was a rail of work clothes that caught Reacher's eye. His own duds were four days old, and being around Chang made him conscious of it. She smelled of soap and clean skin and a dab of perfume. He had noticed, when she leaned close for a look at the phone book, and he wondered what she had noticed. He picked out pants and a shirt, and found socks and underwear and a white under-shirt on a shelf opposite. A dollar per for the smaller stuff, and less than forty for the main items. Overall a worthwhile investment, he thought. He hauled it all to the counter in back and dumped it all down.

The store owner wouldn't sell it to him.

The guy said, "I don't want your business. You're not welcome here."

Reacher said nothing. The guy was a stringy individual, maybe sixty years old. He had caved-in cheeks covered in white stubble, and thin gray hair, unwashed and too long, and tufts in his ears, and fur on his neck. He was wearing two shirts, one on top of the other. He said, "So run along now. This is private property."

Reacher said, "You got health insurance?"

Chang put her hand on his arm. The first time she had touched him, he thought, apropos of nothing.

The guy said, "You threatening me?"

Reacher said, "Pretty much."

"This is a free country. I can choose who I sell to. The law says so."

"What's your name?"

"None of your business."

"Is it Maloney?"

"No."

"Can you give me change for a dollar?"

"Why?"

"I want to use your pay phone."

"It isn't working today."

"You got your own phone in back?"

The guy said, "You can't use it. You're not welcome here."

"OK," Reacher said, "I get the message." He checked the tags on the items in front of him. A dollar for the socks, a dollar for the un-dershorts, a dollar for the T-shirt, nineteen ninety-nine for the pants, and seventeen ninety-nine for the shirt. Subtotal, forty dollars and ninety-eight cents, plus probably seven percent sales tax. Total damage, forty-three dollars and eighty-five cents. He peeled off two twenties and a five and butted them together. He creased them lengthwise to correct their curl. He placed them on the counter.

He said, "Two choices, pal. Call the cops and tell them commerce has broken out in town. Or take my money. Keep the change, if you like. Maybe put it toward a shave and a haircut."

The guy didn't answer.

Reacher rolled his purchases together and jammed them under his arm. He followed Chang out of the store and stopped in the vestibule to check the pay phone. No dial tone. Just breathy silence, like a direct connection to outer space, or the blood pulsing in his head.

Chang said, "Coincidence?"

Reacher said, "I doubt it. The guy probably disconnected the wires. They want us isolated."

"Who did you want to call?"

"Westwood, in LA. I had a thought. And then another thought. But first I think we better check the motel."

"The motel guy won't let us use his phone."

"No," Reacher said. "I think we can pretty much guarantee that."

They approached the motel's horseshoe from the south, so the first thing they saw was the wing with the office in it. There were three things on the sidewalk under its window. The first was the plastic lawn chair, unoccupied, but still in its overnight position.

The second thing was Keever's battered valise, last seen in room 215, now repacked and waiting, all bulging and forlorn.

The third thing was Chang's own suitcase, zipped up, its handle raised, also repacked and waiting.

Chapter 21

Chang stopped walking, like a reflex, and Reacher stopped alongside her. He said, "No room at the inn."

She said, "Their next move."

They walked on, getting closer, changing the geometry, seeing deeper inside the horseshoe, seeing groups of men, just standing around and waiting, filling the empty parking slots, kicking the curbs, standing in the traffic lanes. Maybe thirty guys in total, including whichever Moynahan it was who had gotten kicked in the nuts. He looked a little pale, but no smaller than before. His hapless relative wasn't there. Probably still in bed, dosed up on painkillers.

Reacher said, "We'll go straight to my room."

Chang said, "Are you nuts? We'll be lucky to get as far as the car."

"I bought new clothes. I need to change."

"Bring them with you. You can change later."

"It was already a concession not to change in the store. I don't like carrying stuff around."

"We can't fight thirty people."

They moved on, and stopped twenty feet from the staircase they needed. There were three guys near it. All of them were looking toward the office, where the one-eyed guy was coming out, and hustling across, waving and gesturing. When he arrived he said, "Mr. Keever's booking has come to an end. As has his associate's, therefore. And I'm afraid they can't be renewed. At this time of year I take empty rooms out of circulation for a day or two, for necessary maintenance. Ready for the harvest."

Reacher said nothing. *We can't fight thirty people.* To which Reacher's natural response was: *Why the hell not?* It was in his DNA. Like breathing. He was an instinctive brawler. His greatest strength, and his greatest weakness. He was well aware of that, even as he ran through the mechanics of the problem in his mind, one against thirty. The first twelve were easy. He had fifteen rounds in the Smith, and wouldn't miss with more than three. And assuming Chang took the hint, she could add another six. Or thereabouts. She was white collar, but on the other hand the range was short and the targets were numerous. Which would leave maybe twelve remaining, after the guns jammed empty, which was more than he could remember taking on before, all at once, but which had to be feasible. A lot would depend on shock, he supposed, which would be considerable, presumably. The noise, the muzzle flashes, the shell cases arcing through the bright morning sunlight, the guys going down.

It had to be feasible.

But it wasn't. He couldn't fight thirty people. Not at that point. Not without better information. He had no probable cause.

He said, "When is check-out time?"

The one-eyed guy said, "Eleven o'clock," and then he clammed up, visibly, like he wished he had never spoken.

Reacher said, "And what time is it now?"

The one-eyed guy didn't answer.

"It's three minutes to nine," Reacher said. "We'll be gone well before eleven o'clock. That's a promise. So everyone can relax now. There's nothing to see here."

The one-eyed guy stood still, deciding. Eventually he nodded. The three men near the stairs stood back, just half a pace, but their intention was clear. They weren't going anywhere, but they weren't going to do anything, either. Not yet.

Reacher went up the stairs behind Chang, and unlocked his door, and stepped inside his room. Chang said, "Are we really leaving? At eleven o'clock?"

"Before eleven," Reacher said. "In ten minutes, probably. There's no point in staying here. We don't know enough."

"We can't just abandon Keever."

"We need to go somewhere we can at least use a phone." He dumped his new clothes on the bed, and opened the plastic packets and pulled off the tags. He said, "Maybe I should take a shower."

"You took a shower two hours ago. I heard you through the wall."

"Did you?"

"You're fine. Just get dressed."

"You sure?"

She nodded and locked the door from the inside, and put the chain across. He carried his stuff to the bathroom and took off the old and put on the new. He put the Smith in one pocket and his toothbrush in the other, and his cash, and his ATM card, and his passport. He rolled up the old stuff and jammed it in the trash receptacle. He glanced in the mirror. He smoothed his hair with his fingers. Good to go.

Chang called through, "Reacher, they're coming up the stairs."

He called back, "Who are?"

"About ten guys. Like a deputation."

He heard her step back. He heard pounding on the door, angry and impatient. He came out of the bathroom and heard the lock rattling and the chain jiggling. He saw figures outside the window, on the walkway, a press of guys, some of them looking in through the glass.

Chang said, "What are we going to do?"

"Same as we always were," he said. "We're going to hit the road."

He walked to the door and slid the chain off. He put his hand on the handle.

"Ready?" he said.

Chang said, "As I'll ever be."

He opened the door. There was a surge outside, and the nearest guy stumbled forward. Reacher put the flat of his hand on the guy's chest and shoved him back. Not gently.

He said, "What?"

The guy got set on his feet again, and he said, "Check-out time just moved up."

"To when?"

"Now."

Reacher hadn't seen the guy before. Big hands, broad shoulders, a seamed face, clothes all covered with dirt. Chosen in some way, presumably, to be the point man. To be the spokesperson. The pick of the local litter, no doubt, according to popular acclaim.

Reacher said, "What's your name?"

The guy didn't answer.

Reacher said, "It's a simple question."

No response.

"Is it Maloney?"

"No," the guy said, with something in his voice. Like it was a stupid question.

Reacher said, "Why is this place called Mother's Rest?"

"I don't know."

"Go wait downstairs. We'll leave when we're ready."

The guy said, "We're waiting here."

"Downstairs," Reacher said again. "With two ways of getting there. The other is headfirst over the rail. Your choice. Either method works for me."

Below them the one-eyed guy was staring upward. Their suitcases had been moved nearer their car. They were side by side on the blacktop, next to the tailgate door. The guy with the big hands and the dirty clothes made a face, part shrug, part sneer, part nod, and he said, "OK, you got five more minutes."

"Ten more," Reacher said. "I think that's what we'll take. OK with you? And don't come up the stairs again."

The guy got a look in his eye, like some kind of mute challenge.

Reacher said, "What do you do for a living?"

The guy said, "Hog farmer."

"Always?"

"Man and boy."

"Same place?"

"Near enough."

"No military service?"

"No."

"I thought not," Reacher said. "You let us take the high ground. Which was dumb. Because thirty guys don't mean squat if they have to come up a staircase two by two. You know we're armed. We could pick you off like squirrels. From inside a cinder block building. Which you can't hurt unless you're packing grenade launchers, which I don't think you are. So don't come up the stairs again. Especially not in the lead."

The guy said nothing in reply to that, and Reacher stepped back and closed the door on him. Chang said, "If our aim is to get out of here alive, I don't think you should be antagonizing them."

"I don't agree," Reacher said. "Because as soon as we're gone, they're going to be asking themselves a question. Are we coming back? It's going to be the subject of a big debate. If we'd gone all meek and mild, they'd have known we were faking. Better to let them believe their stonewalling worked."

"It did. Like you said, we don't know anything."

"We know something. I said we don't know enough."

"What do we know?"

"We know the clerk just called in a situation report. He told his boss we'd be gone by eleven o'clock, but that wasn't good enough for the guy. The compromise wasn't acceptable. He wanted us gone right now. Hence the ten guys with the new message. Which was a message we didn't get last night. Last night we were welcomed with open arms. So what changed?"

Chang said, "The woman in white."

"Exactly. The same guy who wants us gone right now didn't want the boat rocked while she was on the premises. But now she's gone, so it's back to business as usual."

"Who was she? And where did she go?"

"We don't know. We don't know about the man in the suit, either. Except they were important somehow. As in, everyone had to be on best behavior when they were around. I saw the clerk tidying up before the car came for the man in the suit. He lined up all the chairs. Before the guy got a look at the place in daylight."

"They weren't investors. Not the kind that actually go inspect an investment, anyway. They didn't have the vibe. I spent a lot of time with investors."

"So what were they?"

"I have no idea. Someone's important guests, or someone's best customers. Or something. How are we supposed to know? Maybe they're fugitives from justice. Maybe this is an underground railroad. But a niche market. Club class only. Peace and quiet and a good night's sleep guaranteed, and all road transfers by Cadillac. For white-collar criminals."

"Would the woman dress up for that?"

"Probably not."

Reacher said, "I agree it has a railroad feel. They get off the train, they spend the night in the motel, they move on the next morning by car. It feels very transient. It feels kind of one-way, too. Like this is a stop on a longer journey."

"From where to where?"

Reacher didn't answer.

Chang said, "So what now?"

"We'll head west and figure that out when your phone starts working."

After ten minutes exactly they opened the door and stepped out to the walkway. The thirty guys were still there below them, still corralled together in small independent groups, twos and threes and fours, collectively surrounding the little green Ford in a rough and distant semicircle. The nearest was the hog farmer, about ten feet from the car. Next to him was the queasy Moynahan. Both of them looked tense and impatient. Reacher put his hand in his pocket, his palm and three fingers lightly on the Smith, and he started down the stairs, with Chang right behind him. They got to the bottom and she blipped the remote and the car unlocked with a ragged thump that sounded very loud in the silence.

Reacher stepped around the hood and looked at the hog farmer and said, "We'll go as soon as you put our bags in the trunk."

The hog farmer said, "Put them yourself."

Reacher leaned back against the Ford, with his hands in his pockets, and his ankles crossed. Just a guy, waiting. All the time in the world. He said, "Apparently you felt comfortable packing them up and hauling them here. So I'm guessing you don't have a constitutional objection to touching our stuff. Or an allergy. Or any other kind of disqualifying impediment. So now's the time to finish the job. Put them in the car, and we'll get going. That's what you want, right?"

The guy said nothing.

Reacher waited. The silence got worse. He could hear wheat stirring in the wind, a hundred yards away. No one moved. Then a guy looked at the next guy, who looked back, and pretty soon everyone was looking at everyone else, short jagged stares, a furious silent argument about trading dignity for results. *Put them in the car, and we'll get going. That's what you want, right?*

Put them yourself.

Eventually a guy behind the hog farmer broke ranks, and stepped forward. A pragmatist, clearly. He walked to the car and lifted the hatchback and put the bags inside, one by one, first Keever's, then Chang's.

He closed the hatch and stepped back.

"Thank you," Reacher said. "I hope you all have a great day."

He opened the passenger door and slid into the seat. Beside him

Chang slid behind the wheel. They closed their doors as one and Chang fired up the engine. She backed out of her slot, and turned the wheel, and took off forward, out into the plaza, and then north past the diner and the store, to the old wagon train trail, where she turned left and headed west, with the road running straight on ahead of her, forever, until it disappeared in the golden haze on the horizon, at that point as narrow as a needle.

She said, "Are we coming back?"

Reacher took his hand off his gun, for the first time since leaving the motel room.

He said, "I expect we'll have to come back."

Chapter 22

They drove three hours, and then stopped for gas and food. Still no cell signal. They figured they might not find one until they were all the way over near the I-25 corridor, deep into Colorado. Another four hours, maybe. In which case they might as well head straight for Colorado Springs, which was where the Ford had been rented, and where planes to LA took off on a regular basis. They agreed LA was next. The telephone was a wonderful invention, but sometimes inadequate. Which meant airport security was in their future, so they stripped the Smiths and dumped their constituent parts in separate trash cans all around the rest stop. Easy come, easy go.

Then Reacher drove the next spell, unlicensed and illegal, but in two hours they saw only two vehicles, neither of which was a cop car. Then Chang took over again, and they drove on, until the golden horizon darkened to gray, which meant civilization was on its way. They talked about what to do with Keever's valise. Reacher, unsentimental about possessions, was in favor of trashing it. But Chang saw it as a talisman. Like a beacon of hope. She wanted to keep it with them. In the end they compromised. They stopped at a FedEx in a strip mall on the edge of Colorado Springs, and shipped the valise back to the yellow house on the dead-end street, in the faded development north of Oklahoma City. Chang filled out the form with the address, and then after a long hesitation she checked the box for *no signature required*.

That afternoon eight men met at the counter inside the Mother's Rest dry goods store. The store owner was already there, with his two shirts and his unkempt hair, and the first to join him was the spare-parts guy from the irrigation store, who was followed by the Cadillac driver, and the one-eyed clerk from the motel, and the hog farmer, and the counterman from the diner, and the Moynahan who had gotten kicked in the balls and had his gun taken.

The eighth man at the meeting came in five minutes later. He was a solid guy, red in the face, fresh from a shower, wearing ironed blue jeans and a dress shirt. He was older than Moynahan and the spare-parts guy and the Cadillac driver, and younger than the motel clerk and the store owner, and about the same age as the hog farmer and the counterman. He had blow-dried hair like a news anchor on TV. The other seven guys stiffened and straightened as he walked in, and fell silent, and waited for him to speak first.

He got straight to the point.

He said, "Are they coming back?"

No one answered. Seven blank looks.

The eighth guy said, "Give me both sides of the argument."

There was some silence and squirming and shuffling, and then the spare-parts guy said, "They won't come back because we did our jobs. They got nothing here. No evidence, no witnesses. Why would they come back to a dry hole?"

The Cadillac driver said, "They will come back because this was Keever's last known location. They'll come back as many times as it takes. Where else can they start over, when they're getting nowhere?"

The eighth guy said, "Are we sure they got nothing here?"

The counterman said, "No one talked to them. Not a word."

The store owner said, "They only used the pay phone once. They tried three numbers, and got no reply from any of them, and then they went away again. That's not what people do, with red-hot information."

"So the consensus is they learned nothing?"

"The what?"

"What you all think."

The Cadillac driver said, "What we all think is they learned less than nothing. They finished up in my store, chasing some non-existent guy named Maloney. They were nowhere. But they'll still come back. They know Keever was here."

"So they did learn something."

The store went quiet.

The one-eyed guy said, "We agreed. It was supposed to look like he wandered off somewhere. We were never going to deny he was here."

The eighth man said, "What was their attitude as they left?"

The hog farmer said, "The guy was throwing his weight around. Some kind of consolation, I figured. Making himself feel better. Playing the tough guy because he knew he was beat. I think the gal was kind of embarrassed by it."

"Are they coming back?"

"I vote no."

"Who votes yes?"

Only the Cadillac driver raised his hand.

The eighth man said, "A six-to-one majority. Which is a fair assessment. I think you're calling it about right. And I'm proud of you all. They came, they learned nothing except what we could afford for them to know, and they went away again. With only a slight chance they'll be back."

The squirming and shuffling turned a little more upbeat. Chests stuck out, and mouths turned down, in self-deprecating aw-shucks grins.

The eighth man said, "But the world turns on slight chances."

The grins turned to solemn nods, seven serious men agreeing gravely with a pearl of wisdom.

The eighth man asked, "Where did they go?"

Seven shrugs, and seven blank looks.

The eighth man said, "It doesn't really matter. Unless they're headed for Los Angeles. The journalist is our only point of vulnerability. That's the only way they can pick the lock, according to what we learned from Keever."

"A million to one," Moynahan said. "How could they even know what they're looking for? How would Westwood even know what he's got?"

"The world turns on million-to-one chances."

"We're supposed to be completely invisible," the motel clerk said. "Aren't we? Isn't that what we pay for?"

"You don't pay for it. I pay for it."

The store went quiet again, until the spare-parts guy picked it up. He said, "OK, isn't that what you pay for?"

"Yes, it is. And more. I pay for assistance as and when I need it. Like the Triple-A. All part of the service."

The hog farmer said, "Going outside of us is a big step."

"Yes, it is," the eighth man said again. "There are considerable negatives. But positives, too. We should discuss them."

Moynahan said, "What kind of assistance?"

"There's a menu. I get what I pay for. From a little to a lot."

The store owner said, "I think we should start with surveillance. At least. If they get near Westwood at the newspaper, then we need to know right away. So we're prepared for what comes next. If the million-to-one goes against us."

The other six watched the eighth man's face, waiting for a shootdown, and when none came they started nodding in agreement, wisely and judiciously.

The eighth man said, "We should take a vote. All in favor of surveillance?"

Moynahan asked, "Is that the low end of the menu?"

The eighth man nodded. "Phones, internet, and physical eyes-on."

"How high does the menu go?"

"All the way to what they call a permanent solution."

"We can do that part ourselves."

"How's your brother?"

"I mean, next time we'll be ready."

"You changing your mind? Now you think there's a next time?"

Silence in the store.

The eighth man said, "Who votes for surveillance?"

Seven hands went up.

"I'm glad you agree," the eighth man said. "Because I already made the call. The surveillance started an hour ago. They sent a man named Hackett. One of their best, they said. Qualified in a number of different areas."

Chapter 23

The car rental company ran a shuttle bus from the returns compound to the passenger terminals, which was convenient, but slow. It added another half hour to an already long day. Reacher and Chang got to the ticket counter in the early evening. There was one LA flight still to go, but it was sold out. No seats at all, and a long queue for standby. Two equipment failures earlier in the day had caused chaos.

Next availability was eight in the morning. No choice. They took it. Chang had an open return, which she used, and Reacher bought his own seat. The clerk told them boarding would start about forty minutes prior, at about twenty past seven in the morning, and until then there was an airport hotel five minutes away by bus.

They walked instead, with Reacher carrying Chang's suitcase rather than rolling it, because he figured the cast-concrete sidewalks would be tough on its wheels. The hotel was a chain, crisp and white on the outside, warm and beige on the inside, with green neon announcing its name and function. There was a small crowd in the lobby. Maybe nine people, not exactly in line for the desk, mostly just standing around, either talking on cell phones, or looking frustrated, or both. *Two equipment failures earlier in the day had caused chaos.* Reacher was not a frequent flier, but he recognized the signs.

The clerk at the reception desk beckoned them closer. She was a young woman in a fitted jacket, with a scarf around her neck. There was some kind of secret urgency in her gesture. She said, "Sir, madam, I have one room left. If you need it, you should probably grab it now."

Chang said, "Only one room?"

"Yes, ma'am, because the airlines had a problem today."

"Is there another hotel?"

"Not in the airport."

Reacher said, "We'll take the room."

Chang looked at him, and he said, "We'll figure it out."

He paid, and got a key card in exchange. Fifth floor, room 501, elevators to the left, room service until eleven, breakfast extra, free wifi. Behind them two couples had lined up, about to be disappointed. Reacher and Chang rode up to five and found the room. It was beige and mint green inside, and adequate in every respect. But Chang was quiet about it. Reacher said, "You can use it."

She said, "What will you do?"

"I'm sure I'll think of something." He carried her bag inside, and left it by the bed. He gave her the key card, and said, "We should go get dinner. Before the waifs and strays take all the tables."

"Let me freshen up. I'll meet you in the restaurant."

"OK."

"Do you need to freshen up? You could use the bathroom first, if you like."

Reacher glanced in the mirror. Recent haircut, recent shave, recent shower, new clothes. He said, "This is about as good as it gets, I'm afraid."

* * *

The restaurant was on the ground floor, separated from the reception area by the elevator lobby. It was a pleasant space, with drapes and carpet and blond wood, compromised only a little by stain-proof and scuff-proof and vinyl-coated finishes on every surface. It was capacious, but almost full. Reacher waited at the hostess lectern, and was led to a table for two near a window. There was no real view. Just yellow lights, and a parking lot full of snowplows, mothballed for the summer.

Chang arrived eight minutes later, face washed, hair brushed, wearing a new T-shirt. She sat down opposite Reacher, looking good, energetic again, clearly invigorated by the simple comfort of running water. But then her face changed, as if suddenly she saw the other side of the equation, which was whatever she had, he didn't.

He said, "Don't worry about it."

She said, "Where will you sleep?"

"I could sleep right here."

"In a dining chair?"

"I was in the army thirteen years. You learn to sleep pretty much anywhere."

She paused a beat, and said, "What was the army like?"

"Pretty good, overall. I have happy memories and no real complaints. Apart from the obvious."

"Which was?"

"The same as yours, I'm sure. The fantastic cascade of bullshit coming down from senior officers with nothing better to do."

She smiled. "There was some of that."

"Is that why you left?"

She stopped smiling.

She said, "No, not exactly."

He said, "I'll tell you if you tell me."

"I don't know if I want to."

"What's the worst thing that can happen?"

She paused a beat, and breathed in, and breathed out, and said, "You first."

"They were shedding numbers, and therefore picking and choosing. My record was mixed, and right then some particular guy had it in for me. Given those two circumstances, it wasn't exactly a huge surprise my file ended up in the out tray."

"What particular guy?"

"He was a light colonel. A fat guy, with a desk job. Public relations, in Mississippi. I was there, with a bad thing going on, and he got all uptight about something ridiculous, and I was mildly impatient with him, verbally, to his face, and he took offense. And got his revenge, simply because the timing worked in his favor. I had gotten away with much worse before, when they weren't shedding numbers."

"Couldn't you fight it?"

"I could have called in some IOUs. But the damage was done. It was a zero-sum game. If I won, the colonel would lose, and all the other colonels wouldn't like that. None of them would want me near them. I would have ended up guarding a radar hut in the far north of Alaska. In the middle of winter. It was a lose-lose proposition. Plus it burst the bubble for me. They really didn't want me there. I finally realized. So I didn't fight it. I took an honorable discharge and walked away."

"When was this?"

"A long time ago."

"And you're still walking."

"That's too profound."

"You sure?"

"Deep down I'm very shallow."

She didn't answer. A waitress came by, and they ordered. When she left, Reacher said, "Your turn."

"For what?" Chang said.

"Your story."

She paused another beat.

"Same as yours, in a way," she said. "A lose-lose proposition. But of my own making. I let myself get backed into a corner. I didn't see it coming."

"Didn't see what?"

"Someone broke into my house. They took nothing, searched nothing, broke nothing, and left nothing. Which I didn't understand at the time. I was working on a money-laundering issue. There was a lot of cash and a mazy chain of shell corporations, like always, but I had the guy. But it was a hard case to prove. Almost impossible, in fact. I was leaning toward forgetting it. There's no point in recommending a prosecution if there's no realistic way of winning it. And then the guy came to see me. I was literally on the point of telling him the file was about to be closed. But he spoke first, and he was two steps behind. He told me if I didn't drop it right away he would claim I had taken a bribe, back at the beginning, to look the other way, but then later on I had changed my mind and stabbed him in the back. And kept the money anyway. He figured my work would be tainted, or even excluded, and he would walk."

"People can say all kinds of things. How could he prove it?"

"He had set up a bank account for me in the Caribbean, in my name, and he wired the bribe money to it. It was right there, large as life. Real money, and a lot of it. It would corroborate everything he was claiming."

"Except he opened the account, not you. There must be records."

"He told me it was a woman who broke into my house. She took nothing, searched nothing, broke nothing, and left nothing. But she used my land line. She opened the account for me, right there in my house, and it's all over my phone bill. Which left me between a rock and a hard place. How could I prove I didn't make that call? I figured maybe the foreign bank would have a recording, or the NSA, but two women's voices might be hard to tell apart on a long-distance line, especially if she was trying to sound like me, which she probably was, because this was a very organized guy. He knew my Social Security Number, for instance, and my mother's maiden name. That's my security question, apparently."

"So what did you do?"

"What he told me to. I dropped the case. Right away. I closed his file. But I was going to anyway. I think."

"Where is the guy now?"

"Still in business."

"What happened to the bribe money?"

"It disappeared. I traced it, like he knew I would. I found it in a shell corporation in the Dutch Antilles. Apparently I had purchased a minority position in a financial vehicle, as a long-term investment. He was the majority stockholder. We were tied together forever."

"So what next?"

"I fessed up. I laid it all out for my SAC. I could see he wanted to believe me, but the Bureau doesn't run on faith. And from that point on I would have been useless as an active agent. My testimony would have been automatically suspect, even years later. I would have been a defense counsel's wet dream. As in, Special Agent, please tell us about the bribe you can't prove you didn't take. So I would have joined you in that radar hut in Alaska. In the middle of winter. It was a lose-lose. So I resigned."

"That's tough."

"You win some, you lose some."

"No, you win plenty, and then you lose one. No second chance."

"I'm not unhappy doing what I'm doing."

"But?"

"I don't know how much longer we can keep on doing it. It doesn't feel like a job for life."

"It might have been, for Keever."

"That's very blunt."

"What was his story?"

"Was?"

"OK, is."

"I heard he was facing a third reprimand. The Bureau is very cautious, and he had a habit of rushing in regardless. No plan, no backup. He was putting cases in jeopardy, they said. As well as himself and his fellow agents. A third strike would have qualified him for Alaska, too. That radar hut would have been getting crowded. So he resigned, ahead of the hearing. I guess he thought it was the only dignified thing to do. And before you say it, sure, I agree, that's probably what he did in Mother's Rest. He rushed in, regardless. He didn't wait for back-up."

The waitress came by, with their plates of food, and with refills for their drinks. When she was gone Reacher said, "But Keever called for back-up. He got that far. We know that. Why call and not wait?"

Chang said, "Impatience? Urgency?"

"Maybe they got to him first. While he was waiting. Maybe he didn't rush in."

"That sounds like a public service message on behalf of hotheads everywhere."

"We don't know what happened."

"I wish he'd rushed out."

"Always a sound policy."

"I bet you never did."

"More times than I can count. Which is why I'm still here, having dinner with you. The chaotic universe. Darwinism in action."

She paused, and said, "May I ask you a question?"

He said, "Sure."

"Are we having dinner?"

"That's what it said on the menu. Lunch was different, and this sure ain't breakfast."

"No, I mean having dinner, as opposed to grabbing road food."

"As in candlelight and piano music?"

"Not necessarily."

"Violin players and guys selling roses?"

"If appropriate."

"Like a date?"

She said, "Broadly, I suppose."

He said, "Honest answer?"

"Always."

"Suppose we had found Keever yesterday, maybe stepping off the train, or fallen over in a wheat field somewhere, with a sprained ankle, somewhat hungry and thirsty but otherwise OK, then yes, for sure I would have asked you out to dinner, and if you had accepted, then we'd be having that dinner right about now, so I guess this half-qualifies."

"Only half?"

"We didn't find Keever. So it's still partly road food."

"But you would have asked me out to dinner?"

"Absolutely."

"Why?"

"You're the sort of person I like to have dinner with."

She was quiet for a long moment, five or six seconds, right to the edge of discomfort, and then she said, "I would have said yes, for the same reason."

"Outstanding."

"So keep it straight in your mind. We're having dinner. Not grabbing road food. That's a fact, not a question."

"Then why did you ask me?"

"To make sure you knew."

No dining chairs were required that night for Reacher. They ate dessert and drank coffee, slowly, relaxed, not rushing at all, both of them choosing to trust the inevitable, and then Chang signed the check, and stood up, and Reacher stood up with her, and she linked her arm in his, like they were an old couple from way back, and they walked out together, slowly, relaxed, not rushing at all, and they waited for the elevator, and rode up to five, and opened the room.

Then it got a little less slow, and a little less relaxed, and a little more rushed. Chang was warm and fragrant, and smooth, and long-limbed, and young but not a kid, and she was strong enough to push back, and she was solid enough not to worry about. Reacher liked her a lot, and she seemed to like him back. Afterward they talked for a spell, and then she fell asleep, and then he did too, the best way he knew.

Chapter 24

Boarding started right on time at twenty past seven in the morning. Chang rolled her bag down the air bridge, and Reacher followed it, all the way to the cheap seats about two-thirds into the plane. Chang put her bag in the overhead and took the window seat. Reacher took the aisle. He said, "How well do you know LA?"

She said, "Well enough to find the newspaper building."

"Maybe he works from home."

"In which case he won't meet us there. I'm sure his address is a secret, if not his cell phone number. He'll pick a coffee shop in the neighborhood."

"Works for me. But which neighborhood? Do you know them all?"

"I suppose we'll have to rent another car. We should get GPS."

"Unless he's in the office and willing to meet us there. We could take a cab."

"We'll get in too early. He won't be there yet."

"OK, we'll call his cell when we land and we'll let him make the decision for us. Coffee shop or office. Rental car or cab."

"If he agrees to see us at all."

"Two hundred deaths. That's a story."

"Which he's already heard, according to you. When Keever's client called him. Who seems not to have made much of an impression."

"There's a difference between hearing and listening. And that's our problem. I doubt if Westwood even knows what he's got. He didn't listen, and his notes don't seem to mean much. It's going to be like picking a lock with spaghetti."

"What if we can't?"

"No such word."

"You're optimistic this morning."

"That's an inevitable consequence. I had a very pleasant night."

"Me, too."

"Good to know."

"What do your friends call you?"

"Reacher."

"Not Jack?"

He shook his head. "Even my mother called me Reacher."

"Do you have siblings?"

"I had a brother, name of Joe."

"Where is he now?"

"Nowhere. He died."

"I'm sorry."

"Not your fault."

"What did your mom call him?"

"Joe."

"And she called you Reacher?"

"It's my name, just as much as Jack. You mean your friends don't call you Chang?"

"I was Officer Chang, and then Special Agent Chang, but that was only at work."

"So what do they call you?"

"Michelle," she said. "Or Shell, sometimes, for short. Which I quite like. It's a nice diminutive. Except not with my last name. Shell Chang sounds somewhere between a Korean porn star and an oil exploration company in the South China Sea and a roll of quarters being dumped in a cash register."

"OK," Reacher said. "Michelle it is. Or Chang."

And then the plane took off, and chased the dawn westward over the mountains.

Seven hours by road to the east, in Mother's Rest, dawn had already happened. The morning train had been and gone. The breakfast rush in the diner was easing. The guy with two shirts had opened his store. The spare-parts guy had opened his too, and was already crammed in behind his counter, sorting invoices into piles. The Cadillac driver was tallying receipts for his seven different accounts, Western Union, MoneyGram, faxing, photocopying, FedEx, UPS, and DHL. The Moynahan who had gotten kicked in the balls and had his gun taken was still home, caring for his brother, who was still a little dazed.

And the one-eyed clerk was coming out of the motel office, and standing and sniffing the air, and glancing all around, at the inside perimeter of the horseshoe, at the parking spaces, at the sidewalk passing the first-floor rooms, at the walkway passing the second-floor rooms. A leisurely visual inspection. Of the light bulbs, all working. Of the lawn chairs, all neatly lined up. All there. All quiet. All serene. 214 was empty. 215 was empty.

They weren't coming back, he thought.

All good.

LAX arrivals was jammed, so Reacher and Chang had to fight their way out to the curb to find a quiet spot to make their call. Chang hid behind a pillar and dialed. And woke Westwood up. Not an early starter. She was embarrassed at first, then placatory, and then she got down to business. She introduced herself again, and said she needed to meet, because something that had looked small to both of them was suddenly not so small anymore. She said there was a credible figure of two hundred deaths. She said as an ex–FBI agent she was taking it seriously. She said her colleague was from the military, and he was also taking it seriously. She said sure, the book rights were still available.

Then she listened to an address, and hung up.

"Coffee shop," she said. "In Inglewood."

Reacher said, "That's close by. When?"

"Thirty minutes."

"We should take a cab. We don't have time to rent a car."

Twenty miles south of Mother's Rest, the man with the ironed jeans and the blow-dried hair took a call on his land line. Triple-A, but not exactly. Their man Hackett had logged the first contact. A cell-to-cell phone call, six minutes long, between Westwood, who was presumably at home, given his hours, and a woman who gave her name as Chang, who was at the airport, judging by the background noise, and who was with a male colleague she described as military. Deaths had been mentioned, and a rendezvous set up, in a coffee shop in Inglewood, which Hackett would monitor.

The cab line was long but brisk, and Inglewood was just the other side of the 405 from the airport, so they got to the designated coffee shop with time to spare. The place was one of many lining the street. Most had tiny outdoor tables and Italian words on their chalk boards, but Westwood's pick didn't. It was a straight-up vinyl-and-linoleum antique, faded over the decades to a dull khaki color. It was about a quarter full, with men on their own, all of them silently reading newspapers, or staring into space. None of them looked like a science editor.

"We're early," Chang said. "He'll be late."

So they took a booth, sitting side by side at a laminate table, on a bench upholstered in tuck-and-roll vinyl, that might have started out deep red and glittery, but was now as khaki as everything else. They ordered coffee, one hot, one iced. They waited. The place was quiet. Just the turning of newspaper pages and the clink of ironstone cups on ironstone saucers.

Five minutes.

Then eventually Westwood arrived. He looked nothing like Reacher expected, but the reality fit the bill just as well as the preconceptions had. He was an outdoors type, not a lab rat, and sturdy rather than pencil-necked. He looked like a naturalist or an explorer. He had short but unruly hair, fair going gray, and a beard of the same length and color. He was red in the face from sunburn and had squint lines around his eyes. He was forty-five, maybe. He was wearing clothing put together from high-tech fabrics and many zippers, but it was all old and creased. He had hiking boots on his feet, with speckled laces like miniature mountain-climbing ropes. He was toting a canvas bag about as big as a mail carrier's.

He paused inside the door, and identified Chang instantly, because she was the only woman in the place. He slid in opposite, across the worn vinyl, and hauled his bag after him. He put his forearm on the table and said, "I assume your other colleague is still missing. Mr. Keever, was it?"

Chang nodded and said, "We hit the wall, as far as he's concerned. We're dead-ended. We can trace him so far, but no further."

"Have you called the cops?"

"No."

"So I guess my first question is, why not?"

"It would be a missing persons report. That's all, at this stage. He's an adult, gone three days. They might take the report, but they wouldn't do anything with it. It would go straight to the back burner."

"Two hundred deaths might get them interested."

"We can't prove anything. We don't know who, why, when, where, or how."

"So I'm buying you breakfast because there's a guy you haven't even reported missing, and two hundred deaths you know nothing about?"

"You're buying us breakfast because you're getting the book rights. You can buy all the breakfasts."

"Except so far this breakfast alone is worth more than the book rights. So far the book rights and fifty cents will get me a cup of coffee."

Reacher said, "You're a scientist. You need to think about it scientifically."

"In what way?"

"Statistically, maybe. And linguistically. With a little sociology thrown in. Plus a deep and innate understanding of human nature. Think about the number two hundred. Sounds like a nice round figure, but it isn't, really. No one says two hundred purely at random. People say a hundred, or a thousand. Or hundreds or thousands. Two hundred deaths sounds specific to me. Like a true number. Maybe rounded up from the high 180s or 190s, but it sounds to me like there's information behind it. Enough to keep me interested, anyway. For instance. Speaking as an investigator."

Westwood said nothing.

Reacher said, "Plus we assume the cops already heard the story, and already dismissed it."

Westwood nodded. "Because you assume Mr. Keever's client called everyone from the White House downward. Including me."

"Which is where we have to start. With the client. We need to find the guy. We need to hear the story over again, from the beginning, like Keever did. Then maybe we can predict what happened next."

"I get hundreds of calls. I told you."

"How many?"

"Point taken."

"And you note them all down. You told us that, too."

"Not in any great detail."

"We might be able to puzzle it out."

"You would need a name, at least."

"I think we have a name."

Chang glanced at Reacher.

"Possibly," Reacher said to her. Then he turned back to Westwood. He said, "It's probably not a real name, but it might be a start. You told us sooner or later you block the nuisance calls. When they wear out their welcome. Suppose a guy got frustrated by that, and tried to start over by coming back to you under a different name and number?"

"Might happen," Westwood said.

Reacher turned to Chang and said, "Show him Keever's bookmark."

Chang dug the paper out of her pocket and smoothed it on the table. The 323 phone number, and *Mother's Rest—Maloney*.

Westwood said, "That's my number. No doubt about that."

Reacher said, "We took it to mean there was a guy in Mother's Rest named Maloney, who was of interest in some way. But there's no such guy. We're sure of that. We asked, and the answers weren't evasive. They were dismissive, and even a little confused. So what if you had gotten sick of Keever's client, whatever his name is, so he decided to start over, and he came back to you under the name of Maloney? And then he called Keever again, and as always told him to check with you, for corroboration, but this time warned him the issue wouldn't be filed under his real name anymore, but under the fake name Maloney? Maybe that's what this note means."

"Maybe."

"You got a third interpretation?"

"I could check," Westwood said.

"We'd appreciate it. We're clutching at straws here."

"No shit. Keever's notes are as bad as mine."

"They're all we've got."

"But even so, with a missing guy and a rumor about two hundred deaths, don't you think you should at least try the cops again?"

"I was a cop," Reacher said. "And I knew plenty more. I never met one who went looking for extra work. So right now they wouldn't listen. Not yet. I can guarantee that. Just like you didn't."

"I could check," Westwood said again. "But I don't see how a fake name will help."

"By leading us to the real name."

"How can it do that? It conceals the real name."

"Check who you blocked just before Maloney started calling. That's the client."

"We'll find more than one candidate. I block lots of people."

"We'll figure it out. Geography could be significant. We know he hired an investigator from Oklahoma City, and we know he reads the *LA Times*. That might narrow it down some."

Westwood shook his head. "My phone number ain't exactly easy to find. I don't pay Google to put it front and center. If your guy is good enough with computers to dig it up off the internet, then he's reading the paper on-line. That's for sure. Guys like that haven't bought physical print for a decade. He could be living anywhere."

"Good to know," Reacher said.

"Meet me in my office in an hour. In the *Times* building."

Chang nodded and said, "I know where it is."

Then the waitress came by and Westwood ordered breakfast, and Reacher and Chang left him alone to eat it.

Less than ten minutes later, twenty miles south of Mother's Rest, the man with the ironed jeans and the blow-dried hair took a second call on his land line. His contact told him Hackett had observed the meeting in the Inglewood coffee shop. He had not been close enough to hear much detail, but he had caught Keever's name, and he had lip-read Chang say they had hit the wall, where he was concerned. Then at the end of the conversation he had inferred a second rendezvous had been suggested, at a location he hadn't caught, but he had heard Chang saying she knew where it was. He would stay on Westwood for the time being, who would no doubt lead him there.

Chapter 25

The *LA Times* was in a fine old art-deco building on West 1st and Spring in downtown Los Angeles. It had security worthy of a government agency. There was an X-ray belt, and a metal detector. Reacher wasn't sure why. Maybe an inflated sense of importance. He doubted if the *Times* was top of anyone's target list. Probably not even on the fourth or fifth page. But there was no choice. He dumped his coins in a bowl and stepped through the hoop. Chang was slower. She still had her suitcase, and her coat.

But eventually they were through, and they got passes from a desk, and rode up in an elevator. Westwood's office turned out to be a square cream room with shelves of books and stacks of newspapers. There was a handsome old desk under the window, with a two-screen computer on it. Westwood was in a chair in front of it, reading e-mail. His enormous canvas bag was dumped on the floor, bellied open, full of more books and more newspapers and a metal laptop computer. Outside the door the hall was loud with the hum of busy people doing busy things. Outside the window the sky was bright with Southern California's perpetual sunshine.

Westwood said, "I'll be right with you. Take a seat."

Something in his voice.

Taking a seat required a little effort. Reacher and Chang cleared stacks of magazines and papers off two spare chairs. Westwood closed his e-mail program and turned around. He said, "My legal department isn't happy. There are confidentiality issues at stake. Our database is private."

Chang asked, "What kind of downside do they foresee?"

"Unspecified. They're lawyers. Everything is downside."

"It's an important investigation."

"They say important investigations come with warrants and subpoenas. Or at least missing persons reports."

Reacher said, "Why did you talk to your lawyers?"

Westwood said, "Because I'm required to."

"Did you talk to your managing editor?"

"He doesn't see a story. We ran background on Keever. He's on a bender somewhere. He's a washed-up old gumshoe."

Chang said nothing.

Reacher said, "I never met the guy. But I met plenty like him. Above average in every way, except loose with impulse control. But those impulses came from the best of intentions. And however washed up he was, he was James Bond compared to the population of Mother's Rest. But still they got him."

"You don't know that."

"But suppose they did. Suppose there's something weird out there, with two hundred dead people. That's a story, right? That's something the LA Times would eat up with a spoon. You could run it for weeks. You could get a Pulitzer. You could get on TV. You could get a movie deal."

"Get back to me as soon as you've got something solid."

"What do you think the chances are of that happening?"

"A hundred to one."

"Not two hundred?"

"Your theories aren't evidence."

"Here's another theory. We walk out of here, leaving behind the hundred-to-one possibility there's a big story out there, but because we're gone it's no longer a *Times* exclusive anymore, which means if the hundred-to-one pays off and it breaks, there's going to be a crazy scramble, with all the papers competing for pole position. So if you're a smart science editor, even though it's only a hundred to one, you can see a tiny advantage in using what you know so far to get somewhat prepared ahead of time. So my guess is as soon as we're back in the elevator, you're going to check the database for calls from a guy named Maloney. Just to put your mind at rest."

Westwood said nothing.

Reacher said, "So what difference would it make if we were still in the room?"

No response for a long moment. Then Westwood turned his chair to face his screens, and he clicked the mouse and typed a few letters in two different boxes. User ID and password, Reacher figured. The database, hopefully. Chang leaned forward. The screen showed a search page. Some kind of proprietary software, no doubt suitable for the job at hand, but ugly. Westwood clicked on a bunch of options. Isolating his own notes, possibly. To avoid irrelevant results. Maybe there were a hundred newsworthy Maloneys in LA. Maybe there were two hundred. Sports stars, businesspeople, actors, musicians, civic dignitaries.

Westwood said, "All theories should be tested. That's a central part of the scientific method."

He typed *Maloney*.

He clicked the mouse.

He got three hits.

The database showed contact made by a caller named Maloney on three separate occasions. The most recent was just shy of a month previously, and the second was three weeks before that, and the oldest was two weeks before the second. A five-week envelope, all told, four weeks ago. The incoming phone number was the same on all three occasions. It had a 501 area code, which no one recognized.

Westwood had made no notes about the subject or the content of any of the three conversations. Instead he had simply routed name, number, day, and time straight to a folder marked *C*.

"Which is?" Reacher asked.

"Conspiracies," Westwood said.

"What kind of thing?"

"It's a fairly wide category."

"Give me an example."

"Smoke alarms are compulsory in homes because they contain cameras and microphones wirelessly linked to the government. With poison gas capsules too, in case the government doesn't like what you're saying or doing."

"Keever wouldn't waste time on a thing like that."

"And I wouldn't ignore something more serious."

"Maybe it wasn't well explained."

"I guess it can't have been."

"You sure you don't remember this Maloney guy at all?"

As a response Westwood clicked his way through to an unfiltered list of all the calls he had received. The screens were big and he had two of them, but even so there was space only for a small part of the calendar year.

Reacher said, "Are we in there?"

Westwood nodded. "From this morning."

"What folder did you put us in?"

"I haven't decided yet."

Chang took out her phone and dialed Maloney's number. The 501 area code, and seven more digits. She put her phone on speaker. There was hiss and dead air as the cellular system hooked her up. Then the number rang.

And rang, and rang.

No answer, and no voice mail.

Chang hung up, after a whole long minute, and the office went quiet.

Reacher said, "We need to know where the 501 area code is."

Westwood clicked off his database and opened up a web browser. Then he glanced at the door and said, "So I guess we're really doing this."

"No one will know," Reacher said. "Until the movie comes out."

The computer told them 501 was one of three area codes given to cell phones in Arkansas. Chang said, "Was there an Arkansas number you blocked about nine weeks ago? Maybe our guy switched from his land line to his cell, simple as that."

Westwood went back into his database, to the unfiltered list of calls, and he scrolled back nine weeks, and said, "How much limbo should we give him? How fast would he have come up with the idea of changing his name and number?"

"Pretty fast," Reacher said. "It isn't brain surgery. But I'm guessing there was some limbo. Most likely because of hurt feelings. You rejected him. It might have taken him a week to swallow his pride and call you back."

Westwood scrolled some more. Ten weeks back. He opened the list of area codes on his second screen, and went back and forth, comparing, line by line, and when he was finished he said, "I blocked four guys that week. But none of them was from Arkansas."

Reacher said, "Try the week before. Maybe he's more sensitive than we thought."

Westwood scrolled again, backward through the next seven days, and then forward again, checking against the list of area codes, and he said, "I blocked two guys the previous week, for a fourteen-day total of six, but still no one from Arkansas."

Reacher said, "We're getting somewhere anyway. The Maloney calls started nine weeks ago, from a guy who had just gotten blocked, in a recent window of time, and in that category there are six possible candidates. Logic says our guy is one of them. And we could be talking to him thirty seconds from now. On his other line. Because you have all the original phone numbers."

Chapter 26

Westwood copied and pasted the six names and num-
bers to a new blank screen. The names were a standard American
mixture. They could have been the first six up for any team in the
Majors, or they could have been any six guys in line at the pawn
shop, or the ER, or the first-class lounge at the airport. Half the numbers were cell phones, Reacher guessed, because he didn't recognize
the area codes, but there was a 773 for Chicago in there, and a 505
for somewhere in New Mexico, and a 901, which he figured could be
Memphis, Tennessee.

Westwood put his phone in a dock on his desk and dialed the first
number direct from his computer. There were speakers in the dock,
and Reacher heard the *beep-boop-bap* of the electronic pulses, and
then nothing but hiss, and then a pre-recorded voice, pitched somewhere between scolding and sympathetic.

The number was out of service.

Westwood hung up and checked the area code on his screen. He
said, "That was a cell phone, in northern Louisiana, maybe Shreveport, or close by. The contract was probably terminated or canceled,

as happens in the normal run of things, and the number will be reissued sooner or later."

He dialed the second number.

Same thing. The dialing sounds, then nothing, then the phone
company voice, its script apologetic, its tone faintly incredulous that
anyone would do anything as pitifully dumb as try to call a telephone
number that was currently out of service.

"A cell in Mississippi," Westwood said. "Somewhere north. Oxford, probably. A lot of college students there. Maybe his parents
threw him off the family plan."

"Or maybe it was a burner phone," Reacher said. "A pay-as-you-go
from a drugstore, that ran out of minutes. Or was trashed. Maybe
they're all burners."

"Possible," Westwood said. "Bad guys have done that for years, to
stop the government building a case. And these days citizens are
learning to do the same thing. Especially the kind of citizens who call
newspapers with hot tips about conspiracies. Such is the modern
world."

He dialed the third number. Another cell, according to the list of
area codes, this one in Idaho.

And this one was answered.

A guy's voice came over the speakers, loud and clear. It said,
"Hello?"

Westwood sat up straight, and spoke to the screen. He said, "Good
morning, sir. This is Ashley Westwood, from the *LA Times,* returning
your call."

"It is?"

"I apologize for the delay. I had some checking to do. But now I
agree. What you told me has to be exposed. So I need to ask you
some questions."

"Well, yes, sure, that would be great."

The voice was pitched closer to alto than tenor, and it was a little
fast and shaky with nerves. A thin guy, Reacher thought, always quiv-

ering and vibrating. Thirty-five, maybe, or younger, but not much older. Could be Idaho born and bred, but probably wasn't.

Westwood said, "First I need to start with a trust-builder. I need you to confirm the name of the private detective you hired."

The voice said, "The name of the what?"

"The private detective."

"I don't understand."

"Did you hire a private detective?"

"Why would I do that?"

"Because it has to be stopped."

"What does?"

"What you told me about."

"A private detective would be no good for that. They'd do the same to him they do to everyone else. As soon as they saw him. I mean, literally. I told you, it's a line of sight thing. No one can avoid it. You don't understand. The beam cannot be beaten."

"So you didn't hire a private detective?"

"No, I didn't."

"Do you use another cell phone, with a 501 area code?"

"No, I don't."

Westwood hung up on him without another word. He said, "I think I remember that guy. Apparently our minds are being controlled by beams."

Reacher said, "What kind of beams?"

"Mind-controlling beams. They come off the bottom of civilian airliners. The FAA requires them. That's why they charge for checked bags now, so people will use carry-on instead, which leaves more space in the hold for the equipment. And the operator. He's down there, too, like an old-fashioned bomb aimer, zapping people. The guy in Idaho won't go out unless it's cloudy. He says obviously the flyover states are especially vulnerable. All part of the elitist conspiracy."

"Except the most-flown-over state is nowhere near Idaho."

"Where is it?"

"Pennsylvania."

"Really?"

Chang said, "Yes, really, because there's a lot of regular East Coast traffic, plus all the shuttles between D.C. and New York and Boston. Now can we move on? Can we dial the next number?"

Westwood dialed the next number, which was the fourth, which was 901 for Memphis. The first land line, probably. They heard the dialing noises, and then the ring tone, loud in the room.

The call was answered.

There was a hollow *clonk* as a heavy handset was lifted, and a male voice said, "Yes?"

Westwood sat up straight again, and ran through the same bullshit as before, his name, the *LA Times,* the returned call, the apology for the delay.

The voice said, "Sir, I'm not sure I understand."

The guy was old, Reacher figured, slow-spoken and courtly, and if he wasn't from Memphis, he was from somewhere very close by.

Westwood said, "You called me at the *LA Times,* two or three months ago, with something on your mind."

The old guy said, "Sir, if I did, I surely have no recollection of it. And if I offended you in any way at all, why then, certainly I apologize."

"No, you didn't offend me, sir. No apology required. I want to know more about your concerns. That's all."

"Oh, I have very few concerns. My situation is blessed."

"Then why did you call me?"

"I really can't answer that question. I'm not even certain I did."

Westwood glanced at Chang, and back to the screen, and took a breath ready to speak again, but there was a muffled sound on the speaker, and another *clonk,* apparently as the handset was wrestled away, because at that point a woman's voice came on the line and said, "Who is this, please?"

Westwood said, "Ashley Westwood, ma'am, at the *LA Times,* returning a call from this number."

"A recent call?"

"Two or three months ago."

"That will have been my husband."

"May I speak with him?"

"You just were."

"I see. He didn't remember the call."

"He wouldn't. Two or three months is a very long time."

"Would you have any idea what the call might have been about?"

"Don't you?"

Westwood didn't answer.

The woman said, "I'm not judging you. If I could tune him out, I would. Are you a political writer or a science writer?"

Westwood said, "Science."

"Then it will have been about granite countertops being radioactive. That's this year's topic. Which they are, as a matter of fact, but it's a question of degree. I'm sure he asked you to write a story about it. You and many others."

"Do you know how many others?"

"A small number compared to the population of the United States, but a large number compared to how many hours an old man should spend on the telephone."

Westwood said, "Ma'am, is it possible he hired a private detective?"

The woman said, "For what?"

"To help him with his investigations into the granite situation."

"No, it would be most unlikely."

"Can you be certain?"

"The facts are not in dispute. There's nothing to investigate. And he has no access to money. He couldn't hire anybody."

"Not even cash?"

"Not even. Don't ask. And don't get old."

"Does your husband have a cell phone?"

"No."

"Could he have gotten one, maybe from a drugstore?"

"No, he never leaves the house."

"Have people died because of the granite?"

"He says so."

"How many, exactly?"

"Oh, thousands."

"OK," Westwood said. "Thank you. I'm sorry for disturbing you."

"My pleasure," the woman said. "Makes a change, talking to someone else."

They heard a slow pause, and a final *clonk,* as the big old handset was put back in its cradle.

Westwood said, "Welcome to my life."

Chang said, "It's better than hers."

Westwood dialed the fifth number. Area code 773, which was Chicago. It rang and rang, way past the point where an answering machine would have cut it short. Then suddenly an out-of-breath woman came on the line, and said, "City Library, Lincoln Park, volunteer room." She sounded very young and very cheerful, and very busy.

Westwood introduced himself and asked who he was talking to. The kid gave a name, no hesitation at all, but said she had never called the *LA Times,* and knew no private detectives. Westwood asked her if the phone they were on was used by other people, and she said yes, by all the volunteers. She said she was one of them. She said the volunteer room was where they left their coats and took their breaks. There was a phone in there, and time to use it, occasionally. She said the Lincoln Park library was a little ways north of downtown Chicago, and it had dozens of volunteers, always changing, young and old, men and women, all of them fascinating. But no, none of them seemed to be obsessed about anything scientific. Not overtly. Certainly not to the extent of calling distant newspapers.

Westwood checked his list, for the name against the 773 number, as recorded contemporaneously in the company database. He said, "Do you know a volunteer called McCann? I'm not entirely sure if it would be Mr. or Ms."

"No," the kid said. "I never heard that name."

Westwood asked, "How long have you volunteered there?"

"A week," the kid said, and Westwood thanked her, and she said he was welcome, and he said he guessed he should let her go, and she said well yes, she had things to do, and Westwood hung up.

He dialed the last number. Area code 505, which was New Mexico.

Chapter 27

The New Mexico number rang four times, and was answered by a man with a quiet, defeated voice. Westwood gave his name and ran through his standard preamble, the *LA Times,* the returned call, the apology for the delay, the sudden revival of interest in the issue. There was a long pause, and the quiet man on the other end of the line said, "That was then. It would be a different story now."

Westwood said, "How so?"

"I know what I saw. At first no one would listen, including you, I'm afraid. But then the police department sent a detective. A young man, casually dressed, but keen. He said he was from a special confidential unit, and he took my report. He said I should sit tight and do nothing more. But then a week later I saw him in uniform, on traffic duty. He was writing parking tickets. He wasn't a detective at all. The police department had fobbed me off with a rookie. To keep me quiet, I suppose. To head me off."

Westwood said, "Tell me again exactly what you saw."

"A spacecraft in the desert, just landed, with six passengers disembarking. They resembled humans, but weren't. And the important thing was the craft looked to have no means of taking off again. It was a landing module only. Which meant those creatures were set to stay. Which begged a question. Were they the first? If not, how many came before them? How many are already here? Do they already control the police department? Do they already control everything?"

Westwood said nothing.

The quiet man said, "So now the story would be psychological, rather than purely scientific. How does an individual cope, when he knows something, but is forced to pretend he doesn't?"

Westwood asked, "Did you hire a private detective?"

"I tried to. The first three I called wouldn't take on extraterrestrial investigations. Then I realized it would be safer to lie low. That's the issue now. The stress. I suppose many of us are in the same boat. We know, but we feel like the only one, because we can't talk to each other. Maybe that's what you should write about. The isolation."

"What happened to the spaceship?"

"I couldn't find it again. I imagine their allies hauled it away and hid it."

"Has anyone died as a result?"

"I don't know. Possibly."

"How many?"

"One or two, conceivably. I mean, a controlled landing implies considerable energy. Flames from retro rockets, and so on. It might have been dangerous, inside a certain perimeter. And no one knows what they do later, after they settle in."

"Do you have a cell phone?"

"No, the radiation is too dangerous. It can cause brain cancer."

"Does the name Keever mean anything to you? Is he one of the folks you called?"

"No, I never heard that name."

"Thank you," Westwood said. "I'll be back in touch."

He hung up.

Chang said, "I know, welcome to your life."

Westwood said, "Welcome to New Mexico."

He deleted the third, the fourth, and the sixth numbers from his temporary list. He said, "Beam boy and granite guy and close en-counters guy aren't it, agreed? Which leaves us the abandoned cell phone in Louisiana, and the abandoned cell phone in Mississippi, and the volunteer room in Chicago. We cut the odds in half, at least."

He neatened up the new three-line layout on his screen. At the top was the Louisiana number, which ten weeks ago had belonged to a person named Headley, according to the database, and below it was the Mississippi number, with the name Ramirez, and below that was the Chicago rec room, one user of which had been the elusive Mr. McCann, according to the database, or Ms. McCann, neither of which the out-of-breath kid had ever heard of.

Westwood printed the page and handed it to Chang.

She said, "Try the Maloney number again."

Westwood dialed it, *beep-boop-bap,* and it rang and rang, and it wasn't answered, and voice mail didn't cut in.

He hung up, after another whole minute of trying.

Reacher said, "We need a list of everything you published in the last six months."

Westwood said, "Why?"

"Because why else would the guy call you? He saw something you wrote. We need to know what it was."

"That won't help us find him."

"I agree. It won't. But we need to know what kind of guy we're dealing with when we get there. We need to know what his problem is."

"All my stuff is on the web site. You can check it, going back years."

"OK," Reacher said. "Many thanks for your help."

"What now?"

"We'll figure something out. Like you said, we cut the odds in half. We have three to choose from. We'll track them down."

"Here's another theory," Westwood said. "I checked Keever's web page, obviously, and Ms. Chang's, too. It all looks very competent. I'm sure you have all kinds of resources available to you, including your own private databases, and reverse phone directories, and possibly your own sources inside the phone companies themselves. Therefore my new theory is you don't need me anymore. My theory is you'll cut me out completely now."

"We won't," Chang said. "We'll keep you in the loop."

"Why would you?"

"We don't want the book rights."

"Why wouldn't you?"

"I'm too busy and he can barely write his own name with a crayon."

Reacher said nothing.

Westwood said, "So I stay in?"

Chang said, "All for one and one for all."

"Promise?"

"Cross my heart."

"But only if it's a good story. Please don't bring me beams or granite or spaceships."

Reacher and Chang left Westwood in his office, and rode the elevator back to the street. Chang had a laptop computer in her suitcase, and all she needed was a quiet space and a wifi connection, and then she could get to work, with her private databases, and her reverse phone directories, and her list of sources inside the phone companies themselves. Which meant a hotel, which meant finding a taxi. There was one parked at the curb across the street, and Reacher whistled and waved at it, but for some reason it took off fast in the other direction without them. Every city had its own hailing protocol, and it was hard to keep track. They walked north toward the children's museum and found cabs lined up and ready to go. The kind of places Reacher knew in LA weren't notably quiet and might not have had wifi, so he let Chang decide their destination. She told the driver West Hollywood, and the guy set out through the traffic.

* * *

Ten minutes later, twenty miles south of Mother's Rest, the man with the ironed jeans and the blow-dried hair took a third call on his land line. This time his contact was in a chatty mood. The guy said, "It was a gift. They met in the *LA Times* office for nearly an hour. Which is an old building with thick walls. But Hackett got lucky. Apparently most of the business was done on the phone, and apparently Westwood uses his phone in a dock on his desk, and his desk is under his window, so Hackett had an amplified signal blasting straight through the glass. His scanner nearly blew up. They made seven calls in total. Two were expired cell phones, one was a cell phone that didn't answer, and one was a public phone in Chicago. The other three were weirdoes they gave up on. Keever's name was mentioned once, and private detectives in general all three times, plus once more to the shared number in Chicago, where Westwood also asked about the name McCann."

The man south of Mother's Rest was quiet for a very long time.

Then he said, "But no real progress?"

"That's for you to decide. They got three possibles. I'm sure one of them was Keever's client, and I'm sure you know which. They got phone data, which can be checked. I've seen things go bad from less."

"I need to know if they contact the phone companies. Like a distant early warning system. And if they do, I need to know what the phone companies tell them."

"That would cost extra, I'm afraid. Phone companies can be secretive. Palms would need to be greased."

"Do it."

"OK."

"Then what happened?"

"Then it got a little comical."

"How so?"

"Westwood stayed inside and Reacher and Chang left."

"Where did they go?"

"That's where it got comical. Hackett lost them. He was posing as a cab driver. No better cover in a city. But Reacher tried to hail him, so he had to take off fast."

"That's not good."

"He has Chang's phone in his system. As soon as she makes a call, he'll know exactly where they are."

Chapter 28

The address in West Hollywood that Chang chose was a motel, not unlike the one in Mother's Rest, except its more glamorous location made it hip and ironic rather than old and sad. Reacher paid cash for a room, which had a desk and a chair and a choice of wired or wireless connection. But best of all it had a king-size bed, flat and wide and firm. They both looked at it, and kissed, meaning it, but only briefly, like people who knew they had work to do first. Chang sat down and plugged in her laptop. She unfolded the paper Westwood had printed. Three names, three numbers. She said, "Are you a gambling man?"

Reacher said, "Louisiana is right next to Arkansas, which could explain why the guy has those two area codes. But so is Mississippi, just the same. Chicago isn't, but a guy with the real name McCann might choose Maloney for an alias. Maybe it was his mother's name. So at this point I would say it's even money."

"Where do you want to start?"

"With the current 501. It might be a recent contract. It might have a real name on it."

"If it isn't a burner."

She opened a search page just as ugly as Westwood's, and typed in the number 501 and seven more digits.

The screen said: *refer.*

Reacher said, "What does that mean?"

She said, "It means it isn't in the reverse directory, but there's information to be had. At a price, from a source in the phone company."

"How big of a price?"

"A hundred bucks, probably."

"Can you afford it?"

"If it comes to anything I'll bill the *LA Times.*"

"Check the others first. In case you need a quantity discount."

Which turned out to be a possibility. The Chicago number came back exactly as advertised, one of a dozen lines into the Lincoln Park branch of the city library, but both the Louisiana cell and the Mississippi cell came back as *refer.*

Information to be had.

Reacher said, "How exactly do we get it?"

Chang said, "We used to e-mail. But not now. Too vulnerable. Too risky for the source. Worse than a paper trail. Now we have to call."

She picked up her phone and dialed. The call was answered fast. There was no small talk. Chang was all business. She gave her name, and explained what she needed, and read out the three numbers, slowly and distinctly, and listened to them repeated back, and said "OK," and hung up.

"Two hundred bucks," she said. "He'll get back to me later today."

Reacher said, "How much later?"

"Could be hours."

There was only one thing to do, to fill the time.

Ten minutes later, twenty miles south of Mother's Rest, the man with the ironed jeans and the blow-dried hair took a fourth call on his land line. His contact said, "Hackett says Chang just made a call. He says they're in a motel in West Hollywood."

"Who did she call?"

"The phone company. She wanted information on three numbers. She paid two hundred dollars for it."

"What information did she get?"

"None yet. Her source said he'd call back later today."

"How much later?"

"Could be hours."

"Can you get it faster?"

"Save your money. Hackett is listening. You'll know when she knows."

"How far away is he?"

"He's heading to West Hollywood now. I'm sure he'll be in place before the guy calls back."

The motel bed was indeed flat and wide and firm. Reacher lay on his back, filmed with sweat, the AC not really cold, the ceiling fan busted. Chang lay beside him, breathing deep. Reacher's theory had always been the second time was by far the best. No more tiny inhibitions, and no more first-time fumbles, yet still plenty of novelty and excitement. But that theory had been shattered. It had been blown apart. *All theories should be tested,* Westwood had said. *That's a central part of the scientific method.* And tested it they had. The second time, an hour ago, had been sensational. But the third time had been better. Way better. Reacher lay there, drained, empty, his bones turned to rubber, relaxed in a way that made any previous notion of repose seem like furious agitation.

Eventually Chang rolled up on one elbow, and traced her fingers over his chest, to his neck, to his face, and down again, as if learning him, as if memorizing the slabs and contours of his body. In turn he was happy with stillness, his hand on the inside of her thigh, unmoving but alive with the thrill of hot skin, damp but velvet smooth, the muscle under it slack, a tiny pulse ticking against his palm.

She said, "Reacher."

He said, "Yes?"

"Nothing. I'm just trying it out."

Her hair was on his shoulder, thick and heavy. Her breasts were crushed against his arm. He could feel the beat of her heart.

She said, "Have you ever been married?"

"No," he said. "You?"

"Once. But it didn't last."

"Like so many."

She said, "What's the longest relationship you ever had?"

"Six months," he said. "Or thereabouts. Postings made it difficult. I got moved too often. It was a lottery. A double lottery, if she was in the service, too. Mostly it was like ships that pass in the night."

Her phone rang.

She pushed off him and twisted upright and padded naked across the room to the desk. She checked the incoming number and answered the call. No small talk. All business. The phone company, presumably. She found a pen, and padded back to the night stand, where there was a pad of motel paper, all brittle and yellowed with age. She carried it back to the desk, and bent down, and started making notes, first on one page, and then on a second, and then on a third. At one point she turned toward him and leaned forward and winked.

He propped himself on his elbows.

She said, "Thank you," and clicked off her call.

He said, "What?"

She said, "Wait."

She woke her computer and clicked and typed and her face was lit by cold gray light from the screen. She put her fingertips on the touchpad and swiped and scrolled and zoomed.

Then she smiled.

He said, "What?"

She said, "All three numbers were burner phones. All pre-paid, all bought at pharmacies. The Louisiana phone is recent. From a drugstore in Shreveport. It had to be registered before it could be used. That's the system now. You buy it, you use it to call an 800 number, it gets assigned an area code local to where you're calling from, plus an available number. Which all happened. Then it was used eleven times, and then it ran out of minutes, and it wasn't topped up fast enough, so it lapsed. It was taken off the air. The number will be reissued about six months from now."

"Who did it call?"

"Westwood, in LA, all eleven times."

"From where?"

"Shreveport. The same cell tower every time."

Reacher said nothing.

Chang said, "And the Mississippi phone was exactly the same, more or less, except it's a little older. It was bought a year ago at a drugstore in Oxford, and registered with a local Mississippi area code, and topped up four times, but eventually abandoned. All usage was in Oxford, all on two towers. Dozens of calls to Westwood, from a school and a dorm, maybe, if he was right, and the guy was a college student."

"Good to know," Reacher said. "But not worth a wink and a smile. So tell me about the Arkansas number. I'm guessing that's where the action is."

Chang smiled again, still naked, still happy, relieved, satisfied, and excited. She said, "The Arkansas number is different. It's a drugstore burner like the others, except it's still on the air, even though it's originally much, much older. It was part of a huge Wal-Mart order from years ago. Back then they came with numbers already built in and pre-assigned. Hence the Arkansas area code, because Wal-Mart's HQ is in Arkansas. But it wasn't sold there. Wasn't sold anywhere, in fact, at least not by Wal-Mart. It got replaced by a newer model, and earlier this year the last of the unsold stock was auctioned off for ten cents on the dollar. About a hundred units, my guy thinks."

"Who bought them?"

"A middleman in New Jersey. A kind of broker. A specialist in such things."

"And he sold them on?"

"That's what middlemen do."

"When?"

"Twelve weeks ago."

"Who did he sell them to?"

Chang's smile got wider.

She said, "He sold them to a mom-and-pop drugstore in Chicago."

He said, "Where in Chicago?"

She turned her laptop so he could see its screen. He craned his neck. Gray light and straight lines. Google Maps, he figured, or Google Earth, or whatever kind of Google it was that showed satellite pictures of city streets.

Chang said, "It's a little ways north of downtown. It's literally right next door to the Lincoln Park branch of the city library."

Still naked, still excited, still smiling, Chang tried the number again, the grandfathered 501 area code, plus seven more digits, but as before it rang and rang without being answered, and without going to voice mail. She gave it a whole hopeful minute, and then she hung up. Then she put her phone on speaker, and called Westwood, and found him in his office at the *LA Times*. She said, "The 501 number is a pharmacy burner that was sold in a store right next to the Lincoln Park library in Chicago. Therefore Maloney is McCann. We're assuming he volunteers in the library, which would give him open access to the 773 number he used before. Then when you blocked him he went next door and bought a cell phone and tried again. We need to know his history. We need to know when he started calling."

Westwood said, "I'll check."

They heard pattering keys, and clicking and scrolling, and breathing. Reacher pictured the twin screens, and the phone in the dock. Then Westwood came back and said, "The first McCann call came in a little over four months ago. There were fifteen more before I blocked him. Then he changed to Maloney, and called three more times. But you know that."

"Got notes on the earlier calls?"

"Nothing. I'm sorry."

"Don't worry. We'll figure it out."

"Keep in touch."

"We will."

She hung up.

Reacher said, "We should find the main number for the library. They must have details on their volunteers. We could get a home address."

She said, "We should shower first. And get dressed. I feel weird doing this with no clothes on."

Reacher said nothing.

The man with the ironed jeans and the blow-dried hair took a fifth call on his land line. His contact said, "The phone company just called her back. Then she called the *LA Times,* immediately. She's all excited about a guy named McCann in Chicago."

There was a long, long pause.

Then the man with the jeans and the hair asked, "Did she speak to him?"

"To McCann?" his contact said. "No."

"But she has his phone number."

"Actually she has two phone numbers. Although one of them seems to be in a public library. Apparently McCann volunteers there."

"She already knows where he works?"

"Volunteering is not the same thing as working."

"Why hasn't she spoken to him?"

"She tried to. She called his cell, but he didn't answer."

"Why wouldn't he?"

"How would I know?"

"I'm asking you, as a professional. I want analysis. That's what I pay you for. What are the possible reasons for not answering a cell phone call?"

"Sudden decease of the cell phone owner, loss of the cell phone under the seat of a city bus or similar, not recognizing the incoming caller ID while in a misanthropic mood, being in a location or environment where taking a call would be socially unacceptable. There are hundreds of reasons."

"What's her next move?"

"She'll keep trying the cell number, and she'll go through the main switchboard at the library to get whatever data is kept on the volunteers."

"Like an address?"

"That might be difficult. There would be privacy issues."

"So what then?"

"She'll go to Chicago. She'll go anyway. If McCann was Keever's client, she'll want to interview him. And she can't expect him to fly out to her."

"And Reacher will go with her to Chicago."

"Most likely."

"I can't let them do that. They're too close already."

"How do you propose to stop them?"

"Your boy Hackett is right there."

"At the moment Hackett is engaged for surveillance only."

"That might need to change. You told me about the menu."

"You need to think about this carefully. Not just the money. It's a big step."

"I can't let them get to Chicago."

"You need to be very sure. This kind of decision benefits from absolute certainty."

"We should have stopped them ourselves, when we had the chance."

"I'll need a formal instruction."

The man with the jeans and the hair said, "Tell Hackett to stop them now. Permanently."

Chapter 29

The shower made for a slow and gentle transition between what they had been doing and what they had to do next. The tub was narrow, but the curtain was on a bowed-out rail, and the spray was wide and warm, and they didn't want to get more than an inch away from each other anyway, so all was comfortable. They washed each other, like a game, top to bottom, slowly, carefully, soap and shampoo, no crevice neglected, and some lingered over. They took their time. There was a certain amount of fooling around. Steam rose, and filled the room, and the mirror fogged.

Then eventually they climbed out and dried off with thin towels, and they rubbed circles in the steam on the mirror, one high up, one lower down, and they combed their hair, Reacher with his fingers, Chang with a tortoiseshell implement she fetched from her suitcase. They collected their clothes from where they had fallen, on the floor and the chair and the bed, and they dragged them on over still-damp skin.

Then it was back to business. Reacher re-opened the drapes, and saw nothing outside except bright sun and blue sky. It was a spectacular day. Southern California, in late summer. Even the band of smog low down looked golden. Chang tried the 501 cell again. As before, it rang endlessly, without an answer. She kept it going. It purred dolefully but relentlessly on the speaker. On and on. Reacher said, "I never had this happen before. Either someone answers or it goes to an answering machine."

"Maybe those old burners didn't have voice mail yet. Or maybe he didn't set it up. Or he disabled it."

"Can you do that?"

"I don't know."

"Why isn't he answering? He can't have it both ways. Either you use voice mail or you answer your damn phone."

"He's given up. No one would listen to him. So he dumped the phone. It's ringing in a drawer somewhere."

Reacher was a need-to-know person, where technology was concerned. He understood faxes and telexes and military radio and the United States Postal Service, but he had never needed to know anything about civilian cell phones. He had never owned one. Why would he? Who would he call? Who would call him? The little he understood came from everyday observation. He pictured the phone in his mind, ringing and ringing. Vibrating too, probably. Ringing and buzzing. Powerful, and energetic. He said, "The battery must be charged. If it went dead the phone would switch off and the network would know. So he must plug it in from time to time."

"So maybe he went out to the store and left it behind."

Reacher glanced out the window and didn't answer.

The phone kept on ringing.

Chang said, "What?"

"Nothing." But in his mind's eye he was getting a lonely picture, of a phone on the floor, alive, hopping around, like a faithful spaniel pawing at its dead master, trying to get his attention, not understanding. Out on the moors, maybe, or in a grand living room. A heart attack, perhaps, or gout, or whatever guys with spaniels died of. But he was a need-to-know data-driven person, so all he said was, "Shut it down and try the library switchboard instead."

Chang killed the call and the room went quiet. She woke her computer and clicked her way to a web page for the Chicago library system. The Lincoln Park branch had its own inquiries number. A 773 area code, plus seven more digits, not far removed from the volunteer room number they had gotten before. She dialed, and got a menu. English or Spanish. Touch one for this, touch two for that. To speak with a person, touch nine.

She touched nine. There was a ring tone, and then a woman's voice came on and said, "How may I help you?"

Chang introduced herself the same way she had to Westwood, the very first time. She said her name, and said she was a private detective, now based in Seattle, but previously with the FBI, and that last part seemed to help. The woman in Chicago seemed impressed.

Chang said, "I understand you have volunteers helping out."

"That's correct," the woman said.

"Do you have a volunteer named McCann?"

"We did."

"But not anymore?"

"We haven't seen him for three or four weeks."

"Did he quit?"

"Not as such. But volunteers tend to come and go."

"What can you tell me about him?"

"Why do you need to know? Is he in trouble?"

"He was my firm's client. But we lost touch. We're trying to reconnect. To see if he still needs our help."

"He's an older man, very quiet, keeps himself to himself. But he does good work. We'd like to reconnect, too."

"Did he have any burning interests, or things on his mind?"

"I'm not sure. He was never exactly a chatterbox."

"Is he local? Do you have an address for him?"

Dead air from Chicago. Then the woman said, "I'm sorry, but I'm really not permitted to give out that kind of information. We have to respect our volunteers' privacy."

"Do you have a phone number for him? At his home? Perhaps you could call him and ask him to call us."

Silence from Chicago. Just tiny plastic clicks. A database, possibly. A long list, on a computer. Lots of scrolling required. M for McCann would be exactly halfway.

Then the woman came back on the line and said, "No, I'm afraid we don't have a phone number for him."

After that they checked Chang's secret private-eye databases for guys named McCann in Chicago, in case he stood out some other way, but they got hundreds of random hits, as was to be expected, Reacher supposed, given ethnic names and historic patterns of migration. Maybe their McCann was one of them, but there was no way of knowing. He was hidden like a grain of sand on a beach.

After that they checked the airlines. There was plenty of choice. LAX to ORD was a big-deal route. There were multiple departures all through the afternoon hours. Which made sense. Folks could get home before their natural bedtimes, two time zones east. Anything later approached red-eye territory.

The major carriers were all charging the same price, to the penny, so Chang went with American, where she had a gold card, and she booked on the phone, through a gold card person. More reliable in urgent situations, she said, and better seats.

Reacher put his toothbrush in his pocket, and she packed her suitcase, with her comb, and her computer, and its charger, and her phone charger.

She zipped it up.

She said, "OK?"

Reacher nodded and said, "Let's go find a cab."

Chapter 30

They stepped out the door and blinked in the bright sun, and stopped by the office to return the key. The clerk seemed perturbed by their early departure, at first worried there was something wrong with the room, and when they told him there wasn't, he seemed to assume they saw the place as a hot-sheets by-the-hour convenience, and got upset all over again. Reacher told him it was an urgent change of plan, that was all, just business, nothing more, but he saw the guy's point. Their hair was still wet from the shower, and the afterglow was coming off them in waves, like nuclear radiation.

There was a cab at the curb across the street. Reacher whistled and waved, the same as before, and this time it worked. The cab pulled a slow curb-to-curb U-turn and came to rest with the rear door handle exactly level with Reacher's hip. The driver popped the trunk and climbed out to help with Chang's suitcase. He was a big guy in a short-sleeved shirt, his forearms roped with muscle, his nose bent from an earlier break, his eyebrows thick with scar tissue. A boxer in his youth, Reacher thought, or just plain unlucky. The guy lifted the suitcase like it was weightless and placed it in the trunk. Chang slid in across the vinyl bench, behind the driver's seat, and

Reacher climbed in beside her. The driver got back behind the wheel and caught Reacher's eye in the mirror.

"LAX," Reacher said. "American, domestic."

The cab took off, slow and steady through the winking sunlight, left and right on the side streets, to Santa Monica Boulevard, where it headed south and west toward the 405.

This time the guy with the jeans and the hair didn't wait for his land line to ring. He wanted to get ahead of the news, so he dialed his contact preemptively. He said, "Is it done?"

His contact said, "Don't worry, it will be."

"So it isn't done?"

"Not yet."

"But Hackett was right there."

"Let us do what we're good at, OK? Two dead in a West Hollywood motel room would have been a disaster. They go to town over a thing like that. There would have been ten squad cars there in a thin minute. They'd have put four detectives on it. It would have been on the evening news. Hackett can't afford that kind of exposure. Too much risk. He has to be able to work again."

"So when?"

"Trust me. They won't get on the plane."

The 405 was busy, as always, but it was moving. Three lanes, keeping pace, all bright colors and clean paint and wax and chrome, and fierce flashing sun, and the tawny hills in the background. The ride was soft. Chang had her window all the way down, and the breeze was warm. It was blowing her hair around. Her T-shirt was damp on the shoulders, where it had rested. The driver was neat and precise in his movements. No slamming around. He was staying in the right-hand lane, going with the flow, as good a way as any, on LA's freeways. They would get there when they got there.

Reacher was leaning back in his seat, still deeply content, still rubbery, and Chang looked the same beside him. She said, "A library volunteer is bound to be local, right? It's a community thing, basically. It's not like we'll have to search the whole of Chicago."

Reacher said, "You should check what Westwood wrote four months ago. We need to know what was on McCann's mind. Before we meet him. We need to know what triggered his first call."

Chang took out her phone, and used her thumbs to ask for the *LA Times* web site. The cell network was slower than wifi, but it got there in the end. She said, "Four months exactly? Or do we assume he researched an earlier piece?"

"Good point," Reacher said. "I guess if McCann is an internet guy, he could have found anything. But listing everything Westwood ever wrote in his life won't help us. Try a three-month window. Four, five, and six months back."

Chang used the site's own search box and typed *Westwood*. She got a bunch of stuff about the LA neighborhood of the same name. So she changed the search to *Ashley Westwood,* in quote marks, which worked much better. First up was a sidebar section on the right, with a photo and a bio of the man himself. The photo looked like it had been taken some years earlier, on a good day. Westwood looked a little younger, and his hair and his beard were a little neater, and less gray. The bio said he had postgraduate degrees in molecular biology and journalism. On the left was a list of his articles. Each one had a headline and a capsule summary. First up was a teaser for his piece on the history of wheat, which was due to be published on the upcoming Sunday. Below that was the piece on traumatic brain injuries they had already seen, in Keever's Oklahoma City bedroom.

Chang swiped at her screen and the list spooled upward. She stopped it eight pieces back, which was four months. The guy was doing a new article every two weeks, approximately, each one fairly long and presumably researched fairly extensively. Which in terms of civilian employment was easier than being a coal miner or an ER doctor, no doubt, but not actually easy, in Reacher's opinion. He had never written anything longer than an after-action report. Which was generally a discipline much shorter in form, and not necessarily researched, or even non-fiction.

First up at the four-month mark was a piece about organic farming. Fruits, vegetables, and staple crops. The headline was provocative, and the capsule summary hinted that big agribusinesses were subverting the definition in order to reap the premium prices without doing the hard work. Two weeks before that Westwood had written about gerbils. Ancient gerbils, to be precise, according to the headline. Apparently new research proved the bubonic plague in medieval Europe had been carried not by fleas on rats, as long supposed, but by fleas on giant gerbils from Asia.

The traffic was slowing up, in the right-hand lane at least. The middle lane and the left lane were passing them by. But the driver didn't move over.

Chang scrolled on down the list. Next up after the gerbils was a five-month-old piece about climate change. The headline said the oceans were rising, and the capsule summary said fractal geometry meant an East Coast seawall would need more concrete than humans had mixed in all their history so far.

Chang said, "Everyone writes about climate change. No need for McCann to pick on Westwood in particular, right?"

Reacher said, "Agreed."

Next up was something called the Deep Web. Which had to do with search engines and the internet. Apparently the Surface Web was easier to navigate. After that came bees. Apparently they were dying out the world over. Without them crops would not get fertilized and everyone would starve. Which was a lot more than two hundred people. Reacher could see about two hundred people right then, out the window, because the traffic was slowing even more. They were still in the right-hand lane. The middle lane and the left-hand lane were still a little faster. A black Town Car came level on Chang's side and kept pace for a second. A gap opened up ahead of it. Its rear window came down, and Reacher caught a partial glimpse of a guy inside, his head turning toward them. For an absurd split second it looked like the guy wanted to tell them something. But then the inevitable happened. The Town Car was in the middle lane, but it was going at the right-hand lane's speed, and behind it a small red coupe didn't slow, inattentive, and it kissed the Town Car's rear bumper. The speed differential was modest, not more than five or ten miles an hour, but even so the Town Car was punted solidly forward, and the passenger's head was slammed back against the seat cushion, and then hurled forward again, all of Newton's Laws of Motion in play, inertia and action and reaction. Reacher was surprised by the force of it all. Maybe whiplash really was a thing. The Town Car motored on into the gap ahead, and the red coupe followed, neither one of them slowing, both of them apparently undamaged. Clearly federal bumpers worked like they should.

There was no fuss. No honking horns, no shaking fists, no middle fingers. All in a day's work, Reacher supposed, in Los Angeles traffic.

The right-hand lane slowed even more. Within seconds the Town Car and the red coupe were way ahead and out of sight. The left-hand lane was moving even better. Reacher leaned forward and asked, "Why aren't you moving over?"

The driver glanced in the mirror and said, "It's all going to jam up soon."

"So why not get ahead before it does?"

"It's a hare and tortoise thing, my friend."

Chang put her hand on Reacher's arm and pulled him back. She said, "Let him do what he's good at. You failed driving, remember?"

She turned back to her phone. The last item in their chosen three-month window was a piece about an ocean corridor parallel to the West Coast, from California to Oregon, which great white sharks used for seasonal migration. Not an issue for most folks, except a Frenchman was proposing to swim through it, on his way across the Pacific from Japan. He would sleep on a chase boat every night, and start over every morning, eight hours a day. Apparently the sharks were a secondary problem. First he would have to traverse the Pacific

Gyre, which was a slow thousand-mile whirlpool, full of dumped plastic and toxic sludge and all kinds of other crap.

Chang said, "The French are crazy."

Reacher said, "My mother was French."

"Was she crazy?"

"Pretty much."

The traffic slowed again, proportionately, the left-hand lane to what the middle lane had been doing, and the middle lane to what the right-hand lane had been doing, and the right-hand lane itself almost to a stop. Still the driver wouldn't move over. He just inched along, stopping and starting, barely faster than walking.

Then they found out why.

Just past Culver City and just before Inglewood, with LAX not far away, the guy pulled off the freeway into a sudden unmarked exit on the right, which led to a narrow road that looked like the entrance to some kind of an abandoned maintenance depot. The cab crunched over debris-strewn blacktop, all alone, between rusty iron sheds, and then it turned and bumped across broken concrete into a dead-end fork, with nothing up ahead but a derelict warehouse, which had a busted door hanging open.

The guy drove straight inside, into the dark.

Chapter 31

The warehouse had rusted iron ribs holding up the roof, and what little light there was inside came from hundreds of tiny bright speckles of sun showing through lacy holes in the siding. It was a big place, close to three hundred feet long, but largely empty, except for unexplained piles of abandoned equipment and scrap metal. The floor was concrete, worn smooth in some places, stained with oil in others, and covered with rusty fragments and pigeon feathers everywhere. The crunch of the tires and the engine noise and the beat of the exhaust came back loud through Chang's open window.

There were no people inside, as far as Reacher could see, which fact the back part of his brain seized upon. One blow to the side of the driver's head would solve the problem. A right-handed haymaker, around and down a little. Unexpected. No warning. Give the guy some whiplash of his own. Get your retaliation in first. Reacher's hand balled into a fist, ready.

And then it relaxed again. The guy drove on, slow and steady, but confident, as if he knew exactly where he was going, as if he had been there many times before, and he said, "The hare and the tortoise, my friend. I just saved us twenty minutes."

At the far end of the warehouse was an identical busted door, hanging open just the same, and the guy drove out through it into the bright light, and over more cracked concrete, between more abandoned sheds, and out a sagging gate onto LAX's northern perimeter road, just outside the big wire fence. Reacher saw the control tower dead ahead, and runways and taxiways and parked planes and little trucks swarming all around, busy and innocent under the high sky and the blazing sun.

The driver said, "We were trespassing, technically, but I used to work in there, back when it was a going concern, so I figure I'm entitled. It saves using the regular way in off the freeway, which will be a real mess right now. It always is, in the afternoon. I lose a buck or two on the meter, but I make it back double because I get a new fare all the faster. My secret sauce. A little local knowledge never hurts."

He turned right on a cargo road, and followed the outside of another big wire fence, and ten seconds later they were back in the river of Town Cars and taxis and friends and relatives all heading for the terminals. A minute after that they were at American, slowing down, pulling over, and stopping. Another minute, and Chang's suitcase was out on the sidewalk, upright, handle raised and ready to go, and the driver was paid and tipped and pulling away again.

Chang got flimsy paper boarding passes from a machine, and then they headed for the security line. They didn't get there. A guy stepped in the way. He was about forty, pink and solid, with short fair hair. He was wearing tan chinos and a blue polo shirt under a blue warm-up jacket. All the garments looked institutional. A uniform, of sorts. He was wearing a lanyard around his neck. It was tangled and the badge on the end was turned the wrong way around. He said, "Ma'am, sir, I watched you walk inside from the curb."

Reacher said, "Did you?"

"You passed by the curbside bag drop and used a no-checked-bags machine."

"Did we?"

"Sir, you have no luggage. Nothing checked, no carry-on, not even a personal item."

"Is that a problem?"

"Frankly, sir, yes, it is. It's unusual behavior. It's one of the things on our list."

"Whose list?"

The guy stared for a second, and then he figured it out and glanced down, to where his ID was hanging backward. He made a little noise in his throat, either irritation or frustration, and he flipped the badge around. Reacher saw a pink thumbnail photograph on the right, and the blue letters *LAPD* on the left, plus a bunch of lines too small and pale to read.

The guy said, "Counterterrorism."

Reacher said, "I agree having no luggage is statistically rare. That's a matter of simple observation. But I don't see why negative inferences need to be drawn."

"I don't make the rules. You'll have to come with me, I'm afraid. Both of you."

Chang said, "Where?"

"To talk to my boss."

"Where is he?"

"In the van at the curb."

Reacher glanced out the sliding doors and saw a dark blue panel van parked in the no-waiting lane, about thirty yards away. Not very clean. Not very shiny.

"Surveillance," the guy said. "And by boss I mean my watch supervisor for the day. Not my real boss. The man in the van has the responsibility. It's that simple. This is pure routine. No big deal at all."

Reacher said, "No."

"Sir, that's not a word right now. This is national security."

"No, this is an airport. This is where people get on airplanes. Which is what we're going to do. With one bag between us. So either arrest us or step aside."

"That kind of attitude is on the list, too."

"Higher or lower than the no luggage thing?"

"Sir, you're not helping yourself."

"In what endeavor?"

The guy got all tensed up, and a pair of LAPD uniforms strolled into view, with all kinds of hardware on their bulky hips. Then the guy breathed out, with the same kind of sound as before, either irritated or frustrated, and he said, "OK, you folks have a safe flight."

And he walked on, diagonally, already scanning the middle distance for new alerts.

Chang's gold card guy had gotten them some kind of preapproved status on their boarding passes, which let them use a special line through security, and keep their shoes on. Reacher put his coins in a bowl, and raised his hands in the scanner, and joined Chang on the other side. They walked to the gate, and found a lounge nearby that more gold card coding let them in, and they waited a good long time on upholstered chairs, which they agreed were the modern-day equivalents of the old mahogany benches at the railroad stop in Mother's Rest, in that both were more comfortable than they looked. Which the modern-day equivalents needed to be, because theirs was not the first flight out. Which Reacher eventually figured was the gold card downside.

Then they boarded, and the gold card guy came through strong again, with seats in the exit row, which meant more leg room, which Reacher obviously appreciated, yet also resented. He understood the theory. In an emergency people would have to exit that way, out through the window and over the wing. Hence all kinds of regulations mandated a minimum space, so people would be comfortable on their way through, except that if such a thing existed as a minimum space for a person to be comfortable, then why wasn't every row just as capacious? It was a regulatory conundrum he couldn't unravel.

Chang said, "This is nice."

Reacher said, "It sure is."

"Why didn't you like that cop in the airport?"

"I liked him fine. I like everyone. I'm a happy, cheerful, and gregarious person."

"No, you're really not."

"I liked him fine," Reacher said again.

"You reacted to him in a negative way."

"Did I?"

"You said no to him, and then you started pushing him. You were practically daring him to arrest us."

"I had a question."

"Which was what?"

"I mean, I thought he was plausible. Very plausible, really. We've both seen it happen. Some upstairs pointy-head writes a list. Based on what, no one knows. Maybe nine times out of ten no luggage means you're a bad guy. Except my guess would be nearer one in a million. His too, probably. But he sticks to the list. Because he has to."

"So what was your question?"

"Have you seen an LAPD photo ID recently? To compare?"

"I can't recall."

"Me neither."

"You think he was phony?"

"I wish I knew. I guess if he wasn't, at least he was proving the mind control thing was bullshit. Otherwise he would have been happy I wasn't checking bags. I would have been leaving more room in the hold for the machinery."

"If he was phony, who could he be really?"

"Maybe he was another Moynahan cousin."

"In LA? How many can there be? I don't buy it."

"Why did he quit when he did?"

"Because you convinced him. He had no probable cause. And most likely he needed some. The legislation is probably weaker than we think it is."

"No, he quit when he did because the cops came close."

"They were his."

"But suppose they weren't. Suppose he was a con man whose job it was to get us in the van. But hey, nothing is that important. He's a pro who wants to work again. He wasn't sure what I was going to do next. I might have gone ballistic. He couldn't risk attention. So he shut it down, because the cops happened to wander close, prowling around, looking for unusual behaviors. In other words, the guy covered his ass and ran."

"Or he was a good soldier who spared you an hour in jail and himself an hour of paperwork by taking a deep breath and counting to ten and walking away."

The plane turned onto the runway, amid noisy billows of dry brown air, and it accelerated slowly, complacently, as if fully aware the mysteries of flight had been worked out long ago, and it lifted off calmly, and glinted in the sun, and sideslipped in the haze, and curved upward on trails of soot, setting a dark but graceful course north and east.

Ten minutes later, twenty miles south of Mother's Rest, the man with the ironed jeans and the blow-dried hair took the call on his land line. His contact said, "We're going to put this right."

"Put what right?"

"We got very unlucky."

"What are you talking about?"

"There was a problem."

"Did they get on the plane?"

At which point the contact went talkative again. Not from high spirits. From a bitter and incredulous should-have obsession. He said, "Hackett set it up perfectly. She booked the flight on the phone, so he had all the details. The timing was perfect. To the second. He watched them leave the motel, in a taxi. He was in the back of a Town Car by then, with a subcontractor driving, and they followed for a spell, and then they got alongside on the 405, and it was a total gimme, including she even had her window open, and the fast lane was moving well for the getaway, and a black Town Car on the road to LAX is invisible, because there are a million of them, so the shotgun was literally coming up, right then, point-blank range, but they got rear-ended by a Ferrari. Like getting kicked into next week, Hackett said. They never saw them again. You can't move backward on a freeway."

"So they're on the plane?"

"It wasn't the earliest flight. They chose it because she has a gold card. Hackett is ahead of them, by thirty-four minutes. I told you, we're going to put this right."

"In Chicago?"

"No extra charge. It wasn't our Ferrari, but it is our reputation."

"Don't let them talk to McCann."

"Understood. Our thoughts exactly."

The flight was long. Not coast to coast, but basically transcontinental. A big slice, if not the whole thing. Chang had her seat reclined an inch, and her legs were stuck out straight, with her lace-up shoes under the seat in front. She was thinking, like he had seen her think before, behind the wheel of the little green Ford, on the long empty road to Oklahoma City. Sometimes half-smiling, and then half-grimacing, as positives and negatives ran through her mind, or strengths and weaknesses, or good outcomes and bad. Without a road to watch her eyes were involved too, narrowing, squinting, widening, shifting focus far and near.

Reacher was trying not to think. He was chasing an elusive memory, right in the twilight between conscious and subconscious. He was looking away from it, not thinking about it, leaving it well alone.

He said, "The library will be closed when we get there."

She said, "We'll hit it first thing in the morning. We'll stay the night in a hotel."

"We should make it a good one. We should stay in the best hotel in town, and send the bill to the newspaper. A big suite. With room service. They'll be happy to pay. Because something is coming. I can feel it."

"What exactly?"

"I don't know. There's something I can't remember, but I know it's important."

"How, if you can't remember?"

"Just a feeling."

"Because the best hotel in town will go on my credit card first. I'll be taking a financial risk."

"They'll be happy to pay," Reacher said again.

"Four Seasons or the Peninsula?"

"Either one."

"I'll call from O'Hare and take whichever is cheaper."

Reacher said nothing.

Chang said, "Exactly how important do you think this thing is, that you can't remember but know is important?"

"I think it's going to give us a shape. Of what we're up against."

"What is?"

"I don't know. It's like I'm trying to match two things. Two things have been identical. But I don't know what. Words, or facts, or places."

"Not places. LA is nothing like Mother's Rest. There's no similarity at all."

"OK."

"Neither is Chicago. Except maybe some of the farmers go there, to do whatever farmers do in Chicago. Is that it?"

"No."

"You better hurry up. We're going to be there soon."

Reacher nodded, absently. *We're going to be there soon.* He pictured the deplaning process in his mind. He liked to think things through, and scope things out. Even something as simple as getting off a plane. It was a lizard brain thing. They would taxi and park, and the seatbelt sign would go off, and people would stand, and wrestle stuff out of the overheads and from under the seats, and they would pack together in the aisle, and eventually shuffle one by one to the door and out to the jet bridge. Then the race would be on for real, down the long wide corridors, past the silvery boutiques, past the food courts, with their laminate tables and their lonely customers.

Which was when he got it.

He said, "Not words or facts or places."

She said, "What then?"

"Faces," he said. "Do you remember that Town Car on the 405?"

"There were a million Town Cars on the 405."

"One of them pulled alongside and kept pace for a second, and then got rear-ended by a red coupe."

"Oh, that one."

"Its window came down. I caught a glimpse of the guy inside."

"How much of a glimpse?"

"Partial, and extremely brief."

"But?"

"We've seen him before."

"Where?"

"In the diner in Inglewood. That brown place. This morning. Where we met with Westwood the first time. That guy was in there. Elbows on the table, reading a newspaper."

Now Chang said nothing.

"Same guy," Reacher said.

"I was trained to think like a defense attorney."

"And whatever you're going to say, the front part of my brain agrees with you a hundred percent. It was a split-second glimpse between two vehicles moving at forty miles an hour, and eyewitness testimony is unreliable at best."

"But?"

"The back part of my brain knows it was the same guy."

"How?"

"The radio chatter is off the scale."

"You hear radio chatter?"

"I listen out for it hard. We were wild animals for seven million years. We learned a lot of lessons. We should be careful not to lose them."

"What is the radio chatter saying?"

"Part of it is tuning up for a fight. It knows nothing good is coming."

"What about the other part?"

"It's having a back-and-forth, working out the implications. Which are basically all or nothing. Either I'm completely mistaken, or that guy has been following us from the start. Which would mean he's tracking us through your cell phone. Which would mean he knows virtually everything so far. And which would mean we better call the Four Seasons or the Peninsula from a pay phone. That way we'll get ahead. And we need to get ahead, because this guy is escalating. He's moving right along. At breakfast this morning in the diner he was observing. Maybe eavesdropping a little, reading lips. Now he's trying to kill us."

"By opening his window?"

"He looked at me. For a split second I thought he wanted to tell me something. He was kind of locking in on me. In a preparatory way. But not ahead of him telling me something. He was acquiring his target. That's what he was doing. Logic says he had a sawed-off shotgun in there with him. For a car-to-car drive-by, like an air-to-air missile. Two rounds to make sure, and then everyone panics and crashes, and he gets away in the fast lane, and afterward he was just one Town Car in a million, like you said."

"That's a very extreme scenario."

"It's all or nothing. What else was he doing, pulling level like that? He's been told to take us out. Which suggests he's versatile. And therefore expensive. Which starts to give us a shape for what's happening in Mother's Rest. They're supplying something. In exchange for money. Enough money to hire a versatile private operative to counter a perceived threat."

"Unless like you said, it was a split-second glimpse at forty miles an hour, two moving vehicles, and eyewitness testimony is unreliable."

"Hope for the best, plan for the worst."

"That wouldn't get us a warrant."

"Warrants are about what you can prove. Not what you know."

"And you know?"

"It's an instinct thing. It's why I'm still here, after seven million years. Darwinism in action."

She said, "What did we do between breakfast time and now to make them escalate?"

"Exactly," he said. "We homed in on McCann."

"Who must therefore be very dangerous to them. And therefore very interesting to us."

"And the library will be closed when we get there."

She said, "If he's the same guy. You could still be wrong."

"But the smart money says we should act like I'm right. Just in case."

"Like Pascal's Wager."

"Costs us nothing if we're wrong, but saves us plenty if we're right."

"Except he's behind us now. He's still in LA."

"Not necessarily. This was not the first flight out."

Chang said nothing. She just took out her phone, and held down a button, and changed it from airplane mode to off completely.

* * *

They landed from the east, after a long lazy loop over the lake and the city. A summer dusk was almost done, still bronze and hot, but darkening. The lights on the runways were bright. They taxied and parked, and the seatbelt sign went off, and people stood up and wrestled things out of the overheads and from under the seats, and they started to pack together in the aisle, Reacher and Chang among them.

Chapter 32

Eventually Reacher and Chang crabbed one at a time down the aisle to the airplane door, and out to the jet bridge, and then out to the concourse, which was packed full of a thousand people either sitting and waiting or hustling fast in every direction. Reacher had the unknown man's face front and center in his mind, like a Most Wanted photograph in the post office, and he scanned the crowds obliquely, in the corner of his eye, looking away, not thinking, trusting his instincts to snag the resemblance, if it was there.

It wasn't. The guy wasn't sitting, wasn't waiting, wasn't hustling in any direction. They walked together through the long concourse corridor, past people waiting outside restroom doors, past people lining up for coffee, past newsstands, past silvery boutiques, past fast-food eateries with their laminate tables and their hunched solo travelers. Reacher scanned ahead for newspapers being read, for elbows on the table, for a familiar slope of shoulders, but he saw nothing. No guy. Not in the building.

They made it to the airside exit, and stepped out to landside, to baggage claim, and onward toward the door for ground transportation, and they saw a wall of pay phones, lonely and ignored, but better still they found a concierge desk, which offered all kinds of helpful services to new arrivals, including hotel bookings made direct. A cheerful woman in a blazer recommended the Peninsula, and made the call for them, and got them a suite, and told them where the cab line was.

It was a warm evening, and the air outside was thick with humidity and gas fumes and cigarette smoke. They waited five minutes, and got a tired guy in a tired Crown Vic, who took off for town as fast as he could. Reacher watched out the window until the airport crowds were gone, but he saw no faces he knew. On the highway he watched the cars around them, but none pulled close or kept pace. They all just rolled along through the evening dark, individually, oblivious, all lit up, in worlds of their own.

Chang said, "We should buy a burner phone."

Reacher said, "And we should tell Westwood to buy one, too. Because that's how our guy got this whole thing started, presumably. He was sitting on Westwood, monitoring his calls. We came to him, this morning. We walked right into it."

"Which proves they're worried about Westwood. Which confirms something Westwood wrote is highly relevant."

"Probably not the sharks and the Frenchman."

"Or the gerbils or the climate change."

"See? We're narrowing it down already."

They came in parallel to the L tracks, and saw the great city huge and high and implacable in front of them, by that time a purely nighttime vista, with a million lit windows against an inky eastern sky. The Peninsula hotel was ready and waiting for them, with a suite twice as large as the service bungalows Reacher had grown up in, and a thousand times plusher. The room service menu was the size of a phone book, and bound in leather. They ordered whatever they wanted, on the assumption the *LA Times* would pay. They ate it slowly, on the assumption they had the whole night ahead, uninterrupted. No need to rush. Better to savor the certainty. Better to bask in the upcoming promise. Through appetizers, and entrees, and desserts, and coffee.

They woke early the next morning, despite the time zones, partly because they had things on their minds, but mostly because they hadn't bothered to close the drapes the night before, and the bedroom faced east, where it caught the morning sun. What was on Reacher's mind was his theory, which had suffered further revision. The fourth time had been better than the third. Hard to believe. But true. Which was bittersweet. Because one day it would have to be average. It had to stop somewhere. Sooner or later. It couldn't keep on getting better forever.

Could it?

Hope for the best, plan for the worst.

Apparently what was on Chang's mind was Lincoln Park, and an irony, because she said, "I'm wondering how to get there. It's pretty close. I'm not sure it's worth renting a car. It might be hard to park. And taxis will add up, and might be hard to find. So overall I'm thinking we should get a Town Car for the day. Preferably black."

"Through the hotel," Reacher said. "Another layer of staying ahead."

"Pick up at nine. We'll be at the library about ten minutes after it opens."

"Outstanding."

Which because of the early hour gave them plenty of time, for a long slow room service breakfast, and long slow showers, after other things best done long and slow, in the morning, including the testing of theories.

Their Town Car was the traditional sedan, black in color, as requested, and waxed to a shine. Its driver was a small man in a gray suit. He professed himself equally happy to drive through traffic or sit at a curb. No skin off his nose. He was getting paid either way. It took him ten minutes to Lincoln Park. The library had a start-of-the-day feel, when they stepped inside. There was a little discreet bustling going on, getting things ready. They asked for the woman they had spoken to on the phone the day before, on the inquiries number, after touching nine, and they got directions from one helpful staffer after another, like a relay race, all the way to a desk labeled *Inquiries,* which stood alone in a side alcove, and which was currently unattended. Its chair was neatly tucked in, and its computer screen was blank. As yet undisturbed. The inquiries lady was late for work.

But all was not lost. Because in the end wall of the alcove was a door, and behind the door were voices, and on the door was a sign: *Volunteer Room.* From inside of which McCann had made fifteen calls, until Westwood had run out of patience.

Reacher knocked on the door, and the voices fell silent. He opened the door, and saw a break room, very municipal, full of inoffensive colors and low chairs with fabric upholstery. In the chairs were five people, two men, three women, different ages, different types.

The phone was on a low table, between two of the chairs.

"Excuse me," Reacher said. "I'm sorry to interrupt. I'm looking for Mr. McCann."

An old guy said, "He isn't here," and he said it in a way that made Reacher assume he knew McCann, possibly well, in order to answer with such authority, and to appoint himself spokesperson on the matter. He was a thin old specimen, with pleated no-iron khaki pants and a full head of white hair, neatly brushed, and a tucked-in plaid shirt, like a retired-person uniform. Retired from an executive position, probably, full of spreadsheets and data, still needing to feel wanted, or wanting to feel needed.

Reacher asked him, "When was the last time you saw Mr. McCann?"

"Three or four weeks ago."

"Is that usual?"

"He comes and goes. These are volunteer positions, after all. I gather he has many other interests."

"Do you know where he lives?"

The old guy said, "I'm sorry, but these are personal questions, and I have no idea who you are."

"A short time ago Mr. McCann hired a firm of private detectives, to help him with a problem. We're the agents. We're here to help him."

"Then you must know where he lives."

Reacher said quietly, "Sir, may we speak alone?"

Which hit the spot, as far as the old guy's ego was concerned. He had been recognized as a cut above. As exactly the kind of man you pulled aside and brought closer to the center. He said to the other volunteers, "Would you give us the room? It's time to start work anyway. You've all got things to do."

So the others trooped out, the younger man and three women, and Chang closed the door behind them, and she and Reacher sat down in places just vacated, in a triangle with the old guy, who hadn't moved.

Chang said, "The agent who dealt with Mr. McCann is missing, I'm afraid. And the first thing we need to do in a case like this is make sure the client is safe. That's our standard operating procedure. But we're going to need help finding him."

The old guy said, "What's this about?"

"We don't know exactly. Maybe you can help us there, too. We think Mr. McCann is all worked up about something. Maybe he mentioned it."

"I know he's not a happy man."

"Do you know why?"

"We aren't close. We don't exchange confidences. We have a working relationship. We talk about library matters, of course, often at length, and we agree on most of them, but I recall very little personal conversation. I get the impression he has family problems. That's as much as I can tell you. I think his wife is long dead and his grown-up son is an issue. Or a challenge, as they would say nowadays."

"Do you know where he lives?"

"No, he never told me."

Reacher said, "Isn't that unusual? Don't people normally talk about where they live? The stores on their block, or how far they have to go for a cup of coffee?"

The old guy said, "I got the strong impression he was ashamed of where he lived."

They left the old guy in the room, and found the inquiries lady at work at her desk outside. She had showed up, just in time. Chang renewed their acquaintance, and showed one of her defunct FBI cards, and it was all going as smoothly as could be, but still the woman wouldn't give up McCann's address. She was unmovable. She was passionate on the subject of privacy. She said a request could be made to the director. But Reacher figured the director would be equally passionate, maybe not on the subject of privacy, but certainly on the subject of possible litigation, and therefore just as unmovable.

He said, "OK, don't tell me the address. But at least tell me if Mr. McCann has an address."

The woman said, "Of course he has."

"And you know what it is?"

"Yes, I do. But I can't tell you."

"Is it local?"

"I can't give you the address."

"I don't want it. I don't care about the address anymore. I wouldn't listen if you told me. I just want to know if it's local. That's all. Which doesn't give anything away. Every neighborhood has thousands of people."

"Yes, it's local."

"How local? Does he walk here, the days he works?"

"You're asking me for his address."

"No, I'm not. I don't want his address. I wouldn't even let you tell me now. I would stick my fingers in my ears and sing la-la-la. I just want to know if it's walking distance. It's a geography question. Or physiology. How old would you say Mr. McCann is?"

"How what?"

"Old. His age is different than his address. You're free to talk about it. You're free to share your impressions."

"He's sixty. He was sixty last year."

"Is he in good shape?"

"Hardly. He looks terrible."

"That's too bad. In what way?"

"He's too thin. He doesn't look after himself. He takes no care at all."

"Is he lacking in energy?"

"Yes, I would say so. He's kind of down all the time."

"Then he wouldn't want to walk too far, would he? Let's say three blocks maximum. Would that be a fair conclusion?"

"I can't tell you."

"A three block radius is thirty-six square blocks. That's bigger than Milwaukee. You wouldn't be telling me anything."

"OK, yes, he walks to work, and yes, it's a short walk. But that's it. I can't tell you anything else."

"What's his first name? Can you tell us that?"

"It's Peter. Peter McCann."

"What about his wife? How long has he been widowed?"

"I think that was all a long time ago."

"What's his son's name?"

"It's Michael, I think. Michael McCann."

"Is there an issue with Michael?"

"We didn't talk about it."

"But you must have pieced something together."

"I would be betraying a confidence."

"Not if he didn't tell you himself. You would be sharing your own conclusions. That's all. That's a big difference."

"I think Mr. McCann's son, Michael, has a behavioral issue. I don't know what, exactly. Not something to be proud of, I think. That would be my conclusion."

Reacher made a sympathetic face, and tried one last time, but still she wouldn't give up McCann's address. So they took their leave and detoured to the reference desk and checked the Chicago phone books. There were too many P. McCanns and too many M. McCanns to be useful. They stepped back out to the street armed with precisely nothing except impressions and guesses.

Chapter 33

They turned left on the sidewalk outside the library door, and found the mom-and-pop pharmacy exactly where it should have been, which was directly adjacent. It was a narrow storefront, with an awning and a door and a small display window, which was full of not-very-tempting items, including elastic bandages and heat pads and a toilet seat for folks having difficulty with mobility. Pharmacy windows were a marketing challenge, in Reacher's opinion. It was hard to think of a display liable to make people rush inside with enthusiasm. But he saw one item of interest. It was a burner cell, in a plastic package, hanging on a peg on a board. The phone looked old-fashioned. The plastic package looked dusty. The price was advertised as super-low.

They went inside and found six more identical phones pegged to a panel otherwise covered with two-dollar cases and two-dollar chargers, and car adapters, and wires of many different descriptions, most of them white. The phones themselves were priced a penny shy of thirteen dollars. They came pre-loaded with a hundred minutes of talk time.

Reacher said, "We should buy one."

Chang said, "I was thinking of something more modern."

"How modern does it need to be? All it has to do is work."

"It won't get the internet."

"You're talking to the wrong person. That's a feature, as far as I'm concerned. And it's a karma thing. We'll have the same phone as McCann. It might bring us luck."

"Doesn't seem to have worked for him," Chang said. But she unhooked a phone from the display anyway, and carried it to the counter, where an old lady waited behind the register. She had steel-gray hair in a bun, and she was dressed with last-century, old-country formality. Way in the back of the store was an old guy working on prescriptions. Same kind of age, same kind of style. A white coat over a suit and tie. Same kind of hair, apart from the bun. Mom and Pop, presumably. No other staff. Low overhead.

Reacher asked the woman, "Do these phones have voice mail?"

She repeated the question, much louder, not directed at him, he realized, but at Pop in back, who called out, "No."

The woman said, "No."

Reacher said, "A friend of ours bought one here. Peter McCann. Do you know him?"

She called out loudly, "Do we know Peter McCann?"

The old guy in back shouted, "No."

"No," the woman said.

"Do you know his son, Michael?"

"Do we know his son, Michael?"

"No."

"No."

"OK," Reacher said. He found a ten and a five in his pocket, and paid for the phone. His change came in coins, expertly reckoned and deftly dispensed. They stopped on the sidewalk outside the store and wrestled the package open. Wasn't easy. In the end Reacher gave up on finesse and tore it in half down the middle. He put the charger in his pocket and passed the phone itself to Chang. She looked it over, and figured it out, and turned it on. It came up with a welcome screen, small, blurred, and black and white. It showed its own number. Area code 501, plus seven more digits. It showed a battery icon, at about fifty percent capacity. Charged at the factory, but not all the way. The icon was like a tiny flashlight battery, tipped over on its side, solid at one end and hollow at the other. Reacher said, "Try McCann again. Maybe this time he'll answer. Maybe his phone will recognize a kindred spirit."

There was no speaker option. Not for thirteen bucks. Chang dialed, and they stood together cheek to cheek, listening, her right ear, his left, and they heard McCann's phone ring. And ring. Endlessly. The same as before. No answer, and no voice mail.

Like a faithful spaniel, not understanding.

Chang ended the call.

She said, "Now what? We search an area bigger than Milwaukee?"

"I was dramatizing for effect. Milwaukee is bigger than thirty-six blocks. It's a pretty nice place."

Then he stopped.

She said, "What?"

He said, "Nothing."

He had been about to say *we should go there sometime.*

She said, "OK, we have to search an area smaller than Milwaukee, but not by much."

"A couple of blocks might do it. If we point ourselves in the right direction. This is a man who looks terrible because he doesn't take care of himself. Probably doesn't eat right, maybe doesn't sleep right. Probably won't go to the doctor, so he doesn't get prescriptions to fill. And he certainly isn't trawling the aisles comparison shopping for vitamin pills. Pharmacies are not on his radar. He doesn't have a favorite. He's indifferent to them all. Therefore he had no particular reason to buy his phone from this particular pharmacy. So why did he? Because he walks past it twice a day, to and from the library. How else would he even notice? They had one phone in the window, all covered with dust. So I think we can conclude he walks home in this direction. Out the library door, turn left, past the pharmacy, and onward."

"To where?"

"I think this is a pretty nice neighborhood. I think the real estate here is solid. But apparently McCann is ashamed of where he lives. What does that mean? You see anything around here you'd be ashamed to live in?"

"I'm not McCann."

"Exactly. It's all relative. The old guy in the volunteer room looks like a retired CEO or something, and I'm sure he's local, and I'm sure he lives in a house. Pretty much impossible to have a shirt like that without living in a house. The two things go together. Practically a requirement. Probably some kind of a nice brownstone on a quiet leafy street. Therefore if it's relative, McCann doesn't live in a house. But not in an apartment, either. Apartments are perfectly legitimate alternatives to houses. Better in some ways. Certainly nothing to be ashamed about. So McCann lives in something less than a house, but not an apartment."

"A broken-up house," Chang said. "A not-very-nice brownstone, on a not-very-leafy street, all divided up into separate rooms. Probably not still cooking on electric hotplates, but close. Which is hard for one guy to admit to another guy, especially when the other guy has a brownstone all to himself. Maybe the exact same brownstone. Same builder, same plan. But his street didn't fall on hard times. Which is way too pointed for testosterone to bear."

"That's how I see it," Reacher said. "Roughly. Maybe not the hormonal stuff. But two or three blocks in this direction, we're going to find a couple of streets of tumbledown row houses, each with about a dozen bells on the door, and those kind of bells usually have labels next to them, sometimes with names on, and with a bit of luck we'll find one of those names is McCann."

There were plenty of names, because there were plenty of labels, because there were plenty of bells, because there were four streets, not a couple, and they were long. The first two turned left and right off the main drag two blocks after the library, and the third and the fourth came another block further out. They were low-rise enclaves between taller buildings, not shoe-horned in but there from the beginning. There was nothing off-putting or unpleasant about them. No trash in the gutters, no busted syringes crunching underfoot, no graffiti, no rot or decay. Nothing overt. But somehow the mysterious and unforgiving calculus of real estate had downgraded them. Maybe there were missing trees, or damp in the basements, or too much window AC. Maybe the breeze blew wrong. Maybe way back a poor widow had split up her house to make ends meet, and then another, and another. Image was a very subtle thing.

They had their Town Car quarter the neighborhood at a slow speed, to establish the search area's boundaries. Then they had the guy park, and they got out to walk. The sun was over the lake, and the light was sharp with reflections. It was already hot, two hours before noon.

Chang took the sunny side of the street, and Reacher stayed in the morning shadows. They moved door to door, separately, unsynchronized, up brownstone stoops and down again, like restaurant workers delivering menus, or missionaries seeking converts. Reacher found that most bell buttons had names against them, some handwritten, some typed, some printed, some embossed on narrow black tape and stuck over previous tenants'. There were Polish names, and African names, and South American names, and Irish names, a whole United Nations right there, but on the first street at least none of the names was McCann.

Twenty miles south of Mother's Rest, the man with the ironed jeans and the blow-dried hair took another call on his land line. His contact said, "She's not using her phone anymore."

"Why not?"

"Hard to say. A precaution, possibly. She's ex-FBI and he's ex-military. They're not babes in the wood."

"In other words you're saying Hackett can't find them."

"No, he found them. He found them real easy. He watched the library. They showed up right on time. They were inside for half an hour, and then they bought a burner phone in the drugstore next door."

"So what is he waiting for?"

"Opportunity."

"They must not talk to McCann."

"Don't worry. That ain't going to happen. I can promise you that."

They crossed the main drag and entered the second street, up brownstone stoops and down again, house by house. Most places seemed to have three floors with up to four separate dwellings on each. The names kept on coming. One place had Javier, Hiroto, Giovanni, Baker, Friedrich, Ishiguro, Akwame, Engelman, Krupke, Dassler, Leonidas, and Callaghan. Perfectly alphabetical, if you changed the order. The first twelve letters. And Callaghan at least was Irish. But it wasn't McCann.

The houses themselves had touches of faded glory. There were remnants of stained glass, and Victorian tile. The front doors were crusted with layers of paint, and most of them had pebble glass panels, with blurred and hazy views of inside lobbies, with shapes that might have been parked bicycles, or baby carriages. Reacher moved on, door to door, one place after another, the end of the street coming close, the search nearly half over, and he didn't find McCann.

But Chang did.

She waved from across the street, from the stoop of a house just like all the others, and he raised his palms in a semaphored question, and she pumped her fist, discreetly, like a golfer after a long but successful putt. He crossed the street and joined her, and she pointed at the bell box, and ran an elegant nail over a ribbon of white paper neatly printed with the name *Peter J. McCann*.

Chapter 34

McCann's digs were listed as apartment 32, which Reacher figured was the second apartment on the third floor, possibly a back room, if they were counting clockwise from the front left, as was likely. A top-floor walk-up, in other words, with no view. In an unremarkable building on a second-rate street. Location was working against the guy.

The street door was stout and securely locked.

Chang pressed McCann's call button. They heard no sound inside. Too far away, presumably. There was no crackling reply over the speaker. Nothing at all. Just a hot quiet morning, with nothing stirring.

Reacher said, "Try his phone again."

Their burner had a redial facility. Not bad for thirteen bucks. Chang hit it and they waited cheek to cheek.

It rang and rang.

No answer.

She killed the call.

She said, "Now what?"

"Too early for pizza," Reacher said. "We'll have to be UPS."

He pressed nine separate buttons, and when the first of them answered he said, "Package delivery, ma'am."

There was a pause, and then the door lock buzzed and clicked.

They went inside, through a hot vestibule with bikes and baby carriages and drifts of Thai menus and locksmiths' cards, into a downstairs hallway that bore traces of family living from a hundred years before, with crown moldings and wallpaper. But the wallpaper was faded and scuffed, and the moldings were cruelly terminated by crude partitions, and the elegant parlor doors had five-lever locks butchered into them, and spy holes, and brass numbers screwed on not exactly level. First on the left was 11, with 12 behind it, further on down the hallway.

The staircase was ornate, and carpeted, and steep. Automatic lights came on as they passed every dogleg. They got to the top, breathing hard. It was hot up there. Unit 32 was the first door they came to. Back corner, on the left.

Reacher knocked.

No answer.

But the way the door rattled in the frame didn't sound right.

Reacher tried the handle.

The door was unlocked.

The door opened straight into a living room, and that was pretty much the whole apartment, right there, dark but small enough for a single glance. There was hot air and a sour smell, and an unmade twin-size bed against one wall, and a windowless RV-size kitchenette and a windowless RV-size bathroom side by side on another. The only light in the place came from a bay window, which was dark with soot and had drapes only half pulled back. The walls were bare, and might once have been white, but they had long ago grayed over, to the color of ash. There was a bar-height eating table, no wider than an oil drum, and a single stool. There was a lone armchair, and an ottoman that didn't match, except it was worn shiny in the same kind of way. And that was it for variety, in terms of furniture. Everything else was tables.

There were five tables in all, each one about the size of a door, about six feet long, about three feet wide, all of them made of wood and stained black. Together they dominated the whole apartment. They were arranged in a line down the center of the room, in a pattern, the first end-on, the second butted up sideways, making a T shape, the third end-on again, the fourth sideways, another T, the fifth and last end-on again, the whole array looking like a rigid backbone running through the dismal space, like vertebrae and stubby ribs.

On the tables were computers, seven of which were desktops and eight of which were laptops. There were other unexplained black boxes, and external hard drives, and modems, and USB hubs, and power supplies, and cooling fans. But above all there were wires, great bales and billows of kinked and tangled cables, like rats' nests gone haywire. And where there weren't either wires or boxes, there were books, high teetering piles of them, all about technical aspects of coding, and hypertext protocols, and domain name allocation.

Chang checked the hallway and closed the door behind them.

Reacher said, "Try his phone."

She hit redial, and he heard a purr of ring tone against her ear, and then the cell network clicked in, and a phone started to ring in the room. It was loud and insistent. It was ringing and buzzing, with a stupid tune and the thick vibration of plastic on wood. McCann's phone was right there, on a table, hopping around under a nest of wire, its little front window all lit up blue. It was plugged in to a charging wire, which was plugged in to a computer.

Chang killed the call.

She said, "Why doesn't he have it with him? A cell phone belongs in a pocket."

Reacher said, "To him it's not a cell phone, I guess. Not in the normal way. It was an alternate number for calling Westwood, that's all. And it did its job. Not its fault there was no result. So like you figured, he gave it up and dumped the phone in a drawer. Except the drawer is a table."

"Plugged in."

"Habit, maybe."

"So where is he?"

Reacher said, "I don't know where he is."

"Keever's door was unlocked, too."

"I remember."

"I think we should take a quick look and get out."

"How quick?"

"Two minutes."

Which wasn't much, but which was enough, because there wasn't much to look at. The kitchen was tiny, with a half-size cabinet that held only a box of off-brand breakfast cereal, and a half-size refrigerator that held only a quart of off-brand milk, and two candy bars. The bathroom cabinet had legal analgesics and over-the-counter cold remedies. There was a chest of drawers full of threadbare clothing, most of it man-made material, and all of it black. There was nothing unusual about the bed. The computer equipment was what it was. All the screens lit up on command, but from that point onward every step of every way needed a password.

No photos, no personal items, no leisure reading, no stacks of mail.

Chang opened the door and checked the hallway.

She said, "Let's go."

She opened the door wider.

There was a guy standing there.

Eyewitness testimony was suspect because of preconditions, and cognitive bias, and suggestibility. It was suspect because people see what they expect to see. Reacher was no different. He was human. The front part of his brain wasted the first precious split second working on the image of the guy at the door, trying to rearrange it into a plausible version of a theoretical McCann. Which was not an easy mental task, because McCann was supposed to be sixty years old and thin and gaunt, whereas the guy at the door was clearly twenty years younger than that, and twice as solid. But still Reacher tried, instinctively, because who else could it be, but McCann? Who else could be at McCann's door, in McCann's building, in McCann's city?

Then half a second later the back part of Reacher's brain took over, and the image resolved itself, crisp and clear, not a potential McCann at all, not even remotely a contender, but the familiar twice-glimpsed face, now three times seen, first in the diner, next in the Town Car, and finally in the there and then, in a dim upstairs hallway in a three-floor walk-up.

Chapter 35

The guy was about forty years old, give or take, right up there on a hard-won plateau in the center of his life, not a dumb kid anymore, but not yet an old man either, and full of accumulated competence and confidence and capability, all wrapped up in experience. He looked to be dead-on six feet tall, and about two hundred pounds. He was wearing blue jeans, coarse and high-waisted, not stylish at all, with a belt, and a white open-neck shirt, and a blue satin baseball jacket. He had fair hair cut short and neatly brushed, and a pink slabby face, and small blue eyes, and an inquiring expression. He could have been a neighborhood electrical contractor, showing up in person to prepare a detailed estimate for a difficult job.

Except for the gun in his hand. Which looked like an old Ruger P-85. Nine millimeter. With a suppressor tube attached. A silencer, about nine inches long. The guy was holding the gun down by his leg. Pointed at the floor. With the suppressor tube it ran from the middle of his thigh to the middle of his calf. Long, and slender.

A random circuit in the back part of Reacher's brain sparked up with a play-by-play: *He flew short-notice from LA, and can't have taken a gun on the plane, so he has operational support in Chicago, at a fairly high level, given that suppressors are illegal in the state of Illinois.*

The front part of his brain said: *Step forward.*

He stepped forward.

The gun came up, and the guy said, "Don't move."

Reacher stepped forward again, all the way to the door.

The guy said, "I'll shoot."

You won't, because you want to shoot me in the room, not in the doorway, because I'm too big to move afterward, and also because in real life suppressors don't work like they work in the movies, with a polite little spit, but with a hell of a bang, not much quieter than a regular gunshot anyway, which will be audible all over the house, if you fire in the hallway.

So you won't shoot.

Not yet.

The guy said, "Stay where you are."

The back of Reacher's brain said: *If he has operational support in Chicago, you should check for reinforcements. Muscle is cheaper than silencers here.*

Which was why he had pushed his luck all the way to the door. To get the angle. But there was nothing in the dim shadows beyond the guy's shoulder. No bulk, no sound, no shifting stance, no breathing.

The guy was alone.

Reacher stood still.

The guy said, "Back inside now."

From the room Chang said, "What do you want?"

You're not going to say you want to shoot us, nothing personal, purely business, because that would induce a measure of last-ditch defense on our part.

The guy said, "I want to talk."

"About what?"

"About what's happening in Mother's Rest. I think I can help you."

And you have a bridge for sale in Brooklyn. I wasn't born yesterday. Reacher stayed right where he was, filling the doorway, angled slightly, his front toe on the seam between the hallway floor and the room floor, with the guy about a yard in front of him, halfway to the staircase railing, and Chang about two yards behind him, still halfway into the room.

She said, "If you're here to help us, why did you bring a gun?"

The guy didn't answer.

Reacher had failed driving, but he had passed everything else. Including unarmed combat. Which sounded like a useful qualification, but wasn't. The whole point of the military had been to engage with hot weapons at minimum risk to the home side. In other words, to shoot the other guy from a very long way away with a rifle, or failing that to shoot him closer by with a handgun. The unarmed combat courses had been afterthoughts. There had been a whiff of embarrassment. Hand-to-hand implied failure at the hot-weapons stage. Worst of all, the pointy-heads couldn't find anything to write in the manual. There were no valid theories. Martial arts didn't work in the real world. Judo and karate were useless without the mats and the referee and the special pajamas. So unarmed combat was brawling, basically. Like a bar fight. Whatever worked.

Chang said, "Put the gun down, and we'll talk."

He won't, because that would give up his only advantage. He would be one-on-one with a giant, which was not appealing, especially because right then the giant was fixing him with the glassy stare of a psychopath.

Whatever worked.

The guy kept the gun where it was.

Reacher leaned forward an inch.

He wants to shoot me in the room, not the doorway. I'm too big to move.

The guy said, "Back up now."

Reacher said nothing.

I'm too big to move.

And then it shifted. The man with the gun was no longer in charge. No longer in control. He was being pushed back. Inch by inch. Because of relentless pressure. Not physically. The tip of the suppressor didn't move. But in his mind the man with the gun felt battered by a sudden and unexplained reversal of fortune, and he felt roasted by some kind of death rays coming out of the psychopath's eyes.

Reacher said, "Don't worry."

Brawling. All in the head. Win them before you get in them.

He said, "Let's see if we can help you out of this mess."

His standard procedure, such as it was, based on what had worked, for a right-handed person facing a right-handed gunman, was to drive slightly forward but mostly counterclockwise, a savage rotation from the waist, explosive, exaggerated like a dance move, with the right shoulder whipping hard around, therefore the right elbow whipping hard around, and the right hand and the right palm, the palm smacking hard against the inside of the bad guy's wrist, and then pushing it, pushing it hard, pushing the gun out of orbit, then clamping on like a claw, the other hand meanwhile coming palm-to-palm with the gun hand, the left against his right, like dancing, like fighting over the gun, but it's not fighting over the gun, it's pushing the gun hand, pushing the gun hand back, and back, all the time dragging the wrist forward with the claw, until the wrist breaks and the gun drops.

But you can save yourself a lot of effort, because he's got a suppressor. That gun is twice as long as his muscle memory thinks it is. Which makes it easy. Go the short route.

Which Reacher did, twisting hard from the waist, but short, keeping his palm hooked close to his body, smacking not the guy's wrist but the suppressor itself, pushing it wide and safe, then grasping it and hauling on it hard.

A standard procedure, so called because it was often used, like a default setting, because ninety-nine times in a hundred it worked. But this was the hundredth guy. He knew what to do. He didn't allow himself to get hauled around off balance by keeping hold of the gun. He let go of it right away. Instantly. He gave it up, no contest. He just dropped it and spun away. It was his only smart play. It was one in a hundred.

It was a smart play because even though it gave Reacher sole possession of a lethal weapon, it gave him possession of it the wrong way around. He had grabbed it by the suppressor, in his right hand, palm outward, and he was still rotating away from the action, and the dead stop and the right-left-right shuffle to get the gun where it needed to be was going to occupy some finite slice of time, and then turning the barrel toward the target was going to occupy another slice, maybe longer, because it was a long barrel, with the suppressor in place. Not point and shoot. More like lashing the guy with a whip. Which would all take what? A second and a half? Two seconds?

During which time a guy smart enough to start such a play will be hitting you in the side of the head. He'll be raining down the blows. Maybe four in your two seconds, if he's any good with the speed bag. Better to let the gun go for the time being. Better to come back to it later. Better to get ready for what you know is coming.

Reacher opened his hand and the Ruger fell away, and he started to unwind his counterclockwise twist, bringing his elbow up backhand, ducking his head down, and the first of the incoming blows bounced off the top of his skull, and then a left hook caught him above the ear, a savage blow, like an iron bar, and then his own elbow arrived in the neighborhood, scything a kind of defensive no-fly-zone through the nearby air, butting aside the next incoming right, and he used its momentum to pull a left hook of his own out of the bag, but the bang above the ear had set back the unwinding process an inch or two, so his blind aim was off, and the punch landed weakly, in that it didn't knock the guy through the staircase railing, but merely bounced him off it.

At which point the guy showed yet more talent. Naturally Reacher was leaning in, waiting to finish it, waiting for the guy to come flopping back, all loose and raggedy and defenseless, but the guy jerked away sideways, at ninety degrees. A supreme gymnastic effort. Remarkable, for a big man. And a lifesaver. With a bonus. Not only had the guy escaped a colossal impact but now Reacher had his weight on the wrong foot, so the guy took advantage, by stepping in a pace and crashing a short left into Reacher's kidney. Which Reacher felt would leave a bruise.

Then the guy stepped back the same pace, like a boxer to a neutral corner. He stood there, alert but not moving, and looking pretty confident. The Ruger was on the hallway carpet, about halfway between Reacher's feet and his. It was aimed at neither one of them. It was pointing to the side, as yet undecided, like an emperor's thumb, neither up nor down.

Not exactly halfway between them.

Closer to Reacher, if anything.

How long to get it?

Long enough to get your head kicked in.

Or shot through the heart. Reacher checked the guy's clothes. The satin jacket was thin, and showed no bulges or heavy weights. It was falling open, with nothing to hide. The blue jean pockets were puffed out innocently. Just air and Kleenex. Therefore his back-up weapon would be on his belt, in a pancake holster in the small of his back. As supplied by his local operational support. Not the fastest draw in the world, but a lot faster than a tall guy bending down and trying to scrabble up a small pistol off the floor, all unbalanced with nine inches of extra metal.

Hence the confidence. Which he wouldn't feel if he was heading for a fistfight. No one had before. But this guy looked pretty good. He had only one minor concern, Reacher supposed. Which was that Reacher didn't really need to pick up the Ruger as such. All he really needed to do was get a foot on it and scrape it backward between his legs to Chang.

That would be a game-changer.

But difficult. And slow. A clumsy, unnatural movement. Plus then the finite slice of time it would take Chang to grab it up herself, and set, and aim, and fire.

Not the fastest draw in the world, but faster than that.

Almost certainly.

So, a concern, but minor.

Time to mess with his head.

Reacher stepped backward. One long pace. The proportions changed. Now the Ruger was nearer the guy. Who then stepped forward. Closer to it. Inevitably. Human nature, right there. Hard to push them back, easy to suck them in. The guy would have made a big point of standing his ground against forward pressure of any kind, but he showed no such determination in the other direction. He stepped right up. His first mistake. A weakness. He didn't understand. He thought any length of rooming-house hallway was as good as any other. In fact he thought his new position was better. Because it put the Ruger right at his feet. He could reclaim it, any old time he wanted to. Then he would have two guns, and Reacher would have none.

Better.

But not really.

Because of the temptation. Because of the urgency. The guy had two weapons within easy reach, but neither one was actually in his hand. So near and yet so far. He was consumed by all the future possibilities. He was thinking ahead, to the heavy solid feel, the ribbed grips rough against his palm, the trigger warm and hard under his finger. Invulnerability. Victory. Job done. So close. After nothing more than dipping down and up again for the Ruger, real fast and swooping, or batting his satin jacket aside and scrabbling around behind his back to the holster, and drawing, and aiming, and firing.

Nothing more than that.

So close. Temptation. Urgency. But either maneuver would take time. A second or so. Maybe more. And either maneuver would be a clear signal. There would be no ambiguity. Reacher would know exactly what was coming next. And he was only two paces away. He was a big guy, but clearly mobile. And how mobile did he need to be? Trying for the Ruger meant a kick in the face. Surely. Reacher would take one step, and *bang*. Right-footed, after a little shuffle. Like punting a football. The target would be right there, in the right place, at the right time, at the right height. On a tee. Begging for it. His face.

And trying for the holster meant a kick in the nuts. Equally surely. He would be fighting with one hand behind his back, literally. His elbow would be bent in a weird position. He would be wide open.

Two weapons within easy reach, but neither one in his hand.

Temptation.

Urgency.

Distraction.

Reacher took half a step closer. Compressing the geometry. Reducing the range. Sharpening the focus. Upping the pressure. Face to face, five feet apart. The guy kept still on the surface. But Reacher could see underneath. The guy was quivering. A physical manifestation of his dilemma. He wanted to duck down or reach around. One or the other. Or both. Uncontrollable. He kept starting and stopping, microscopically. Trying it this way, trying it that way. Little shakes and judders. His eyes were moving. Up and down, up and down. So near and yet so far.

Reacher said, "What's your name?"

The guy said, "Why?"

"We seem to have made each other's acquaintance. We might as well introduce ourselves formally."

"Why?"

"Might be a smart move on your part. Might make me think about you as a person. Not just an opponent. I might not hit you so hard. That's the conventional wisdom these days. Victims need to humanize themselves."

Shakes and judders. Eyes going up and down.

So near and yet so far.

The guy said, "I'm not a victim."

Reacher said, "Not yet."

Behind him Chang said, "This doesn't need to end badly. Step back and raise your hands. Then we'll talk. And we can fix this. You haven't done anything to us yet."

The guy didn't answer. His eyes were going up and down. Reacher could see he wanted to use the Ruger. And why not? It was his original weapon of choice. For a reason, presumably. And it had the suppressor. It was operationally superior. Sentimentally superior, too. Which maybe the guy didn't know yet, in the front part of his brain. But it was working on him. He could pick up the Ruger, and he'd be right back at the beginning. Like starting over. Like nothing happened. He could pick up the Ruger and make himself whole again.

Reacher said, "What's your name?"

The guy said, "Keith Hackett."

"I'm Jack Reacher. I'm pleased to meet you."

The guy didn't answer.

Reacher said, "But you already know our names."

No reply.

"So that's the price. Like my colleague said, this doesn't have to end badly. Not for you, at least. All you have to do is tell us who told you our names. Who gave you this job. Who you call every night, with a progress report. You tell us that, and we'll let you walk away."

No response.

"It's a simple concept, Mr. Hackett. You tell us, you walk away. You don't tell us, you don't walk away. Maybe you can't walk away. These things are unpredictable. Injuries can be serious."

No answer.

"Think of those old signs for crossing the street," Reacher said. "When they did them with words. Walk or don't walk, Mr. Hackett. That's the issue here."

The guy waited a beat, suddenly still for the very first time, and then he went for the Ruger. He powered down, faster than gravity, his eyes on the prize, his hands already moving, rehearsing the scoop, his face averted, because of what he knew must be coming, but what he hoped could be beat.

It couldn't. The guy's face was turned away high and back, so Reacher's boot caught him under the chin, like a monstrous uppercut from a heavyweight with a horseshoe in his glove. The guy went over backward and laid out full length, but to his credit he knew he was dead if he stayed there, so he skidded once, and then crabbed and scrambled away, all elbows and knees, and he got himself upright, shrugging and blinking and pawing the air. He didn't look good. He had a broken jaw, obviously. Missing teeth. Which were serious injuries. But neither, in a technical sense, a referee would say, were also debilitating injuries, under the current circumstances. Unless the guy was planning to start his victory feast anytime soon.

Reacher watched the guy's right hand. He figured it could move only one of three ways. Smartest would be straight up in surrender. Dumbest would be another fist. Therefore the second-dumbest would be the same as the second-smartest, which would be to go for the holster.

The guy went for the holster.

Didn't get there.

His arm moved back, and his elbow came out, and he flattened his hand to slip it behind his back, and his left hand moved in awkward sympathy, counterbalancing, and his shoulders opened up, and he went as flat and two-dimensional as if he was pasted on the air. Like a paper target. Like a paper target on a wall in an unarmed combat class. Whatever worked. Reacher stepped in a short pace and head-butted the guy full in the face, from fully three feet away, plenty of arc through the dim hallway air, plenty of power, plenty of acceleration, a colossal, driving impact, and then suddenly the guy wasn't there anymore and Reacher was using every muscle in his body to stop himself from following through and head-butting the floor.

Then across the stairwell a room door opened and a white-haired woman stuck her head out. An automatic light came on because of her.

She asked, "Who are you people?"

Chapter 36

The neighbor was a noble old bird, thin and faded, but animated. She seemed to be on the ball. Like many of her generation she tended toward courtesy, and a reluctance to disbelieve. Overtly, at least. Purely out of politeness, Reacher supposed.

He said, "We're putting in a new computer for Mr. McCann. But it's hot up here. This guy fainted."

"Would you like me to call for the ambulance?"

"No, we'll get him inside and give him a glass of water."

"It would be no trouble."

"Ma'am, it's an insurance thing. He's a freelance contractor. It's tough on these guys. He's got an insane deductible. He doesn't want a hospital bill."

"Is there anything else I can do?"

"Not a thing, ma'am."

Reacher grabbed Hackett under the arms and started dragging him toward McCann's room. Chang nudged the Ruger with her foot, discreetly, pushing it to safety a few inches at a time. The neighbor started to close her door, and then she changed her mind and opened it again, the same confidential twelve-inch gap, and she said, "I thought Peter always installed his computers himself."

Then she closed up for good and the hallway went quiet.

Chang picked up the Ruger and carried it the rest of the way. Reacher got Hackett inside. Chang closed the door. Hackett had plenty of maxillary damage. That was for damn sure. Pretty much all the facial bones. Some doctor was headed for the lecture circuit. But the guy was breathing pretty well. For the moment, at least. Until various internal items swelled up and clotted. After that it was a gamble.

Chang said, "When will he wake up?"

Reacher said, "I have no idea. Somewhere between two hours and never."

"You hit him very hard."

"He hit me first. Twice in the head and once in the back."

"Are you OK?"

He nodded. He was OK. But not spectacular. His kidney hurt bad. Movement was not pain-free. And his head hurt worse. There was a sharp pain above his ear. It had been a hell of a blow. Maybe the worst he had ever taken.

The head-butt had been unwise, under the circumstances.

"We can't wait here two hours," Chang said. "Anything could happen."

"We need to find McCann, and waiting here is as good a way as any."

"You're not thinking," she said. "Do you have a headache?"

"Not yet. But I will. Why?"

"How did they find us here?"

"I guess this guy followed us. In retrospect it was obvious we would start at the library."

"But then we took the Town Car. On a crazy route. Looping all around the neighborhood, to get our bearings. There was no one behind us. There was no one following. How could there be?"

"How, then?"

"They have better information about McCann than we do. Somehow. Maybe he's done business with them. They have his address, at least. Maybe that's why the door was unlocked. Like Keever's door was unlocked. Maybe Hackett has already been here once this morning."

Something in her voice.

Reacher picked up the Ruger and checked the chamber and dropped the mag. Brassy nine-millimeter rounds winked at him. But not enough brassy nine-millimeter rounds.

The mag was one short.

He sniffed the chamber. Sniffed the muzzle.

The gun had been fired.

Chang said, "They didn't want us to talk to McCann. There were two ways of stopping us. They chose both."

Reacher checked Hackett's pulse. In his neck. It was there, but slow. Deeply unconscious. Or comatose. Was there a difference? Reacher wasn't sure.

Chang said, "We should assume reinforcements sooner or later."

Reacher said, "This guy could tell us things."

"We don't have time."

"So at least let's get what we can."

They got a fancy cell phone, as thin as Chang's, and a rental car key, and a hotel key card, and eighty-five cents, and a wallet, all from the pockets, and a Heckler & Koch P7, from the holster on the back of the belt. The P7 was small enough to hide, but big enough to use. It shared the same Parabellum rounds as the Ruger, which was logistically sensible. The wallet contained more than a hundred dollars in cash, and a California driver's license, and a bunch of credit cards. Chang kept the cell phone, for the call log, and Reacher kept the cash, for future expenses, and the P7, for a number of reasons. They wiped what they were leaving behind, and everything else they had touched. They put their loot in their pockets.

Chang said, "Do we need anything else?"

Reacher took a last look around.

He said, "One more thing, perhaps."

"Which would be what?"

"I think we can forget about organic food and honey bees. Look at this place. There's sugary breakfast cereal and factory milk. And two candy bars. That's what he eats. He wears polyester pants. He doesn't care what he puts in his body and he's not a tree-hugger. Therefore the *LA Times* article he reacted to was the Deep Web thing. About the internet. Which would make total sense, with all these computers."

"You want to take a computer?"

"Did you hear what the neighbor lady said? Before she closed her door?"

"She said she thought Peter installed his computers himself. You hadn't convinced her. It was a very polite parting shot."

"She got the words right. Computers are installed, are they not? And she called him Peter. I would have expected an old lady like that to call him Mr. McCann. They must be good friends. Like long-time neighbors sometimes are. In which case maybe they talk about personal matters. And if she knows about computers, maybe he's told her what's on his mind. Because she'd understand."

"We don't have time to ask her. There could be more of these guys in this building at any minute. And then the cops."

"I agree," Reacher said. "We don't have time to ask her. Not here, anyway. Therefore she's the extra thing I want to bring with us. The neighbor. We should take her out for a cup of coffee. Away from here. And we should ask her there."

It was not a fast process. Not a high-speed getaway. There was some skepticism. Some reluctance. In the end Chang had to play the FBI card, literally. Then there was a search for a coat, even though they told her the weather was warm. But it was a matter of manners. She said she wasn't completely old-fashioned. She wouldn't insist on gloves and a hat.

Then came the long, unsteady walk down the steep flights of stairs, and out to the street, where it was the Town Car that overcame her last real reluctance. Its gleaming black paint and its driver in his neat gray suit finally sealed the deal. It was governmental. She had seen such cars on the evening news.

Then came Reacher's search for the right kind of place. Many pleasant candidates were rejected. Finally one was chosen, a traditional Chicago coffee shop, perhaps discreetly updated by a respectful grandson and heir. It had a pleasant atmosphere as well as a full roster of all the required virtues. Which were nearby parking for the Town Car, and inside seating, and a TV screen on the wall.

McCann's neighbor seemed happy with it. Maybe it reminded her of the places she used to frequent. She folded her bony self into a booth, and let herself be hemmed in by Chang, who slid in next to her. Reacher sprawled on the opposite bench, sideways, as unthreatening as he could be.

All-around introductions revealed her name to be Mrs. Eleanor Hopkins, widow, previously a wife and a laboratory researcher at the university, not only technically literate, but the technical literature with which she was familiar was written, she said, in a very small number of very small ways, in some of the cracks and the edges, by herself, or by people she knew. Or knew of, or might have known of, if she had taken some other job at some other time. She said her career had overlapped an interesting period, in terms of technical progress.

Then she said Peter McCann had lived in her building for a good many years, and they had grown close, in a gruff and occasional and good-fences kind of a way. She said she had last seen him three or four weeks ago. Which often happened. Which was not a cause for concern. She went out very rarely, and it would be a matter of sheer coincidence if she met him in the hallway. And he was gone a lot, anyway, often for days at a time. She had no idea where. She had never inquired. She was his neighbor, not his sister. Yes, he was an unhappy man. Things often turned out badly.

The TV on the coffee shop wall was tuned to local news. Reacher watched it in the corner of his eye. Mrs. Hopkins ordered coffee and a slice of cake, and Chang told her it was possible Mr. McCann had gotten himself into some kind of trouble. Of a sort no one knew. Did she?

She didn't.

Reacher asked, "Did he seem obsessed about something?"

Mrs. Hopkins asked, "When?"

"Recently."

"Yes, I would say he did."

"For how long?"

"About the last six months."

Outside there were distant sirens, and the dull beat of helicopter blades, maybe a mile away. Reacher asked, "Do you know what Mr. McCann's problem was?"

"No, I don't. We spoke very little of personal matters."

"Was it connected to his son?"

"It might have been, although that tended not to be an up-and-down situation."

The TV screen showed a helicopter shot of green lawns. Trees. A park.

Reacher asked, "What was the issue with his son?"

Mrs. Hopkins said, "He didn't talk of it in detail."

"Did you know he hired a private detective?"

"I knew he intended to take concrete steps."

"About what?"

"I don't know."

"Did you and he talk about technical matters? Given your background and his evident interest?"

"Yes, we talked frequently about technical matters. Over coffee and cake, sometimes. Like this. We explored the issues together. We rather enjoyed it. I helped him grasp the basic structures, and he helped me understand the uses to which they are now often put."

"Was his obsession a technical obsession?"

"I think not at its core, but there were technical aspects."

"Was it something to do with the internet?"

On the TV, under the unsteady green picture, was a ticker-tape ribbon, with the words *Shooting Victim Found in Park*.

The old lady looked up and said, "By a dog walker, I expect. That's how it usually happens, I think. In parks."

Reacher said, "What was McCann's interest in the internet?"

"There were aspects he wanted to understand. Like most laymen he thought of things in physical terms. As if the internet was a swimming pool, chock-full of floating tennis balls. The tennis balls representing individual web sites, naturally. Which is wrong, of course. Web sites are not physical things. The internet has no physical reality. It has no dimensions, and no boundaries. No up or down, no near or far. Although one might argue it has mass. Digital information is all ones and zeroes, which means memory cells are either charged or not charged. And charge is energy, so if one believes Einstein's $e=mc^2$, where e is energy, and m is mass, and c is the speed of light, then one must also believe that m equals e divided by c^2, which is the same equation expressed differently, and which would imply that charge has detectable mass. The more songs and the more photos you put on your phone, the heavier it gets. Only by a trillion-billionth of the tiniest fraction of an ounce, but still."

On the TV screen the helicopter camera zoomed tight on a group of low bushes. There were uniformed cops standing around, and police tape, and a suggestion of a half-concealed figure on the ground, black shoes and black pant legs, under leafy branches. The ticker still said *Shooting Victim Found in Park*.

Reacher asked, "What exactly did McCann want to understand?"

The old lady said, "He wanted to know why some web sites can't be found. Which was fundamentally a question about search engines. His image of the swimming pool became useful. He imagined millions of tennis balls, some bobbing up on the water, some trapped deeper down by the weight of the others. So I asked him to imagine a search engine as a long silk ribbon, being pulled up and down and in and out, weaving through the balls every which way, sliding over their wet fuzzy surfaces at tremendous speed. And then to imagine that some balls had been adapted, to have spikes instead of fuzz, like fish hooks, and that other balls had been adapted to have no fuzz at all, to be completely smooth, like billiard balls. Where would the silk ribbon snag? On the spikes, of course. It would slide over the billiard balls completely. That's what Peter needed to understand about search engines. It's a two-way street. A web site must want to be found. It must work hard to develop effective spikes. People call it search engine optimization. It's a very important discipline now. That said, it's equally hard work to be a billiard ball. Staying secret isn't easy either."

Chang said, "Secret web sites imply illegality."

"Indeed," the old lady said. "Or immorality, I suppose. Or both at once. I'm naïve about such things, but one imagines pornography of the most unpleasant sort, or mail-order cocaine, and so forth. It's called the Deep Web. All those smooth billiard balls. Millions of them. No spikes, no hooks, nothing but going about their business with no one watching. The Deep Web might be ten times bigger than the Surface Web. Or a hundred. Or more. No one knows. How could they? Not to be confused with the Dark Web, of course, which is merely out-of-date sites with broken links, like dead satellites whirling through space forever. Which makes the Dark Web more like ancient archaeology, and the Deep Web more like the wrong side of the tracks. Not that either one is actually dark or deep or either side of any actual tracks, you understand. The internet is not a physical place. There are no physical characteristics to it at all."

On the TV screen an ambulance rolled into the overhead shot, slowly over the grass, lights flashing forlornly, being followed by what looked like a coroner's wagon. People got out, and joined the cops.

Chang asked, "So how can a person find secret web sites?"

"A person can't," the old lady said. "Not from the outside, anyway. You can't use a search engine, because the sites are smooth. You need the exact address. Not just CoffeeShop.com, but something like CoffeeShop123xyz.com. Or much worse, of course, in reality. A unique resource locator combined with a super-secure password, all rolled into one. Apparently such addresses circulate through certain communities by word of mouth."

On the TV screen a dark blue Crown Vic bumped over the grass and parked. Two men in suits climbed out. Detectives, presumably. The ticker changed to *Lincoln Park Homicide*. Reacher could hear more helicopters in the air, about a mile away. Rival channels, late to the party.

He asked, "Did McCann tell you what kind of a web site he was looking for?"

The old lady said, "No."

On the screen men squatted by the black-clad figure on the grass. Detectives and the medical examiner, Reacher supposed. He knew the drill. He had squatted by horizontal figures many times. Some had been alive. This one wasn't, he knew. There was no urgency. No hustle. No shouting voices. No backboards, no IV lines, no breathing tubes, no chest compressions.

Lincoln Park Homicide.

The old lady said, "That's Peter, isn't it? Why else would you be asking me about him? Why else would the FBI be interested in me?"

Chang didn't answer either question, and Reacher said nothing, because as the old lady spoke the TV picture changed. To a house. An undistinguished brownstone, on an undistinguished street. Peter McCann's brownstone. The old lady's house. Where they had been, moments before. It was recognizable. It was familiar. The front of it was all lit up by flashing red lights. Cops were running up the stoop.

Much too soon for a connection to have been made. The cops in the park hadn't even looked in McCann's pockets yet. They hadn't found a wallet, hadn't checked the driver's license, didn't know who he was, and didn't know where he lived. They were still waiting for the all-clear from the medical examiner. Reacher knew how it worked. He had sat back on his heels many times, just waiting. Death had to be pronounced, before the body became evidence.

Not yet connected. A separate investigation. The ticker changed to *Anti-Terror Cops Storm Chicago Dwelling.*

Reacher turned back to the old lady and asked, "Did you call 911?"

The old lady said, "Yes, I did."

"When?"

"As soon as I closed my door on you."

"Why?"

"I didn't like the look of you."

"Neither one of us?"

"You especially. You don't look like what you say you are. Not like an FBI agent on the television."

"I was undercover. Pretending to be a bad guy."

"Your act was convincing."

"So you called 911."

"Immediately."

"What did you say?"

"I had armed terrorists in my house."

"Why that?"

"This is Chicago. That's the only way to get a response in less than four hours."

Chang said, "We should probably get going."

Reacher said, "No, let's stay a little longer. Five more minutes can't hurt."

They got refills of coffee, and the old lady wanted more cake, so Reacher and Chang got more too, to keep her company. The TV changed to a split screen, with the park on the left, and the house on the right, over individual labels saying *Lincoln Park Homicide* and

Terror Alert, both of those labels centered over the main ticker, which said *Busy Day for Cops.*

The second cup of coffee was as good as the first. As was the cake. A body bag showed up in the park, and an ambulance arrived at the house. The body bag was zipped up and carried to the coroner's wagon, and EMTs came out of the ambulance and ran up the stoop and in the house. Later they came out again with an injured man on a gurney. Hackett, presumably, although it was hard to be sure. The guy's face was bandaged from the neck up, like an Egyptian mummy, and his clothes were covered with a sheet.

Then like a slow-burn visual effect in a movie the cops drove out of the park, and four long minutes later they showed up at the house, in the same cars, all the way from the left of the screen to the right, a short electronic hop but a circuitous real-world route. The same detectives got out and rushed up the stoop and went inside the house, and a minute later they came back out again, talking urgently on their cell phones.

The ticker changed to *Official Says Cases Are Connected.*

Reacher said, "Ma'am, I'm very sorry for your loss, and I'm very sorry for the intrusion you're about to suffer. The Chicago PD will want to ask you questions. And it's not like it is in the television shows. The FBI can't come in and take over their case. We have to leave them alone. So we'd appreciate it if you don't even tell them we've talked. There are all kinds of sensitivities there. Better not to tell them about us at all. Even about us being at the house earlier. They don't need to know we beat them to it."

"Are you asking me to lie to them?"

"I will, if they ask me who told them terrorists, and why."

"Then very well, I will, too," the old lady said.

"Do you really have no idea what McCann's problem was?"

"I told you, I'm his neighbor, not his sister. You should really ask her."

"Who?"

"His sister."

"He has a sister?"

"I told you before."

"I thought it was a figure of speech."

"No, she's real. They're very close. She'd be the one he shared secrets with."

Chapter 37

They sent Mrs. Hopkins home in the Town Car, and told the driver that was the last of his engagements for the day, and therefore he was off-duty thereafter, free to go home, or back to the garage, or wherever else it was he was supposed to go. The guy took the news cheerfully. But Reacher figured his last engagement wouldn't be his finest. He figured they wouldn't make it all the way. They would get within a couple of streets of the old lady's house, and then they would hit the roadblocks. If the old lady could produce proof of name and address, she would be allowed to continue on foot. Or in the back of a real government car, depending how much sooner or later they wanted to talk to the neighbor. Either way she would end up cool and comfortable, plied with water and coffee, talking to polite young women.

Safe enough.

Chang switched on her cell phone. Also safe enough. Hackett's tracking operation was out of business, at least temporarily. And they needed maps, and satellite images, and flight schedules, and search engines. Mrs. Hopkins had told them Peter McCann's sister was a woman named Lydia Lair. She was younger by a number of years.

She had married a doctor and moved away, to a tony suburb outside of Phoenix, Arizona. Her husband was rich, but McCann had asked for nothing except her time and her ear. There was a street address for her, a scribbled note intended for the old lady's Christmas card list, still wedged in a pocket diary in her purse. But there was no phone number. Chang found the husband's practice on-line, but the medical receptionist wouldn't give out a home number. The phone company database said it was unlisted. Neither husband nor wife showed up anywhere in Chang's secret databases. Google brought nothing back either, except one anodyne image of the couple at a charity event. Dr. and Mrs. Evan Lair. A kidney foundation. He was in black tie, and she was in an evening gown. She looked in good health. She glittered with diamonds, and her teeth were very white.

Then it became a three-way decision, between how soon they would need to get to Phoenix, and how long they could wait for a gold card flight, and how long the police would wait before notifying the sister. If they ever did. She was not the next of kin. That would be the son. He would be their primary focus. They would want to tell him first. And if they did, they would leave it to him to call his aunt. They would see that as his responsibility. Which he might or might not discharge, depending on his challenges.

All of which meant one way or the other she might or might not be getting the call just as they touched down in Phoenix. Which was still OK, either way. Bad news was bad news. Didn't matter when you got it. As long as she didn't have time to start up with a scheme whereby she should fly to Chicago and take charge of everything personally. She had to be gotten to well before that happened. Before she was coached into nothing but bumper stickers, by victim support officers, or well-meaning friends.

The best travel bet was outside Chang's comfort zone, on an airline she didn't have a card for. But it was the first and most satisfactory option. It gave them just enough time to stop by the Peninsula to dump the P7 and grab Chang's bag. And one other thing. They fired up Hackett's captured phone and checked the call log. All incoming traffic was from one number alone. Its area code was 480.

Chang checked her computer.

She said, "That's a cell phone in Phoenix, Arizona. Where we're going."

A very expensive quickie with her phone company guy told them the Phoenix number was a burner cell bought from a local Arizona Wal-Mart just a week ago, and registered immediately, right outside in the Wal-Mart parking lot. Bought with cash, and as one of six at a time, which were purchasing behaviors suggestive of a customer who was comfortable with the theory and practice of untraceable communications.

Reacher said, "He'll dump that number soon. He'll move on to the next."

Chang nodded. "As soon as Hackett doesn't call him when he should. Or as soon as he turns on CNN and sees what's going on here."

"So maybe we should call him first. While we still can."

"And say what?"

"Whatever might produce an advantage. We need to keep him off balance. We need all the help we can get."

"You want to upset him."

"Can't hurt. Whatever stray emotions we can bring to bear."

"OK, try it."

He lit up Hackett's phone, and found the right screen, and pressed the green button. He heard the numbers spooling outward into the ether, and then he heard a short hissing silence, and then he heard a ring tone.

And then he heard an answer.

A voice said, "Yes?"

It was a man's voice, from a big chest and a thick neck, but the syllable was snatched at and the full boom was bitten back short, because of breathy haste and enthusiasm. And anticipation. Like a gulp or a gasp. This guy had caller ID, and he wanted Hackett's news, and he wanted it bad, and he wanted it right then. That was clear. So the celebrations could begin, presumably.

Reacher said, "This is not Hackett."

The voice paused, and said, "I see."

"This is Jack Reacher."

No answer.

"Hackett got McCann, but he didn't get us. In fact we got him. He was good, but not good enough."

The voice said, "Where is Hackett now?"

Some kind of a flat, monotone accent. Eastern European, maybe. A big guy, for sure. Probably pale and fleshy, maybe short of breath.

Reacher said, "Hackett is in the hospital. But handcuffed to the bed, because the police found him before the doctors. Right here in Chicago. We took his phone and his back-up weapon, but we left him with the gun that killed McCann. Unconscious, in a suspected terrorist den. The cops found him there. I know, don't ask. Bad data. They were misinformed. But because of it they'll be sweating him hard. They'll be telling him Guantanamo is in his future. Or rendition, to places where bad things happen. He'll be so desperate for a deal he'll give you up in a heartbeat. Nothing you can do to him the government won't do worse. So you have that to worry about. Plus you have us to worry about. You started a war. Which was dumb. Because you'll lose. And it won't be pretty. We're going to beat you so hard your kids will be born dizzy."

"You think?"

"We already beat Hackett. He went down easy. Was he the best you had? I hope not, for your sake. Because you're next. We know your name, and we know where you live. And we're on the way. The time for looking over your shoulder starts now."

There was a long indrawn breath on the other end of the line, as if more words were coming, perhaps many, but in the end none were spoken. Instead the call cut off, and Reacher heard nothing more. He pictured the electronic chip being pried out of the phone, being snapped in two by a blunt thumbnail, the pieces being dumped in the trash.

Chang asked, "Who was he?"

Reacher said, "He didn't talk much. Only nine words. But he sounded big and heavy, and Russian, and fairly verbal, and reasonably smart."

"Russian?"

"From around there. Georgia, or Ukraine. One of those new countries."

"Verbal, with only nine words?"

"I told him I wasn't Hackett, and he said, I see. Measured, and calm. Or said in order to appear measured and calm. This is a guy who understands how words can mean all kinds of different things."

"Do we really know his name and where he lives?"

"I might have been glamorizing our situation a little. Or exaggerating for effect. As in, we fake it till we make it. Because we will know, sooner or later. Somehow. Maybe your phone guy could list his calls by location. There's only a week's worth, on that number. He can't have strayed far from home. We could zero in."

"Would the information lead to physical harm or serious injury?"

"That would be its sole purpose."

"Then my phone guy won't do it. That's his deal."

"Do you have to tell him?"

"He would put two and two together after the fact. Then he would go work for someone else. I can't let that happen."

"Even for Keever?"

"Keever would understand. So should you. You had a code. A deal is a deal."

"Works for me," Reacher said. "I guess. I expect we can figure it out some other way. After we talk to the sister. Who might figure it out for us. Depending on how much she knows. And whether it means anything to us."

"Nothing else does. This is not a small thing in a wheat field any-more. Hackett is from California, and he has armorers in Illinois, and his boss is in Arizona. This is a nationwide organization. They'll be watching the airport. You told them we're coming."

"That's why I told them. We won't find them otherwise."

"It's a risk."

"Everything is a risk. Getting on the plane is a risk. All the other passengers have phones. Think of the songs and the pictures. Think of the extra mass."

In any event the jet engines coped perfectly with the challenge the on-board phones presented. Their plane took off smoothly and climbed away, just like every other plane that day at America's busiest airport. Reacher was confident they had not been followed, certainly airside. But their real names were in an airline's computer, and their ETA was widely advertised. Hope for the best, plan for the worst.

They had seats together over the leading edge of the wing. Window and middle. Not the exit row. That was two behind them. Reacher was at the window. Chang had taken the middle, voluntarily. Next to her on the aisle was a woman with ear buds.

Reacher said, "I was thinking about the Moynahan cousins. Or brothers, or whatever they were."

Chang said, "And?"

"There were two of them, and they were a hundred times less trouble than Hackett on his own."

"How are you feeling?"

"Like I got hit three times. Which is my point. As opposed to zero times before. I agree with you about Hackett in California and the gun guys in Illinois and the boss in Arizona. It's a national organization. But I don't see how Mother's Rest can be a part of it. Those folks are a far lower standard. They can't be a local division. They would be the weak link in the chain. They'd stick out like a sore thumb."

"So what are they?"

"Clients, possibly," Reacher said. "McCann hired Keever. Maybe Mother's Rest hired someone, too. Maybe that's what happens now. Maybe bad guys outsource their muscle to national organizations. Maybe they outsource everything. Why not? It's a service economy."

Chang said, "Then the sister could be in danger. Theoretically. Because organizations behave like organizations. They ask for a detailed brief. Did Mother's Rest know McCann talked to his sister? If so, she's in the brief. She's a loose end. Because we are, too. We could meet. And organizations don't like loose ends to meet. Cover-your-ass is way too important."

Reacher said nothing.

Chang said, "What?"

"I wanted to say I'm sure the sister is OK. She has to be, logically. I mean, Keever was there just a couple of days, and now we're asking if someone knows his client's sister's address? The odds against would be enormous, surely. Big numbers."

"But?"

"Being on a plane is a helpless feeling. Things can prey on your mind."

The Phoenix airport was properly titled Sky Harbor International, and it was a safe harbor, at least airside. Because of the metal detectors. Landside was a different ball game. So Reacher and Chang got off the plane and walked away from the exit, toward more distant gates. Where they stopped in at a coffee shop and sat on high stools and waited. For the last Chicago passenger to be in a hotel bus. For anyone waiting out there for Chicago passengers to have long ago given up and gone home.

Then they strolled out, window shopping, infinitely slow, watching for belated recognition, for phoned-ahead alerts, but seeing nothing. The airport was spacious, and crowds were thin, and folks were relaxed. After Chicago it felt like Sunday. They stopped short of the airside exit and looked at shoes and sweatshirts and turquoise jewelry, until the next plane landed, and a crowd of disembarking passengers bore down, maybe a hundred people, from Minnesota, Reacher thought, with a hundred carry-on bags, and he and Chang slipped in ahead of the last stragglers, and they hustled through the baggage hall in a loose mobile crowd, through the last of the air-conditioned chill, and out to the taxi line, into the baking desert heat. But the wait there was not more than a breathless minute. No one paid attention. No one shuffled, and no one looked at them, and no one looked away.

They took the cab to the car rental compound. No one followed. Reacher had no driver's license, so Chang lined up and rented a mid-sized Chevrolet. It was bland and white, for anonymity, and it had GPS, for getting around. They waited at the document booth and scanned ahead. No idling cars at the curb. No one else around. It was too hot for pedestrians.

They drove random and incoherent directions for ten minutes, and then they set the GPS for the tony suburb. Where the doctor lived, with McCann's sister. They found news radio, but there was nothing from Chicago. No time for it. Apparently Phoenix had problems of its own. The GPS took them north, and then east toward Scottsdale, then into a suburban street that led to another, and finally to the right development.

Which had a gatehouse at its entrance.

The gatehouse was built in a decorative style, with a hipped roof and cactus plantings, and a red-striped barrier coming out on the right, and a red-striped barrier coming out on the left. Like a fat bird with two skinny wings.

A gated community. Rich people. Taxpayers. Political donors. The Maricopa County sheriffs on speed dial.

They waited at the curb, a hundred yards short.

It was three in the afternoon. Five, in Chicago.

There was one guard behind the glass.

Reacher said, "We should have figured."

Chang said, "If she's heard about her brother, we'll never get in. Not if that guy has to call the house first. Which I'm sure he does."

Reacher said, "You have an FBI card."

"It's not a badge. He'll know the difference."

"He's a rent-a-cop."

"He's a human being with a pulse. That's all it takes."

"Mrs. Hopkins was impressed by it."

"Different generation. Different instincts about the government."

Reacher said nothing.

Chang said, "You OK?"

"My head hurts."

"What do you want to do?"

"Let's try to get in."

"OK, but any problems, we withdraw gracefully. We live to fight another day. The sister is a bridge we can't afford to burn."

She drove on and turned in, and stopped ahead of the barrier, right next to the sliding glass partition. She buzzed her window down. She flipped her hair and turned her head and smiled. She said, "We're here for Dr. and Mrs. Evan Lair."

The rent-a-cop was an elderly white man, in a gray polyester uniform. A short-sleeved shirt. Thin, mottled arms.

He hit a red button.

He said, "I hope you folks have a wonderful afternoon."

The barrier went up.

Chang drove on through. She buzzed her window up again and said, "I wouldn't want to pay money for security like that."

Reacher said, "The landscaping is nice, though."

And it was. There were no lawns. There was nothing that needed water. There were artful rivers of stone, with cactus leaves slashing through like blades, and mists of pale red flowers, and steel sculptures, still bright and uncorroded in the bone-dry air. The land was flat, and the lots were large, and the houses were set at different angles, this way and that, as if they had arrived on the scene by accident.

Reacher said, "It should be up ahead on the left. A quarter-mile, maybe."

Which was where a lot of cars were gathered. All different makes, all different models, all different colors. Most of them expensive. They were cheek by jowl on the driveway, three across, three deep, then spilling out bumper to bumper to the street outside, all clustered, all packed in tight, all randomly misaligned, with empty curbs ahead of them, and empty curbs beyond them, as if the house at that location was uniquely and strongly magnetic.

Maybe thirty cars in total.

Which was why the barrier had gone up with no questions asked.

There was a message at the gate.

A house party.

Or a cocktail party, or a pool party, or whatever other kind of a party could bring thirty cars over at three o'clock on a hot afternoon.

The mailbox at the end of the crowded driveway said *The Lairs' Lair*.

Chang parked beyond the last of the curbside cars. They got out in the heat and looked back. The house itself was handsome, wide and confident, one story, a complex roof, part adobe, part rough-hewn hunting lodge, showy enough to at least whisper wealth and taste, but by most standards not really showy at all. Whatever was happening at the house was happening in the back yard. Which was not on view. There was a head-high wall running all around. An architectural feature, made to look the same as the house. Same siding, same color. Same everywhere in the association. The front yards were all open, but the back yards were all buttoned up tight. Private. Nothing to see. But Reacher felt he could hear a pool. He could hear splashing, and muted watery yelps. The kind of sounds people make in pools. Breathlessness, and the shock of cool water. Which would make sense. It was three o'clock in the afternoon. It was more than a hundred degrees. Why else would people come over? The pool, the patio, maybe the kitchen and the family room, in and out of sliding doors. Cans of beer in tubs of ice.

Chang said, "We did some research in the Bureau. I wrote some of it myself, actually. I'm like Mrs. Hopkins. The research was into cars. We worked out a ratio, for any given venue, between the value of the cars parked outside and the amount of money changing hands inside."

Reacher said, "You think there's money changing hands in there?"

"No, I'm telling you based on my hard-won expertise valuing cars that there are some very wealthy folk in attendance here. And quite a mixture. Those are not just girl cars. There are some couple-cars here. Even some boy cars, straight from work. This is a heavyweight crowd."

They walked closer.

There was a gate in the back yard wall, near the garage. Wide enough for a ride-on mower. Specified years before, presumably, by an architect who thought people would always want lawns. Now used as a regular in-out walkway. A landscaped path. Rivers of stones. Knee-high solar lights. The gate standing open a foot. Glimpses of people beyond, packed together, gauzy, sunlit, moving a little.

A woman coming out of the gate.

Carrying a bag to her car, briskly, busily, officially.

Not McCann's sister. A friend or a neighbor. A co-host or a co-organizer.

Walking fast.

Coming close.

Stopping, and smiling.

Saying, "Hello, welcome, so good of you to come, please go in."

Moving onward to her car.

Chapter 38

Reacher and Chang used the decorative path, past the plantings, between the solar lights, through the gate, and into the back yard. They saw a broad rectangle of spectacular desert landscaping, with wood arbors and climbing vines for shade, and huge terracotta pots and fallen amphorae spilling out with flowers, and stately saguaro cactuses standing alone in gravel beds. They saw a swimming pool made of dark plaster, shaped like a natural pond, edged with rocks, and fed by small splashing waterfalls. They saw teak furniture, richly oiled, with fat colorful cushions, and sun umbrellas, and outdoor dining tables.

They saw about forty people, men and women, some young, mostly older, some dressed in bright Arizona clothes, some in bathing suits, some in cover-ups, all clustered in groups, talking, laughing, clutching plates and glasses. Some were wet, and there were others still in the water, ducked down neck-deep and talking, or floating, or horsing around. At a table under a vine was a young woman of about thirty, long and lithe and golden tan, in a thin shirt over a bikini, relaxed and smiling, but luminous, and in some unstated but obvious way the center of attention. Behind her on one side was a man, gray-haired but well preserved, wearing khaki shorts and a loud Hawaiian shirt, and behind her on the other side was a dark-haired woman with bright eyes and a wide smile, wearing an ankle-length shift made of pale linen. The familiar ease between the three of them made it clear this was a daughter and her parents, and the old Google image seen on Chang's phone made it clear the parents were Dr. and Mrs. Evan Lair.

Reacher pointed discreetly and said, "Check that out."

There was a long table set up near the house, and it was stacked with gifts, most of them large and boxy, all of them wrapped and rib-boned in monochrome whites and silvers.

Chang said, "This is a wedding."

"Looks like it," Reacher said. "Their daughter's, presumably. The girl at the table. I guess she's McCann's niece."

Then McCann's sister was on the move, after a last laugh and smile and affectionate squeeze of her daughter's shoulder. She drifted from group to group, chatting, sparkling, leaning in, smiling, kissing, hav-ing the time of her life.

Chang said, "She hasn't heard from Chicago yet. How could she have?"

Reacher said nothing.

McCann's sister moved on, group to group, taking a glass from a passing tray, putting her hand on other people's arms, putting the glass back on another tray. Then she caught sight of Reacher and Chang standing alone and awkward near the gate, underdressed in terms of quality, overdressed in terms of quantity, unknown and unexplained, and she changed course and headed toward them, still smiling, eyes still bright, a happy hostess's welcome all over her face.

Chang whispered, "We can't tell her. Not now."

The woman came close and extended a slim and manicured hand. She said, "Have we met? I'm Lydia Lair."

She looked like her Google picture at the charity ball. Like a million dollars. Chang shook her hand and gave her name, and then Reacher did, and the woman said, "I'll ask you the same question I've been asking all afternoon, which is, do you know our daughter from school or from work? Not that it makes the slightest bit of difference, of course. It's all one big party. But it's something to say."

Reacher said, "Ma'am, we're here for something else entirely. Perhaps we should come back later. We wouldn't want to crash a wedding. Might bring seven years of bad luck."

The woman smiled.

"I think that's mirrors," she said. "And this isn't the wedding. Far from it. Not yet. This is a kind of pre-pre-pre-wedding breakfast bride's-side-only party sort of thing. So people can start to get to know each other ahead of the rest of the week's events, so everyone gets energized for the big deal at the weekend. My daughter says everyone does it now. But you know how it is these days. The weddings last longer than the marriages."

And then she laughed, a happy sound, as if certain her joke didn't apply to her, as if certain her daughter's marriage would last forever.

Chang asked, "Would this evening be more convenient?"

"May I know what it's about?"

"Your brother, Peter."

"Oh dear, I'm so sorry, but I think you might have wasted a trip. He isn't here. He didn't come. We expected him, obviously, but it's a long flight. How do you know Peter?"

"We should get into that later this evening. If that's convenient. Because right now we're holding you up. And we've taken far too much of your time already. We should let you get back to your guests."

McCann's sister smiled appreciatively, and started to turn away. But a new thought struck her, and she turned back, different. She said, "Is Peter in trouble? Are you police officers?"

Chang did the only thing she could, as a woman with a code, which was to ignore both questions completely, and respond with a statement that resembled an answer. She said, "We're private investigators."

"Did Keever send you?"

"Ma'am, now we really need to talk. But we can't pull you away from all of this."

"Is Peter in trouble?"

Chang did the same thing again. She said, "Ma'am, we're here to be briefed. Our job is to hear about Peter from you."

McCann's sister said, "Come with me."

They walked through the house to a dark-paneled study, shuttered tight against the sun, with club chairs and a river stone fireplace. They sat down, the women perched almost knee to knee, Reacher leaning back. McCann's sister asked, "Where should I begin?"

Reacher said, "Tell us what you know about Keever."

"I never met him, obviously. But Peter likes to talk things through, so during the selection process I felt I got to know all the candidates to some extent."

"How many candidates were there?"

"Eight to start with."

"Did the process take long?"

"Almost six weeks."

"That's thorough."

"That's Peter."

"How often do you talk?"

"Most days."

"How long are the calls?"

"Some days an hour."

"That's a lot."

"He's my brother. He's lonely."

"Why did he need a private detective?"

"Because of Michael, his son. My nephew."

"People say there are issues."

"That's the wrong word. That's a polite way of saying difficult. Which is already a polite way of saying something worse. Michael is the opposite of difficult."

"What would be the right word?"

"Michael didn't make it all the way to the end of the assembly line. A couple of things didn't get bolted on. I try not to blame the mother. But she wasn't well. She died less than ten years later."

"Which things got missed?"

"Are you a happy man, Mr. Reacher?"

"Can't complain. Generally speaking. Right now I feel pretty good. Not in relation to the current part of our conversation, you understand."

"On a scale of one to ten, what's the worst you've ever felt?"

"About a four."

"And the happiest?"

"Compared to the theoretical best ever?"

"I suppose."

"About a nine."

"OK, four at the bottom and nine at the top. What about you, Ms. Chang?"

She didn't answer right away. Then she said, "The worst I've ever felt would be a three. And I was going to say eight for the best. But now maybe nine. I think."

She looked at Reacher as she said it, in a certain way, and McCann's sister caught the glance. She said, "Are you two sleeping together?"

No response.

"Honey, if you're sleeping together, make it a nine for sure. Always safer. But no higher. Ten gives them performance anxiety. But right now between the two of you we have a swing from either three or four at the low end to a pair of nines at the high end, even though one of the nines is really an eight, but we're too polite to say so. But you get my drift. You're normal people. If you swung from two to seven you'd still be normal, but you'd be seen as a little dour and reserved. Understand?"

Chang nodded.

"Now suppose your needle is jammed on zero. Doesn't move at all. Zero at the bottom and zero at the top. That's Michael. He was born unhappy. Born without the capacity to be happy. Born without any concept even of what happiness is. He doesn't know it's there."

Chang said, "Is there a name for that?"

"They have names for everything now. Peter and I discuss them endlessly. None of them really fits. I like an old-fashioned vocabulary. I think of it as melancholy. But that sounds too weak and passive. Michael has depth of emotion. Just not range. You feel joy or passion, and he feels the same intensity, but it's all hammering away down at the zero level. And he's intelligent. He knows exactly what's happening to him. The result is endless torment."

"How old is he now?"

"He's thirty-five."

"What are the outward signs? Is he hard to get along with?"

"The opposite. You hardly know he's there. He's very quiet. He does what you tell him. He hardly speaks. He sits for days staring into space, chewing his lip, his eyes darting around. Or else he's on his computer, or fiddling with his phone. There's no aggression. He never gets upset. Upset would imply an emotional range."

"Can he work?"

"That's been part of the problem. He has to work, to qualify for housing. It's part of the deal. And he can work. There are things he's good at. But people find him draining. They don't like to be with him. Productivity goes down. Usually he's asked to leave. So he's in and out of the programs."

"Where does he live now?"

"Right now, nowhere. He went missing."

* * *

At that point the bride-to-be came in, looking for her mother. A thin shirt over her bikini. Peter McCann's niece. Michael McCann's cousin. Up close she was still luminous. She glowed. She was close to perfect. Pre-natal care, perinatal care, post-natal care, pediatrics, nutrition, education, orthodontics, vacations, college, postgrad, a fiancé, the whole nine yards. Her assembly line had worked just fine. The American dream. A spectacular result. And she looked happy. Not silly, not giggly, not hyped up, and not an airhead. Just deeply and serenely content. With room at the top for ecstasy. Her needle ran from maybe six to ten. She had gotten everything her cousin hadn't.

McCann's sister went back out to the pool with her. She promised to return as soon as she could. Reacher and Chang sat quiet in the darkened den. They heard the sounds of the party, muted by walls and distance. Splashes and yelps and the clink of glasses, and the rolling murmur of conversation. Chang said, "We should call Westwood in LA. We should update him. A deal's a deal. Plus we're going to need another hotel."

Reacher said, "Tell him we need everything he has on the Deep Web. All his notes. Or maybe tell him to come out here to explain it all in person. We might not understand his notes. He can get on a plane. He's getting the book deal."

Chang put her phone on speaker and dialed, and she gave the guy the play-by-play, everything that had happened since she last called, from the West Hollywood motel. She mentioned Chicago, the library, the mom-and-pop pharmacy, McCann's street, McCann's house, Hackett, the neighbor, the Lincoln Park homicide, the flight to Phoenix, and finally the sister. And then the son, in the long term trapped between zero and zero, and in the short term missing.

Westwood said, "They call it anhedonia. The inability to experience pleasure."

"The sister makes it sound worse than that."

"And Keever's job was to find him and bring him home?"

"We assume so. We didn't get that far in the story. We were interrupted."

"I don't see how the Deep Web or two hundred deaths are involved. This feels like the crime desk, not the science desk. Or one of those human tragedy stories."

"It could be all three. We don't know yet."

"Where are you staying?"

"We haven't figured that out."

"OK, I'll call you when I land."

The line went dead.

Reacher said, "Apparently Michael spends time on his computer, or fiddling with his phone. Maybe that's the Deep Web connection. Maybe he's in some weird kind of chat room all the time. Maybe he has a whole life no one else knows about."

"He's depressed, not weird."

"Depressed means what it says, which is pushed down below the normal position. Which implies a range. Which Michael doesn't have. Which is weird. Or unusual, to be polite. But he's intelligent, she said. Maybe there are support groups on-line. Maybe he started one."

"Why would it need to be secret?"

"Because of search engines, I guess. Employers check on-line. I read about it in the newspaper. And not just employers, probably. Probably all kinds of people. Relatives, possibly, or doctors. There's no privacy anymore. Things can come back to bite you. If Michael posted something that showed he wasn't making progress, he could lose his housing. Or someone might decide he needed supervision."

Then the door opened and Lydia Lair came back in. Peter McCann's sister, Michael McCann's aunt, and the mother of the bride. She sat down in the same chair and Reacher asked her, "How did Michael go missing?"

She said, "That's a long story."

Twenty miles south of Mother's Rest, the man with the ironed jeans and the blow-dried hair took the call on his land line. His contact said, "This is your screw-up now."

"In what way?"

"There were things you didn't know."

"What things?"

"I promised you they wouldn't talk to McCann. And I delivered. Can't talk to a dead man. But it came at a cost. I lost Hackett."

"How?"

"Reacher took him out. Or both of them together. Either way, it shouldn't have happened. Not theoretically possible."

"Is he dead?"

"He's in the hospital."

"Are you going to let them get away with this?"

"No, I'm not. I'm going to make an example. This is an image business. Very competitive. Brand strength is everything. So I'll split it with you fifty-fifty."

"Split what?"

"The cost of not letting them get away with it."

The man with the jeans and the hair paused a beat, and then he said, "You didn't let them talk to McCann. For which you have my grateful thanks. It was a job well done. But with respect, that concluded our business. Any feelings you retain for Reacher or Chang are now personal to you, surely."

"Hackett is handcuffed to the hospital bed. He's in police custody."

"How much does he know?"

"Bits and pieces. But they won't prove anything. Hackett has no evidence with him. No data. Reacher stole his phone, and he left his computers in the car. Which was provided by our friends in Chicago, complete with a driver. So we still have his hardware. We fired up the phone sniffer again. Chang is back on the air. She just called the guy at the *LA Times*. From a suburban location right here in Phoenix."

"Why there? Because of you? Are they coming for you?"

"Reacher called me on Hackett's phone and told me so. Plus it would be an easy prediction anyway. But not if you listened to Chang's call to the *LA Times*. They're here for a completely different reason altogether."

"Which is what?"

"There were things you didn't know."

"What things?"

"The kind of things that will make you happy to split with me fifty-fifty."

"Tell me."

"Peter McCann had a sister. Lydia McCann, as was. Now Lydia Lair, married to a doctor. She lives here in Phoenix. In a suburban location. The brother and the sister talked all the time. He told her everything. According to what Chang just said to Westwood, it could be that talking to the sister is the same thing as talking to McCann himself."

"We can't let that happen."

"We?"

"OK, fifty-fifty. Of course."

"I'm glad we see eye to eye."

"But with one extra thing."

"Which would be what?"

"Tell me how McCann died."

"Hackett shot him."

"In greater detail."

"Hackett went to visit him very early in the morning and walked him out of the building at gunpoint. To the local park. There was no one around. He shot him in the back of the skull with a silenced nine."

"Was there a lot of mess?"

"I wasn't there."

"Probably exited through the face. But the brain was dead by then. No further heartbeat. No blood pressure. Effective, but not visual. Are you going to do the same thing with Reacher and Chang?"

"I'm going to do whatever the hell works. Split fifty-fifty. Which could be expensive. Because apart from anything else, we also have to do it fast. They could be talking right this minute."

Chapter 39

The long story about Michael McCann's disappearance
began with a desire to visit Oklahoma. Michael announced it one day,
in his slow, halting, disappointed way, and his father didn't let himself fall in the trap of worrying about it, not then, not immediately,
because he knew it was unlikely to happen. These things rarely did.
But then Michael further announced he had researched housing policy in Oklahoma, which was different from Illinois, in that part-time
work could qualify. Which might be more sustainable.

Peter McCann's reaction had been mixed. Obviously at the top of
the pole was the sheer terror of imagining Michael alone and adrift in
an unfamiliar environment. But underneath that was a tiny green
shoot of optimism. Finally Michael had spent some computer time
productively. He had researched housing policy in another state. He
had even drawn a conclusion. *Which might be more sustainable.*
Which was almost like making a plan. Certainly it showed a solid
flicker of initiative. It was evidence of self-motivation, which some
long-ago shrink had said would be the first sign of improvement.

So all in all Peter McCann had been holding it together.

His sister said, "Then Michael announced he had a friend in Oklahoma. Which was a big deal. He had never had a friend before. He had never even used the word. We figured it happened through an internet forum. Which was worrying, I guess. But Michael is thirty-five years old. He's not retarded. His IQ is way up there. He knows what he's doing. He's sad, that's all. So Peter asked what questions he could and then bit his lip."

Reacher said, "And what happened?"

"Michael went to Oklahoma. A little place not far from Tulsa. He texted at first. Then less frequently. But he was OK, as far as we knew. Then one day he texted to say he was coming home soon. He didn't say exactly when, and he didn't say why. We haven't heard from him since."

"When did Peter call the police?"

"Pretty soon afterward. Then he called everybody."

"Including the White House?"

"I advised him not to. But of course no one anywhere was listening to him. There are half a million mentally challenged homeless men in America. No one would consider searching for an individual among them. How could they? Why would they? Michael is not aggressive and he isn't on medication. He isn't dangerous."

"Didn't they at least check with the friend?"

"I'm sure you know how it is. In your own jobs. Suddenly all you have is a name that doesn't mean much, and a hazy half-remembered address no one can find."

"So the friend has not been identified?"

"No one even knows whether it was a man or a woman."

"What about the social housing?"

"There wasn't any. Clearly Michael had been staying with the unknown friend. Probably not working at all, even part-time."

"And then what happened?"

"Obviously Peter wouldn't give up. He went to work on his own. First he got help from the phone company. He can be very persistent. They tracked Michael's phone. The last day they can see it move southwest, from one cell tower to the next, from around Tulsa to

Oklahoma City, at what looks like an average speed of about fifty miles an hour. Which was a bus, Peter thinks. He thinks Michael took the bus from Tulsa to Oklahoma City."

"Why?"

"To get the train to Chicago."

Reacher nodded. The train.

Inevitably.

Chang said, "There are other trains out of OC."

McCann's sister said, "Peter thinks Michael was coming home. Peter's certain of it. And sure enough, at first the phone moves north in the right direction at the right speed. But then it switches off."

"Because it got too far away. We had the same thing. The last cell tower is about ninety minutes north of Oklahoma City. Then you're in dead air forever."

"It never came back on again."

"Did Peter tell the cops?"

"Of course."

"What did they say?"

"They say the phone hunted for a signal so hard it ran down the battery. Then Michael didn't get a chance to charge it before it got stolen in Chicago. Just because he hasn't visited his dad doesn't mean he isn't back in town. And so on and so forth. Or alternatively the phone was stolen in Tulsa or OC and some other guy took it on the bus and the train, but he didn't have the code to unlock the screen, so he quit trying and trashed it. Meanwhile Michael is still in Oklahoma, or perhaps he went somewhere else entirely, possibly San Francisco."

Reacher said, "Why San Francisco?"

McCann's sister said, "There are a lot of homeless men in San Francisco. Cops think it's a magnet. They think people go there automatically, like it's still 1967."

"How does Peter rate that possibility?"

"As a possibility, but nothing more."

"So then he hired Keever?"

"He started the process."

"Searching on-line?"

"At first."

Reacher said, "Tell us about his interest in the internet."

But then the daughter came back in the room, to tell her mom people were leaving. The two of them went out together to say good-bye, and Reacher heard the outside hubbub change in frequency to a long slow goodbye tone, and then he heard car doors slamming and engines starting, and vehicles pulling away.

Five minutes later the house was absolutely silent.

No one came back to the shuttered study. Reacher and Chang waited alone in the gloom. Five more minutes. Nothing doing. They opened the door and looked out. An interior hallway, empty. Silver-framed photographs on the wall. A family story, in chronological order. A couple, a couple with a baby, a couple with an infant, a couple with a kid, a couple with a teenager. All three of them growing older, frame by frame.

There was no sound.

No voices, no footsteps.

They moved out of the study to the hallway. They felt entitled. Or allowed. Or at least no longer inappropriate. The guests were gone. No more need to hide. They turned toward what they felt was the center of the house and took quiet tentative steps. The silver-framed photographs started up again. A fresh batch, in a new location. But the same old story. A couple with a college student, a couple with a muddy college student in a soccer uniform holding a cup, a couple with a graduating college student.

No voices, no footsteps.

They moved on, past a room with padded walls and a giant screen and a forest of upright loudspeakers. And three separate chairs, each one of them with its own reclining mechanism, and its own cup holder. A home theater. Reacher had never seen one before, in a home.

No sound.

They came out in an arched antechamber ahead of the living room. Where the architecture changed from adobe to hunting lodge. The ceiling soared overhead, with knotty boards rising to an angled peak, in a shallow upside-down V. Black iron chandeliers hung down, with bulbs made to look like candles. There were sofas made of thick brown leather, deep and wide and sprawling, with plaid blankets folded over their backs, for color.

They heard a car on the driveway.

Metallic thumps, as doors opened and closed.

Footsteps on the rivers of stone.

The front door opened.

A heavy tread in the hallway.

Dr. Evan Lair walked into his living room. He saw Reacher, saw Chang, and stopped. He said, "Hey, guys," in a way that was part welcome, part question, perfectly amiable, completely accepting, but with a tiny edge of impatience, as if what he really meant was *I thought all the guests had gone.*

Then his daughter came in behind him, still in the shirt and bikini, and she put her hand on his back and said, "It's something to do with Cousin Michael. Mom has been talking to them."

Then she maneuvered onward and stepped up close, and put out her hand, and said, "Hi, I'm Emily," and they all shook and introduced themselves, and said congratulations all around.

Then McCann's sister came in, kind of dusting her hands, and she said, "I'm sorry, but we took a slice of cake and a glass of tea to the man at the gate. The least we could do. He had a busy afternoon on our behalf."

Reacher said, "Did you give him a guest list beforehand?"

"We have to."

"Then you should have given him only half a slice of cake. He let us in without checking it."

Evan said, "Is Michael still missing?"

Emily said, "Dad, you know he is."

"And Peter is finally looking for him now? Is that what this is?"

"Uncle Peter has been looking for him all along."

"Well, he isn't here. Neither one of them is here."

Reacher said, "We apologize for the intrusion."

"Sit down," Emily said. "Please."

They ended up two and three on opposite sofas, Reacher and Chang cradled in the corners of one, with ice tea in glasses, on coasters on coffee tables made to look like old steamship trunks, and across from them on the other sofa was the Lair family, all in a line, with Evan and Lydia at the ends, and Emily in the middle, long and lithe and golden tan.

Reacher said, "Peter did very well with the phone company. That kind of information is hard to get."

Peter's sister said, "It's Chicago. It was a friend of a friend in the union."

"And Peter being a thorough guy, he won't have summarily dismissed the phone theft scenarios before or after the train ride. In Tulsa or OC or Chicago. Not completely out of hand. But he will have thought it at least equally likely something happened along the way."

"On the train?" Emily said.

"Or not. We know that train, as it happens. It stops once before Chicago. At a little country place called Mother's Rest."

No reaction from McCann's sister.

Reacher said, "Mother's Rest is way out in the middle of nowhere. It's also Keever's last known location. I think Peter concluded Michael got out of the train there. Hence his phone never came out the other side of the dead zone. I think he sent Keever to check."

"Well, that's good, right?" Evan said. "If he's there, Keever will find him."

Reacher said nothing.

McCann's sister said, "He's had no luck yet. Peter hasn't had a report in three days. Nothing doing. Unless he's due to call me with the good news right about now." Which seemed to make her conscious of the time, because she patted her wrist, looking for a watch, and then she squinted far into the kitchen to see the microwave clock.

She said, "It's after suppertime in Chicago."

She pointed near Reacher and said, "Hon, pass me the phone."

The phone was on the steamer trunk, near his ice tea. It was bigger than some, and curvier, and heavier. Better plastic. Still cordless and modern, but first-generation. If it ain't broke, don't fix it. It had a transparent window for speed-dial labels, with a space at the top for its own number, which someone had filled out in elegant pencil, the 480 area code and seven more digits. He passed it across, and McCann's sister took it, and checked it for a dial tone.

She said, "The line is working."

Evan asked, "How big of a place is Mother's Rest?"

Reacher said, "Very small."

"Why is it called that?"

"No one knows."

"How can it take three days to search a very small place?"

"Depends how thorough you are. You could spend three weeks poking around, opening every door, looking under every bush. Which is what's on my mind. It's a footsore picture. It's old-fashioned police work. The phone company trace, through a pal in the union, the railroad schedules, the guess about whether he stayed on board or got out, the physical search of a physical location. Time and space. Steel and iron. Shoe leather and late nights. Smart people would call it analog."

"I suppose sometimes it has to be that way."

"But we heard Peter was obsessed with the internet. He called a science journalist in LA a total of eighteen times to talk about it. Was that separate? How is that connected to a place that doesn't even get cell service?"

McCann's sister said, "It wasn't separate. It was parallel. He thought it might be a clue to where Michael was. He thought that Michael might talk to similar people on secret sites. Maybe he was heading somewhere for a reason. Maybe there had been discussions. We had high hopes of Mr. Westwood for a time. He might have held the key. But Peter was very persistent. And persistence can be a negative thing in the end. As you say, eighteen calls. I tried to warn him."

"Did he find the sites anyway?"

McCann's sister said, "I'll get more tea."

She stood up and picked up the jug from the steamer trunk, and the jug caught the phone and sent it spinning in place, frictionless, plastic on leather. Reacher saw the neat pencil handwriting, rotating slowly, like a bicycle spoke coming to rest. Area code 480, and seven more digits.

Phoenix, Arizona. Where we're going.

We're on the way.

The time for looking over your shoulder starts now.

Half a slice of cake.

He said, "Evan, may I ask you a personal question?"

Dr. Lair did what most guys do, when facing such an inquiry, which was to pause a quizzical beat, and shrug in mock innocence, and say, "Sure."

"Do you keep a gun in the house?"

"Is that important?"

"Just a matter of interest."

"As a matter of fact I do."

"May I see it?"

"That's a strange request."

His daughter, Emily, was half-turned sideways, sitting cross-legged, watching the exchange, back and forth from one face to the other, like tennis.

So was Chang.

Reacher said, "Is the gun in the bedroom?"

Lair said, "As a matter of fact it is."

"It would be better in the hallway. Dead-of-night home invasions are rare. Plus you'd be too sleepy to be effective. Are you right-handed?"

"Yes, I am."

"Then within six feet of the front door on the right-hand side would be favorite. In a drawer or a cabinet. Or grips-up in a decorative vase. On a table. I imagine that would work."

"Are you also a security consultant?"

"We aim to offer a wide range of services."

Emily said, "He's right, Dad. The bedroom is pointless."

Chang said, "Technically our advice would be to conceal a separate firearm in each major zone of the house. The bedroom certainly, but also the kitchen area, the living area, the entrance lobby, upstairs if you have one, the basement if you have one, and the garage."

Emily said, "Where's best if you only have one?"

Only have one, Reacher heard.

"Go with the math," Chang said. "Most problems come in the front door."

"Seriously?" Lair said. "I should move it?"

"Better ask Mom," Emily said.

And right then McCann's sister came back, with a fresh jug of tea and cake on a plate, and she said, "Ask me what?"

"Whether my daddy should move his gun to the hallway."

"Why on earth would he want to do that?"

"On the advice of one logical daughter and two security consultants."

"How on earth did the subject come up? Is it important?"

We can't tell her. Not now.

Reacher said, "No, it was just professional interest, that's all," and a minute later the matter evaporated like a bubble of soap, quickly forgotten, except by Chang, who flashed a question, eye to eye: *What the hell is going on?*

Reacher scratched his nose, absently, with the edge of his forefinger, the rest of his hand cupped below, hiding him mouthing *Turn your phone off.*

McCann's sister said, "Are you OK?"

Reacher said, "Tell us about the web sites Michael was using."

Chapter 40

McCann learned two things fast, his sister said, when he started looking at his son's computer. The first was that software could be booby-trapped so that opening an internet history was the same thing as erasing an internet history. Unless you opened it right, which he didn't, obviously. Because he didn't know how. But like a lot of downloaded programs it wasn't perfect. It had a tiny glitch. It left the first screen visible for about half a second. Then it was gone. Blank. No more.

The second thing he learned was how short of a time half a second was. But also how long. A fastball could get there and back again in half a second, easy. And plenty could be retained in the memory. It was a question of trusting, not thinking. Some ancient trick of mind and retina and after-image. Better to look away, and glimpse it on the edge.

Except it meant nothing. Just long lines of characters, as if someone had rolled a ball along the top part of a keyboard. Completely random.

McCann's sister said, "So Peter being Peter, he learned what he could about what he was up against, which turned out to be the Deep

Web. About which there wasn't much useful to learn. We had some scary conversations. We thought we were in charge. Relatively speaking. But we weren't. There was a whole secret world we knew nothing about. It was ten times bigger than ours. People were in there, talking. Doing weird stuff we wouldn't understand. It was like a science-fiction movie."

Reacher said, "Was there one thing in particular Westwood was supposed to help with, or was it a general inquiry?"

"No, it was very specific. There's a widespread feeling among Deep Web people that the government must be building a search engine capable of finding their web sites. We felt there was a hint in Westwood's article that it already exists. Peter wants Westwood to confirm or deny, and if so, help get him a chance to use it."

"Is that likely?"

"Personally I don't think there's a hope in hell, but leave no stone unturned. His son is missing. My nephew."

"Is it conceivable Peter could have left things out when he was talking to you? Were his stories always completely joined up?"

"What do you mean?"

"You hadn't heard the words Mother's Rest, for instance."

"No, I hadn't."

"Did he ever say anything about two hundred deaths?"

Emily said, "Two hundred what?"

Her mother said, "No."

Reacher said, "He talked to Keever about both those things. And Keever went to Mother's Rest. So it was important somehow. Yet he didn't mention it to you."

"What happens there?"

"We don't know."

"Peter's my big brother and I'm his little sister. He never forgets it. Never lets me forget it, either. Not in a bad way. In the best way. The only reason he would leave things out would be to spare me unpleasantness."

No one spoke.

Chang got up.

She said, "I need the ladies' room," and Emily pointed it out, and she wandered away in the right direction.

Reacher said, "Do you guys have plans for dinner?"

McCann's sister said, "I haven't thought about it yet."

"We could go out."

"Who?"

"All of us."

"Where?"

"Anywhere you like. Right now. My treat. Let me take you out to dinner."

"Why?"

"Sounds like you've been working hard all day."

Chang reappeared at the edge of the living room. She caught Reacher's eye and said, "Men's room is right here, if you need it."

He said, "OK."

"I can show you, if you like."

"I'm sure I'll find it when the time is right."

Emily said, "She wants to talk to you in private."

So Reacher got up and joined Chang in the outer hallway. She said, quietly, "You think Hackett's friends are coming?"

"We should have been more cautious with the phone. They could have equipment all over the country. If so, we just sold out the sister. We gave Westwood chapter and verse. So we can't leave them alone. Not here. Not now. Either we get them out or we babysit them all night. Close personal protection. A wide range of services."

"I'd rather get them out."

"I already offered them dinner."

"The guy on the gate is useless."

"Which way is the bedroom?"

"The other wing. Through the living room again."

"You try asking them to dinner. Maybe they thought it was weird from me."

"It's weird from either one of us. We don't know them. And they're in the middle of a high-precision wedding countdown. Two strangers suddenly taking them out for a bucket of chicken would make their heads explode."

"I said anywhere they want. Doesn't have to be KFC."

"Same difference. Doesn't matter where we go."

They heard a car on the driveway.

Metallic thumps, as doors opened and closed.

Footsteps on the rivers of stone.

Modern automotive design puts no more than four seats behind regular wide-open doors. Some sedans might be five-seaters, and some trucks were seven-seaters, but no tough guy grows up wanting to sit on the transmission hump, and no one is effective in the way back of a minivan. So worst case would be four incoming. Best case would be one. Likelihood was either two or three. Reacher turned instantly and headed across the living room, charting his course many steps ahead, as straight as possible, setting himself to graze the corners of tables and the arms of chairs, like a downhill slalom against the clock. The Lair family was still all in a line on the sofa, frozen, not understanding, Lydia, Emily, Evan, the linen shift, the shirt and bikini, the shorts and the loud Hawaiian, all watching, so Reacher patted the air as he passed them by, telling them to stay where they were, and then he hustled onward, out the far side of the living room, into a short hallway, past more silver-framed photographs of unknown people, maybe relatives, including a thin man and a sad boy, perhaps Peter and Michael McCann, and finally onward into the bedroom.

The back of his brain said *women usually take the side near the bathroom* and he sidestepped and scrambled around a pillow-stacked king-size bed to a night table with nothing on it but an alarm clock and an unread book.

He heard them kick down the front door.

He wrenched open the drawer under the book and saw reading

glasses and headache pills and a box of tissues and a Colt Python with a six-inch barrel. Hatched walnut grips lacquered to a soupy shine, an immense blued-steel frame, brawny .357 Magnum rounds in the wheel. One hell of a nighttime gun. Smart in some ways. No complexity. No safety, no jams. But dumb in other ways. It weighed three pounds. Too heavy to lift while blinking awake. And the recoil would blow a sleepy arm through the headboard.

Reacher took it and checked the cylinder. All there. A six-shooter. Six rounds.

He heard boots in the hallway.

Inside the front door. Moving six feet to the right. Two people. A third would be coming around the back. If there was a third. Along the decorative path, past the plantings, between the solar lights, through the gate.

Please go in.

No spare rounds in the drawer.

A six-shooter.

Reacher stepped back to the bedroom door. Still he heard boots in the hallway. Then he moved out, past the silver-framed photographs again, edging sideways, Python at arm's length, eyes on the front sight, crisp and clear, everything else blurred, the light soft, the house shuttered and shaded against the sun, and full of dim shadows.

He stopped at the mouth of the living room. On his left was the Lair family, still on the sofa, but starting to stir. Shock was giving way to fear. And in Emily's case, outrage. She was going to break forward. Her folks were going to break back. On his right was the sofa he and Chang had sat on, and beyond it was a partial view to the door.

He saw the bulk of a moving shoulder. A silhouette, against the light. Tense and pumped up and ready to go.

On his left through the slider he saw a guy in the back yard. Behind the wedding gifts. Then out in clear air. Black T-shirt, black pants. And a Ruger P-85, with a suppressor tube fitted. Carried easy, down by his side, from above his knee to the top of his boot. Which was also black. They were dressed the part. That was for damn sure.

Where was Chang?

Reacher did not want to fire without knowing where she was. Not a Magnum round. Not in her general direction. Too many dim shadows. Too much dazzling contrast. Too many crazy outcomes. Rounds could deflect off bone and go through walls. Plural. They could exit the building completely, and break a window down the street.

Where was she?

Emily was drawing breath, ready to start yelling and screaming, bikini and all, in Reacher's view a natural primeval reaction, the instinctive defense of family and territory, plus in her case a measure of righteous indignation, as in, this was her special week and who the hell did they think they were anyway? Evan was a calm man, accustomed to calamity, trained in science and reason, in tests and evidence and careful diagnosis, and he was a smart guy, and all his circuits were sparking, but he couldn't make anything fit in his mind, so his body was left waiting for a final decision. Lydia was pressed back in her corner, the wife and mother, the sister and the aunt, retreating into herself, Reacher thought, or into an earlier version of herself, perhaps the true McCann version, raised tougher, maybe in the kind of place where splintering wood and a heavy tread was never good news.

Then the guy in the yard opened the slider and stepped inside, and the back of Reacher's brain showed him the whole chess game right there, laid out, obvious, like flashing neon arrows, in immense and grotesque detail, the snap pivot left and the round into the meat of the yard guy's chest, where it was less likely than a head shot to go through-and-through, which was good, given a neighborhood behind them full of wooden fences, but where it was more likely to soak the Lair family with thick pink mist, from behind, hair and all, which wasn't good, because it would be traumatic, especially during such a week, except on reflection Reacher figured the week was already pretty much a disaster from that exact point onward, given that the chess game said there would be a dead guy at that very moment sliding to the floor of their private house, even as the homeowner-owned

Python was snapping right again for two rounds at where the silhouette of the shoulder had been, which two rounds might or might not hit anything, but which would give a second's cover for the scramble around the sofa and the capture of the dead guy's Ruger, for a total of three rounds expended and fifteen gained.

But Reacher made none of those shots or moves, because by then he knew where Chang was. She was being pushed into view, toward the living room from the front door, struggling, two guys holding her, her hands trapped behind her back, a palm clamped over her mouth, a gun at her head. Another Ruger, with another suppressor. Unstable and unwieldy in its present role, because of its length. But no doubt effective.

Reacher put the Python on the floor behind him, very quietly, in the shadows against the hallway baseboard, under the last of the silver-framed photographs.

Then he stepped into the living room.

Chapter 41

The guy from the yard tracked around part of a curve, and the two from the door came in and took up position on the same arc, wide apart, Chang suddenly shoved forward, sent sprawling, all the way to the Lairs' sofa, where she landed and steadied herself and turned around and perched on the edge. Reacher sat on the arm, slow and casual, wanting to look like less of a threat, wanting to anchor himself at that end of the room, knowing a standing guy will be told to sit, and often where, whereas a sitting guy was rarely moved. Evan was next to him, and then came Emily, sitting back, and Chang, sitting forward and breathing hard, and Lydia, sitting back. What had been spacious for three was crowded for five. They made a unified target. Three Rugers against them, fanned out wide, like a field-of-fire diagram in an old infantry manual.

Three Rugers, three guys. Black clothes, scalped hair, pale skin. Big enough and heavy enough, but also somehow bony. Tight cheekbones. Hard times in their DNA, from not too long ago. From Europe, maybe. Far in the marshy east. Every man against his neighbor, for the last thousand years. They stood there, rock steady, at first calming down and taking stock and checking boxes, and then thinking hard about something new. Normally Reacher might have said they looked like they knew what they were doing, but the truth was right then he thought they didn't. Not a hundred percent. Not anymore. They were improvising. Or preparing to improvise. Or at least considering it. As if their own chess game had come to a fork in the road. Arrows to the left, arrows to the right. Options. Freedom of choice. Always dangerous.

They didn't move. Didn't speak. There was maybe a hint of a smile. Then the guy in the middle said, "We were told we would find a man and a woman talking to another woman."

Good English, close to a regular American accent, but with dull Slavic undertones. Eastern Europe for sure. Moody, put-upon, a guy whose life was a sea of troubles.

No one answered.

The guy said, "But what we actually find is two men and three women. One of which is Chinese. Which is all very confusing. So tell me, which among you has been talking to who?"

Chang said, "I'm American, not Chinese. And we've all been talking. To each other. Everyone to everyone else. All ways around. Now you tell us something. Who the hell are you and what the hell are you doing here?"

The guy said, "One of you is somebody's sister."

No response.

The guy said, "We don't know if the somebody is a Chinaman. That information would have helped, I guess."

No response.

"Which one of you is somebody's sister?"

"Not me," Reacher said.

"You got a sister, wise guy? Maybe you should tell me where she lives."

"If I had a sister, I would. Save me kicking your ass myself."

The guy looked away, to the other end of the sofa. To the three women there.

He said, "Which one of you is the sister?"

No response.

"Which one of you is the woman who spoke to the sister?"

No response.

The guy looked back the other way.

He said, "Which one of you is the man who spoke to the sister?"

No response.

The guy said, "There are many combinations. Like a test at the Institute of Mathematics. How many socks do I need to guarantee a pair? But in this case one answer at least is obvious, even to the dullest student. We could kill you all. That would guarantee the correct result. That would be a sufficiently large number of socks. But it would be five dead for the price of three. And that price was agreed upfront. Count your change before you leave the store. No renegotiation after the fact. Those are the fat man's rules."

Silence.

The guy looked at Evan, and said, "What do you do for a living?"

Evan started once, and started again, and got it out third time around. He said, "I'm a doctor."

"Do you work for free?"

"No, I guess I don't."

"Dumb question, right? Doctors working for free?"

"Some doctors work for free."

"But not you, right?"

"No, I guess not."

"Do you think I should work for free?"

Evan breathed in, breathed out, floundering.

The guy said, "Doctor, it's a simple question. I'm not seeking a medical opinion. Do you think I should work for free? When you don't?"

"Does it matter what I think?"

"I want us all to be comfortable. I want us all to agree. A person should get paid for the work he does. I need your backing on this."

"OK, a person should get paid."

"For what?"

"For the work he does."

"Should he get more for five things than three things?"

"I guess he should."

"But how can he, when the price was fixed upfront? There is no more blood in that stone. Which is bad news for us. But good news for you. We'll do only what we've been paid to do. No free samples. You stand a chance of surviving."

A forty percent chance, the back of Reacher's brain told him, immediately and automatically, if the shooting was random. But why would the shooting be random? Their brief was a man and two women. In which case Evan's odds rose to fifty-fifty. And Chang's fell, from forty percent to thirty-three.

The guy said, "Of course the flaw in the plan is we might leave the wrong two alive. Which would not be acceptable. I'm sure you have professional standards of your own. The problem needs to be solved another way. We need to think laterally. We need to find a way to get paid. Help me out here."

Evan said, "There's no money in the house."

"Doctor, I'm not asking a man to pay for his own execution. That would be harsh. I'm asking you to think laterally. What is there in the current situation that could provide some element of recompense for me and my partners?"

Evan said nothing.

"Be creative, doctor. Loosen up. Think outside the box. If not money, what else?"

No answer.

The guy looked at Emily and said, "What's your name, sweetheart?"

Evan said, "No."

The guy looked at Chang.

He said, "Her, too."

Emily pulled her shirt tight around her and drew up her knees and scrabbled backward on the sofa. Evan leaned in front of her. The guy in the middle stared him down and said, "If you behave yourself we'll shoot you first. If you don't, we'll leave you alive and make you watch."

The three guys were equally spaced along the rim of a quarter circle. Like the bases loaded. But much closer. They were in a room, after all, not a ballpark. A spacious room, but still. The guy at first base on the right was maybe seven feet from Reacher. At third on the far left the furthest guy was fifteen feet away. And the guy on second was halfway between the other two, doing all the talking, on a straight line between Reacher and the front door, about twelve feet distant.

Three guys. No doubt the Maricopa County DA would call them invaders. As in, *a home invasion turned tragic tonight, in an exclusive gated community northeast of town. Film at eleven.* The cops would call them perpetrators. Their lawyers would call them clients. Politicians would call them scum. Criminologists would call them sociopaths. Sociologists would call them misunderstood.

The 110th MP would call them dead men walking.

The guy on second said, "Let's get this show on the road."

Emily was wedged hard against the back of the sofa, pressed against the plaid wool blanket, her knees drawn up, her arms wrapped tight around her shins. Altogether she looked like a person half her size. Chang wasn't going anywhere, either. She was planted in place, her hands flat on the sofa by her sides, her legs out straight, her lace-up shoes way out in front of her, her heels literally dug into the rug, like a cartoon roadrunner skidding to a stop.

The guy on second said, "I'm getting impatient here."

Wet lips.

Moving eyes.

Urgent.

No response.

Then Reacher breathed out and raised a placatory don't-shoot palm, and he half-stood, slow and calm, unthreatening, the complete opposite of sudden, and he kept himself half-turned away from the guys with the guns, and half-turned toward the group on the sofa, and he said, "Come on, Emily, let's get this done. They're going to

nail you one way or the other. Might as well make it easy on yourself."

She said, "What?"

He leaned past Evan and grabbed the kid's wrist and pulled her
upright. Immediately Evan stood up to fight him, and Chang too, and
McCann's sister, all of them breathless and panicked and unbeliev-
ing. Suddenly there was a small knot of people all vertical and active,
clustered together on the rug between the sofas, moving, swaying,
bumping, glancing desperately left and right.

The moment of truth.

The three guys did nothing. Their smart play at that point would
have been to start blasting away, there and then, no hesitation, recognizing that the situation was turning to shit right in front of their
eyes. But by then they were heavily invested in a plan of their own
devising, in a course of action, in a procedure, in the promise of extreme future physical pleasure, and the two major components of
that coming nirvana were knotted tight in the swaying crowd, col-
lateral damage just waiting to happen, and they didn't want them
damaged. Not so soon. They wanted them just the way they were,
whole, aware, reacting, all smooth tan flesh and bikinis and T-shirts
and low-cut jeans. So they didn't shoot. They didn't think. Not with
their brains, anyway.

So far so good.

Reacher nudged Evan one way and Chang the other and pulled
Emily out of the crowd. He reeled her in, all thrashing knees and elbows, and he turned her around and shoved her onward, hard, into
the hallway with the silver-framed photographs of the unknown relatives.

He said, "The bedroom is that way."

Evan scrambled past him, grabbing at his daughter, and McCann's
sister jostled him, almost as quick, and Chang piled in behind her,
with the first-base guy following, some sudden concern on his face
about the emerging chaos, and behind him the second-base spokesperson crowded in, with the third-base guy coming in from the rear.

Eight people in total, clumsy, stumbling, forced nearly to single file, funneling into a dark narrow hallway.

Reacher dropped down in the crowd and scooped up the Python, two-handed to stop it skittering on the polished wood, and he snugged the butt in his palm, solid and reassuring, and he fit his finger in the guard, against the trigger, hard and substantial, and he brought the gun up, three pounds of weight, and he put his left hand on the top of Lydia Lair's head, and buckled her knees, and forced her down, and he aimed over Chang's right shoulder and fired, at the center of the man-on-first's face.

There were many factors that made a handgun either accurate or not accurate. The velocity of the round and the length of the barrel were the most important, aided or not by aerodynamic subtleties like the degree of spin imparted by the rifling grooves, which either worked well or didn't, depending on the bullet. Precision of manufacture was influential, with careful machining of quality metal much preferred over casting from leftover slag. Not that anything much mattered at seven feet. A pore to the left or a wrinkle to the right was immaterial. The human face was a big enough target, generally hard to miss at close quarters, and the man-on-first's was no exception.

It was a through-and-through, obviously, given the short range and the power of the Magnum round. Twenty feet behind the guy's head the wall instantly cratered, the size of a punch bowl, and a ghastly split second later the contents of the guy's brain pan arrived to fill it, with a wet slap, all red and gray and purple. Meanwhile the guy himself was going down vertically, as if he had stepped into an elevator shaft, and Reacher was turning fractionally left, from the waist, shoulders braced, looking for the third-base guy, the furthest away, because some back-of-the-brain calculation was telling him the guy had a better line of return fire, and he wasn't drooling as bad as the second-base guy, so maybe he was less invested in the upcoming entertainment, and therefore more likely to start blasting, even at the risk of damaged goods.

Reacher eased the trigger home, and he felt the mechanism turn, gears and cams and levers, effortless, and the gun fired, in his mind a considered shot, a decent interval after his first, but in the real world almost a double tap, a fast *bang-move-bang,* a craftsman going about his business, calmly, using his natural-born gifts. It was a through-and-through again, inevitably, in the guy's upper lip, out the base of his skull, shattering the slider window, and exploding a pile of wedding presents on the table in the yard outside, in a cloud of paper fragments, white and silver, like confetti a few days early. The broken glass came down like a waterfall, governed by gravity, and therefore at the same downward speed as the third-base guy, who was also governed by gravity. Reacher saw an inch of their synchronized descent, and then he whipped away to the right, to find the second-base guy.

Because at that point the race was really on, and Reacher was losing. One guy was nothing, and two guys were never really a problem either, but a third guy could get tricky. The *bang-bang* of his pals going down tended to concentrate his mind, and worse than that gave him time to get his head in the game, to react, to finally realize *oh yeah I've got a gun in my hand,* to bring the gun up, slower than usual, because of the fat suppressor tube, because the gun was twice as long as his muscle memory thought it was, and also heavier, and therefore less controllable, which was all good, because his traverse was a whole lot shorter than Reacher's needed to be. He was almost there already. Just inches away. Game almost over. But Reacher kept on moving, in what felt like hopeless slow motion, like forcing the back of his hand through molasses on a cold winter's day, his left eye on the Python's front sight, his right eye on the hole in the end of the suppressor tube, which was still elliptical, but only slightly. It was an inch away from dead on.

The Python was a foot away from dead on.

Reacher chopped it downward, like cracking a whip backhand, mainly for extra speed and power, but also because the guy was widest at the shoulders, and aiming was a luxury Reacher could no longer afford. The Python was a double-action weapon, which meant the same trigger pull cocked the hammer and then dropped it, so he started early, getting the cylinder turning while the gun was still moving, seeing the hammer come up, feeling the cams and the levers, waiting, then firing, trusting millisecond timing and momentum and deflection and complex four-dimensional calculations.

In other words, a wing and a prayer.

But it worked, apparently.

Because the guy didn't fire back, and a red chunk came out of his neck. Big enough to feed a family.

A triple play.

Unassisted.

Baseball immortality.

Behind the guy the bullet smashed its way in and out of a powder room and shattered a lamp in the hallway. The guy himself went down in a heap, with what should have been a thump and a clatter, but Reacher heard none of it, because a Magnum's downside was deafness, at least temporary, especially inside. Around him the others were helpless with shock, as if frozen in place by a camera strobe or a flash of lightning. McCann's sister was on her knees, her mouth wide open in a scream Reacher couldn't hear, and Emily was crouched against the base of the hallway wall. Understandable. A Magnum inside was like a stun grenade. Three times.

Then the hiss and the roar dulled a little, and people started moving. Chang went for Emily, and Evan helped his wife up and then shouldered his way through for a look at the living room, whereupon he turned around and started herding people back toward the bedroom again, shaking his head emphatically, saying, "We can't go in there," over and over again. Not because of personal discomfort, Reacher supposed, the guy being a doctor and so on, but to spare his family the sight. Although he supposed they had been in a butcher's shop, and survived the experience. Although three guys was a lot of dead meat. Or maybe he was worried about crime scene integrity. Too much TV.

The Lair family sat on the bed, smaller somehow, except for their eyes, all of them panting hard, all of them trying to hold it together. Chang paced. Reacher wiped the big old Colt and left it on Evan Lair's night stand.

Lair said, "We should call the police. We have a legal responsibility."

Chang said, "Yes, sir, that would be my advice. You need to get out in front of this."

McCann's sister said, "Peter's dead, isn't he?"

No answer.

"They got him and now they came to get me. Because they think I know what he knows. Or knew. Everyone thinks that. That's what you think."

Chang said, "We have no proof or first-hand evidence about Peter. It would be most improper for us to tell you anything. And Michael must be told first, anyway."

"I expect he's dead, too."

"We have no information."

The room went quiet.

Then Evan said, "What are we going to do?"

Reacher said, "About what?"

"We have dead people in our house."

"They won't come out smelling of roses. So they'll call it a righteous shooting. A home invasion, silenced weapons, threats of sexual violence. We're not going to jail over this. We're going to get a pat on the head instead. Except I don't really care for that kind of thing. I would be just as happy not to be mentioned at all. Like I wasn't here. You should take the credit. Play around with the gun. Get your prints on it again. They'll give you a free year at the country club. You'll get new patients. The badass doc."

"Are you serious?"

"I don't care how it turns out. They'll never find me. But I would appreciate a head start. Ms. Chang and I have a lot to do. It would help us if you would sit tight for about thirty minutes, before you call

911. Tell them any story you want. Tell them you were in shock. Hence the delay."

"Thirty minutes," Evan said.

"Shock can last that long."

"OK."

"But when it comes to the story, tell them only two of them had guns."

"Why?"

"Because I'm going to take one with me. And some cops can count that high."

"OK, thirty minutes. Two guns. If I can. I'm not good with uniforms."

Reacher looked at Emily and said, "Ma'am, I'm very sorry your big week got ruined."

Emily said, "I owe you my thanks."

"Think nothing of it."

He headed out, behind Chang, who stopped to hug McCann's sister, and to say, in response to her mute inquiries, "I'm very sorry for your loss."

Then they closed the door on them and headed down the hallway, past the photographs, to the living room. First up was the first-base guy, but he had collapsed at an awkward angle. His suppressor was in the pool of blood coming from what was left of his head, and suppressors have wadding inside, or very fine baffles, either one of which would leak blood forever, so they passed the guy by. The third-base guy was a detour, so Chang ducked down to the second-base guy, the guy who had done all the talking, and she scooped up his Ruger, white collar or not.

And then she stopped.

She whispered, "Reacher, this one is still breathing."

Chapter 42

Reacher squatted by the horizontal figure. Chang knelt beside him. The guy was on his back, his legs splayed, his arms in disarray. He was unconscious. Or deep in shock, or in a coma. Or all of the above. His neck was a mess. Half of it was missing. He smelled of dirty clothes and sweat and the iron stink of blood. He smelled of death.

But there was faint respiration, and a thready pulse.

"How is that even possible?" Reacher whispered. "A piece the size of a porterhouse steak came flying out of him."

"Obviously not a vital piece," Chang whispered back.

"What do you want to do?"

"I don't know. We can't call the ambulance. They'll bring the cops with them. They always do, for gunshot victims. We wouldn't get a head start. But on the other hand this guy looks pretty bad. He needs a trauma surgeon, as soon as possible."

"Evan is a doctor."

"But what kind? He'd take one look and call the ambulance himself. Immediately. And then he'd call the cops himself. Also immediately. He's shaky on the thirty-minute thing anyway."

"We could walk out and leave the guy here. Who would know?"

"Too hard on Evan. Potentially. This guy might live thirty minutes. Then the story would leak. He'd be the doctor who ignored a dying man so he could go sit in his bedroom."

Reacher put his fingertips high on the guy's neck, on the intact portion, above the wound, one on each side, behind the ears, near the hinges of the jaw.

He kept them there.

Chang said, "What are you doing?"

"Compressing the arteries that feed his brain."

"You can't do that."

"What, it was OK to murder him the first time, but not the second time?"

"It's wrong."

"It was right the first time, when he was a piece of shit who was about to rape you at gunpoint. Did he change? Did he suddenly become some kind of a saintly martyr we should rush straight to the hospital? When did that part happen?"

"How long will this take?"

"Not long. He wasn't well to begin with."

"This is so wrong."

"We're doing him a favor. Like a horse with a broken leg. No one could fix this neck."

Her phone rang.

Loud and clear. Penetrating. She juggled it out and hunched away and answered it. She listened. She whispered. She clicked off.

Reacher said, "Who was that?"

"Westwood has landed at Sky Harbor."

"Good to know."

"I said we'd call him back."

"Probably best."

"The family will have heard the phone. They'll know we're still here."

"They'll think it's one of these guys. In a pocket. They'll ignore it."

"Is that guy dead yet?"

"Nearly there. It's peaceful. Like falling asleep."

Then he sat back, and checked for a pulse, and didn't find one.

He said, "Let's go."

Their car was on the curb a hundred yards away, in what had been the closest spot when they arrived. Then the tide had gone out and left it high and dry. It was all alone. Chang drove. She U-turned across the road and headed back the way they had come. The development was quiet. Stunned by heat. The air shimmered everywhere, blue and gold, like liquid.

The gatehouse had both barriers up. Both red-striped poles were vertical. Like a fat bird dressed for the oven. Wide open, both ways, in and out. No guard behind the glass.

Chang stopped the car.

She said, "Check it out."

The blacktop was hot under Reacher's feet. He could have fried an egg on it. He heard the buzz of flies six feet away. The sliding window was open. Where the guard leaned out to talk. *I hope you folks have a wonderful afternoon.* The AC was running hard, trying to cope.

The guard was on the floor. All tangled up around the legs of his stool. Short sleeve shirt. Mottled arms. Open eyes. He had been shot once in the chest and once in the head. Flies were feasting on his blood. Blue and iridescent. Crawling. Already laying eggs.

Reacher walked back to the car.

He said, "The old guy. Not going to get any older."

"Makes me feel better about the assisted homicide."

"Makes me wish I had found a butter knife in the kitchen and cut his head off."

Chang drove out the gate, and took random lefts and rights. They heard no howling sirens in the distance. No commotion. Just the perpetual Phoenix traffic, three shiny lanes, like a slow river, rolling along forever.

"Where to?" she said.

"Let's go find a cup of coffee. And there's a call you need to make."

They pulled in at a strip mall in Paradise Valley. There was a big-name coffee shop sandwiched between a store selling leather belts with silver buckles, and a store selling china plates with fancy patterns. Chang got iced coffee, and Reacher got hot. They sat at a sticky table in back.

Reacher said, "Tell Westwood to pick a hotel. Somewhere convenient, to suit his budget. Tell him we'll join him there in two hours."

"Why two hours?"

"Do you guys have a Phoenix office?"

"Of course. Lots of retired FBI in Phoenix."

"We need local knowledge."

"About the guys at the house?"

"About their boss. Who was also Hackett's boss. A provider of outsourced security, for what is no doubt a varied roster of clients. The service economy at work. Physically he sounded like a big guy to me. On the phone. And then the guy who did all the talking at the house called him the fat man. Did you hear that? He was moaning about not getting paid, and not being able to renegotiate afterward, and he said those are the fat man's rules. So we need a name. An Eastern European Phoenix-area crime boss who runs Eastern European muscle locally and people like Hackett elsewhere. And who could plausibly be called fat. Behind his back, presumably. Known locations would be good, too."

"Why?"

"I want to pay him a visit."

"Why?"

"For Emily. And for McCann's sister. And the guard in the gatehouse. And my back hurts and I have a headache now. Some things can't be allowed to continue."

Chang nodded. "And some things have side benefits."

"Exactly."

"Mother's Rest will be left wide open. We'll be canceling its security contract. By cutting off its head. Before we go back there."

"Is that the kind of information your local person would have?"

"I would, if someone called me about Seattle."

She took out her phone and dialed, first Westwood, about the hotel, and then she scrolled through her contacts and found her local number. A spare bedroom, presumably. Close by. In Mesa or Glendale or Sun City. Fitted out with matching shelves and cabinets, and a desk, and a chest of drawers. And a computer and a telephone and a fax machine and a printer. Investments, for a new career. *We have offices everywhere.*

Reacher got up and headed for the men's room, where he checked himself in the mirror, for blood, whether his or not, or other signs of mayhem. Always prudent. Once he arrested a guy who had his victim's tooth stuck in his hair, front and center, like a pale yellow bead from a salon near the beach. Then he washed his hands very thoroughly, and his wrists, and his forearms, with plenty of soap. To get rid of the gunshot residue. Also always prudent. Why make it easy?

Back at the table Chang said, "He's Ukrainian and his name is Merchenko."

Reacher said, "Is he fat?"

"Apparently he's colossal."

"Do we know where he does business?"

"He has a private club south of the airport."

"Security?"

"We don't know."

"Can we get in the club?"

"Members only."

"We could apply for jobs. I could be a bouncer."

"What could I be?"

"Depends what kind of club it is."

"I think we can guess."

"Works for me aesthetically," Reacher said. "We should go look at the place. Right now. Better to see it in the daylight."

South of the airport was not all badlands, but it was brighter and brasher than what they saw on the way. Merchenko's club was a metal building about the size of Yankee Stadium. But square. It filled its own block, sidewalk to sidewalk. The walls were painted pink and softened in shape by hundreds of giant foil balloons, also pink, some in the shape of hearts, and some in the shape of lips, all of them somehow fixed to the siding. Lacing in and out between them were miles of neon, right then bleached gray by the sun, but at night no doubt pink. What other color would the neon be? The door was pink, and it had a pink plastic awning above it, and the name of the place was *Pink*.

Chang said, "Should we risk going around the block?"

"It's early," Reacher said. "Should be safe enough."

So she turned left off the frontage, and drove down the right-hand side. Same huge size. Same pink. Same lips and hearts. Which were kind of drunk-friendly, Reacher thought. Better than swaying the other way, into traffic.

Then they saw the building did not fill the whole block. Side to side, maybe, but not front to back. It stopped short, and the rear part of the block was a delivery yard. Which made sense. A club that size would need all kinds of consumables. Like an ocean liner. And it would generate all kinds of trash and recycling. Which would need regular pick up. The yard was fenced, with some kind of superior hurricane wire, interwoven with pink screens, so it wasn't see-through. The fence was topped with floppy rolls of razor wire, to keep climbers out. But two ten-foot lengths were hinged to fold inward, which made sense because of the truck traffic in and out, food and drink and garbage.

One of those gates was open.

"Stop," Reacher said.

Chang did, and then backed up discreetly, for a better view.

She said, "I don't believe it."

Inside the gate was a line of head-high trash containers, and then next came an area outside the kitchen door, with fake green grass laid on the concrete, and a token picket fence, and a white metal garden bench, and a big canvas sun umbrella. For chefs and waiters to smoke in comfort.

Sitting on the bench was a fat man.

He was smoking a thick cigar and talking to a Hispanic guy, who was wearing a wife-beater and a do-rag, and standing rigidly to attention, his gaze fixed on a spot in the air just above the fat man's head.

But fat was too small a word, and plainly inadequate for the occasion. The man on the bench was not plump or big-boned or overweight or even obese. He was a mountain. He was huge. Over six feet, and that was side to side. He dwarfed the bench. He was wearing an ankle-length caftan, gray in color, and his knees were forced wide by his belly, and he was leaning back, perched with his ass on the very front part of the seat, because in the other direction his belly wouldn't let him fold up ninety degrees to a normal sitting position. There were no recognizable contours to his body. He was an undifferentiated triangle of flesh, with breasts the size of soft basketballs, and other unexplained lumps and bulges the size of king-size pillows. His arms were resting along the back of the bench, and huge dewlaps of fat hung down either side of dimpled elbows.

All in all he was colossal, which was the word Chang's contact had used. His head was tiny in comparison with his body. His face was pink and shiny from the sun, and his eyes were small and deep set, partly because he was squinting against the light, and partly because his face was swollen tight, as if someone had stuck a bicycle pump in his ear and given it ten long strokes. His haircut was the same scalped style as the three guys at McCann's sister's house.

Chang said, "He could be a brother or a cousin. Maybe it's a fat family."

"He looks like the boss," Reacher said. "Look how he's talking to that guy. He's giving him a real hard time."

And he was. No histrionics. No shouting. Just a steady stream of words, unending, conversational, and therefore probably all the more cruel and effective. The guy in the do-rag wasn't enjoying himself. That was for damn sure. He was holding himself rigid, staring at the air, riding it out.

Chang said, "We have to be sure. Maybe Merchenko delegates. Maybe there are underbosses. Maybe this is a brother or a cousin taking care of staff relations for him."

Reacher said, "Did your contact mention family members?"

"She didn't say."

"Can you check?"

Chang dialed her phone. Reacher watched the fat man. He wasn't going anywhere. Not yet. He was still talking. Chang asked her question and listened to the answer. She hung up the phone.

She said, "We don't know of any family members."

"He looks like the boss," Reacher said again. "Except there's no security. No guys with sunglasses and wires in their ears. There would be one at the gate, surely. Bare minimum. This guy is supposed to be a crime boss. He's in full view of the street. We're just sitting here. No one has tried to chase us away."

"Confidence, maybe," Chang said. "Or overconfidence. He thinks we're dead by now. Maybe he's got nothing else to worry about. He could be the apex predator here. Unchallenged."

"If he's the guy."

"We shouldn't assume."

"I wish we could. I could hit him from here."

"Really?"

"Figure of speech. Not with a handgun. To be certain I'd want to be closer."

"Inside the yard?"

"Ideally."

"Maybe there are guards behind the gate."

"Could be. But it's an image thing with these guys. They like to be seen behind a human wall. Or not seen."

"So maybe he's not the guy."

"He sure looks like the guy. He looks like a fat man, and it looks like he's making rules."

"We have to be certain."

"We'll never be certain. Unless I ask for ID. Which he might not have. I don't see a pocket in his dress."

"It's a caftan. Or a muumuu."

"What's a muumuu?"

"What he's wearing."

"We need to know. This could be solid gold. He's right there."

"Which is the problem. It's too good to be true."

"Could be confidence. Like you said. Could be pure routine. Maybe his security is inside. Maybe they're used to him ducking outside for a smoke. It's early, and they know no one's around. Maybe he doesn't like them close. Or maybe he thinks staff relations are best done in private."

"How long will he stay there?"

"It's a big cigar. But maybe he smokes it a bit at a time."

"We'll never have a better chance."

"And it can't last much longer."

"But we have to know."

Reacher said nothing.

The fat man kept on talking. Maybe getting more intense. He was jabbing his head with every beat. The fat on his neck was jiggling. The rest of his body was implacably still. Not made for gesture.

Reacher said, "I think he's summing up. I think he's arriving at a conclusion. We don't have much more time. We need a decision."

Chang said nothing.

Then she said, "Wait."

She raised her phone and Reacher saw a picture swim on the screen. The sidewalk, the pink fence, the open gap. An odd angle, unsteady. Camera mode. Then the trash containers, the fake garden, and the fat man.

She touched the screen and the phone made a sound like a shutter. Then she swiped and dabbed and typed and dabbed again, and the phone made a sound like a *whoosh*.

She said, "I'm asking my contact for visual ID."

Reacher said, "She better hurry. This can't last much longer."

The fat man kept on talking, and jabbing, and jiggling. The guy in the do-rag kept on taking it. Then the fat man's fingers started scrabbling at the top slat of the bench. Possibly the beginning of a long and complicated procedure designed to get himself up.

Reacher said, "We're losing him."

The fat man threw his cigar on the ground.

Chang's phone dinged.

She checked the screen.

She said, "Oh, come on."

"What?"

"She wants me to zoom in. She wants a close-up."

"What is this, the Supreme Court?"

She raised her phone again and did something with her fingers, like the opposite of a pinch, and she got the fat man as big as she could, and steadied him in the center of the frame, and clicked the picture. Reacher turned around to get the Ruger off the floor in back. Just in case. He heard the *whoosh* of her text, or her e-mail, or whatever it was. He kept the gun low and smuggled it between the seats to his lap. A solid weapon. Nothing fancy. The firearm equivalent of a domestic sedan. Like the rental Chevrolet they were sitting in. The suppressor was an aftermarket item, with a custom mount. The magazine was two rounds short. From the old guy in the booth. The chest and the head. *I hope you folks have a wonderful afternoon.*

Reacher waited.

Then the fat man levered his hips forward. A special technique, clearly. He was going to jack himself straight, like a plank, and then walk himself upright with his hands. Or push off from behind, and hope to totter away. Neither maneuver easy. But one or the other obviously possible. The guy hadn't spent his whole life in the same spot.

Reacher said, "We're out of time."

But then the Hispanic guy spoke.

Maybe a heartfelt statement, full of apology and contrition, full of promises of future reform, and likely polite, and certainly short, but apparently there was something in it the fat man wanted to either rebut or comment on further, because he settled back down, amid much asynchronous wobbling and shaking, and he started talking again.

Chang's phone dinged.

She checked the screen.

She said, "We're a hundred percent sure that's Merchenko."

Chapter 43

She drove twenty yards down the street, and then she U-turned, sidewalk to sidewalk, and came back slow, easing to a stop on the curb just shy of the first possible line of sight out the open half of the gate. Which put Reacher about sixty feet from the target. Twenty to the gate, and forty in the yard. A right-hand turn. He opened his door, and climbed out. There was no easy way to hide a silenced pistol, so he carried it down by his leg, long and threatening, mid-thigh to mid-calf. Completely unambiguous. But the acoustic benefits would be worth it, he hoped, during business hours, close to the center of America's sixth-largest city.

Six paces on the sidewalk, and then he turned in at the yard. No guards behind the gate. The trash containers dead ahead. Then the garden. Then the fat man. Still talking. Not looking. Not yet. The Hispanic guy still standing, chin up, eyes level, still taking it. Reacher kept walking, brisk but not urgent, the gun still down, his heels loud on the concrete, so loud it was impossible the fat man wasn't already staring at him, but he wasn't. He was still talking, audible now, the same flat tones from the telephone, scolding, belittling, humiliating, his head jerking above the vast wattle of his neck.

Then he was staring. He turned his head, completely independent of his immobile body, and his mouth came open, and Reacher stepped over the token foot-high picket fence, to the shiny grass, and he raised the gun, and he took one step more.

In the tall tales told by firelight there was always a brief and laconic conversation. Because the bad guy had to be told why he had to die, as if reference to injured parties like Emily Lair and Peter and Lydia McCann and the gate guard's grandchildren could conjure up spirits and console them, and also because the bad guy had to be given the chance to either repent or snarl further defiance, either of which could turn a story classic, depending on the hero's next reply.

But tales were tales, and not the real world.

Reacher said nothing, and shot the fat man in the head, twice, a double tap, *pop pop,* and then he watched the kitchen door.

Which stayed shut.

The suppressor worked pretty well, out in the open air.

Reacher turned back, and stepped over the foot-high fence.

Behind him the Hispanic guy said, "Gracias, hombre."

Reacher smiled. Pretty much manna from heaven for that guy. Pretty much exactly what he was praying for every minute. To the letter. His exact words. *Dear Lord, please send someone to shoot this bastard in the head right now.* A miracle. He would go to mass on Sunday.

Reacher walked away through the yard, the same route, the same speed, brisk but not urgent. He wiped the gun as he went, on his shirt, and dumped it in the first trash container he came to. Then he continued, out through the gate, and as soon as Chang saw him she eased the car forward, and he climbed in, and she drove away.

Westwood had chosen a fancy place out by Scottsdale, and traffic was slow because of the afternoon rush hour, so it was getting dark when they arrived. They found the guy in the bar, looking just the same, with his tousled hair and his tangled beard, in his papery clothes full of zippers, with his enormous satchel at his feet. He was reading a book about marijuana. Maybe his next subject after wheat.

Chang settled in to give him the so-far play-by-play, and Reacher went to wash more gunshot residue off his hands. When he got back Westwood asked him, "Do you believe journalists have ethics?"

Reacher said, "I'm sure it varies."

"You better hope I'm one who doesn't. Because a reasonable interpretation of what Ms. Chang just told me is you committed four homicides today."

"One of them twice," Reacher said.

"Not funny."

"Feel free to go home whenever you want. They're your book rights, not mine. Someone else can pick over the story after it happens."

"Is there a story?"

"There are only three parts we're not sure about."

"Which are?"

"The beginning, the middle, and the end."

Westwood was quiet for a long moment. Then he said, "I heard the name Merchenko before. Back when I was working on the Deep Web piece. Allegedly he offered a menu of services. He would guarantee invisibility for your web site, and he would handle problems if they arose. It was like a subscription thing. The Ukrainians were into online stuff early. I didn't write about him in the paper because nothing was proved. Legal wouldn't let me."

"How many clients did Merchenko have?"

"People said ten, or thereabouts. Kind of boutique."

"That guy wasn't boutique. He wouldn't know boutique if it ran up and bit him on his fat ankle. He had a strip club bigger than Dodger Stadium. It was pink and covered in balloons. He liked excess. He liked volume."

"Ten is what I heard."

"Then the volume must have come from revenue. Those ten clients must have been earning a fortune."

"Possible," Westwood said. "The Deep Web could be five hundred times bigger than the surface web. Very little of it makes money, I imagine, but very little of it needs to, in a universe that large. To earn a fortune overall, I mean."

Chang said, "Has the government built a search engine capable of seeing the Deep Web?"

Westwood said, "No."

"That was what McCann was calling about."

"Then he was asking the wrong question. Or the right question the wrong way. I start to tune out when a caller talks about the government. Like a litmus test for common sense. I mean, who builds search engines? Software writers, that's who. Coders. A tough project needs the best coders, and the best coders are rock stars now. They have agents and managers. They get paid a lot of money. The government can't afford them. The alternative is kids. Rock stars still in their hungry years. But the government doesn't hire them either. Too far outside its playbook. Those kids are weird."

"What would have been the right question the right way?"

"He should have looked at Silicon Valley, not the government."

"Has someone in Silicon Valley built a search engine capable of seeing the Deep Web?"

Westwood said, "No."

"McCann felt there was a hint in your piece."

"I asked what the motivation would be, for one of the big guys like Google. Which is not obvious. It would help law enforcement, but there's no money to be made. By definition. If Deep Web people wanted advertising and promotion, they could come up to the surface web and grab it right now. The point is they actively don't want it. They're actively declining to become customers. And they always will. A better search engine will drive them deeper down. That's all. It will turn into an arms race, with no money to be made, ever. Why would anyone do that?"

"McCann called you eighteen times. The hint must have been positive."

"I said someone else would do it. He must have thought I meant the government. But I didn't. The big guys like Google weren't always big. Once they were two kids in a garage. Or a dorm room. Some of them set out to be billionaires from the get-go, but some of them didn't. Some of them just got caught up in solving an interesting problem, which happened to be worth billions later. It's a personality thing. It's about the solving, not the problem. It's a compulsion. Who knows where it will strike?"

"Are you saying some kid in a dorm room has built a search engine that can see the Deep Web?"

"Not exactly," Westwood said. "Not a kid, not a dorm room, and not exactly built. Like I told you, it's a compulsion. They can't explain it. But sooner or later a problem speaks to them, and they have to solve it. They won't be beat. But nine times out of ten there's no commercial application, so they get a day job and it becomes a hobby. But they keep coming back to it every now and then. They keep tinkering. It will never be finished, because of time and money. But that's not a problem, for a hobby. In fact that's the point of a hobby."

Chang asked, "Who?"

"He's a start-up guy in Palo Alto. Already a veteran figure. Twenty-nine years old. Currently doing well with retail payment systems. But as an undergrad someone told him he couldn't search the Deep Web, and that was all she wrote. It was like a red rag to a bull. Some weird intellectual spark. No money in it, he knew. Always a hobby. He admits it was mostly arrogance. Some geeks are like that. They need to be better than the other geek."

"How far along is he now?"

"That's an impossible question. How could he know? He can see some of it, clear as day. But is that all of it, or only a tiny part?"

"I don't understand why you didn't say more in your piece. This is a big part of the story, right? Progress has been made."

"The guy wouldn't let me. He was scared of retaliation from the Deep Web people. Some of those sites really don't want to be found. He was the guy who told me about Merchenko. A hobby project makes him an easy target. He's not a team. He's just one guy. And he was right to be scared, according to you. I wasn't sure at the time. It could have been drama. They're in a world of their own."

Reacher said, "We need to meet this guy."

"Not easy."

"Right now all we have is second-hand hearsay. But the consensus seems to be that Michael McCann used the Deep Web, and Michael McCann got off a train in a place called Mother's Rest. We need to know if one thing led to the other. Did he get off the train because of the internet, or was he going to get off anyway?"

"You think Mother's Rest is luring people in through the Deep Web?"

"We saw two people arrive by train. They spent a night in the motel and were driven away the next morning in a white Cadillac."

Chang said, "They don't even have cell service. They can't be an internet powerhouse, surely."

Westwood paused a beat, and then he said, "We should go somewhere more private."

Twenty miles south of Mother's Rest, the man with the ironed jeans and the blow-dried hair was pacing. Waiting for his phone to ring. Trying not to jump the gun. The last time he called ahead of schedule he had been made to feel small. *Let us do what we're good at, OK?* Not that they had been. Not yet.

Couldn't wait.

He picked up the phone.

He dialed.

He got no answer.

Westwood had called ahead with the reservations, not knowing, so he had gotten Reacher and Chang a room each. On realizing his mistake he was neither embarrassed nor worried about the overspend. He simply chose the room with the stronger wifi and called it an office. He pulled his metal computer out of his bag and set it up on a desk. Reacher and Chang sat on the bed.

Westwood said, "You mentioned Mother's Rest before. Way back at the beginning. And you were right. A smart science editor would try to get a jump. So I did. It's a grain-loading station and a trading post. There's some technical stuff in the record. But a good reporter likes two sources. So I checked Google Earth, and sure enough, it's right there on the satellite pictures. Right where it should be. And it looks exactly like a grain-loading station and a trading post. But it's in the middle of absolutely nowhere. It's like LA County had one crossroads and the rest of it was empty. It was fascinating. So I messed around a little. I zoomed out to check how far it was from anywhere else, just for the fun of it, and I happened to see a neighbor about twenty miles south. The only neighbor. Even more isolated. So naturally I zoomed in to take a look."

He turned his computer to face the bed.

He said, "And this is what I saw."

What he saw was bright daylight, of course, even though it was dark outside. Satellite photographs were not live. Or up to date, necessarily. Things can change. Or not. Reacher guessed the things on the screen hadn't changed in years. He was seeing a farm, surrounded by a sea of wheat. The farm had a dwelling and a bunch of outbuildings. As far as could be told from a vertical straight-down harshly-shadowed view, everything looked solid and squared away. The place was more or less self-sufficient. There were hogs and chickens and vegetable gardens. There was what looked like a generator building, for electricity. The house itself looked sturdy. It had a place to park cars at one end, and four satellite dishes at the other. And what looked like a well. And a phone line.

Westwood said, "I remembered the satellite dishes later. What are they for?"

Reacher said, "TV."

"Two of them are. The other two are looking at different birds."

"Foreign TV."

"Or satellite internet, maybe. All the bandwidth they want to pay for. Very fast. Doubled up for safety. With their own electricity. That would be an internet powerhouse right there."

"Can we tell by the way the dishes are set?"

"We'd need to know what day and time Google clicked the picture. To work out the angle of the shadows."

"Then we need to look from the inside. We need the search engine. If they're posting from there, we need to read what they're saying."

"All I can do is ask."

"Tell him Merchenko is dead. Tell him you had him whacked, as a service to software developers everywhere. Tell him he owes you a favor."

Westwood said nothing.

Reacher turned back to the screen.

He said, "Where is this place exactly?"

Westwood said, "Twenty miles south of Mother's Rest," and he leaned around from behind and pinched and swiped, making the farm smaller and the wheat bigger, no doubt intending to continue until Mother's Rest itself slid into view above, to show the distant geographic relationship. But before that happened the picture was clipped across the bottom corner by a dead-straight line, and Reacher said, "What's that?"

Westwood said, "The railroad track."

"Show me."

So Westwood came around from behind the screen and set it up properly. The farm and the railroad, centered, in their correct proportions. Maybe three-quarters of a mile apart. The middle distance, for most human eyes.

Reacher said, "I remember that farm. From when I arrived. It was the first human habitation the train passed in hours. Twenty miles before it finally got to Mother's Rest. They were running a machine with lights. A tractor, maybe. At midnight."

"Is that normal?"

"I have no idea."

Chang said, "We figured the Cadillac drove twenty miles. Remember that? Twenty miles there, and twenty miles back. Now we know where it was going. There's nowhere else it could go, twenty miles from Mother's Rest. So that's where the folks from the train went. The man and the woman, with their bags. But then where?"

No one answered.

Westwood said, "Do farmers use the Deep Web?"

"Someone does," Reacher said. "We need the search engine."

"The guy gets paid for his time."

"No one likes to work for free. That's something I learned."

"He won't come here. We'll have to go to San Francisco."

"Like it's still 1967."

"What?"

Reacher said, "Nothing."

Ten minutes later he was alone with Chang, in the room with the weaker wifi.

Chapter 44

They woke early the next morning, with open drapes and things on their minds, the same way they had the previous morning in Chicago, just twenty-four hours before. Reacher was revising his theory again, spellbound with the upward progression. It was beyond expectation. Maybe beyond comprehension. Whereas Chang was preoccupied with getting out of town. She was watching morning television on a local Phoenix affiliate, which had shoved recipes and fashion aside in favor of crime. One presenter was reporting on the fatal shooting of a suspected organized crime figure behind a downtown strip club, which involved much breathless speculation laid over meaningless pictures, mostly of the closed gate in the pink fence, above a ticker that said *Moscow Comes to Phoenix,* which Reacher figured would annoy Ukrainians everywhere, the two countries being entirely separate now, and proud of it, at least in one direction.

The other presenter had the bigger story. No longer *a home invasion turned tragic tonight,* because tonight was now yesterday, and tragic was now inspiring. Apparently a well-respected local doctor residing at the address in question had used a home-defense weapon and killed three intruders, thereby saving his family members from a fate worse than death. Evan Lair was seen on camera, in the far distance, at the limit of a shaky zoom, waving questions away. His reluctance to talk was seen as sturdy old-fashioned modesty. His legend was building. He was halfway to becoming the badass doc, buoyed up by grainy nighttime videotape of gurneys coming out of the house, bathed in flashing red light. There were distant live shots of Emily, now out of the shirt and bikini, now in jeans and a sweater, and Lydia, who was looking down at the ground.

Then a third presenter broke in to say she was hearing from the police department that the events might be linked, in that the three dead men from the house were known associates of the dead man at the strip club. And a fourth presenter broke in to say she had early word from the DA's office, that the shootings at the house would likely be seen as justified, and that as far as the strip club incident was concerned, the murder weapon had been recovered from a nearby garbage receptacle, but there were no fingerprints on it, and therefore there were no suspects at this time, and the inquiry would continue.

Up next, ten things to do with chicken.

Chang said, "You OK?"

Reacher said, "Top of the world. Except my head still hurts."

"No reaction?"

"To what?"

She pointed at the screen. "All that."

"My ears are still ringing a bit."

"That's not what I mean."

"I leave people alone if they leave me alone. Their risk, not mine."

"You're not upset?"

"Are you?"

"What was the machine you saw at the farm at midnight?"

"It was a dot in the distance. It had a light bar. Like a bull bar, but above the cab. Four rectangular lights, very bright. Could have been a jacked-up pick-up truck. More likely a tractor. It was working hard. I could see exhaust smoke in the lights."

"Could it have been a backhoe?"

"Why?"

"That was the day Keever disappeared."

Reacher said, "It could have been a backhoe."

"That's why I'm not upset. It could have been me, if things had been different. Suppose Michael had gone missing in Seattle. McCann would have called me, and then later I might have called Keever, for back-up. Right now you could be hanging out with him, looking for me."

"Perish the thought."

"Could have happened."

"You would have handled it better."

"Keever was a smart guy."

"Was?"

"I guess I have to face it."

"Smart, but not smart enough. He made a mistake. You might have avoided it."

"What mistake?"

"Maybe the same mistake I'm about to make. He underestimated them. If they buried him on the farm with the backhoe, then Merchenko wasn't involved. Not at that stage. That was all their own work. No help required. Maybe they're better than we think."

"They didn't look it."

"Hope for the best, plan for the worst."

That morning eight men met at the counter inside the Mother's Rest dry goods store. As before, the store owner was already there, still in two shirts, still unkempt and unshaven. As before, the first in to join him was the spare-parts guy from the irrigation store, and then came the Cadillac driver from the FedEx store, and the one-eyed clerk from the motel, and the hog farmer, and the counterman from the diner, and the Moynahan who had gotten kicked in the balls and had his gun taken.

The eighth man arrived five minutes later, with his ironed jeans and his blow-dried hair. The first seven guys said nothing. They waited for him to speak.

He said, "The news is not good. Our faith was misplaced. The menu system did not function as expected. It did not do the job for us. As of now we're on our own."

Some shuffling, from the first seven. Not yet worry, but indignation. As in, *it was all his own idea when it was looking good. Now it's we and us and ours?* The hog farmer said, "Is that what I saw on CNN this morning? From Phoenix? The Russian guy?"

"He was Ukrainian. And it wasn't just him. The other three were his, too."

"What about the first one? Was his name Hackett?"

"He's in the hospital in Chicago. With a cop at the door."

"So none of them got the job done?"

"I told you that."

"Going outside of us was a big step."

"It cost us nothing. Except money. They're still out there, but they always were out there. They left, and now they're coming back. We'll deal with them here."

"They'll bring the cops."

"I don't think so. They put Hackett in the hospital. I know that for sure. It was probably them in Phoenix, too. Which means they can't talk to the cops. Any police department in the country would arrest them immediately. As a precaution. Until the smoke cleared. They'll come here alone."

More shuffling, from the first seven.

The Cadillac driver asked, "When will they come?"

The man with the jeans and the hair said, "Soon, I expect. But we all know the plan. And we all know it works. We'll see them coming. We'll be ready."

Reacher and Chang joined Westwood downstairs for breakfast, and Westwood said he had called the guy in Palo Alto and set something up for happy hour. In Menlo Park. Although he expected the guy to be late. He was that kind of guy. Then he had booked flights from Sky Harbor to SFO. Three seats in business class, all that remained. And a hotel. Two rooms only, which helped. His department's budget was cut every year. Reacher thought he had the nervous air of a gambler, deep in the hole, but about to win big.

When it was time they took a cab to the airport, where their fancy tickets got them in a lounge, where Reacher ate breakfast again, because it was free. They boarded the plane at the head of the line, and got a drink before taxi and takeoff. Better than the rows in back. Even the exit rows.

The flight itself was neither long nor short, but somewhere in between. Not a hop or a skip, but not a major portion of the earth's circumference either. Less than New York to Chicago. The cab ride was easy, because it was basically out of town, not that the Santa Clara Valley was sleepy anymore. It was the center of the world, all the way past Mountain View, and people drove like they knew it. The upcoming happy hour was in a bar near a bookstore in Menlo Park, and they found it at the second attempt. They were early, but not early enough to get to the hotel and back, so they paid off the cab and got out.

The bar caused a moment of psychic concern, because every inch of it was painted red, and its name was *Red,* and the back of Reacher's brain spun through fantastical conceits, trying to work out how Westwood was either a cop or a bad guy, tormenting him with the ghost of *Pink,* like something out of Shakespeare or Sherlock Holmes, but then he calmed down and figured the geek would have chosen the spot, and therefore the connection was coincidental. And not exact, anyway. The place was ironic, not tacky. The paint had a somber mid-century tone. Like military issue. There were dirty white-stenciled hammers and sickles, distressed and abraded to make them look old, and framed headlines from *Pravda,* and Red Army helmets, all battered and scratched. The sign at the door was written with a backward R, to make it look Russian, which caused a minor echo of panic. Was it a reference to Merchenko? No, surely Westwood knew the difference between Russia and Ukraine. But were there Ukrainian-themed bars, for a pedantic tormentor? Or would he have to settle for Russian anyway?

No, the geek chose it.

Chang said, "You OK?"

Reacher said, "Thinking too hard. Bad habit. Bad as not thinking at all."

"Let's wait in the bookstore."

Reacher tripped at the curb. Just a stumble. He didn't go down. More of a scuff than a trip. As if there was a lump, or an uneven surface. He looked back. Maybe. Maybe not.

Chang said, "You OK?"

He said, "I'm fine."

Westwood said he had been in the bookstore before. A signing, for an anthology he was in. Science journalism. An award-winning piece. The store was a cool place, in every way, from its refrigerated temperature to its customers. Westwood wandered one way, and Chang another. Reacher looked at the books on the tables. He read when he could, mostly through the vast national library of lost and forgotten volumes. Battered paperbacks mostly, all curled and furry, found in waiting rooms or on buses, or on the porches of out-of-the-way motels, read and enjoyed and left somewhere else for the next guy. He liked fiction better than fact, because fact often wasn't. Like most people he knew a couple of things for sure, up close and eyeballed, and when he saw them in books they were wrong. So he liked made-up stories better, because everyone knew where they were from the get-go. He wasn't strict about genre. Either shit happened, or it didn't.

Chang came back, and then Westwood, and they wandered back to the bar and got ready to wait. Being early gave them a choice of tables, and they took a four-top near a window. Reacher got coffee, and the others got sodas.

Westwood said, "This won't be good news, I'm afraid. Even if the guy bites. The Deep Web is not an attractive place, overall. So they tell me. Not that I spend time there myself. But you might not like what you see."

Reacher said, "It's a free country. And Michael was McCann's son, not mine. I don't care what he was into."

A clock on the wall ticked up to a Cyrillic twelve, the top of the hour, and vodka went down in price by half. Happy hour. The first new person through the door was a young woman in her twenties, flushed, unmistakably new at something, but good at it.

The second person through the door was the guy from Palo Alto.

Dead on time. Not late at all. He was small, white as a sheet, thin as a specter, always moving, even when he was still. The twenty-nine-year-old veteran. He was dressed all in black. He saw Westwood and headed over. He nodded three ways and sat down. He said, "The Valley likes irony, but you got to agree happy hour in a Soviet shrine is the ultimate contradiction in terms. And speaking of the former USSR, my blog alerts tell me a Ukrainian named Merchenko was a mob hit last night. Which is a happy coincidence. But he will be replaced. The market will fill the void. So I'm still not going public."

Westwood said, "Neither are we. Not until long afterward, in the newspaper. By which time there will be so much to bury you won't even be close to the top of the list. You have my word. You won't be public. All we need is to search. In private. For a missing individual and his possible destination."

"Search where?"

"Chat rooms, mostly. Maybe commercial web sites."

"I don't want to become a public resource."

"I'm happy not to pay you."

"Then I would be doing it for friendship, which makes the obligation worse."

Reacher said, "Can you do it? If you wanted to?"

The guy said, "I've been doing it since it was called the undernet. And the invisible web. It got harder, but I got better."

"The destination might be hard to crack."

"Cracking is easy. It's finding that's hard."

"So what would get you to give us an hour of your time? Apart from getting paid?"

"Do you have a motive, apart from getting paid? Does anyone, really?"

"As a matter of fact I'm not getting paid."

"Then why are you doing it?"

"Because some guy thinks he's pretty damn smart."

"But you're smarter? And you have to prove it?"

"I don't have to prove it. I want to prove it. Now and then. Out of respect. For the people who really are smart. Standards should mean something."

"You're trying to steer me to the same conclusion. A battle of egos. Me against them, as coders. Good try. You know me well, even though we've only just met. But I've gone beyond. I'm happy there. I'm better than them. I know that. I'm secure in that knowledge. I no longer feel the desire to show it. Not even now and then. Not even out of respect. Not that I don't respect the way you feel. The old me would have agreed with you."

"What would the new me agree with?"

"Tell me about the missing individual. Is he interesting?"

"Thirty-five-year-old male, crippled by what the doctors call anhedonia, and his aunt calls his happiness meter stuck on zero. Otherwise normal IQ. Functional some of the time."

"Lived alone?"

Reacher nodded. "In sheltered housing."

"Disappeared?"

"Yes."

"Sudden new friend prior to disappearance?"

"Yes."

The guy said, "Thirty-two seconds."

"For what?"

"I'll find him in the Deep Web inside thirty-two seconds. I know where to look."

"When can you do it?"

"Tell me about the aunt."

"She married up. A doctor. She has a beautiful daughter. But she still loves her nephew. And seems to understand him."

"I like her image of the happiness meter."

"We agreed mine is four to nine."

"I've gone beyond. I hit ten now. All the time."

"That's the molly talking."

"The what?"

"I read it in the paper."

"I haven't taken molly for two years."

"Something else now?"

"Everything else now. Got some stress."

"Just remember, speed kills. That's what they told us, back in the day."

"I won't go public. You understand what that means?"

Reacher nodded. "There won't be a trial."

"Was it you with Merchenko?"

"Admit nothing, even on your deathbed. You might suddenly get better."

"One night only," the guy said. "No coming back to check on things. I need space of my own."

"When can you do it?"

"Now, if you like."

"Where?"

"At my house. You're all invited."

Chapter 45

The guy from Palo Alto had a thing on his phone that summoned cars to the curb within minutes. Riding four to a car was deemed unseemly, so he pressed twice and got two. He rode with Westwood, to catch up on old times, and Reacher and Chang followed, in a Town Car all their own. The guy's house was a 1950s box remodeled in the 1970s to look like the 1930s. Reacher figured it had a triple layer of ironic authenticity all its own, and was therefore worth more than all the money he had made in his life.

Inside it was clean and all silver and black. Reacher had been expecting a tangled riot of computer gear, like they had seen in McCann's apartment in Chicago, but in the den there was nothing but a small glass table and a lone no-brand desktop. There was a tower unit, and a screen, and a keyboard, and a trackball, none of which matched. There were only five wires, all cut to the right length, none tangled, all neatly placed.

The guy said, "I built it myself. There are various technical hurdles and some serious data incompatibilities to overcome. It's like visiting a foreign country. You have to learn their language. And their customs, more importantly. I wrote some browser software. Based on

Tor, which is what they all use. Which was written by the United States Naval Research Laboratory, ironically. To provide a safe haven for political dissidents and whistleblowers, all around the world. Which is the law of unintended consequences, right there, biting the world in the ass. Tor stands for The Onion Router. Because that's what we're dealing with here. Layers upon layers upon layers, like the layers of an onion, in the Deep Web itself, and inside all of its separate sites."

He sat down and fired up his machine. There was no fancy stuff on the screen. No pictures of outer space, no icons. Just short lines of green writing on a black field. All business, like an airline check-in desk, or a car rental counter.

The guy said, "What's the missing individual's name?"

Chang said, "Michael McCann."

"Social Security Number?"

"Don't know."

"Home address?"

"Don't know."

"Not good," the guy said. "There are preliminary steps to be taken. I need what I call his internet fingerprint. It's an algorithm I wrote. Some of this, some of that. The precise minimum required to be definitive. Elegant, really. We can start with something as simple as his cable bill. But there are other ways. Do we know his next of kin?"

"That would be his father, Peter McCann. His mother is long dead."

"Do we have an address for Peter McCann?"

Chang told him. The undistinguished brownstone, on the undistinguished street. Lincoln Park, Chicago. Apartment 32. The guy typed a command and what looked like a portal appeared, into the Social Security Administration's mainframe. The real government deal. Reacher glanced at Chang, and she nodded, as if to say *it's OK, I have one, too.* The guy entered Peter McCann's data and found his Social Security Number instantly, which instantly led to Michael's, because they were nominated for each other's survivor benefits. Next of kin. Michael's Social Security Number led to his address, which was also in Lincoln Park, Chicago.

Then the guy came out of Social Security, and went into some other complex database. He entered Michael McCann's Social Security Number, and his address, and the screen re-drew into a long list of alphanumeric codes. The internet fingerprint. Michael McCann, and no one else.

The guy typed a new command, and the screen came up with a title page, crudely formatted out of plain green writing on a black background, but with tabs and spaces and centering, so that it looked vaguely like a commercial product. Or a prototype. Which it was, Reacher supposed. In a way. Potentially. It looked inviting enough. Like bright emeralds on velvet. The most prominent word on the page was *Bathyscaphe*.

"Get it?" the guy said.

"A submarine," Chang said. "Capable of going all the way to the ocean bed."

"Originally I called it Nemo. After the guy in *Twenty Thousand Leagues Under The Sea*. He commands a submarine named Nautilus. I liked him because nemo is Latin for nobody. Which seemed appropriate. But then they made a movie about a fish. Which ruined it."

He typed another command, and a search box came up.

He said, "OK, start your engines. Thirty-two seconds is the wager."

He pasted a whole lot of stuff into the search box. Not Michael McCann's name, but some of the long alphanumeric codes from the previous database. The fingerprint. Better than a name, presumably.

The guy clicked the go tab, and a clock started running in Reacher's head.

Five seconds.

The guy said, "One day it will be much faster. The raw search is good, but the page search is piped out to the find-and-replace function from an old word processor."

Twelve seconds.

The guy said, "But please don't get the wrong impression. In absolute terms it's fast enough. But the Deep Web is very big. That's the issue. And I don't have Google's advantages. No one is clamoring for my attention. They want the opposite. But I'm down there. Right now. I'm among them. They can't see me, but I can see them."

Twenty-five seconds.

The guy said nothing.

Then the search stopped.

The screen changed to a list of links.

"We found him," the guy said. "Twenty-six seconds. Well below the promised thirty-two."

"Pretty good," Reacher said.

"I gambled. I narrowed the field. I knew where I might find him."

"Which was where?"

"I hope Mr. Westwood explained about me. The rabbit holes we go down are sometimes chosen for us. Not necessarily on merit."

Reacher said, "The solving, not the problem."

"Searching the Deep Web is technically elegant, but being in it can be unpleasant. It has a bit of everything, but ultimately it's a three-legged stool. A third of it is a vast criminal marketplace, where everything is for sale, from your credit card number to murder. There are auction sites where hit men compete for jobs. Lowest bid wins. There are sites where you can specify how your wife should die, and there are contractors who will give you a custom quote."

Chang asked, "Where did you find Michael McCann?"

The guy said, "The second leg of the Deep Web stool is pornography of the nastiest sort. Stomach-turning, even for me, and I'm not exactly a mainstream person."

"Is that what he was into?"

"No, I found him in the third leg."

"Which is what?"

"It was an easy guess. Because of the anhedonia. Because of the happiness meter stuck on zero. The third leg of the Deep Web is suicide."

* * *

The guy from Palo Alto said, "I browse those boards from time to time. As an anthropologist, I hope, not a voyeur. Not a spectator at the zoo. I imagine Michael McCann was on the low end of typical. Born depressed, and if his mother is long dead, she died when he was young. Not a good combination. I'm sure he wanted it all to end. Every day. We can't imagine how sure and certain these people are. These are not temporary ups and downs. These people hate their lives, deeply and sincerely, and they want them to stop. They want to catch the bus. That's the phrase they use. They want to catch the bus out of town. But it's a big step. Some of the boards are about support. Which is why I asked about the sudden new friend. They call them suicide partners. They do it together. They hold hands and jump, so to speak. The boards hook them up. There's a lot of discussion about compatibility. Is Michael's partner missing, too?"

Chang said, "We don't know. We don't even know if it was a man or a woman. Near Tulsa, Oklahoma, we think."

Westwood said, "What do they talk about on the other boards?"

"They talk about how. Endlessly. That's their big question. There's plenty of data out there. They discuss it like scripture. Best of all is a shotgun to the head. Instantaneous, as far as we know, and ninety-nine percent effective. A handgun in the mouth is ninety-seven percent. Shotgun to the chest, ninety-six, and a handgun to the chest about eighty-nine. Which is about the same as hanging yourself. Setting yourself on fire scores about seventy-six. Setting fire to your house is about seventy-three. No one really wants to go lower than that. Meanwhile jumping in front of a train is back up there at ninety-six, and jumping off the roof is at ninety-three, and driving into a bridge support is about seventy-eight. But make sure you wear your seatbelt. You can get thrown clear. Unrestrained drivers score about seventy straight. You have to be there, when the engine comes in through the dashboard. And last but not least, ever popular, right back at the top, second only to the shotgun, is cyanide. Better than ninety-seven percent effective, in about two minutes. But it's two minutes of hideous agony. And that's the problem right there. All the best ways are violent. Some folks can't handle that. Men as well as women. And some don't have the circumstances. If you live in the city, you don't have your uncle's old varmint gun in the back of the barn. If you can't drag yourself to the bathroom, how can you drag yourself to the railroad track?"

"So what do they do?"

"They talk, endlessly. About the holy grail. Swift and painless. Like falling asleep and never waking up. That's what they're looking for. They had it once. Or their parents did. A bottle of sleeping pills, and a glass of scotch. Or a hosepipe through the window of the family Buick. You fall asleep and you never wake up. Guaranteed. But not anymore. Now the family Buick has a catalytic converter. No more carbon monoxide. Not enough, anyway. You get a headache and a rash. Your scotch is the same as ever, but your sleeping pills aren't. They're safe now. Take them all at once, and you'll sleep a day and a half, but you won't wake up dead. Life has gotten very protected in America. Which gives these folks a problem. It's what drove them to the Deep Web in the first place. The stigma, of course, but mostly because the solutions to their problems started to look like gray areas. In the surface world there would have been liability issues, and social responsibility, and all the rest of that lawyer stuff. As in, now your Buick is no good anymore, the new preferred source of carbon monoxide is the little hibachi grills you buy at the supermarket. A foil pan with charcoal, and a metal grill, all shrink-wrapped and ready to go. You get six or eight in your bedroom, and you put them high on shelves, and you light them all up, and the monoxide pours out, like liquid, heavier than air, and it pools on your bedroom floor, and the level rises up to the bed, and it snuffs you out. Swift and painless. Like falling asleep and never waking up. The holy grail. Except also one of the grills probably sets the wall on fire and the building burns down and whoever suggested the method gets hit by five hundred lawsuits."

Chang said, "What other laws are they breaking?"

"It comes back to what they can handle. Even the hosepipe through the window was too rough for some. It's cold in the garage, and it's uncomfortable in the car, and the whole thing looks weird. Although carbon monoxide leaves a good-looking corpse. Cherry red. Looks healthy. Makes the mortician's job very easy. But some folks want to die at home. Inside the house. The holy grail is in bed. So the next new thing was gas of a different kind. Plus an interesting medical fact. May I ask you a question? If you have to hold your breath too long, what is it that makes you desperate to breathe again?"

"I'm running out of oxygen, I guess."

"That's the interesting fact. It isn't the absence of oxygen. It's the presence of carbon dioxide. Kind of the same thing, but not exactly. The point is, you could suck up any kind of gas, and as long as it wasn't carbon dioxide, your brain would be happy. You could have a chest full of nitrogen, no oxygen at all, about to kill you stone dead, and your lungs would say, hey man, we're cool, no carbon dioxide here, no need for us to start pumping again until we see some. Which they never will, because you'll never breathe again. Because you'll never need to. Because you have no carbon dioxide. And so on. So those folks started sniffing nitrogen, but you have to go to the welding shop and the cylinders are too heavy to lift, so then they tried helium from the balloon store, but you needed masks and tubes, and the whole thing still looks weird, so in the end most folks won't be satisfied with anything less than the old-fashioned bottle of pills and the glass of scotch. Exactly like it used to be. Except it can't be anymore. Those pills were most likely either Nembutal or Secanol, and both of those substances are tightly controlled now. There's no way to get them. Except illegally, of course, way down where no one can see you. There are sources. The holy grail. Most of the offers are scams, naturally. Powdered Nembutal from China, and so on. Dissolve in water or fruit juice. Maybe eight or nine hundred bucks for a lethal dose. Some poor desperate soul takes the cash to Money-Gram and sends it off, and then waits at home, anxious and tormented, and never sees any powdered Nembutal from China, because there never was any. The powder in the on-line photograph was talc, and the prescription bottle was for something else entirely. Which I felt was a new low, in the end. They're preying on the last hopes of suicidal people."

Reacher said, "But you imply there are honest offers, too. You said most, not all."

"Secanol has gone completely. Nembutal is the last chance. Now the holy grail all by itself. The only legal use for Nembutal in the United States is large-animal euthanasia. Some gets stolen, and some veterinarians are bent. Why not? A lethal dose for a human would be two small bottles. Easy to ship. FedEx would take care of it. Nine hundred bucks, for what gets splashed on the floor when you're killing a mule. You'll take that deal."

He saw houses still lived in, and houses converted to offices, for seed merchants and fertilizer dealers and a large-animal veterinarian.

Reacher said, "Show us exactly where Michael McCann was posting. We want to read what he said."

Chapter 46

They pulled chairs close to the glass table and crowded around the screen to read. Michael McCann was signed up for two suicide boards. In both cases he posted under the name of Mike. He wrote flatly, laboriously, as if numbed, as if exhausted by his burdens. His spelling was good, and his grammar was formal. Not naturally, Reacher thought, but as if he had been told there was a special way to do it, out in the public domain. Like public speaking. You put on a shirt and tie.

The first board was the hook-up board. Michael was looking for a sympathetic companion. Not that he needed help. Not all of the time. More that he felt he could give it. At least some of the time. In many months he had brief conversations with two candidates, and then seemed to settle on a third, who went by the name of Exit. They began messaging often.

Meanwhile the second board was the how board, which sometimes strayed into other discussions. Michael contributed now and then, with measured words, and never with anger or haste. He defended his right to catch the bus. He showed up in a thread about how to take Nembutal. He was anxious for guidance. In its commercial form its taste was said to be bitter. Best to mask it with juice, or chase it with scotch, which enhanced its efficiency anyway. It was always wise to take an anti-emetic beforehand, like a sea-sickness pill. No one wanted to throw up and be left with a less-than-fatal dose on board. No one wanted to wake up twenty hours later, with it all to do again.

Michael also commented in a thread about the reliability of Nembutal suppliers. He had been ripped off more than once. The market was a jungle. All a con man needed was a good web site. No one could know exactly who he was. A guy in Thailand was supposed to be kosher. And then someone posted that MR had delivered, exactly as promised, genuine stuff that tested right. Another poster backed him up. MR were good people, he said. The real deal. Michael queried: *MR?* The first guy came back to the board and said: *Mother's Rest.*

Then over on the hook-up board, a day later, Michael told Exit he had checked the Mother's Rest web site, and he thought Exit should look at it too, because there was much to discuss, especially on level five.

No further details.

Reacher said, "What's level five?"

The guy from Palo Alto said, "Think of the onion. Many layers. Deeper and deeper. The Web itself, and every site on it. The sign-in page is usually level two. Level four is usually the first page of merchandise. Therefore level five is likely to be special merchandise."

On the board, Exit had replied, and said level five was interesting. But that was late in the sequence, and the discussion went no further. It was overtaken by Michael's physical move to Oklahoma. To Exit's place, near Tulsa. His suicide partner. To get ready. Reacher assumed the discussion was continued in person.

He said, "Can we take a look at the Mother's Rest web site?"

The guy said, "We'd have to find it first."

"You did OK before. You were six seconds under."

"I knew where to look. This next one will be measured in minutes. If we're lucky."

"How many minutes? What's the wager?"

"Twenty," the guy said.

He typed commands and loaded up with search terms and keywords. He hit the go tab, and the clock in Reacher's head started running. Everyone pushed back from the glass table, and stretched, and got comfortable, and got ready to wait.

Westwood said, "The two hundred deaths could be two hundred Nembutal customers. I'm not sure what to think about it. From a news perspective, I mean. Is it a scandal? It's legal in Washington and Oregon."

"Not the same thing," the guy from Palo Alto said. "You need two doctors to sign off. You need to be about a hundred years old with a terminal disease. These guys wouldn't qualify. And mostly they're pissed about it."

"Then it becomes an ethical debate. Do we respect a person's choices, plain and simple, or do we feel obliged to judge his reasons?"

"Not his reasons," Chang said. "That's too intrusive. But I think we should judge his commitment. There's a big difference between a short-term panic and a long-term need. Maybe commitment proves reasons. If you hang in there through all the hoops, it must really mean something to you."

"Then perhaps this current system is a good thing. In its way. Inadvertently. There are plenty of hoops. They're certainly earning it."

Reacher said, "But what is Mother's Rest earning? Two hundred Nembutal shipments at nine hundred bucks a pop is less than two hundred grand. Over the whole life of the project, presumably. Less the wholesale cost and the shipping. That's a hobby. And you can't pay guys like Merchenko out of hobby money. Something else is going on there. Has to be. Because."

He stopped talking.

Chang said, "Because what?"

"We think the guy was killed there."

"What guy?"

"At the beginning. With the backhoe."

"Keever?"

"Yeah, Keever. Why kill Keever over a hobby? There has to be more."

"Level five could be special merchandise. Could be worth more."

Reacher glanced at the screen. Still searching. Seven minutes gone. He said, "I'm trying to imagine what could be so special. To be worth Merchenko money."

The guy from Palo Alto said, "They all have my sympathy."

Reacher said, "Mine, too. I take the point about burning down the building with hibachi grills. But otherwise we should let them do what they want. They didn't ask to be born. It's like taking a sweater back to the store."

Chang said, "Except it shouldn't be either too easy or too difficult. Which somehow obliges the rest of us to set the bar. Is that fair on any of us?"

Westwood said, "This is exactly what I was afraid of. It's an ethical debate. I could have written it in my office. On standby for a slow month. There was no need to spend travel money. I'm going to get my butt kicked for this."

Twelve minutes gone.

They got drinks, not exactly served, but collected from the kitchen. Which was very retro. It looked vaguely like some of the places Reacher could remember as a kid. Family quarters on a dozen bases all around the world, different weather outside the window, same cabinets in the kitchen. Some mothers made a big show of scrubbing them down with disinfectant, immediately on the first morning, but Reacher's mother was French and believed in acquired immunity. Which had worked, generally. Although his brother had gotten sick once. More likely a restaurant. He was starting to date.

Chang said, "You OK?"

He said, "I'm fine."

Eighteen minutes gone.

They went back to the den, and the clock ticked on. Nineteen minutes. The guy from Palo Alto said, "We didn't agree on the stakes. For the wager."

Reacher said, "What did we say the first time?"

"We didn't."

Twenty minutes gone.

Reacher said, "We don't want to outstay our welcome."

The guy said, "The program will get there. I'm a better geek than they are."

"What's the longest search you've ever run?"

"Nineteen hours."

"What did you find?"

"The president's schedule on an assassin site."

"Of the United States?"

"The very same. And the schedule was current when I started the search."

"Did you call it in?"

"That was a dilemma. I'm not a public resource. And as a matter of fact there was no more information to be had. A site that took me nineteen hours to find would have so many mirrors and decoys the servers might as well be on Venus or Mars. But the Secret Service wouldn't have taken that on trust. They'd have torn my stuff apart for their own guys to look at. They'd have tied me up for a year, talking and consulting. So no, I didn't call it in."

"And nothing happened."

"Thankfully."

Twenty-seven minutes.

Still searching.

Then the search stopped.

The screen changed to a list of links.

Chapter 47

The list of links showed one direct URL for the Mother's
Rest web site, and four sub-pages, and one external reference, which
the guy from Palo Alto wanted to check first, because he said it was
unusual. He managed to retrieve an isolated chat-room comment
made by a poster named Blood. It said *I hear Mother's Rest has good
stuff.* It was on a secure board the guy didn't recognize. The context
wasn't clear. But it wasn't a suicide board. It belonged to some other
community. An enthusiast site, by the feel of it.

No other data.

Dead end.

The guy from Palo Alto said, "We'll go straight to the mothership.
No pun intended."

He didn't use the trackball. It wasn't that kind of software. It was
all typed commands. The guy seemed to like it that way. Old school.
He was a veteran. And he was fast. His bone-white fingers pattered
up and down. Almost a blur.

The screen re-drew into a full color, full service web site.

There was a photograph.

The photograph was of a road running dead straight ahead,

through an infinite sea of wheat, forever, until it disappeared in a golden haze on the horizon, at that point as narrow as a needle. It was the old wagon train trail. The road west out of Mother's Rest.

And it was an allegory, obviously. At the top of the page was written: *Take The Journey With Us*. At the bottom was written: *Mother's Rest. At Last.*

The first sub-page link was an *About Us* piece. They were a community dedicated to providing end of life choices. The very best goods, services, care, and concern were solemnly promised. Trust was guaranteed. Discretion was a given.

The second sub-page link was the sign-in page. For community members. User name and password. Probably hard to break. But no need, because the third link bypassed it altogether, and led straight down to level four.

The first page of merchandise.

There were three items on offer. First was a non-sterile oral Nembutal solution in a 50ml bottle, going for $200. Second was an injectable Nembutal solution in a 100ml bottle for $387. Third was a sterile oral Nembutal solution in a 100ml bottle for $450. Safely lethal doses were quoted as 30ml through a needle, or 200ml by mouth. Time to a deep sleep was quoted as less than a minute, and time to death was quoted as less than twenty. Reacher figured the injectable solution was a hard sell. If a guy was into needles, he could OD on heroin at a tenth of the price. He figured the sterile oral would be the best seller. Nine hundred bucks for a peaceful exit. Sterile sounded clean, somehow. The holy grail. But the non-sterile was a better value. Only eight hundred, at the risk of getting stomach flu the day after you were dead.

Delivery was thirty bucks, with a tracking number, and payment of the whole balance was required prior to dispatch, through Western Union or MoneyGram. Checks or money orders were not accepted. The Nembutal would arrive in a plain package. It should not be refrigerated, but kept tightly sealed and stored in a cool dry place.

Next came a button that said: *Click Here To Order.*

Chang said, "Reacher was right. This page doesn't pay Merchenko."

Westwood said, "We should take a look at level five."

It took some time to get there. Like dial-up used to be. Although Reacher was sure things were happening lightning-fast behind the scenes. The guy's code, battling the site's defenses, one warrior against a horde, millions of feints and penetrations every second, burrowing in, driving down through the layers.

The page came up.

Michael McCann's friend Exit had called it interesting. And it was, Reacher supposed. Depending on what a person needed. It offered a concierge service. Members were invited to travel to Mother's Rest, by train from Chicago or Oklahoma City. They would be met at the station by a representative, and they would spend the night in a luxury motel. Then came transfer by luxury sedan, to the Mother's Rest HQ. There they would find a private annex, with a suite inside designed to resemble a luxury hotel, with a calming bedroom ambience. There they could get comfortable, and at a time of their choosing an assistant would administer a Nembutal drink, and then withdraw. Or, if preferred, for those concerned about gulping a bitter liquid, the assistant would administer a regular sleeping pill, and then press a button, and an old 1970s small-block Chevy V-8 would start up outside, distant and inaudible, but its sweet rich exhaust would be piped to the room, to do its gentle work.

Members were invited to inquire as to the cost of the service.

It would be substantial, Reacher thought. He pictured the guy from the train, in his suit and his collared shirt, with his fine leather bag, and the woman, in her white dress, fit for a garden party in Monte Carlo. Both rich. Both sick, possibly. Both headed for a dignified end. He saw them in his mind, different people, different days, but the same physical gesture. At room 203's dusty window. Standing with their arms held wide, their hands still on the drapes, staring out at the morning, as if in wonder.

Their last morning.

Chang said, "Michael and his friend. Is this what they did?"

Westwood said, "This is my story. Right here. I'll ask if this is the future. It could be, a hundred years from now. Chaos, overpopulation, no water. There could be one of these on every street corner. Like Starbucks. But I'll have to see it for myself. Having spent the travel money."

"Maybe," Reacher said. "After we check it."

"What's to check? We know what's there. Veterinary Nembutal goes out by parcel service, and high-end clients come in by train. And who can seriously say either thing is wrong? I could ask if the Deep Web somehow predicts what's coming next. Maybe it has to. It's human desire, after all. Nothing more. Unfiltered and unregulated. Somehow organic. The book rights for this one are in the philosophy section. Because this is how these things happen. We've seen these things happen. A hundred years from now this could be normal."

"Keever didn't think it was normal yet. He could have shrugged his shoulders. He could have changed his name to Wittgenstein and gotten out of the way of progress. But he saw something wrong."

"Do you?"

"I'm not sure. But Keever was sure."

"What could be wrong?"

"I don't see how Michael and his friend can have afforded the concierge service. Not if they saved up all their lives. So where the hell are they?"

The guy from Palo Alto said, "Are we done?"

Chang said, "We are, and thank you very much."

Reacher said, "You're the man. You're down there among them. They can't see you, but you can see them."

Westwood said, "Send me an invoice."

The guy said, "I'll get you a car," and he pressed his phone.

People got up, and Reacher took a step toward the door, and another, and then the floor on the left slammed upward at a crazy angle, just canted itself to forty-five degrees, some immense force, instantaneous, and he thought *earthquake* and it tipped him over and smashed him into the door frame, across the chest and the neck, like a blow from a two-by-four, followed by a clatter to the floor, and a desperate glance around, for Chang, and whatever else was coming next.

Not an earthquake.

He sat up.

Everyone else squatted down.

He said, "I'm OK."

Chang said, "You fell over."

"Maybe a board was loose."

"The boards are fine."

"Maybe there's a warp."

"Do you have a headache?"

"Yes."

"You're going to the emergency room."

"Bullshit."

"You forgot Keever's name. You had to say the guy who was killed with the backhoe. That's classic aphasia. You forgot a word and you worked around it. That's not good. And before that you tripped near the bookstore. And you keep drifting off. Like daydreaming, or talking to yourself."

"Do I?"

"Like it's all spacey in there."

"How is it normally?"

"You're going to the emergency room."

"Bullshit. Don't need it."

"For me, Reacher."

"Waste of time. We should go direct to the hotel."

"I'm sure you're right. But do it for me."

"I've never done it before."

"There's a first time for everything. I hope not just this."

Reacher said nothing.

"For me, Reacher."

The guy from Palo Alto said, "Go to the emergency room, man."

Reacher looked at Westwood and said, "Help me out here."

Westwood said, "Emergency room."

The guy from Palo Alto said, "Tell them you're a coder. No waiting time. Some of those companies make big donations."

They did as the guy said, and claimed a status Reacher did not have. And was never likely to have. Right down there in terms of probability, with quilter, or scrapbooker, or tenor in the choir. But it got him seen in ninety seconds, and ninety seconds after that he was on his way for a CT scan of his head. Which he said was bullshit, don't need it, waste of time, but Chang hung in there, and they fired up the machine, which was nothing much, a kind of electric buzz, just X-rays, and then a wait for a doctor to look at the file. Which Reacher said was bullshit, waste of time, the same things over again, and Chang hung in again, and eventually a guy showed up with a file in his hand and a look in his eye. Chang and Westwood stayed in the room.

Reacher said, "The CT in CT scan stands for computed tomography."

The guy with the file said, "I know."

"I know what day of the week it is and I know who the president is. I know what I had for breakfast. Both times. I'm proving there's nothing wrong with me."

"You have a head injury."

"That's not possible."

"You have a head. It can be injured. You have a cerebral contusion, in Latin *contusio cerebri*, in fact technically two, both coup and contre-coup, caused, quite clearly, by blunt trauma to the right side of the head."

Reacher said, "Is that the good news or the bad news?"

The guy said, "If you'd taken that punch on the upper arm, you'd expect one hell of a bruise. Which is exactly what you got. Not on the outside. Not enough flesh. The bruise is on the inside. On your brain.

With a twin across the hall, because your brain bounced from side to side in your skull like a goldfish in a test tube. What we call coup and contre-coup."

Reacher said, "Symptoms?"

"Will vary with the severity of the injury and the individual, but to some degree will include headache, confusion, sleepiness, dizziness, loss of consciousness, nausea, vomiting, seizures, and difficulties with coordination, movement, memory, vision, speech, hearing, managing emotion, and thinking."

"That's a lot of symptoms."

"It's the brain."

"What about mine in particular? Which symptoms will I get?"

"I can't say."

"You have my paperwork right there. An actual picture."

"It can't be interpreted exactly."

"Case closed, right there. You're only guessing. I've been hit in the head before. This is no different. No big deal."

"It's a head injury."

"What's the next part of your speech?"

"I think the scan justifies admission overnight for observation."

"That ain't going to happen."

"It should."

"If the guy hit me in the arm you'd tell me I'd be OK in a couple of days. The bruise would go down. You'd send me home. You can do the same thing with my head. It happened yesterday, so tomorrow will be a couple of days. I'll be fine. If it is what you say it is anyway. You could have gotten that file mixed up with somebody else."

"The brain is not the same thing as an arm."

"I agree. An arm is not protected by a thick layer of bone."

The guy said, "You're a grown-up. This is not a psychiatric facility. I can't keep you here against your will. Just sign yourself out at the desk."

And then he turned around and headed out, ready for the next in line. Maybe a coder, maybe not. The door swung shut behind him.

Reacher said, "It's a bruise. It's getting better."

Chang said, "Thank you for having it checked. Let's go find the hotel."

"Should have gone direct."

"Reacher, you fell over."

He walked carefully, all the way to the cab line.

Chapter 48

People said that on a map San Francisco looked like a thumb sticking up south to north, shielding the Bay from the Pacific, but Reacher thought it curved more like a raised middle finger. Although why the city should be mad at the ocean, he didn't know. The fog, maybe. But either way, the hotel Westwood had chosen was at the tip, where either the thumbnail or the fingernail would be. Right on the waterfront. It was dark, so the view was a void, apart from the Golden Gate Bridge, which was all lit up, on the left, and then further out on the right was the distant twinkle of Sausalito and Tiburon.

They checked in and washed up and met in the restaurant for dinner. It was a pretty room, with plenty of crisp white linen. There were couples and foursomes in there. They were the only threesome. Trysts and deals were going on all around them. Westwood got the internet on his phone and said, "Forty thousand suicides every year in America. One every thirteen minutes. Statistically we're more likely to kill ourselves than each other. Who knew?"

Chang said, "If five of them every nine days use the Mother's Rest concierge service, that's a couple hundred a year. Like Keever's note. We already saw two."

Reacher said, "What would you pay for that?"

"I wouldn't, I hope."

"If it's nine hundred bucks to do it yourself in bed, then what would be reasonable? Five times as much? Say five grand?"

"Maybe. For the pampering. Like going to the spa instead of filing your nails at home."

"That would be a million dollars a year. Better than a poke in the eye with a sharp stick."

"But?"

"Their proposed hit list this week alone was Keever, McCann, you, me, and the Lair family. Seven people. Which is not a problem, apparently, because they rent a Ukrainian tough guy to do the heavy lifting. That's a big reaction for a million bucks."

"People get killed for a dollar."

"On the street in a panic. Not as a strategic imperative. I think there's more in this than a million bucks. But I don't see how. Folks wouldn't pay ten or twenty grand. Or more. Would they? They could buy their own 1970s Chevy. They could buy a garden shed and drill a hole."

"This is not necessarily a rational decision. And it's totally based on not buying your own Chevy. That's the point. Full service."

"So what would they pay?"

"I don't know. It's hard to picture it. Imagine you're a rich guy, and you want out. One final luxury. Discreet people in the background, making sure it all goes OK. Care and concern, and hands to hold. It's a major event in your life, obviously. You might pay what you paid for your car. Which is probably a Mercedes or a BMW. Fifty grand, maybe. Or even eighty. Or more. I mean, why not? You can't take it with you."

Westwood said, "When are we going there?"

Reacher said, "When we've made a plan. It's a tactical challenge. Like approaching a small island across an open sea. It's as flat as a pool table there. The grain elevators are the tallest things in the county. I'm sure they have all kinds of ladders and catwalks. For maintenance. They'll post lookouts. They'll see us coming ten minutes away. And if we come by train, they'll be lined up on the ramp, just waiting for us."

"We could drive in by night."

"They would see the headlights a hundred miles away."

"We could switch them off."

"We wouldn't see our way. It's pitch black at night. It's the countryside."

"The roads are straight."

"Plus at the moment we're unarmed."

Westwood said nothing.

After dinner Westwood went to his room and Reacher and Chang took a stroll outside, on the Embarcadero. Near the water. The night was cool. Literally half of the Phoenix temperature. Chang had nothing but her T-shirt. She walked pressed up hard against him, for warmth. It made them clumsy, like a three-legged creature.

Reacher said, "Are you holding me upright?"

She said, "How do you feel now?"

"Still got a headache."

"I don't want to go back to Mother's Rest until you feel better."

"I'm fine. Don't worry."

"I wouldn't go back there at all if it wasn't for Keever. Who am I to judge? They're meeting a need. Maybe Westwood is right. Maybe we'll all be doing it in a hundred years."

Reacher said nothing.

She said, "What?"

"I was going to say I would save the money and choose the shotgun. But that would be tough on whoever found me. There would be a lot of mess. Same with the handgun. Same with hanging myself, or jumping off the roof. Stepping in front of a train isn't fair to the engineer. Even drinking the Kool-Aid in a motel room isn't fair to the maid. Maybe that's why people choose the concierge service. Easier on the folks they leave behind. That's worth a premium, I guess. But I still don't see how it adds up to Merchenko money."

"I don't see how we get back there. It's like they have a ten-mile-high razor-wire fence. Except laid down flat."

"We should start out in Oklahoma City."

"You want to take the train?"

"I want to keep our options open. We'll figure out the fine print later. Tell Westwood to book the flights."

Reacher woke very early the next morning, before Chang, and he slid out of bed and shut himself in the bathroom. He had given up on his previous theory. Forever. It had been proven categorically wrong. Repeatedly. There was no ceiling. There was no upper limit. There was no reason why it should ever stop.

Which was good to know.

He stood in front of the mirror and twisted and turned and checked himself over. He had new bruises from falling down. The old bruise on his back where Hackett had hit him was vivid yellow and the size of a dinner plate. But he wasn't pissing blood, and the ache was going away, and the stiffness was easing. The side of his head was still tender, and a little soft, but not exactly swollen. Not enough flesh, like the doctor had said. His headache was moderate. He wasn't sleepy. He wasn't dizzy. He stood on one leg and closed his eyes, and didn't sway. He was conscious. No nausea. He hadn't thrown up. No seizures. He walked a line of tiles, from the tub to the toilet, and back again with his eyes closed, and he didn't stray. He touched his nose with his fingertip, and then rubbed his stomach while patting his head. No problems with coordination or movement, beyond his innate and inevitable slight clumsiness. He was no ballet dancer. Neat and deft and dexterous were adjectives that had never applied.

The door opened behind him and Chang stepped in. He saw her in the mirror. She looked soft and sleepy. She yawned and said, "Good morning."

He said, "To you, too."

"What are you doing?"

"Checking my symptoms. The doctor gave me a hell of a list."

"How far did you get?"

"I still have to do memory, vision, speech, hearing, managing emotion, and thinking."

"You already passed managing emotion. I've been quite impressed. For a guy. Who was in the army. Now tell me three famous Oklahomans, since that's where we're going."

"Mickey Mantle, obviously. Johnny Bench. Jim Thorpe. Bonus points for Woody Guthrie and Ralph Ellison."

"Your memory is fine." She retreated to the tub and held up two fingers. "How many?"

"Two."

"Your vision is fine."

"Not a very stringent test."

"OK, stay where you are and tell me who made the bathtub."

He looked. There was small faint writing near the overflow hole.

"American Standard," he said, because he already knew.

"Your vision is fine," she said again.

She whispered something very softly.

"On the plane?" he said. "I'm totally up for that."

"Your hearing is fine. That's for sure. What's the longest word in the Gettysburg Address?"

"Which symptom is that?"

"Thinking."

He thought. "There are three. All with eleven letters. Proposition, battlefield, and consecrated."

"Now recite the first sentence. Like you were an actor on a stage."

"Lincoln was coming down with smallpox at the time. Did you know that?"

"That's not it."

"I know. That was for extra credit on memory."

"We already did memory. Remember? Now we're doing speech. The first sentence."

"The guy who founded Getty Oil was descended from the guy the town of Gettysburg was named for."

"That's not it either."

"That was general knowledge."

"Which is not even a symptom."

"It relates to memory."

"We did memory ages ago."

He said, loud like an actor, "Fourscore and seven years ago our fathers brought forth on this continent a new nation, conceived in liberty, and dedicated to the proposition that all men are created equal."

It sounded good in a bathroom. The marble gave it echo and resonance.

He said, louder, "Now we are engaged in a great civil war, testing whether that nation, or any nation so conceived, and so dedicated, can long endure."

She said, "Has your headache gone?"

He said, "More or less."

"Which means it hasn't yet."

"It's on its way out. It was never a big deal."

"The doctor thought it was."

"The medical profession has gotten very timid. Very cautious. No sense of adventure. I lived through the night. I didn't need observation."

Chang said, "I'm glad he was cautious."

Reacher said nothing.

Then Westwood called on the room phone to say his travel people had booked seats on United, the only direct flight of the day. But no rush, because it left halfway through the morning. So they ordered room service coffee, to be delivered right away, and then room service breakfast, to be delivered in exactly one hour's time.

* * *

Very early in San Francisco was a couple hours into the day in Mother's Rest. Not the difference between city and country habits, but merely time zones. Mother's Rest was ahead. The general store was doing business. The diner had a few last stragglers. The motel maid was hard at work. The one-eyed clerk was in the bathroom. The Cadillac driver was in his store, and Western Union and MoneyGram and FedEx were busy.

But the spare-parts store was closed. For the irrigation systems. And the diner had no counter service. Those two guys were on a metal walkway on top of what they called Elevator Three, the old concrete giant, the biggest they had. With binoculars. And a simple system. There were two roads in, one from the east and one from the west, which was the wagon train trail, running crossways, almost directly below them. But there were no roads in from the north or the south. Just the railroad tracks. The system split the risk heavily in favor of the roads. The guys sat across from each other, one looking west, one looking east, and once every five minutes or so they would turn, and scan the railroad to the north and south, a leisurely sweep from close to far, just in case someone was walking in, or using some weird self-propelled machine, like an old Western movie. It became a ritual. A chance to stretch.

Except at train time. Then the role was harder. They were looking straight down on the train, more or less, so they could see the far side. Almost. Certainly they would see someone force a door and jump down on the blind side, like an old spy movie. But at the same time equal attention had to be paid to the roads. Always. Intrusion by vehicle was judged far more likely.

Which meant apart from once in the morning and once in the evening, the binoculars were trained on the far horizon, for early warning, through the dust in the air, fine and golden close by, then a haze in the distance.

Visibility, about fifteen miles.

You know the plan.
You know it works.

They checked out, and a doorman got a cab, and they squeezed in, three across the rear seat, with a measure of regret in some, but not in Westwood, who was a little unsettled. He said, "That was a very weird hotel. Only in San Francisco, I guess. All the time I was showering they had some guy reciting the Gettysburg Address through the bathroom ventilator."

Chapter 49

The flight was fine and the Oklahoma City hotel the *LA Times* had booked was a grand old three-spired confection, built a hundred years before and gone a little musty, but rescued by a refresh about a decade in the past. It was adequate in every respect, and most of all it retained the kind of service Reacher wanted. He said to Chang, "Go chat with the concierge and tell him you're the kind of person who likes to get to know a town by walking all over. But tell him naturally you're concerned about safety. Ask him if there are parts you should avoid."

She came back ten minutes later with a paper tourist map, printed by the thousand for convention folk, and marked up by the concierge with a ballpoint pen. Certain inner-city neighborhoods were walled off by a thick blue line. No-go areas. Like a napkin sketch of East Berlin in the old days. One particular quadrant was both walled off and then re-emphasized with an *X* so vigorous it scored through the paper.

Chang said, "He told me not to go there day or night."

"My kind of place," Reacher said.

"I'm coming with you."

"I was counting on it."

They ate early, a late-afternoon equivalent of brunch. Plain ingredients, dressed up fancy. The coffee was good. Afterward they waited an hour for the sun to set. The long plains day came to an end. The streetlights came on. Headlights came on. The bar noise changed from afternoon quiet to evening buzz.

Reacher said, "Let's go."

It was a long walk, because the city fathers knew which side their bread was buttered. Convention business had to be protected. The wild frontier was many blocks away. The street life changed as they walked, from occasional busy workers heading home briskly, to a stoop culture with knots of people hanging out in doorways doing not very much of anything. Some of the stores had been shuttered at the close of business, and some looked like they had been boarded up for years, but others were still open and doing a trade. Food, soda, loose cigarettes.

Chang said, "You OK?"

"Doing fine," Reacher said.

He navigated by instinct, looking for the kind of place where people could gather and cars could double park for a moment. There were cars at the curbs, and some in motion. There were tricked-out Japanese coupes, and low-riders, and enormous old aircraft-carrier sedans from Buick and Plymouth and Pontiac. Some had custom modifications, with wide mag wheels, and chrome pipes, and blue chassis lights underneath. One car was lowered waist-high, with the motor sticking up through a hole in the hood panel, vertical like a miniature oil rig, with a huge four-barrel carburetor and a giant chrome air filter about level with the roof.

Reacher stopped and looked at it.

He said, "I need to see those satellite pictures again."

Chang said, "Why?"

"There's something wrong with them."

"What?"

"I don't know. Something in the back of my mind. Not a regular memory thing. I'm OK."

"You sure?"

"Ask me a question."

"Teddy Roosevelt's vice president."

"Charles Fairbanks."

"I thought he was a movie actor."

"I think that was Douglas."

They moved on, past sagging wood houses set close together, past weedy front yards behind wire fences, some empty, some full of trash, some with chained dogs, some littered with bright bicycles and tricycles and other children's toys. They found a diagonal street that cut the corner between one not-quite-main drag and another. It was wide enough for three lanes, but the curbs were parked solid. It was long enough to slow down, and stop, and speed up again.

Reacher said, "This should be fine."

There was stoop activity, but most of it was happening about halfway down the street. Young guys, maybe twelve years old, milling around in groups, scanning left and right for traffic.

Reacher said, "OK, here's where we pretend we suddenly realize what we've gotten ourselves into, and we beat a hasty retreat."

They turned around and hustled back to the not-quite-main drag behind them. They turned the tight right and walked on, roughly the same direction they had been headed, behind the street they had seen. They stopped when they guessed they were level with the invisible knot of twelve-year-olds, who they figured were hanging out a long lot's length to their right. Plus the depth of their own back yard, plus the depth of their own house, plus their own front yard, and the sidewalk. About four hundred dark feet, Reacher figured.

He said, "Let's go see what they have for us."

Chapter 50

They picked a boarded-up house with a broken chain on its gate. They went in, swift and decisive like they belonged, and they slipped down the side of the house, and through its back yard, to its back fence, which shared a blunt angle with the back yard of a house on the diagonal street. Probably not the house they were looking for, but close. Reacher forced a wire panel out of its frame and they slipped through, unobtrusive except for the white gleam of their faces in the yellow evening gloom.

They walked through the new back yard and checked the view between the house and its neighbor. They were one short. All the commerce was taking place one lot to the left. There was a chain-link fence separating the yards. Easily climbed, at the cost of metallic chinking and clinking. Chang was agile. Better than Reacher. He was built for bulldozing, not gymnastics.

The back yard they climbed into was ill maintained. Not really maintained at all, to be accurate. It was full of thigh-high grass and weeds. The rear of the house had one lit window.

Reacher said, "Keep your right hand in your pocket when you can. Make them think you have a weapon."

"Does that work?"

"Sometimes."

She said, "Are they dope dealers?"

He nodded. "Like drive-through hamburgers. They use juveniles to carry the baggies and the cash back and forth to the cars. Young enough not to get arrested. Although that part might have changed. Might be just a myth these days. Especially in Oklahoma. They probably try them as adults now."

The lit window was on the right. Probably a living room of some kind. On the left was a window and a door, both dark. A kitchen, presumably. They swished through the miniature prairie to the door. Reacher tried the handle. Locked. He stepped sideways and looked in the window. A dim space, piled high with trash and dirty dishes. Pizza rinds, and empty cans. Red Bull and beer.

Reacher took another sideways step and pressed against the wall. He looked in the lit window, half an eye, at an angle. He saw two guys. They were sprawled on separate sofas, staring at their phones. Their thumbs were moving. They were playing games, or texting. On a low table between them were two duffel bags. Black nylon, new but poor quality. The kind of thing that costs five bucks in a store selling cameras for ten and telescopes for twenty. On top of one bag was a bulk pack of rubber bands from an office supply store.

On top of the other bag was an Uzi sub-machinegun.

Reacher crept back and rejoined Chang at the kitchen door.

He whispered, "We need to find a rock."

"For the window?"

He nodded.

"What about that?"

He looked where she was pointing. A grudging yard of concrete patio. A square item with rounded corners. Slightly humped. A hole in the center. Some kind of tough material. Plastic, or vinyl, or a blend. A base for a sun umbrella.

He whispered, "Can you throw that?"

She said, "Sure."

He smiled. No kind of a willowy waif. He said, "One second after I kick the door."

She picked it up.

He got in position.

He whispered, "OK?"

She nodded.

One step, two, three, and he smashed his heel through the lock and the door burst open, and as he fell inside he heard the living room window shatter and the umbrella base crash to the floor. He danced through the kitchen to the living room and found the guy on the left still holding his phone, and the guy on the right with his hand moving fast toward the Uzi, but it was suddenly hooking short, because his shoulders were suddenly hunching and flinching away, a reflex reaction to the loud crash behind him, and the brittle shower of glass on his head and his neck, and the blur of a large back yard object flying through his field of vision.

Also flying through his field of vision was Reacher's right boot, which caught him on the side of the face and laid him out like an old raincoat tossed down on a shiny floor. Which was game over, right there, because from that point onward all Reacher had to do was scoop up the Uzi, click the selector to auto, clamp the grip safety, and aim the muzzle at the left-hand guy's heart.

He said, "Stay still," and the guy did.

No sound from the hallway. Summertime, a warm evening, everyone out on the street.

The guy said, "What is this?"

Reacher said, "This is where we take your guns and money."

The guy glanced at the bag with the rubber bands on top. A reflex. Involuntary. Chang stepped in behind them. Fist in her pocket.

Reacher said, "Search them both."

She did. Fast and thorough. Quantico training. She came up with nothing of interest from either guy except a car key and two handguns. The car key was for an Audi and the handguns were a Glock 17 and a Beretta 92. Both nine-millimeter weapons. Same as the Uzi. Their ammunition logistics were neat and tidy, if nothing else.

Reacher said, "Look in the bags."

She did. The bag the Uzi had been sitting on held thousands of small glassine packets, full of dirty brown powder. Heroin, presumably, cut and cut and cut again, now packaged and ready for street-level sale.

The bag with the rubber bands held money.

A lot of money. Sour greasy bills, fives and tens and twenties, loose and bricked and rolled, some torn, some crumpled, all jammed in tight. Hence the rubber bands, Reacher guessed. Once he had read a book about a cartel accountant, who spent five grand a month on rubber bands alone, just to package all the cash.

He said, "Where's the Audi?"

The guy said, "Out front. Good luck with that."

"You're coming with us. You're going to carry the bags."

"Bullshit."

"Get over yourself. You win some, you lose some. We're not the cops. You're still in business. You'll make this back in a couple of weeks. Now move your ass."

The guy got a bag in each hand, and Reacher pushed him ahead to the hallway, one hand on his collar, the other jamming the Uzi in the small of his back. Chang carried the Glock in her right hand and the Beretta in her left. The hallway was long and filthy, and there were street sounds up ahead. Trash talk, laughter, scuffling feet, moving cars, all boxy and dulled by the heat and the distance, and the closed front door.

"Ten seconds more," Reacher said. "Stay smart and live long."

He hauled the guy to the side and let Chang duck ahead and open the door. Then Reacher pushed the guy outside, and the talk and the laughter stopped. There were eleven people out there, some in the yard, some on the sidewalk, some in the gutter, one of them a little boy about two years old, three of them women under twenty, two of them hard men about thirty, and the other five skinny kids about twelve, the back-and-forth gofers. On the street a car drove by, slowly, just posing, with a loud bass line flexing the panels. Then it was gone, and Reacher pushed the guy ahead, and his people stepped up, ready to fight, but the guy said, "Leave it."

Chang blipped the key, and a black sedan flashed its lights. It was smaller than a Town Car, but not compact. Chang opened the rear door, and Reacher made the guy drop the bags on the seat. Then he turned the guy around and shoved him back toward the house. He kept the Uzi leveled. Chang got behind the wheel. Reacher backed into the passenger seat. Chang took off hard. Reacher pulled the heroin bag off the back seat and emptied it out the window as she accelerated away. Tiny glassine packets blew everywhere, shiny and brown, like a plague of dead locusts, like a whirlwind slipstream. Folks ran in the road, scooping them up, chasing the car, leapfrogging ahead of each other, trying to grab whatever they could, with the guys from the house running around too, trying to restore order, trying to reclaim what was theirs. And that was all Reacher saw, because Chang spooled a fast left turn at the end of the diagonal street, and after that its residents were lost to sight.

Chapter 51

They dumped the Audi in an off-street convention garage four blocks from the hotel, doors unlocked, key in, and they zipped the guns in the money bag, and carried it back to Westwood's room. Where they hammed it up a little, at first, with slow reveals, like a magic show. Like rabbits from a hat. First the Beretta, and then the Glock, and then the Uzi, each one greeted with enthusiasm, and then finally the bag falling open, and the avalanche of money on the bedspread.

Westwood said, "I'm changing my mind about the philosophy section."

He and Chang set about counting the cash, and Reacher checked the guns. All were fully loaded, plus one in the chamber. Sixty-seven rounds in total, all interchangeable. The Uzi was in good working order. Most Uzis were. Simple machines, built for what combat was, not what it should be. Like, some would say, the Kalashnikov. The handguns were different. Especially, some would say, the Beretta. They were precision instruments. Beautifully engineered and hard as nails, but still requiring some kind of basic minimal care. Which dope dealers generally didn't give, in Reacher's experience. Their cash spent the same as anyone else's, but sometimes their weapons misfired. Fact of life. Poor maintenance. Or none at all. Both the Glock and the Beretta looked dry and felt gritty. Durable machines, and almost certainly OK, but almost wasn't enough. Not for the kind of thing that made you pick up a gun in the first place. It was a circular argument. It was a Zen question. Was a weapon you couldn't trust a weapon at all?

"Reacher, look at this," Chang said.

He looked. Appearances had been deceptive. Evidently. The lone greasy fives and the rough bricks of tens and the loose rolls of twenties were real enough. But they weren't the whole story. Not even most of it. They were an afterthought. They had been thrown in the bag as a thin extra layer on top of the main cargo. Which had been bricks of official bank-banded hundred dollar bills. All fresh and fragrant and crisp and new. And thick. A hundred bills in every brick.

A hundred hundreds was ten thousand bucks.

Per brick.

There were a lot of bricks.

He said, "How much?"

She said, "More than two hundred and thirty thousand dollars."

He was quiet for a very long time.

Then he said, "Can I see the satellite pictures of that place again?"

Westwood's computer was already wide awake and working, and the image was still in his internet history, so even though he said the wifi was slow, the picture was on the screen in seconds.

Reacher took a look.

As before, he saw a farm surrounded by a sea of wheat. Fences, beaten earth, hogs, chickens, and vegetable gardens. A house and six outbuildings. Parked cars, and satellite dishes. A generator shed. Faint traces of power lines looping between some of the buildings, and a phone line marching in on poles. The well head, and its shadow. Better than an architect's drawing, because it was the actual as-built reality, not just the intention.

He did what he had seen the others do, and slid paired fingers around on the touchpad to make the picture move, and un-pinched it to make it bigger. He started where the cars were parked, and pretended one was moving. He followed it out of the farmyard, into the mouth of a dirt road, east toward the railroad track, and then north at the corner of a field. The field ran unbroken more than ten straight miles, and then the dirt road turned west at its far corner, and then north again, all the way up to Mother's Rest itself, where it came in as a narrow and insignificant tributary at the dead end of the same wide plaza that later ran onward to the elevators. It was a private driveway, essentially, twenty miles long. It went nowhere else.

He drove the virtual trip in reverse, twenty miles back to the farm, and he parked where he had started. He un-pinched the picture until the farm filled the screen, side to side and top to bottom. Nearest the railroad was the hog pen. It had a large shelter, probably made of wood, and a fenced area in front about six times as big, all churned up and pockmarked by heavy feet. All mud and slime. There was a barn a little bigger than the hog shelter. Those two structures had no power. The generator shed was easily identifiable. It had an intake snorkel through the wall, and a top-hat exhaust vent in the roof. Diesel, for a plant that big. Some immense installation. Thumb-thick cables spider-webbed out, sagging from eave to eave, to the house, and the other three buildings.

Reacher said, "Let's assume the biggest structure is the house. With the cars and the satellite dishes. But which structure is the suicide suite?"

The others crouched next to him, shoulder to shoulder, one on each side.

Westwood said, "The suicide suite is probably the next biggest. Bedroom, living area, bathrooms, and so on."

"With power, for heat and AC and dim ambient lighting. Maybe soft music. All the comforts of home." Reacher pointed. "That one?"

"Almost certainly."

"So where's the small-block Chevy V-8?"

"In one of the other outbuildings. Remote and soundproofed."

Reacher nodded. "I was in West Texas once, and I saw them being used to drive irrigation pumps. Back when gasoline was cheaper than water. Regular car engines, pulled out of wrecks, I guess. They poured a concrete pad, and bolted the thing down, like it was still under a hood somewhere. They painted them bright yellow, so they didn't get hit by tractors or plows. But they were noisy, out in the open. So sure, you'd want to build walls around the concrete pad, and a roof. You could stuff the walls with something, and line the ceiling. Some kind of a sound-absorbing material."

"And you'd need power," Westwood said. "They don't run it all the time. Just when needed. It would be embarrassing if it didn't start. So you'd need a battery charger hooked up, permanently, on a trickle setting. Just to be sure."

"So which building?"

Westwood pointed. "That one or that one."

"Where's the exhaust pipe?"

Silence, for a beat.

Westwood said, "Maybe we can't see it."

"We can see the power lines. We can see the phone line, just about. The power lines might be an inch thick. Probably a little less. A car exhaust is at least two inches. Maybe three. Take a look underneath sometime. Metal, because of the heat, and therefore welded in sections. But where is it? There's no pipe running into the suicide suite. Not from any other building."

"Maybe they buried it."

"The damp would rust it out in weeks. It would leak exhaust. They'd be running to the muffler shop all the time. If they wanted to hide it they'd bring it in knee-high through a flower bed and grow climbing shrubs on it. Maybe roses. Which would make it even easier for us to see. But it isn't there. It doesn't exist. Their web site is a lie."

Westwood leaned forward and made the picture bigger, and bigger, until it was crude and blurred and pixelated, as big as he could get it. He moved it around, carefully, slowly, and he followed all four walls of all seven buildings.

No exhaust pipe. No two structures were connected by anything more substantial than an electric cable.

Reacher said, "Two hundred and thirty thousand dollars to spend. This is like working for the Pentagon again. We can afford to make a new plan."

The new plan was made slowly, with care, in depth and in detail, over the rest of that evening, and some of the night, and all the next morning. Computers helped. The plan had five moving parts, and all of them had to be synchronized exactly, and all of them were tricky, and all of them were vital. But because of technology what in the past would have taken days took merely hours. Both Westwood and Chang had laptops, and even Reacher got in the picture, with Chang's phone. He was getting wifi. He was clicking and scrolling with the best of them. And when the time came to call people, when Westwood and Chang got busy on their cells, he used the land line on the night stand, and between them they got things done about ten times faster than back in the day.

The rest of the plan was a shopping list. At the top was a legitimate state resident. Not to be bought, as such, but merely rented. Or bribed, to be technical, to go buy the rest of the stuff on the list. Most of which couldn't be done without an Oklahoma driver's license. In the end the hotel concierge volunteered. He saw himself as a fixer, and a man of the world. He was no doubt attracted by the money on offer. He had no qualms. The cash was real. He was breaking no laws. He was protected by the Second Amendment.

He delivered in the late afternoon, by which time everything else was nailed down. They had rehearsed, and brainstormed, and gamed it all out. They had probed, and questioned, and sometimes started over. They had played it from the bad guys' side, and scoped out their options. They had pondered the wild cards. What if it rained? What if a tornado blew in? All that remained was for Reacher to approve the purchases.

There were three main items. That was all. The temptation had been to go crazy, like kids in a candy store. Then logic had chipped away, and they had ended up where Reacher liked to be anyway, with everything they needed, and nothing they didn't. All three selections were Heckler & Koch products. A P7 pistol for Westwood. Like Hackett's back-up gun. Point and shoot. Nine millimeter. Smaller than an average handgun. To go in his hiking boot, in an ankle holster, also supplied.

The other two items made a matched pair. Two identical MP5K sub-machineguns. One for Reacher, and one for Chang. Bigger than an average handgun, but not by much. Some revolvers were longer. Pistol grips, matching front grips, fat and bulbous. A futuristic design, much loved by SWAT teams and counterterrorist squads everywhere. Single shot or full auto, and full auto could hit as high as nine hundred rounds a minute. Which was fifteen bullets a second.

Hence the rest of the delivery was ammunition. All nine-millimeter Parabellum, interchangeable between all three weapons, but at that point pre-loaded into four P7 magazines and twenty-four MP5 magazines. More would have been hard to carry.

Reacher took the guns apart and put them back together again, and dry-fired them, sometimes with his little finger, which he felt was more sensitive to mechanical nuance.

All three worked.

Plus a small bag of stuff from a hardware store.

"Everything OK?" Chang asked him.

"Looking good," he said.

"You OK?"

"Feeling good," he said.

"Happy with the plan?"

"It's a great plan," he said.

"But?"

"Something we used to say in the MPs. Everyone has a plan till they get punched in the mouth."

Westwood checked his watch. A complex thing, made of steel, with many dials. It was five o'clock in the afternoon. He said, "Seven hours left. We should eat. I'm sure the restaurant is open."

"You go ahead," Reacher said. "We'll get room service. We'll knock on your door when it's time."

Chapter 52

From the metal walkway on top of the old concrete giant
the dawn was vast, and remote, and infinitely slow. The eastern horizon was black as night, and it stayed that way, until at last a person with straining wide-open eyes might call it faintly gray, like the darkest charcoal, which lightened over long slow minutes, and spread, side to side and wafer-thin, and upward, like tentative fingers on some outer layer of the atmosphere, impossibly distant, the stratosphere perhaps, as if light traveled faster there, or got there sooner.

The edge of the world crept into view, at least to the straining wide-open eyes, limned and outlined in gray on gray, infinitely dim, infinitely subtle, hardly there at all, part imagination, and part hope. Then pale gold fingers probed the gray, moving, ethereal, as if deciding. And then spreading, igniting some thin and distant layer one molecule at a time, one lumen, lighting it up slowly, turning it luminous and transparent, the glass of the bowl, not white and cold, but tinted warmer.

The light stayed wan, but reached further, every new minute, until the whole sky was gold, but pale, not enough to see by, too weak to cast the faintest shadow. Then warmer streaks bloomed, and lit the horizon, and finally the sun rose, unstoppable, for a second as red and angry as a sunset, then settling to a hot yellow blaze, half-clearing the horizon, and throwing immediate shadows, at first perfectly horizontal, then merely miles long. The sky washed from pale gold to pale blue, down through all the layers, so the world above looked newly deep as well as infinitely high and infinitely wide. The night dew had settled the dust, and until it dried the air was crystal. The view was pure and clear in every direction.

The Cadillac driver was on the walkway, with the Moynahan who had gotten hit in the head and had his gun taken. The guy was still feeling bad, but there was a schedule to keep. He was wearing an old-style leather football helmet in lieu of a splint. For his cheekbone. The Cadillac driver was facing west, with the new sun weak on the back of his neck. Moynahan was squinting east against the glare, watching the road. He had seen no nighttime traffic. No headlights. Everything else was wheat. Then came the curvature of the earth.

Same in the west. The road, the wheat, the far horizon. No nighttime traffic. No headlights. No excitement. The third morning. Directly below in the plaza early risers were heading for breakfast. Like ants. Trucks were parking, like toys. Doors were slamming. Folks were calling good morning, one to the other. All familiar sounds, but dull and indistinct, because of the vertical distance.

After twenty minutes the sun had pulled clear of the horizon, and was already curving south of east, setting out on its morning journey. Dawn had become day. The sky had gotten brighter, and bluer, and perfectly uniform. There was no cloud. New warmth stirred the air, and the wheat moved and eddied, with a whispered rustle, as if waking up. From the top of Elevator Three to the horizon was fifteen miles. A question of elevation, and geometry, and the flatness of the land. Which meant the guys on the walkway were at the exact center of a thirty-mile circle, floating high above it, the whole visible world laid out at their feet. A golden disk, below a high blue sky, cut in equal halves top to bottom by the railroad line, and side to side by the road. From the walkway both looked narrow and crowded by the wheat. Like thin pencil lines, to the naked eye, scored completely straight with a ruler. The lines met at the railroad crossing, directly below them. The center of the disk. The center of the world.

The Cadillac driver was sitting with his knees up, to steady his binoculars. He was watching the far end of the road, all the way west. If something was coming, he wanted maximum warning. Moynahan had his right hand up, to blot out the sun, and his left hand held his binoculars to his eyes. A little shaky. Not easy, with the helmet. His technique was to scan back and forth, near to far. He wanted to make sure he hadn't missed anything.

Their walkie-talkie hissed at them. Moynahan put his binoculars down and picked it up. He said, "Go ahead."

The man with the jeans and the hair said, "I need you boys to stay up there until the morning train. Your replacements are late."

Moynahan looked at the Cadillac driver. Who shrugged. The third morning. Panic had turned to routine.

Moynahan said, "OK."

He put the walkie-talkie down.

He looked at his watch and said, "Twenty minutes."

He picked up his binoculars and raised his right palm against the sun.

He said, "I got something here."

The Cadillac driver took a last look at the empty west and turned around. He put his right hand up for shade. The binoculars shook a little. The eastern horizon was bright. The sun was still low enough to roil the air. Worse, with the telephoto optics. There was a tiny square shape on the road, somehow rocking from side to side, but in place. No apparent forward motion. An optical illusion, because of the binoculars. It was a truck, doing maybe forty-five miles an hour. Mostly white. Coming straight at them.

The Cadillac driver said, "Keep an eye on it. Make sure there's nothing behind."

He turned back west and pulled up his knees.

He steadied his binoculars.

He said, "Shit, I got something, too."

Moynahan said, "What is it?"

Best guess, it was a red car. Just a dot, tiny in the distance, with low sun winking in its windshield. Close to fifteen miles away. Same thing as the east, rocking in place, no forward motion. An illusion.

He said, "How's yours doing?"

"Still coming on."

"Nothing behind it?"

"Can't tell. Not yet. It could be a whole convoy."

"Mine, too."

They watched. Distant vehicles on a dead-straight road, head-on, the image magnified but flattened by the binocular lenses. Roiling air, urgent side-to-side rocking, no forward motion, plumes of dust.

Moynahan picked up the walkie-talkie. He clicked the button and when he got the go-ahead he said, "We've got incoming vehicles east and west. Moderate speed. Probable ETA about the same as the morning train."

The man with the jeans and the hair said, "This is it. No brainer. They want us worried about three things at once."

The Cadillac driver turned and checked east, because Moynahan was on the radio. The truck was still there. Still square, still rocking. No apparent forward motion. Mostly white. But only mostly. There were flashes of other colors.

Familiar purples and oranges.

He said, "Wait."

Moynahan said, "Wait one, boss."

The Cadillac driver said, "It's FedEx. For me."

Moynahan said, "East is clear, boss. It's only FedEx. West is still unknown."

The man with the jeans and the hair said, "Keep an eye on it."

"Will do."

Moynahan put the walkie-talkie down. He checked on the FedEx truck, just briefly, and then turned to look west. Maybe two heads would be better than one. The car was still coming. Still far away. Just reflected sun and flashing chrome, and a hint of red. Weak new thermals off the blacktop ahead of it, and a low billow of dust behind it. It could have been anything.

The Cadillac driver broke off and checked the railroad line. Nothing in the north. No walkers. No self-propelled machines. But the southern horizon was winking silver. The morning train, fifteen miles away. Coming up from Oklahoma City. A tiny pinprick disturbance in the air.

He checked east. The FedEx truck was still there, rocking in place.

He said, "I just realized. I'm going to miss the delivery. I'm stuck up here."

Moynahan said, "Long way to come back tomorrow." Then he gestured west, with his chin. "This is the slowest car in the world."

"It's not slow. They're timing it. They want to get here with the train. So our attention is divided two ways. Which is why they're coming in from the west. They don't need to use the crossing."

"How far is the train now?"

"The car is closer."

"But the train is faster."

The Cadillac driver didn't answer. It was like the crap they asked in high school. *If a car is twelve miles away and traveling at forty-eight miles an hour, and a train is fifteen miles away and doing sixty, which will get here first?*

Both of them. It was coordinated. It was a no brainer.

The car kept on coming. The train kept on coming. Vectoring in. Collision course. Way below them in the plaza folks were reporting for duty, scurrying like ants. Guys were coming out of the diner. Getting into their trucks. Smart move. They were sending out a holding party. A roadblock, maybe a mile out. Always better to deal with a problem somewhere else. Unless the car was a decoy. Maybe they were on the train. Like an old Western movie. The sides of the cars fall open, and all kinds of sheriffs burst out on horseback. There would be four guys on the ramp to meet them. Plus one on the blind side, just in case. Should be enough. *You all know the plan. You all know it works.*

Now the train was big enough to see. It was sunlit on one side, and shadowed on the other. Like the truck and the car it seemed to be jerking side to side, without actually going anywhere. The air was boiling all around it, like a luminescent slipstream.

The car was still coming. Two pick-up trucks were ready to meet it. About a mile out of town, parked side by side, one in each lane. Lined up exactly. Proud. Almost ceremonial. Like stone lions at a mansion gate.

Then they heard the *whap-whap-whap* of rotor blades.

Chapter 53

Moynahan and the Cadillac driver danced around like crazy men, twisting and turning, like men attacked by bees, looking up, searching the sky for the helicopter. And finding it in two different places.

There were two helicopters.

They were coming in nose down, fast and low, one from the north and east, which was half to the right, and one from the north and west, which was half to the left. *Whap-whap-whap.* Both looked to be painted black. Glassy cabins, but smoked windows. Below them the wheat was thrashing and boiling in long straight lines, the start of a massive letter *V,* where the tip of the *V* looked to be right where they were. The top of Elevator Three.

The car was still coming. The train was still coming.

Their walkie-talkie hissed. The man with the jeans and the hair said, "Stay eyes-on at all times. I need to know what gets out of these things. And where."

Then the call cut off. They could see the guy far below, tiny and truncated in shape by the downward perspective. His was striding around, his radio up at his face.

Whap-whap-whap.

The car was still coming. The train was still coming. Both getting close. No need for binoculars. Not anymore. The rotors were getting louder, beating out of sync, and the scream of the turbines was breaking through.

Everything getting very close.

Less than a minute, maybe.

A whole bunch of things happened. Moynahan and the Cadillac driver spun around and around, trying to see it all. Trying to stay eyes-on. First the right-hand helicopter pounced ahead on a wide track to the east, sliding in again behind the town and heading due south, full speed, which was pretty damn fast.

Toward the farm.

Then the car reached the roadblock and stopped. It was a red sedan. Domestic. Cheap but supernaturally clean. Therefore a rental. Two of the guys from the diner were leaning down, talking in through the window.

Then the left-hand helicopter pulled away west, and hovered in place, like it was waiting, and then it came back again. Right over the plaza. Hovering low. Real low. Lower than the old concrete giant. They were looking down on it. The noise and the updraft tore at their clothes and knocked them about. The downdraft blasted dirt and crap everywhere. Like a dust storm, right there on Main Street.

Then the FedEx truck crossed the railroad crossing, about thirty yards ahead of the train. Thirty yards from getting T-boned by a thousand tons. The guy didn't even speed up. It was his regular route. He knew what he was doing.

Then way in the south the right-hand helicopter dropped over the far horizon. On approach to the farm, they guessed, because what else was there?

And then right at their feet the train came in, loud and long, hot and brutal, hissing and clattering and humming and grinding, but for once in its life drowned out by the thump of the blades and the whine of the jets.

The guys from the diner were still talking through the car window. The train doors opened.

Whap-whap-whap.

No one got out.

Nothing on the blind side.

Whap-whap-whap.

The train doors closed.

The train moved away, sliding out from under their feet, slowly, slowly, car after car.

The guys from the diner were still talking.

The last car rolled away and grew smaller, rocking, as tired rails yielded an inch.

The jets screamed and the helicopter rose up high.

The FedEx truck crossed the railroad crossing again and headed home. Moderate speed. ETA whenever.

The helicopter wheeled away, and banked over, so its downdraft blew sideways, pushing them across the walkway, blasting them with airborne dust and deafening noise. In the south the other helicopter came over the horizon and mirrored the same maneuver. Up, and then over, and then away. Nose down, low and fast. Getting smaller all the time. Flying a brand-new *V,* where the new tip was pointed far away.

It got suddenly quiet. There was nothing to hear, except the wheat. And the wheat was soothing.

Their walkie-talkie hissed.

Moynahan got it and said, "No one got out of the helicopter. It didn't even land. No one got out of the train either. Nothing on the blind side."

Out on the road the guys from the diner were backing their trucks away. The red sedan was nosing through. Coming to town.

Moynahan said, "What's up with that?"

The man with the jeans and the hair said, "He claims he's a customer. He brought a lot of money. We're going to take a look."

* * *

They brought the guy to the diner, but before they let him in they talked among themselves about the helicopters. Everyone was there, apart from Moynahan's brother. The one who had gotten kicked in the balls and had his gun taken. The discussion was brief, and there was no consensus. There were two trains of thought. Either it was general reconnaissance ahead of a further incursion at a future date, in which case it had likely involved cameras and thermal imaging and ground-penetrating radar, or it was the actual search for Keever itself, which they had long predicted would include the air, in which case it would involve pretty much the same technology, but it would find nothing either, because of the hogs.

Brief.

No consensus.

Either they were coming back, or they weren't.

No vote was taken.

The guy they showed in looked healthy. Like a guy from the National Geographic channel. Scruffy gray hair, scruffy gray beard. Forty-five, maybe. Weird kind of clothes with a lot of zippers. Bootlaces like mountain-climbing ropes.

He said his name was Torrance.

He said he had ditched his ID. Not just an insurance thing. Although there were certain clauses in his policy. But mostly he wanted to leave people guessing. That was his aim. No trace at all. His paper trail stopped seven hundred miles ago. A small fire, in the bathroom sink in a Nevada motel. All gone. He had driven onward only by night, to minimize risk. He wanted to leave people unsure. And inconvenienced. Seven long years, before a legal presumption.

The man with the jeans and the hair said, "You'll forgive us for being cautious, Mr. Torrance."

Then he looked at the Moynahan who had gotten hit in the head, and he said, "Where's your damn brother?"

Moynahan said, "I don't know."

"I need him here."

Their usual policy for messages in a meeting was last in, first out.

Moynahan had been last in. He had been slow, down the old concrete giant. Because of his head. Because of his balance.

He said, "OK, I'll go find him."

He headed for the street.

The man with the jeans and the hair looked back at Westwood and said, "Mr. Torrance, I guess our first question would be whether you're wearing a wire."

Westwood said, "I'm not."

"Then you'll be happy to unbutton your shirt."

Westwood did. A sturdy chest, plenty of flesh, curly gray hair. No microphone.

The man with the jeans and the hair said, "Our second question would be how you found us."

"On-line," Westwood said. "Through a board. A buddy of mine named Exit told me."

"We knew her."

Her. Knew.

Westwood said, "She told me she was coming here with her friend Michael. Also a buddy of mine. He posted as Mike."

"She did. We knew Mike, too."

"I figured what was good enough for them was good enough for me."

"Our third question would be what you planned to do with your rental car. That's a bright red paper trail right there."

"I wondered if I paid extra one of you would get rid of it for me. You could dump it all the way over in Wichita or Amarillo. It would get stolen pretty quick."

"Such a thing could be arranged. And if it ever showed up, in the barrio or wherever, it would only add to the mystery. Or make people think homicide."

"That's what I figured."

"As you know, we provide end of life choices. And choice means exactly that. We don't judge. We don't make people state their reasons. We don't offer counseling, and we don't try to change your mind. But you have arrived in an unconventional manner. So we need to ask why. Exceptionally."

Westwood said, "I've had enough. I never asked to be born. I haven't really enjoyed it, to be honest."

"Specifically?"

"I owe a lot of money. I can't pay. I can't face what comes next."

"Gambling?"

"Worse."

"The government?"

"I made some errors."

The man with the jeans and the hair looked at his crew. All there, apart from the Moynahan brothers. Five guys. They shuffled, and grimaced thoughtfully, and nodded vague assent.

The man with the jeans and the hair looked back at Westwood and said, "I think we can help you, Mr. Torrance. But I'm afraid it will cost all of what you brought."

Westwood said, "I want the gasoline engine. That's how I want to do it."

"It's a popular option."

"Is it leaded gas?"

"It runs on unleaded now. Special cylinder heads. The carbon monoxide is the same as it always was. It's the catalyst that takes it away, not unleaded. And the smell is better. The benzene makes it sweet. It's a nice way to go."

"What do other people choose?"

"Most choose both. Certainty of outcome is considered paramount. Hence all the statistics they study."

"Should I do both?"

"No need for it. The gasoline engine is a hundred percent effective. You can trust it."

Then the guy looked at the street door.

He said, "Where did the Moynahans get to?"

Last in, first out.

The spare-parts guy from the irrigation store said, "I'll go find them."

He headed out.

The man with the jeans and the hair looked back at Westwood and said, "It's an odd question, Mr. Torrance, but would you like to join us for breakfast?"

Westwood thought about it and then said yes, and the counterman temporarily put aside his community membership in favor of his professional duties, by stepping back there and setting up a fresh pot of coffee. The Cadillac driver said he better go check on his delivery first, back in a minute, but the store owner and the hog farmer and the one-eyed guy from the motel all sat down right away. The waitress came over and took their orders. Coffee was poured, and plates were delivered. Then the store owner got up again and said he wanted to run next door to get something. Heartburn medicine, the others thought. He too said he would be back in a minute.

But he wasn't.

Neither was the Cadillac driver.

Or the Moynahans, or the guy gone looking for them.

The man with the jeans and the hair stared at the door. He said, "What the hell is going on here? People keep leaving and not coming back."

He got up and stepped to the window. There was nothing out there. As in, nothing at all. Just stillness. No traffic, no pedestrians. Nothing moving. Hot sun, empty streets.

The guy said, "We have a problem. Out the back, right now. Mr. Torrance, excuse us. We'll come by for you later."

And then he ran, through the kitchen, followed by the hog farmer and the counterman and the one-eyed clerk, to the alley in back, where the counterman's crew-cab was parked. They piled in and took off, back to the plaza, south to the far end, into the mouth of the narrow dirt road. Like a private driveway, twenty miles long.

Westwood stood alone in the silent diner. Until the street door opened and Chang came in, followed by Reacher.

Chapter 54

The biggest chunk of the money had gone for the helicopters. Two air limousines, touting for corporate business out of Kansas City. Like Town Cars in the sky. No chance of getting them to land. Not on unapproved sites. No chance of them letting anyone rappel out on ropes. Their insurance wouldn't permit it. But they were happy to fly there and back empty. They were happy to add a little drama. For a video shoot, they were told. They got the exact GPS coordinates direct from Google. Timing was the tricky part. So the cameras could roll. But they had computers in the cockpits. It might be possible.

The second-biggest chunk of the money was carried by Westwood. Enough to impress. His cockpit computer was a rented Ford's speedometer and his wristwatch. High school, not postgrad. *If a car needs to travel fifteen miles in fifteen minutes, how fast must it go?* All tied to the train, of course. He found an AM station with traffic-and-weather-together, which said the railroad was on or close. To schedule, presumably. He could do no better.

Meanwhile Reacher and Chang were in the FedEx truck. They had called the depot in Oklahoma City and said they had a super-rush urgent overnight package for a place called Mother's Rest. They were told the latest time they could bring it. They came five minutes before. They found the night driver smoking in the alley. He said Mother's Rest was on his regular route. He agreed official bank-banded bricks of hundred dollar bills were wonderful things. Especially with a little psychology thrown in. *Take as many as you want. Whatever you think is fair. All we want to do is ride in the back.* And arrive at train time exactly. Which the guy said he could do. No problem. With his eyes shut. It was his regular route. They could ride up front if they wanted, and then hop in the back when they were getting close by.

And then hop out again, hopefully unnoticed, behind the Cadillac driver's store, amid all the helicopter mayhem and the train panic and the Westwood confusion. If the timing worked. Which it had, apparently. There had been plenty of mayhem. That was for damn sure. And no one in the store. Which was a bonus in the short term. But a burden in the long term. It was one more thing for later.

Which began with whichever Moynahan it was Reacher had kicked in the balls. They saw the guy limping along a cross street, heading in the direction of the diner or the store. Or the motel, conceivably. He went down easy, hog-tied tight with five of the cable zips from the hardware store, and gagged with one of the rags from the same source, and dumped in the abandoned CPA's office next door to FedEx, which had not been furnished with much of a lock.

Then came the guy's brother or cousin or whatever he was, wearing a ridiculous leather hat, looking for something. He went down too, just as easy, five cable ties, one rag, and a berth on the CPA's floor, right next to his relative. Then came the spare-parts guy. From the irrigation store. Looking for the first two. This time there was no conversation about football. Just the ties, a rag, the floor.

Regular folk kept well out of the way. They stayed indoors. Some kind of an ancient instinct, presumably. Maybe because of the submachineguns. They looked alien. Like movie props. Nothing to do but hide. The 911 service was the same thing as disconnected. The cops were a long way away. And it was hot anyway. More comfortable inside, with the AC.

The Cadillac driver walked right into it. He thought his store was still his. Ties, rag, floor. They had to go further to find the dry goods owner. They got him coming out the back of his building, holding a small bottle of Pepto-Bismol. Ties, rag, floor.

Then the well ran dry, when the crew-cab screamed away from behind the diner.

Leaving Westwood all alone.

Who said, "They agreed to the gasoline engine."

Reacher nodded. "They'll keep the con going to the end. Whatever it is."

"I assume the farm is where they went."

"Where else is there?"

"Are we ready?"

"We've done what we can."

"I'll get us there."

"I know you will."

"And that's where you'll ditch me, right?"

Chang said, "We won't ditch you. Unless you want to be ditched."

"I don't."

Reacher said, "I wish I could send you ahead. Instead of me. You're a grown-up. I don't care what happens to you. Come if you want. Stay with us all the way. But stay with us on my left-hand side."

"Why that?"

"I'm right-handed. I like freedom of movement."

"Understood. Let's go."

In the normal way of business it would have been called a test drive. An unfamiliar piece of equipment, driven briefly and experimentally by an intending purchaser. Except that Reacher was not an intending purchaser. He rarely purchased anything, and nothing that wasn't consumable, and certainly not farm equipment. The salesman knew. And Reacher wasn't driving it, either, because he couldn't. He didn't know how. He got over the first problem with the sub-machinegun, and the second with Westwood, who had once learned how to drive such a thing because science editors sometimes got sucked into judging science projects, which sometimes led to hands-on involvement in neighborhood do-gooder bullshit, which often meant shoveling some kind of actual shit, and mechanically was always the best way to handle that.

It was a New Holland backhoe, from the farm equipment dealer north of the wagon train trail. Westwood chugged it back through the plaza and onward past the motel. If not a test drive, at least a courtesy loan. Without the courtesy part. But a loan nonetheless. Reacher had no intention of keeping it. On the back it had a claw arm and a digging shovel, very narrow, with two aggressive teeth. An entrenching tool. On the front the bucket was broad and tall, but shallow. More like a bulldozer blade. It was clearly a versatile machine. All kinds of things could be bolted on. It was brand-new, brightly painted, and completely clean. It had a new-backhoe smell. The cab was just about wide enough for three, but there was only one seat. Westwood was in it, because he had to be. There were all kinds of levers and pedals. Chang was standing sideways on Westwood's left, and Reacher was jammed in sideways on his right. The engine was roaring. The thing was built for hard work and short back-and-forth distances, between hole and pile, but there were road-going gears in there, too. Westwood had it wound up to about thirty miles an hour when they left the plaza.

Not into the mouth of the private driveway.

Into the wheat.

Westwood had the front bucket set a couple of feet off the ground, with the bottom edge jutting forward. Like a metal chin. It smashed the wheat down, like a blunt scythe, and thick golden clouds of dust and fragments filled the air, like an ongoing linear explosion, and stalky debris thrashed the underside, and on the edges of the furrow the wheat swayed back in waves and brushed the windows. The land was flat in a global sense but where the rubber met the dirt it was uneven and lumpy. The backhoe was pitching fore-and-aft like a boat, and bouncing on its tires. They were soft, and they bulged and floundered on every bump. Westwood was hammering up and down in his seat. Reacher and Chang were hanging on sideways, like subway riders on a runaway train.

The metal chin hammered on.

Dust and fragments howled all around them.

Thirty miles an hour.

Twenty miles to go.

Elementary school.

Forty minutes.

But better than taking the private driveway. Which could be mined. Or at least spiked. And which definitely involved a straight head-on ten-mile approach to a right-angle corner, where any sane defender would mount a fifty-caliber machine gun. Arriving by car on the dirt road would be like coming up the motel stairs two at a time. *We could pick you off like squirrels.* Better to have some freedom of movement. Which meant an off-road vehicle. Which meant a battering ram. Hence the front bucket. Which was also bulletproof, and the size of a twin-bed mattress. Heavy steel, for humping jagged rocks. There was a sliver of visibility over the top. As much as they needed. For the wheat, anyway. So far, so good. The plan was working. Except for one small unintended consequence. Mainly because of the slamming around.

Reacher's headache was coming back.

Most of the way the farm was out of sight behind the wheat, so they steered by the sun. Not exact, but close enough. First visual contact happened about a quarter-mile from where they were aiming, and just about right on time. A house and six outbuildings. Fences and beaten earth. A phone line on poles. The diesel generator's top-hat exhaust.

And the stink of hogs.

Like a chemical weapon.

Westwood looped away, and came back head-on, and stopped about two hundred yards out. The engine died back to an idle. Last fragments of wheat settled back to earth.

Quiet.

All alone.

Reacher felt like a predator above a water hole.

Then the water hole started shooting back.

Three weapons firing. Long guns. All the same. Distinctive. Flat solid barks, and the crack of fast bullets in the air. NATO rounds out of M16s, if Reacher was a gambling man. All of them so far missing. Understandable. It was a deceptive shot. Two hundred yards, absolutely flat, eye to eye. Except it was absolutely curved, because it was part of a spherical planet. Hence the miscalculation.

Westwood said, "Should we back off?"

"No," Reacher said. He counted in his head. He said, "Move up fifty yards. Now. Put the pressure on. They're coming up to a magazine change."

"Fifty yards forward?"

"Now."

Westwood moved it up.

A ragged lull. Pretty slow. No infantry training. That was for damn sure. Then the pot-shots started again. All of them misses.

Until a single hit.

Right in the center of the front bucket. A tiny thrill through the framework. The bullet, collapsing. Then the sound, arriving late, a sonorous *clang*.

Reacher said, "I'm impressed."

Chang said, "By what?"

"Finally they hit a target only slightly smaller than a barn door.

Thereby revealing the front bucket is indeed bulletproof. So we're good to go."

Westwood said, "Now?"

"No time like the present."

Chang said, "Take care, Reacher."

"You too, Chang."

They opened their doors and jumped down to the ground, one on the left, and one on the right.

Chapter 55

Westwood had quoted from his recent research and said old-style wheat grew about four feet tall, but it was being bred down to a brawnier plant with more seeds, just two feet high. In which case the local farmers were still old-style. The wheat was easily four feet tall. Not that Reacher needed it for cover. Very little cover was required against guys who couldn't hit a target only slightly smaller than a barn door. But surprise was always a good thing. So he crawled. Some visible disturbance, but gentle, and hard to locate precisely where, from two hundred yards. The nighttime dew had not burned off. His knees and elbows got thick with mud. There were new clothes in his future. That was clear. Even without the mud. The smell of the hogs was pretty bad. The air was thick with it. It was bound to get in the fabric. So, a new outfit tomorrow. A good idea anyway, he thought, with Chang around.

Then he thought, this ends today.

Chang won't be around tomorrow.

After a hundred lateral yards he curved tight toward the farm, aiming to get closer to it as he moved around its perimeter. As close as possible. Less than a hundred feet would make him happy. He was a big admirer of the MP5K. It was a slightly swollen handgun that worked like a much-miniaturized rifle. Set to single shot, it stood a chance of hitting at ninety feet. Or eighty. Or seventy-five. Which would be a bonus.

Five minutes in he risked raising his head to check where he was. Which was in a pretty good spot. He had moved around the dial counterclockwise, from the ten to beyond the eight. And he had gotten much closer. And sure enough, the countervailing defenders, being uncertain of their marksmanship, had grouped at a point physically nearest the main threat, but consistent with their own safety. They perceived the main threat to be the backhoe, and the nearest cover was an outbuilding near the fence, about the size of a single-car garage. Three guys were hiding behind it. Which put them exactly side on to Reacher. Clear as day. A classic flanking maneuver. West Point would have been proud.

The counterman from the diner was there. And the one-eyed clerk from the motel. And the hog farmer, who had led the deputation up the stairs. Big hands, broad shoulders, clothes all covered with dirt.

All of them with M16 rifles.

Reacher waited. His head hurt, both sides.

Chang crawled the other way, and got closer sooner, because her role was not to outflank. Her role was to wait for the backhoe to move, and then open a second front with a sustained burst of fire. Which would drive them into cover, where Reacher would shoot them in the back.

That was his plan. She had been dubious. But his plan had worked so far. He had predicted four early prisoners and gotten five. And he predicted at the farm they would shoot but miss, and he was right about that, too. But even so she had asked him again if this part would work. No, he had said, it won't. They'll fall back to the house. A managed retreat. They must have a position prepared. Something hardened. Like a safe room.

She had asked, then why are we doing it this way?

He had said, because we might get lucky.

She crawled on. She wanted to get closer. She knew the numbers. A thirty-round magazine would be gone in two seconds. She wanted to make both of them count. She wanted to get lucky. If she hit one and he hit one, that was two less for later. Which was good.

Which were words she had never spoken, before she met him.

She crawled on, getting closer. The smell of the pigs was bad. In her head she lined herself up with the satellite image. She was at the eleven o'clock position. The hog pen was at the three. It stank. It told her two things. This was no genteel resort. Not possible. Some folks couldn't come close. Not without gagging.

And Keever was buried there. She knew. In the hog pen. They couldn't dig in the fields. Even a low-speed version of how Westwood had driven would be visible from the air. And they would worry about the air. They had Keever's wallet. They had seen his FBI cards. Defunct, like hers, but they didn't know that.

She felt close to him.

She raised her head. She saw a fence and an outbuilding about the size of a single-car garage. The backhoe sat alone, idling, knee deep in the wheat, far to her right. The outbuilding was their only cover against it. At least one of them would lean out and fire. Right in front of her.

She put two spare magazines on the ground. Lined up and ready to go.

She wanted to get lucky.

She clicked her fire selector to auto.

She lined up her sights.

She waited.

Westwood kicked the engine to life and pulled levers, and pushed others, and he brought the front bucket vertical, and moved it up, until he could see nothing out the windshield but its painted rear surface. Safety over visibility. His part of the plan was fluid from that point onward. Reacher had told him to hold the wheel straight and drive slowly forward. Blind. Keep on going. Through the fence if necessary. Don't worry. Don't stop. Unless something else happens first.

Fluid.

The future of journalism. The internet had changed everything. Now news was personal. The reporter had to be in the story. A first-hand account. The reporter had to *be* the story.

Blogs, features, platforms, book deals.

He dipped the clutch. He rattled the lever into gear.

He set off forward.

Reacher heard the backhoe move. He felt dizzy. He was on his knees, but he was swaying. He raised his head. Two fences. Two out-buildings. Six guys. Double vision. He smacked the heel of his hand against his forehead. He tried again.

Better.

Way to his left the backhoe rolled forward. The big slack tires gave and flexed. The three guys stood back-to, pressed up against the rear of the building. Rifles at port arms. Then the counterman rolled around the corner and inched along the end wall. He got to the next corner and took a cautious look. He raised his rifle.

Reacher aimed. The H&K was essentially a twelve-inch tube with a pistol grip at both ends. Very precise. Iron sights.

The counterman aimed at the backhoe. And waited. Behind him the one-eyed guy slid toward the opposite corner.

The backhoe rolled on. The tires squelched. The wheat brushed the bottom of the bucket, and sprang back up.

Reacher's head hurt. Both sides. *A cerebral contusion,* contusio cerebri, *in fact two, both coup and contre-coup.* Arcing and sparking between them, like electricity.

Then Chang fired.

Full auto. Nine hundred rounds a minute. Impossibly fast. A brief blur of sound, like a manic sewing machine. Two seconds. A whole mag. Dirt stitched up in a line and a splinter of wood blew off the building.

The one-eyed guy ducked back.

The counterman craned further around his corner, looking for the new source of danger. Reacher's gun tracked his move. Rear sight, front sight, target.

Reacher fired. Single shot. Range, eighty feet. Nine-millimeter Parabellum, 124 grains, full metal jacket. Muzzle velocity, more than eight hundred miles an hour. Time to target, less than a fifteenth of a second. Virtually instantaneous.

The round hit the guy high on the back, dead center, at the base of the neck. A spine shot. Lucky. Reacher had been aiming lower, at center mass. The biggest part of the target. Always safest. With an in-built advantage. Center meant center. There was stuff on the edges, side to side, and especially up and down. The legs and the head. Misses had somewhere to go. The guy went down. Just a slow fall forward into the corner of the building, which tipped him around and dumped him on the floor.

The hog farmer hit the deck. Out of sight. Behind the wheat. Smart guy. But the one-eyed clerk took a step. Raised his gun. Fired. The bullet cracked in the air and smashed through the wheat about thirty feet to Reacher's right.

Chang fired again.

A second magazine. Good for her. Resolve and determination. The same manic purring. Dirt kicked up and splinters flew.

Then silence.

The one-eyed guy slid back to the corner and leaned around and aimed at where the sound had been.

The backhoe rolled closer.

Some small part of Reacher's mind didn't want to shoot at the one-eyed guy. *He's a poor old handicapped man.* Didn't seem fair. Except right then he was a poor old handicapped man pointing a lethal weapon at Chang. So Reacher aimed. About ninety feet. He kept his focus tight on the front sight. A needle post in a hooded ring. He stared at its paint. At its every molecular pit and detail. Razor sharp. The rear sight was a blur. The target was a blur. For maximum accuracy. How he was trained. The front sight was everything. Eventually it would all come together. Blur, post, blur. And it did. Three things merged. Linear. Rock steady.

He fired.

Same thing. A rising trajectory. This time ninety feet, not eighty. Twelve percent more time in the air. Twelve percent more rise. The round hit the one-eyed guy in the base of the skull. The medulla oblongata. The first tentative swelling of intelligence. A tiny bud, from a hundred million years ago. The lizard brain. About an inch thick. The round went through it in a thousandth of a second. Full metal jacket. The hydrostatic pressure blew it apart. The guy was dead before the sound of the gunshot even cleared the fence. He went down like a slamming door.

The backhoe rolled closer.

The hog farmer ran.

Reacher clicked up to full auto and stood straight and fired, whipping the muzzle through the guy, like flicking paint. The rest of the mag, twenty-eight rounds, a sewing machine of his own. But he missed with all of them. All low. No steady footing. Off balance. Dizzy. Temporarily. He shook his head and came back fine.

Chang fired again. A third magazine. Full auto. But way high. Roof shingles blew off the building. The guy ran full speed out of sight.

The backhoe rolled closer.

Then Reacher ran, plunging through the wheat, smashing through the stalks, striding, wading, floundering, angling toward the backhoe's path. Westwood saw him through the side glass and stopped. Chang ran in from the other side and didn't stop. She looped all the way around and hugged Reacher tight.

She said, "You OK?"

He said, "I'm hanging in there."

"You got two."

"With two to go. There were four in the crew-cab."

"How do we do it?"

"First we find them."

"You said a safe room."

They got back in the cab, left and right, flanking Westwood, standing sideways. No view out the front. Westwood said, "Where would they build a safe room?"

"They didn't build one," Reacher said. "They already had one. I'm sure every farm in the state has one. Hardened against tremendous impacts."

Chang said, "A tornado shelter."

"Exactly. Under the house. With a secondary exit somewhere else. In case the house falls down on the trapdoor. Every basement should have one. I'm sure these guys do. They need the versatility. Probably a tunnel to another location entirely. With a hidden escape hatch. That's what we need to find first. So we can park a truck on it."

Westwood kicked the engine to life again and pulled the same levers, but in reverse order, and the front bucket tilted backward, and came down, until he could just about see over the top of it. A narrow slot. No longer completely safe, but a reasonable compromise.

He waited.

Reacher said, "No time like the present."

The backhoe lurched, and settled to a moderate speed. Bucking on its clumsy tires. A hundred and fifty yards out. A hundred. Heading for the fence. Closer. And closer. And then smashing through it, rails tossed aside, left and right, hickory splinters in the air, and then onward, around the first outbuilding, on its left, past the dead one-eyed guy, into the beaten-earth compound. Where they slowed down, and then stopped. And waited. No longer a predator above a water hole. Now a combatant in an arena.

No one shot at them.

No response.

Reality was pretty much the same as the Google image. Except looking across, not down. Dead ahead was the house, and closer by on the right was the suicide suite. On the left was the generator shed and a small building the size of the place the three guys had hidden behind. Way beyond the house in the east were the hog shelter and the barn. Kind of separate. The driveway let out before them. Where the phone line came in on poles.

No exhaust pipe.

No movement.

Westwood took his gun out of his boot.

Reacher said, "The next part is strictly voluntary."

"I know."

"Stick together and start at the house."

They climbed down from the cab.

No one shot at them.

No response.

Nothing at all, except the stink of the hog pen.

They walked across the beaten dirt, toward the house, three in a line, Chang on the left, Westwood in the middle, and Reacher on the right, his head hurting like someone was sticking an ice pick in his ear.

Chapter 56

Reacher stood guard on the front porch while Chang and Westwood went inside to search. He kept a close watch. The secondary exit could be anywhere. Sudden surprises could come from any direction. But they didn't. Nothing happened. Two minutes later Chang came back out and said, "We found the main entrance. Westwood has it covered. It's a zoo in there."

She took his place on the porch and he went inside and found Westwood in a bedroom corridor. He was guarding the inside of what once might have been a linen closet. Now it was full of an angled hatch set at forty-five degrees between the back wall and the floor. Angled at forty-five degrees, because it capped a staircase, presumably. To an underground room, no doubt. It was closed, but like all storm doors it would open outward. So the wind could never blow it in.

Reacher judged the distance, the width of the corridor plus the depth of the linen closet to the mid-point of the angled hatch, and then he went to find the living room, where he saw what Chang meant about a zoo. It was like Peter McCann's place in Chicago, but ten times more complicated. There were screens everywhere, at least twenty of them, and dozens of keyboards, and tower units, and tall racks of humming components, and piles of hard drives, and fans and connectors and power strips, and blinking lights, but most of all wires, miles of them, some bundled, some tangled, some coiled.

None of which Reacher wanted right then.

He headed onward and found a living area and looked at a sofa. A big old thing. Three-seater, easy. Plus extravagant curlicued arms. Long enough. He half carried it and half dragged it back the way he had come. Into the bedroom corridor. Where he stood it upright and walked it forward and dropped it back down, sideways, jammed between the hatch cover and the opposite wall.

One hole sealed.

Then they stood together on the front porch and figured out where the second hole would be more or less by dead reckoning, and a lot of pointing and gesturing and visual explanation. The house was rectangular, like most houses, which meant the shelter would be too, running in the same direction. Had to be, surely. An architectural no brainer. And human nature said if the main door was at one end, the escape hatch would be at the other end. So the tunnel would follow the spine of the house, perpendicular to the gable wall, running outward under the compound, toward the generator shed, or possibly the smaller building next to it.

The generator shed would make more sense. A poured concrete base, properly engineered, easy to integrate with the mouth of the tunnel. Aboveground was a working environment, often checked. Clean, efficient, and safe. No junk piling up. The perfect escape hatch. For all the right reasons.

But for all the wrong reasons they would choose the smaller building. It wasn't just nature they hoped to outrun. People too, in a worst-case scenario. There would be no point climbing out in a logical place.

The smaller building had double doors, like an old-style garage. The lock was rusted in the open position, which Reacher felt boosted the building's case. No lock at all would be safest. Keys could go missing. No point escaping by the skin of your teeth, and then spending the night locked in a barn.

They pulled the doors wide and saw a tangle of junk. Scrap metal, mostly, and some old cans of paint. There was a paint-spattered drop cloth dumped on the floor. Not a working environment. Not often checked. Not clean, efficient, or safe. Not a likely location.

Except.

The tangle of junk was somewhat artful. There was a void where logic and gravity would not have put one. And there were other voids, somehow linked up, as if a person could hustle through one after another, and get all the way outside, double quick.

The main void was right above a slight hump in the paint-spattered cloth.

Reacher pulled the cloth aside and they saw the same kind of hatch they had found in the house. Not angled this time, but set down flat in the floor, and cemented all around.

It was closed.

"Outstanding," Reacher said.

Chang went to find a truck with the keys in, and Reacher and Westwood got busy shoving metal aside, so she could get it in when she found one. She came back with the same crew-cab they had seen racing out from behind the diner. She drove it in and sawed it back and forth until she had the left front wheel centered on the hatch.

Second hole sealed.

Chang got out of the truck and looked at the metal and said, "What the hell is this stuff?"

Which was a good question.

The metal was all mild steel, some of it square-section tube, some of it solid rod, some of it one-eighth sheet bashed into strange curled shapes. All of it was rusty, and most of it was smeared black in places with some kind of paint or stain. Most of the tube and all of the rod was welded up in what looked like bolt-together sections of fence.

Some of them were about four feet by two, and some of them were about four by four, and some of them were about six by three. All of them were dumped and tangled in a ragged pile.

And none of them made sense. The fence they had busted with the backhoe was post-and-rail, made of wood, with barbed wire stapled on. There was no metal fence on the property. None in the whole county, as far as Reacher had seen. Maybe the state. And the sections didn't match. They were not a uniform size. There was no coherent way to bolt them together. No point in having a fence where one short section was three feet tall, and the next six, and the next four. Plus some of the bolt holes ran the wrong way. Some were aligned vertically, and some horizontally.

Some sections had hinges.

Not a fence.

Chang said, "Oh my god. They're cages."

The one-eighth sheet had been cut into strips, and then rolled and beaten and welded into shapes. Rusty and smeared black, like all the rest. There were hinged hoops about three inches around, with U-shaped eyes brazed on.

Manacles.

There were hinged hoops about six inches around, with long spikes brazed on.

Slave collars.

There were crude iron masks, and pincers, and nails.

"The black stains," Chang said. "I think they're blood."

They backed out the double doors and stood in the sun. It felt cold. They turned and looked back at the house. And the suicide suite next to it.

Reacher said, "The next part is strictly voluntary."

He started walking. Chang went with him. Westwood paused a beat, and then hustled to catch up.

* * *

The suicide suite was an outbuilding about half the size of the house. It had a concrete foundation, about knee high, stained orange by rain splashing mud out of puddles. Then came siding made of heavy tarred boards. The roof was shingle. Conventional construction, square and solid, built to last. A power line as thick as Reacher's finger looped in under the eaves.

No windows.

The door was locked.

Reacher said, "Ready?"

"Not really," Chang said, in a voice that sounded small and full of defeat. He remembered her leaning close, in the Cadillac driver's store, looking at the phone book. Looking at M for Maloney. He remembered piles of packages. Two had come direct from foreign manufacturers. German medical equipment made from sterile stainless steel, and a high-definition video camera from Japan. He remembered the guy from Palo Alto, puzzling over the stray chat-room message from the guy named Blood. *I hear Mother's Rest has good stuff.* On a board the guy from Palo Alto didn't recognize. Some other community. An enthusiast site, by the feel of it. Deep down in the Deep Web.

Reacher stepped back and strode forward and punched his heel through the lock. The door smashed inward and bounced back off the wall. He stopped it short with spread fingers and stepped inside.

A vestibule. A smell. Worse than the hogs. Ahead was a small kitchen, with mugs and bottles of water. And wires and cables and plugs and connectors, all piled and tangled, used and forgotten. A working place. To the left was a small lobby with a door on the right and a door at the end. The door on the right was a bathroom. Neither clean nor dirty. An efficient space. Communal. On the wall beyond were coat hooks. A line of four. Loaded, but not with coats.

With rubber aprons.

They were smeared brown and black.

Reacher tried the door at the end of the lobby.

Unlocked.

His head hurt.

He said, "Ready?"

"Not really," Chang said again.

A small voice, full of defeat.

He opened the door. Pitch dark inside. A bad smell. Cold. The empty sound of a large space. Hard surfaces. Some obstructions. He patted the wall, looking for a switch.

He found one.

He turned it on.

He saw the woman in white.

Not heading for a garden party in Monte Carlo. Not heading to City Hall for her fifth wedding. Not heading for a private annex with a calming ambience, where she could get comfortable and drink Nembutal, or lie in bed while an old V-8 engine did its gentle work.

None of the above.

She was chained by the wrists to a white-tiled wall.

Slumped down, and hanging low.

Blood spatter all around.

Stone dead.

Reacher was no kind of a competent pathologist, but he figured she had been beaten to death with a baseball bat. There was one on the floor, crusted with blood. Going black, like the stains on the metal. She had livid bruises and broken bones. Her skull was mis-shapen. Her hair was matted. Her white sheath dress was filthy with blood and vomit.

She was faced by an array of video equipment. Three television cameras on sturdy tripods, and video lights on stands, with pegged sheets of translucent diffuser. Wires snaked all around the floor. The white tiles made a kind of stage. They covered the last third of the side walls, and the whole of the back wall, and the last third of the floor. An arena. They would light up bright. Plenty of definition. Plenty of detail.

White tiles, smeared pink.

There were microphones above the stage.

Two of them.

Stereo.

There was a sheet of paper clipped to a camera stand. An e-mail, printed out. It said, *I would like to see a bossy bitch beaten with a bat. Like a CEO type. Keep it going as long as possible. Legs first. You should make her say sorry Roger, sorry Roger, over and over again. I would be willing to pay a hundred thousand.*

Some other community. An enthusiast site.

The enthusiast site was called Mother's Rest, the same as the decoy. Westwood and Chang managed to get the computers up and running. Back in the house. It was all video streaming. Pay per view. A lot of money. The cheapest was the price of a car. *Starved to Death* was the most expensive. Because of the time it took, presumably. Lots of working hours. *Pregnant and Bayoneted* was next. *Gut Shot* was costly. There were most-popular lists. And recently viewed lists. In all kinds of different categories. Male victim, female victim, couples, young, old, black, white, cutting, stabbing, beating, power tools, extreme insertion, medical experiment, electricity, drowning, and shooting.

There was also a custom business. Level five. Community members were invited to write in with their requests. As detailed as they liked. Whole scripts, if they wanted. Every attempt would be made to satisfy. It all depended on the right actor coming along. No payment was required until the face and the price had been agreed on.

Chang scrolled to the end of a catalog page and said, "Check this out."

A small voice, full of defeat.

Reacher looked. The latest addition to the Mother's Rest video library was red hot, brand-new, and now available for instant streaming. It was called *Thin Man All Ribs Broken First.*

The guy from the train. In the suit and the collared shirt. With the fine leather bag.

He was a thin man.

Reacher's head hurt.

Chang scrolled backward, from brand-new to recent, and stopped on *Sad Couple With Something to Be Sad About.*

She said, "This has to be Michael McCann, and his friend Exit. Doesn't it?"

Reacher said nothing.

Westwood said, "Look at this." He was in some kind of root directory. He pointed at the lines of numbers. He said, "Let's call them movies. Because that's what they are. They're snuff films. Some of them are very long. The shortest is two hours. The oldest is from five years ago and the newest was put up yesterday."

Then he ran his finger down the screen and stopped close to the bottom. He said, "Guess how many movies they made before McCann first called me."

Reacher said, "Two hundred."

"Now two hundred and nine."

Reacher said nothing.

Westwood said, "You want to see *Death by a Thousand Cuts*?"

"No."

"I wonder what they would have called my movie."

"*Hack Attack,* probably. Stabbed to death by pens."

"How long does the con last? When do people figure this out? Only after they step in that room?"

Chang said, "I think they figure it out when the Cadillac driver opens their door and they smell the pigs. I think that's when the guns come out."

"We should ask," Reacher said. "We know where the con men are."

They walked through to the bedroom hallway. To the one-time linen closet. To the sofa, jammed sideways between the hatch and the opposite wall.

Reacher said, "It would be easier to move the truck."

Chang said, "You OK?"

He nodded. "Under the circumstances."

They went out the front, and walked where they figured the tunnel ran, to the small building with the double doors. Chang got in the crew cab and pulled it forward. She got out and left it idling. She looked at the hatch and said, "How do you want to do this?"

Reacher said, "I doubt if they're crouching right there, right now. But plan for the worst. Westwood opens the lid and stands back, and we aim straight down the hole. OK?"

She nodded. Westwood nodded. Reacher took up position, right of dead center, with his H&K ready. New mag, full auto. Chang mirrored him exactly, left of center.

Westwood bent down and grasped the handle.

He threw open the door and jumped back.

There was no hole.

Chapter 57

The hatch assembly had been bought in a store and then brought home and cemented down on a flat concrete floor. No hole, no stair head. No penetration of any kind. A continuous unbroken slab. The same pebbly surface on the left of the hatch, and the right of the hatch, and under the hatch.

Like a blind eye.

A fake.

A decoy.

Reacher said, "My fault. I wasn't thinking."

Westwood said, "Spilled milk. But we need to know where it really is."

"No," Chang said. "We need to know if they used it yet."

Which question was immediately answered by a supersonic *crack* in the air and a hiss of rifling whine and the granular punch of a NATO round passing through a wooden wall, a yard from their heads. Followed instantly by the blast of the rifle itself. Sound waves were slower than bullets. But in this case not much later. Which meant the rifle was close. A hundred feet, Reacher thought. Which was closer than close. It was heading toward point-blank range, even for these guys.

They hustled inside, and another round punched through the wood, leaving a bright spot of sun. And another, eight feet away. Through-the-wall tactics. Sight unseen. Purely random. This was the A-team, Reacher thought. These were the guys who could hit the side of a barn. He walked past tangles of metal to the far back corner. Invisible from the outside. And fairly invulnerable. Not protected by any kind of a physical shield, but protected by the lottery of aiming blind. The walls weren't worth a damn, but numbers never lied.

He kicked out the back wall siding, low down near the floor, a gap two feet high, and four feet long, and then five, as he punched more boards clear. Big enough to crawl out. First Westwood, then Chang. Another round punched through. Then Reacher. They backed off, keeping the building in line. Behind them was nothing but wheat. To the right of behind them was the building near the broken fence. With the dead guys. The backhoe was parked directly right of them. About twenty yards away. Ahead on the right were the movie studio and the house. Ahead on the left was the generator shed. Plenty of places.

But all of them the wrong side of open ground. Twenty yards minimum. Twenty steps. A long way. Not impossible. It depended on the other guys. How they aimed. How they were trained. If they were trained. A guy who was taught the front-sight mantra might focus so hard he could lose his peripheral vision. Just in the moment. It was possible a guy could walk away unnoticed. It was possible a guy in a gorilla suit could walk away. It would depend on the degree of focus. A person might get away with it.

But three people wouldn't.

Reacher whispered, "Stay here. Don't move. I'll come back out and get you."

Chang said, "Back out of where?"

"I'm going back in the building."

"That's crazy."

"Not really. Look at what kind of shooters they are. It's a math thing. To do with probability. I'm no less safe going right where they're aiming."

"That's nuts."

"It's a big wall. What are the chances? I'm more likely to develop a rare heart condition on the way there."

"I'm coming with you."

"OK, but Westwood stays here. War correspondents maneuver with the second wave."

Westwood said, "Is that what I am?"

"No, I'm trying to make you feel good. You're thinking of the book rights."

"Not completely."

"Either way, stay here."

Reacher and Chang walked back to the building, and crawled back inside. The spots of sun made a large constellation. Mostly high. Reacher's taller brother might have had a problem. But Reacher himself would have been untroubled, and Chang unscathed. Another round passed through, a punch, a *whang,* another spot of sun, high and way to the left, another losing ticket.

Reacher said, "If it's truly random, all locations are equally likely. Even locations that have been hit before."

He put his eye to a spot of sun and squinted out.

He said, distorted because his cheek was pressed against the board, "We need to see their muzzle flashes. Then we can chase them off. I want them running."

Another round passed through, punch, *whang,* sun. Perfect height, but ten feet too far to the right.

"I see one of them," Reacher said.

Dust in the air. He scraped a blink against the wood.

They waited.

Another round. Punch, *whang,* sun. High and left.

Reacher peeled away from the wall. He said, "I got them both. They're both the same. The back left corner of the movie studio. About a hundred and ten feet. They're taking turns, rolling around the corner and bringing their guns up. It's like a movie about the Marines. One of them is the hog farmer and the other one has hair like a weather guy on TV."

"Can we get them from here?"

"We can waste a magazine shutting them up for a minute. Then we can move down to the front corner of the movie studio."

"And do what? Sneak around from corner to corner? Front to back? It's an awful long way. It's a rectangular building. Most buildings are."

"Marines would go through the building. They'd come out the end wall. That's what anti-tank weapons are for."

"What would we do?"

"We would take a chance. We would wait for a magazine change."

Chang said, "Not good enough."

"You wouldn't like the good-enough plan."

"Are you asking me apologetically?"

"You bet your ass."

"What is the good-enough plan?"

His head hurt.

He said, "It's a pact with the devil. It guarantees one, but only one. The other guy runs. And apart from that, it's going to be unpleasant."

Reacher fired first, because Chang was the faster runner. He stepped between the open doors and aimed at the back left corner of the studio, about two-thirds up, and he saw some splinters, but not enough for two whole seconds. But it shut them up. Chang took over, a mag of thirty, full auto, two whole seconds, and Reacher ran, for the near front corner of the studio, where he reloaded and fired down the length of the building, corner to corner, another whole mag, while Chang ran and joined him, pressing in behind him, out of breath.

"Ready?" he said.

She didn't answer.

They slipped in the studio door. The vestibule. The smell. The small kitchen, with the mugs and the bottles of water.

They waited.

They heard a noise. A guy rolling around the corner. Like a movie about the Marines.

They waited.

They heard the shot. Aimed at the now-empty and now-distant building. Maybe a hit, maybe not. Either way, Reacher leaned out the studio door and fired half a mag back. No expectations. No time for finesse. But enough time for a message.

Your opponents are now in the building.

Right in your business.

Reacher and Chang backed in, backward past the bathroom, backward past the aprons, backward through the door at the end. The lights were still on. The woman in white was still there. She hadn't moved. They stood facing away, like cameramen who had turned to answer a question.

They waited.

The hunters were now the hunted. Their prey was luring them into a bottleneck. They had to show themselves, single file in a narrow hallway, with the lights on. Like walking up a motel staircase two by two. The smart money said don't go in. Not ever. But they would. They had to. It was their domain. And still their future. All the guys Reacher had ever known, fraud, theft, homicide, and treason, right up to the very end believed there was some chance of getting away with it, and therefore something should be salvaged, if possible. No one wanted to start over with nothing. These guys might save most of their inventory. And their equipment. Reacher assumed high definition cameras were expensive.

So one of them would step inside. But only one. The surprise ending worked only once.

They waited.

Human nature.

The hog farmer showed up. Big hands, broad shoulders, clothes all covered with dirt. Peering around the corner, very cautious, committed to nothing at all except a brief glance. Pressing hard against the wall. Nothing showing. A shoulder, perhaps. Or a nose. Peering again, around the corner, a little farther, leaning out an inch.

Reacher shot him in the forehead. The gentlest touch on the trigger, barely there, in and out, a purring stitch of ten. Game over. Which the last guy heard, obviously, and therefore the last guy was now running. He was all alone. Suddenly prey to primeval fears. Suddenly free to act on them. No witnesses.

In military circles aggressive pursuit was much admired, and any excuse to get out of the room was a good one, so Reacher ran too, with Chang right behind him.

Chapter 58

They hurdled the hog farmer and spilled out the studio
door and headed half left, aiming around the end of the house to the
mouth of the driveway. Because the driveway was the goal. Had to
be. Human nature. Escape. The only way out. Everything else was
wheat.

They saw him sixty feet ahead, running, looking back, his M16 in
one hand and nothing in the other. He was a stocky guy with a red
face and big waves of hair all scooped up around his head. He was
wearing blue jeans that looked starched. He got near the driveway
mouth and glanced back. They ducked in closer to the house. The
guy was all alone in the landscape. The hog pen was behind him, and
then nothing but wheat before Missouri. The driveway was on his
right. Twenty miles to Mother's Rest.

The guy stood still.

Chang said, "Can you hit him from here?"

Reacher didn't answer.

She said, "You OK?"

He said, "Ninety percent."

Which was how he saw it. There was nothing wrong with him.

Nothing specific. No broken bone, no bleeding wound. But nothing was working right. Not exactly. *The brain is not the same thing as an arm.*

Chang said, "How do we do this?"

Reacher counted back in his head. The rounds aimed at the small building. Punch, *whang*. How many?

Memory.

He stepped out a pace.

The guy with the jeans and the hair raised his rifle.

An M16 at sixty feet. Theoretically a problem. Any competent rifleman could hit with a long gun at sixty feet. Less than forty barrel lengths, for an M16. Practically touching distance. But the guy wasn't a competent rifleman. That had been proved. At the small building. And now he had been running. Now he was breathing hard. His chest was heaving. His heart was thumping.

Reacher stood still.

The guy fired.

A miss. A foot high and a foot wide. Reacher heard the buzz of the round in the air, and then a distant thump far behind him as it hit a building. The small place near the broken fence, probably. With the dead guys.

He stepped back into cover.

He said, "Sooner or later he'll run out of ammunition."

Chang said, "He'll reload."

"But not fast."

"Is that your plan?"

"I need you with me. Just in case."

"Of what?"

"Two heads are better than one. Especially mine right now."

"You OK?"

"Not really. But then, how good do I need to be?"

"I'll go do it."

"I can't let you."

"Not woman's work?"

Reacher smiled. He thought about the women he had known.

"Just a personal thing," he said. "Habit, mostly."

"How do we do it?"

"I'll draw his fire. He'll miss every time. I promise. When he clicks on empty I'll hose him down. Meanwhile you'll be running closer, so if I miss, you won't."

Chang said, "No, we'll both draw his fire. We'll do this together."

"Not efficient."

"I don't care. That's how we're doing it."

They stepped out. The guy was still there. All alone in the vastness. Jeans, hair, M16 rifle. Sixty feet away. Chang aimed her gun, one eye closed. Reacher stood still, arms held wide, looking up at the sky, his gun hanging upside down off his trigger finger. *Take your best shot.* The guy did. He raised his gun, held still, and aimed, and fired.

And missed.

Missed both of them.

Chang fired back. Single shot. The spent case spat through the air. The bullet missed. But the guy backed off. Five clumsy paces, backward. Then ten.

Chang fired again. Another case glittered through the air. Another miss. The wheat moved in waves, heavy, and slow, and silent.

The guy raised his rifle.

But he didn't shoot.

Chang said, "Is he out of bullets?"

Reacher's head hurt.

He said, "He doesn't know. He lost count. So did I."

Then he smiled.

He said, "Do we feel lucky?"

He raised his gun. Two grips, held easy, somewhere between firm and gentle. The front sight, and the blur beyond. He blinked. He had focus, but it was not molecular. Plus he had a microscopic thrill in his arms. Through his whole body. *Difficulties with coordination, move-*

ment, memory, vision, speech, hearing, managing emotion, and thinking.

He lowered his gun.

He said, "We should get closer."

They made up the distance the guy had retreated. Slow and easy. Heart rate low, breathing normal. The guy added ten more paces. The jeans and the hair, moving backward, toward the hog pen.

Reacher and Chang got closer.

The smell was bad.

But better than the movie studio.

The guy backed off ten more paces.

And jammed up hard against the hog pen fence.

Reacher and Chang stopped.

The guy raised his rifle.

And then lowered it again. He stood against the fence, all alone, the rails at his back, small and absurd in the emptiness. The sun was high in the south. Far behind the guy his hogs moved out of their shelter. Fat and smooth, glistening with slime. Each one the size of a Volkswagen.

Reacher walked forward. Chang kept level.

The guy dropped his rifle and raised his hands.

Reacher walked forward. Chang kept level.

Fifty feet. Forty. Thirty.

Twenty feet.

The guy had his hands in the air.

In the tall tales told by firelight there was always a brief conversation. Because the bad guy had to be told why he had to die.

Reacher said nothing.

Tales were tales, and not the real world.

But the guy spoke first.

He said, "Their lives were forfeit. Surely you see that. They had given their lives away. Their decision was made. They were already gone. They were mine to use. And they got what they wanted anyway. In the end."

Reacher said, "I don't think they got what they wanted. That wasn't the holy grail."

"It was an hour or two. At the very end. After the end, as far as they were concerned. They had made their decision."

"How many hours was the guy you starved to death? Or was it a woman?"

The guy didn't answer.

Reacher said, "One practical question."

The guy looked up.

"Where are the bodies?"

The guy said nothing. But he glanced back. Reflex. Involuntary.

He glanced at the hogs.

Reacher said, "Then why did you bury Keever?"

The guy said, "The hogs had already eaten that day."

Reacher said nothing.

The guy said, "It was a custom order from Japan. An excellent match. All I'm doing is meeting a need. You can't blame me for other people's tastes."

Reacher said nothing.

The guy's hands came down an inch. He wanted his shoulders free to work the normal way, and his neck, and his head, for body language, for gestures, for cajoling, for explaining. For bargaining, and for offering. All the guys Reacher had ever known. Right up to the very end. They believed they would get away with it.

Chang raised her gun. Reacher watched her. Black hair, hanging loose. Dark lively eyes, one closed, one tight on her front sight. The needle post in the hooded ring.

She said, "This is for Keever."

The bad guy had to be told.

She said, "It could have been me."

She touched the trigger. Twenty feet. Instantaneous. She hit him in the throat. Full metal jacket, through and through. The bullet would fall to earth way out in the wheat, where it would never be found. It would be plowed under, lost and forgotten, and it would return to its constituent elements, lead and copper, part of the planet, the same way it started.

The guy gurgled, a lone tubercular cough, very loud, and blood foamed and sprayed from his wound. For a second he stayed upright, just a guy leaning on a rail, and then everything gave way all at once, and he went down like liquid, in a sprawled puddle, all arms and legs and jeans and hair.

Reacher said, "Where were you aiming?"

Chang said, "Center mass."

Reacher smiled.

"Can't beat center mass," he said.

He walked twenty feet, and found the guy's collar, and the back of his belt, and he hoisted him up, and he dumped him over the fence.

The hogs came running.

Chapter 59

They didn't want to take the crew-cab back to town, because they didn't want to sit where those guys had sat, so they rode the backhoe, as before, Westwood driving, Reacher and Chang face to face above his head, but this time on the dirt road. Which was slow, but more comfortable. They parked in the dealer's lot. The salesman came out. The backhoe was examined. It was a little stained by crushed wheat, and a little scratched on the sides. There was a little dirt caked on. And the front bucket had a dimple, where the bullet had struck. Not new anymore. Not exactly. Reacher gave the guy five grand from their leftover money. Easy come, easy go.

Then they walked south through the plaza. The sun was warm. A kid threw a ball against a building, and hit the rebound with a stick. The same kid they had seen before. They stopped by the motel office, where Westwood booked a whole bunch of rooms. For himself, and his photographers, and all kinds of assistants and interns. The new help at the desk was a teenage girl. Maybe ready for college. She was fast and efficient. She was cheerful and bright.

Reacher asked her, "Why is this town called Mother's Rest?"

She said, "I'm not supposed to tell you."

"Why?"

"The farmers don't like it. They've done their best to bury it."

"I won't tell them you told me."

"It's a corruption of the old Arapaho Indian name. One word, but it sounds like two. It means the place where bad things grow."

Westwood gave Chang the key to his rental car, and said goodbye. Reacher walked with her to the diner, where the red Ford was parked.

She said, "You were headed for Chicago."

He said, "Yes, I was."

"You wanted to get there before the weather turned cold."

"Always a good idea, with Chicago."

"You could take the seven o'clock train. Eat lunch in the diner. Sleep all afternoon in the sun. In a lawn chair. I saw you, the very first day."

"You saw me?"

"I was walking by."

"I told you. I was in the army. I can sleep anywhere."

"Are you going to follow up with a doctor?"

"Maybe."

"I'm driving to Oklahoma City. I'll drop the car at the airport. I guess Westwood's interns will bring him another. I can fly home from there."

He said nothing.

She said, "You OK?"

He said, "We were just in Chicago. Maybe I should go someplace else."

She smiled. "Go visit Milwaukee. All thirty-six blocks."

He paused a beat.

She said, "You OK?"

"Will you come with me?"

"To Milwaukee?"

"Just a couple of days. Like a vacation. We earned one. We could do what people do."

She was quiet for a long moment, five or six seconds, right to the edge of discomfort, and then she said, "I don't want to answer that question here. Not in Mother's Rest. Get in the car."

He did, and she did, and she started the engine. She put the lever in gear, and turned the wheel, and they drove away from the diner, and the dry goods store, to the old wagon train trail, where they turned left and headed west, with the road running straight on ahead of them through the wheat, forever, until it disappeared in the golden haze on the far horizon, at that point as narrow as a needle.

About the Author

LEE CHILD is the author of twenty *New York Times* bestselling Jack Reacher thrillers, with ten having reached the #1 position. All have been optioned for major motion pictures; the first of which, *Jack Reacher,* was based on *One Shot.* Foreign rights to the Reacher series have sold in almost a hundred territories. A native of England and a former television director, Child lives in New York City.

leechild.com
Facebook.com/LeeChildOfficial
@LeeChildReacher

To inquire about booking Lee Child for a speaking engagement, please contact the Penguin Random House Speakers Bureau at speakers@penguinrandomhouse.com.

About the Type

The text of this book was set in Life, a typeface designed by W. Bilz and jointly developed by Ludwig & Mayer and Francesco Simoncini in 1965. This contemporary design is in the transitional style of the eighteenth century. Life is a versatile text face and is a registered trademark of Simoncini S.A.